MAJOR STEPTON'S WAR

Major Stepton's War

by MATTHEW VAUGHAN

Doubleday & Company, Inc., Garden City, New York
1978

Library of Congress Cataloging in Publication Data

Vaughan, Matthew.
    Major Stepton's war.

      1. United States—History—Civil War, 1861–1865—
Fiction. I. Title.
PZ4.V367Maj [PR6072.A9]   823'.9'14
ISBN 0-385-13607-2
Library of Congress Catalog Card Number 77–11369

For My Father

In the fall of 1863 a force of Southern Cavalry, drawn from several Regiments but all impressed into the 1st Virginia Cavalry, attacked the peaceful working town of North Adams. The raid was led by Major Gervase Stepton, who apparently died soon afterwards while taking refuge in the nearby woodlands. Major Stepton and his men wished to capture bullion stored in the Bank at North Adams, whether for their own purposes or that of the Rebel States. They were frustrated in their design by the intrepid gallantry of the town's inhabitants. Several citizens were butchered, killed by armed cavalrymen as they went about their lawful business. While many who follow the profession of arms may admire, and even applaud, the bravery of Colonel Mosby's raiders, this attack was more akin to the outrages perpetrated by Quantrill. Indeed, it is known that Major Stepton met "Colonel" Quantrill while he was serving on Lee's staff in Richmond during the early years of the War. How appalling that he should have followed the example of "Colonel" Quantrill rather than that of his great and chivalrous Commander.

History of the Town of North Adams
(Boston, 1904)

In November 1863 a small detachment of the Regiment was wiped out by immensely superior Federal Forces while performing a desperate raid on North Adams in Massachusetts. This town afforded a genuine military objective, for it contained a storehouse for Federal bullion, and acted as a railhead for the movement of munitions and other military stores. Major Stepton, a native of Sweetwater, Virginia, whose home was ravaged during the Seven Days' Battles, was captured at Antietam and imprisoned in the notorious camp at Fort Delaware. After his escape he made his way to Canada, and organised the raid with some of his fellow captives. The small force was totally destroyed, and the Federal forces acted with flagrant disrespect for the rules of civilised warfare. The place of Major Stepton's grave is unknown.

*A History of the 1st Virginia Cavalry
in the War Between the States*
(Richmond, 1897)

MAJOR STEPTON'S WAR

Witness to a Lawful Act

January 1859. Gervase Stepton walked up and down in front of the line of cadets from the Virginia Military Institute. Their admirable discipline was not reflected by the remainder of the crowd, many of whom were seated on the ground, smoking, laughing, even drinking. The breeze from the Shenandoah was cold, and the image of the Blue Ridge Mountains to the east was sharp. One of the cadets allowed a smile to pass across his face. Gervase walked quickly toward him, but their adult commander moved more quickly. He spoke with a grating, gravelly voice, which removed the smile.

"Stedman, a man is going to die. He is going into the presence of his God, sir, and I would ask you to comport yourself with the dignity that is appropriate to the occasion." He turned to Gervase. "Stepton, I should tell you to keep a better control of your men. This is no holiday."

"No, sir," replied Gervase. His own hands were sweating. He felt excitement; his heart pounded. It was not every day that one saw a man hanged. Then he looked up into the adult's eyes, which were cold, colder than the icy water of the Shenandoah.

"Die, Stepton. And after this man dies, how many more? It is a terrible matter to die for one's faith. Give him that respect, at the least. And when you die, pray that you have an audience about you. It makes the passing easier. To die alone is the worst of fates." Inwardly, Gervase winced. This man deserved to die a thousand times over; he wished to overthrow order. He was a

murderer, a fanatic. Not that old Jackson wasn't a fanatic too.
Oh, he could talk about war with vigor and freshness. But he
had not seen death since Mexico. Gervase was not afraid of
dying, and he was excited by the prospect of death, of watching
a man whom he despised swing at the end of a rope. Jackson
beckoned him closer. The noise of the crowd rose. There were
women present, and they squealed and laughed. "Close in the
company," said Jackson. Gervase shouted an order, and the company formed a half circle. Jackson raised his voice.

"You are about to see a man die," he said. He softened his
voice: "I can be confident that you will all address your Maker
on his behalf. Some of you, perhaps, think this man is dying because he came to free the Negroes. He is dying for no such thing.
He is dying because he came to break the law. The law is the
mirror of God's will in human society. It is the order that sus-
tains us all. Some of you may own slaves; some of you may despise slavery. That has nothing to do with this affair. He is to die
on the altar of the law. And it is right that he should end thus."
His voice attained a terrible intensity. He gazed around at the
crowd, splayed on the cold earth: human muck, spread out like
animal dung. Eating, shouting, swearing, joyful, some dejectedly
singing hymns, lost individuality. The marines guarding the
scaffold stood rigidly at attention. The executioner, dressed in
sober black, stood waiting, testing the rope in his hand, knotted
with precision, awaiting its burden. Jackson let his voice sink
lower, without losing the tremulous intensity. "Pray for him."
Why should they? thought Gervase. He was only seventeen, Gervase Stepton, scion of the Virginia aristocracy, heir to broad
lands, Sweetwater Mansion, many slaves, son of a father who
could cite Virgil and a mother whose life was a poem of retained
gentility. His feelings were intuitive passions, celebrations of the
glory of stability. Why should he care for this dabbler in divin-
ity? Why should he heed the sober words of his Presbyterian
commander?

Suddenly a shudder of anticipation swept over the crowd.
Cards were dropped, skirts lowered, oaths fell silent, murmurs
rippled through tongues. "Here comes the nigger lover. Here's
the bastard at last." The executioner looked forward, and Gervase motioned the cadets back into line. Gervase felt nothing but

exhilaration. He peered at the group that was walking toward the scaffold—soldiers, a clergyman, several men in frock coats; in the midst a nondescript figure, without a beard, without presence, whose eyes shot about as if in terror, yet a terror that was not truly fear. But he seemed a *nondescript* man. As the party passed close to him, Gervase heard the murmur of prayer—not the prayers he knew himself, ordered, graceful Episcopalian prayers, but rather a gabble, addressing God as if from the gutter. He supposed the man had enough to pray for to his Maker. He saw Jackson's head sunk in prayer too: They were of a kind, he surmised. Solemnly, the cortège mounted the scaffold, and the executioner moved forward to maneuver the condemned man into place. He shook himself free, and the sinister official looked at the quiet, bearded officer in charge of the proceedings, Colonel Lee. The latter shook his head slightly, though what to indicate Gervase could not guess. The nondescript man looked up. At that moment a cry broke out: "Nigger lover!" The doomed figure took up the challenge. Yes, thought Gervase, he's always been good with his mouth; why do they let him use it? But that too is fair, he reflected. We must allow that decency to our enemies, especially at their moment of death.

"Yes, I'm a nigger lover," he shouted, voice strained, tense, almost hysterical, afraid yet triumphant. "I rejoice to be a nigger lover. Look at you, whoremongers and gamblers in the presence of the Angel of Death. You kill me now, but how many of you will be alive in ten years? I ask you—no, tell you—to think of that. You lie on the ground now, but soon a deal of you will be under it, food for worms. And why? Yes, why? Think on that! Because you treat your fellow men, black men, as if they were things, property, owned, objects, nothingness compared with yourselves. Many of you, I warrant, are churchgoers, worthy men, I'll guess. Yes, indeed. And yet you spit in the face of God hourly; you make filth in the face of God. *They* have mothers, they have children, they have husbands and wives—but you ignore this. Here I am surrounded by soldiers and politicians and clergymen. Yet darkness will come to you all—darkness until the fire of God bursts forth and burns you all up. Don't think that the fire won't burn. It will burn you all with a foretaste of the hell you hand out to the blacks you say you own. I spit on you

all." And spit he did. Gervase was a young man, relishing his
mere seventeen years, and he flinched from the vulgarity of this
act; he flinched from the contempt it symbolized, and instinc-
tively he raised his hand to the soft skin of his cheek and wiped
away the hot phlegm from his flesh from under his blond hair
and rejoiced in the thought that he would know how to die like a
gentleman, and that it was more important to die like a gentleman than a hero. He was glad that his uniform was creased so
precisely, and his boots polished highly, because that denoted a
style, a style his father had taught him, and that he had been
taught by *his* fathers, all the way back to those cavaliers who
had sailed over to Virginia after the carnage and disorder of
Naseby. Gervase tried hard to feel some sympathy for John
Brown (what a nondescript name—just as the man himself!) as
a human being, before God equal, but try as he could, no sympathy flowed into his veins. The man was vulgar; he paraded his
absurd beliefs; he saw no virtue in tolerance; all was black or
white, and black was good and white was evil. Even Lincoln was
not that simple.

The clouds now obscured the Blue Ridge Mountains, and the
wind soughed along the Shenandoah. Nature was rehearsing its
tragedy, thought Jackson. The Lord is preparing his pageant.
Well, that's what I brought my boys to see, and let the Lord
make them learn their lesson, because they'll learn it in blood
soon enough. He reflected: Why did God permit America to
grow, prosper, and divide itself? So that it might be a moral lesson to the world; so that the effete nations of the Old World, of
decaying Europe, might see how men could still die for belief
and belief alone. He detested Brown; he was a threat to order, to
that static frozen structure that God had decreed from eternity.
Black was black and white was white and property was property
and nation was nation and sanctity was sanctity and love was
love and there could be no deviation from that ideal order:
What was, was what it was, and he would see his sword red and
a thousand Yankees swinging at the end of a rope before he
would allow the least deviation or swerve from this. He knew his
boys would die for their country, for Virginia, on a hundred battlefields choked with the bloody dead and the screaming dying,

in the valleys, by the riverbanks, in the shattered woodlands.
But, gradually but inexorably, they had to be taught that what a
man died for was belief—not style, not some silly pictures of
home and mother, not some mere social order, but belief—belief
in an unswerving God who rewarded constancy with eternal
bliss. Now look at young Gervase Stepton, his face creased with
distaste—thinking that his father would not spit, but failing to see
that Brown had a worthiness of constancy before the stern face
of the unrelenting God. Brown was superior, yes, sir, to these
gamblers and whoremongers who made a holiday to see him die.
And the world would marvel at America, because it could embrace an ideal as a man embraced a naked virgin and hold it
until its love burst all bounds and expired in the supreme passion
of rectitude.

The executioner had positioned Brown over the trap and
pinioned his arms behind him—thin arms, whipcord tough. Before the hood went over his head the wind tousled his hair, just
as his mother's hand had done when he was a baby without belief or passion. Gervase stared at those eyes before they disappeared under the fatal black—they were, he could see even from
his distance, dark and determined and confident. He shouted and
the sentence was cut off: "I am the instrument of . . ." and then
there was a muffled sound. The executioner, his face blank,
anonymous, professional, stepped backward from the trap. The
wind took a great leap through the valley of the Shenandoah and
the boards opened and he dropped down, snapped to a halt,
swung there, manhood erect, in a moment of great silence, which
was suddenly broken, before Jackson could assemble his cadets
for prayer, by a great yell, a yell that was soon to be heard on
the battlefields of the West, of Virginia, of Pennsylvania—what
"they" were to call the rebel yell.

And there was Gervase, fascinated, excited, pitiless in his seventeen years, elegant in his dress, severe in his style, profound in
his patriotism, indifferent to the newly released soul twittering
and gibbering above them in the windy air, committing himself
to God knows what ideal of sweet images from sweet water and
Sweetwater and his mother and father and sisters and drinking
in the great silence and wholly misinterpreting it in his arrogant

innocence and not realizing for a moment, as, indeed, none of them did, that at that moment Brown had won a victory for his cause, precisely because he realized it was a cause and they did not. The rope creaked, and Colonel Lee made a movement with his gauntleted right hand so that they would disperse. Amen.

1

The Forging of an Arm

"You got a black horse?" asked Colonel Stuart.

"Yes, sir, Colonel," replied Gervase.

"'Colonel' or 'sir' will do, Stepton," replied Stuart. "I don't ignore compliments, but time's too short for an excess of them. You're a gentleman, and you are a Virginian, and you are from the Institute, so that's enough for me." He paused. "I've a letter here from General Jackson about you. It reads well enough. What did you think about your lecturer in military science? Although I shouldn't ask." Gervase was somewhat at a loss to reply. "You can't say. Wait and see, wait and see, boy." Gervase checked his resentment at being called "boy." His father abstained even from calling Negroes "boy." But he recognized that Stuart was motivated by affection rather than condescension. "James Ewell Brown Stuart": Even now the name was being abbreviated to JEB, with affection, with the anticipation of later victories and myth. Already he had put a plume onto his hat, which gave him a dashing air, a new Prince Rupert of the South, a romantic of war, forming a regiment whose uniform had black facings and whose troopers all rode upon great black horses, like his own mare "Virginia." Yet the man radiated an earthiness too, as Gervase noted as Jeb shifted his rump to break wind noisily. The sound was short, sharp, and audible. Gervase was a Puritan who did not like to think that great commanders were lumps of flesh as well as burning souls.

"Pray do not be a prig, Stepton," smiled Jeb. "Colonels fart,

officers fart, and—as you doubtless already know—the men fart.
But we are all men, Gervase. We all feel happiness, we all feel
pain, and we all feel fear. So be as brave as you wish, but be
brave sensibly. And don't think I'm a god. I am just your commanding officer. See?" Gervase nodded, with restraint.

"Still," Jeb added, "you won't be seeing too much of me, Lieutenant. Your training will be in the hands of Major Jones. Major
William Edmonson Jones here." He waved with studied noncha-
lance at a dour figure standing by the side of his table, which
was itself before the flapping tent in the sunlight. The major
nodded without a smile. "You'll soon find what the men call
Major Jones. I wouldn't have any other name for a training
officer. If the men like the man who trains them there's something wrong with a regiment. Gentleman or no gentleman, Lieutenant Stepton, Major Jones will have the skin off your arse in no
time." Gervase was by now habituated enough to life in the
Army—all three weeks of it—not to resent this form of address,
nor be offended by it. He was not of an overscrupulous turn of
mind. Nor was Stuart. Of others he could not say. Major Jones,
in a voice high-pitched and ludicrous if one did not know his
reputation, now took up the tale. "Lieutenant Stepton, you'll be
in the company of Major Collins. Pray report to him in the lines
immediately." Gervase turned away. He was still but nineteen.
Major Jones called after him. "I didn't see your salute to your
commanding officer." Jeb grinned. Jeb often grinned. "You will
always salute your commanding officer. I will not tolerate such
impertinence and slackness again. Indeed, if officers . . ."

"Let it go, Major," said Stuart. Jones flushed. He looked down
at Stuart. "Always 'let it go,' Colonel," he said, with some
justifiable bitterness. "It is easy enough to be lenient when one is
not responsible for training . . ." "You were right, Grumble,"
replied Stuart, "you were right, as always. But let it go. He's
new."

"More important to learn the customs of the service."

"Salute me, Gervase," said Stuart. "Then go and leave Major
Jones and me to talk about discipline. And now you'll know who
the men mean when they say Grumble: The best training officer
in the Army." Gervase saluted smartly.

Gervase led his stallion Avenger down the lines in the direc-

tion Grumble had indicated. He already thought of Jones as
Grumble; the Army was perfect in its choice of names, and he
had no doubt that he would hate the man for weeks and then be
very grateful to him when the clash of arms occurred. He was
accustomed to think in such resounding phrases, because men in
his society always used them in public speeches. They relished
the sonority of rhetoric. His father, too, seemed to split his world
of words between an easy and direct colloquiality when he
talked with his family, and the "high" style when he was showing to an admiring world his "public" face. It certainly was not
hypocrisy: It was a decorous separation of the areas of being,
and a fastidious selection of the words and tone appropriate
thereto. For Gervase the war was an excitement, a festivity. Before he had arrived at Stuart's camp north of Richmond he had
returned to Sweetwater, on the day after Virginia had seceded
from the Union. He had expected his father to share his exhilaration (for his father could whoop along too, riding, or hunting,
or dancing, or even when campaigning in politics). Gervase was
disappointed. His father was somber; his face, delicate in color-
ing beneath his rich white hair, was creased in lines of anxiety,
his eyes puckered, as they sat at a table by one of the small pillars in front of the house. His mother was resting, as was her
wont in the early afternoon; certainly no politics would make her
change her habits. She lived by habits, so that, eventually, they
were more than habits to her, but sacred rules, as if she were a
secular nun. She was always elegant, suavely romantic, and studied in the minutiae of social ritual. "You're off to war, Gervase?"
his father had asked, looking out over the soft green field that
sloped gently down to the meander of the Sweetwater, where the
cattle moved with a similar placidity, as if they understood the
social rituals too.

"But of course, sir," Gervase replied, his voice neutral, because
he realized that his father was not asking a question, but seeking
the ratification of the expressed word, a sacrament of patriotism.
"I'm going to Colonel Stuart's cavalry. Brigadier Jackson wrote
to him on my behalf." His father remained silent for a while,
flicking a small stick at his left foot, for his knees were crossed.
He seemed strangely indecisive. Gervase felt that he must express a little more of his own vigorous exhilaration. "We'll have

them beat by Christmas. Why, sir, almost every officer in the federal Army has resigned his commission to join us. We *are* the old United States Army."

"Yes, indeed," his father replied. "*Arma virumque cano . . .* I sing of arms and the man. The glory is understood. But you won't find this war too glorious, and you won't have them beat by Christmas. Oh, they won't have us beat either, but that won't matter to them." Gervase flushed.

"Do you doubt our skill at arms, sir?" His father smiled at him—a small, melancholy smile, the smile of the elder man sending away his son to return a victor or come back on his shield and knowing the probabilities a little too well.

"No, I don't doubt your skill at arms. Nor James Stuart's. Nor Robert Lee's. Perhaps I am a little more skeptical of our President's skill in diplomacy." Already they doubted Jeff Davis—the eternal battle between soldiers and statesmen. "I can add numbers together, however. And I can see those factories in the North. We don't have many factories in the South, Gervase. And wars are fought with guns, with bullets, with iron and steel. Where will we find the iron and steel to arm our soldiers? And, unlike many of my friends, I don't underestimate Mr. Lincoln. No, sir. He'll stick it to the end. And, my dear boy, that's all the Yankees have to do: stick it to the end. Look out there." He pointed toward the river. "We're fighting for our land—more than that, for the *idea* of our land, the style of our life. Not so the Yankees. They are fighting for the idea of this continent. They are fighting for the future, and we are fighting for the past. The past may be more elegant, more beautiful, even more *true;* but the past is the past, and it has the disadvantage of having gone by forever. The Yankees want to move too fast, but move they will. Don't you see that slavery is merely a peculiarity in the middle of the nineteenth century? We pin our banner to a cause that might have stirred the heart of Aristotle. No longer, though."

Gervase had the intelligence, but not the will and the feeling to follow his father's reasoning. Gervase was not willing to think of the war in terms of the movement of civilizations. It was the danger to his country; the call of his friends; the ecstasy of proffered action—these moved him sufficiently for him to shut out his father's somber speculations. How could some soot-caked factory affect the clash of armies? That was a clash of wills, and he was confident that the will of Virginia would be equal to that of a crowd of New Englanders and Irishmen. But he did not choose to argue with his father; the habits of agreement were too fixed in his mind. Not that his father had not actively encouraged disagreement, for he had taught his son to argue and debate as well as to ride and hunt and dance and converse. He had trained him for the full life, and the vigorous life of the mind was an intrinsic part of civilization as he understood it. He even gave him the books of Emerson to read, which he did, echoing his father's style. They read the essay on Nature together, and, after some paragraphs, burst into laughter. But then, fair as ever, his father had said: "The man has some sound ideas at heart. He just can't write. He likes the great belch of windy language. Clarity, Gervase, clarity is the supreme virtue of the pen. If you have to choose between profundity and clarity, always choose clarity. Though please remember that it is profound ideas that change the world in the end." His father was always too fair to his opponents. As he was fair to him, to his mother, to the slaves. Gervase, being younger, did not suffer from the paralysis of decency and fairness. Yet. His father stood up as the breeze quickened over the fields. As if in silent obedience, some of the cows rose lumberingly to their feet. His father held out his hand and kept his son's enclosed in his.

"Let us take farewell before your mother comes. I don't ask you to be brave, because I know that you will be. I merely ask you to be sensible. Learn the arts of war before you risk yourself too much." He paused and released his son's hand. "Incidentally, if you are joining James Stuart you might find a somewhat interesting man as your comrade in arms. He's a lawyer from Bristol. Shot a man while he was at college. Of course, unlike yourself, he has no training in war, so he'll be a mere private—to start with, sir, not for long. Now, *he'll* have no illusions about chivalry, though I don't say he'll not be chivalrous. Look out for him, I say. His name is John Mosby. And here is your dear mother." Was there a touch of irony in the description? Gervase never knew, because he never chose to inquire. But she came out into the sunlight, still dark-haired as when his father had met her in

Charleston, billowing white, radiant, her feature continually
caught by some vision that lifted her head high, never question-
ing, always accepting, an embodiment of Nature in its minute
glories of sun and flower and waterspaces, her limbs and hands
delicate and fragile and her physical being neat and co-ordinated into that incarnated harmony that Gervase recognized as
Woman, rather than women. She would not speculate; it was for
such as her that he would fight.

The officers' tents, in neat rows not too close together, were
upwind of the horse lines, and Gervase handed over Avenger to
a private who seemed well aware of what to do, and yet treated
Gervase with that peculiar mixture of familiarity, equality, and
respect that was the mark not only of Stuart's, but also of all the
best southern regiments. Gervase watched his horse trotting and
then walking in the unfamiliar grip, pulling its head against the
rein, man and beast transforming even a walk into a brief contest
of will. Gervase turned and found a saber point at his throat,
held by a small, dark-haired man with bright blue eyes. He drew
back the weapon and made as if to plunge the blade in Gervase's
chest. As the point came in, slowly, Gervase swept it aside with
his elbow (for the blade did not look very sharp) and leaped
forward at his adversary. The other cast aside the weapon and
embraced him.

"Roscoe," cried Gervase, "you *are* a silly bastard!"

"Watch it," replied Roscoe Stedman, who had been at Lexington with Gervase. "Don't let the brigadier hear you speaking like
that. And save it for the Yanks." They wrung each other's hand.
"I've got you in my tent. Thought you might like to be with
friends?" Roscoe sprang over to the tent flap (he never seemed
to move slowly) and pulled aside the taut canvas after untying
the knots. Three beds were along the sides. Two were covered
(neatly) with kit; one was bare—his. But his kit would be
delivered, and he knew how to lay it out properly, if not to the
complete satisfaction of Major Jones.

The great advantage of the southern Army, in particular the
Army of Northern Virginia, was that it was recruited upon a re-
gional basis. So, too, was the Army of the North—but in, say,
Ohio, men knew each other rather less well than they did in the
organic communities of the South. Gervase had grown up with

Roscoe. They had haunted the woods together as boys, discovering their first snake, first raccoon, first woodchuck; they had contested as to who could shoot the first squirrel, the first deer, the first partridges. They had both fallen in love with the same girls, shyly, then more boldly; they had talked together of their deepest experiences in the humid summers, with circumspection, decency, and the occasional explosive excursion into lust; they had fought each other, and worn each other's blood as a proud motto on the knuckles; they had listened to Jackson together at Lexington. The web of their lives intermingled; skeins interwoven. They would—or so they hoped—die for each other, although neither would voice such a vaunting sentiment. And they knew most of the other officers and many of the men. Stuart had been a guest at both the Stepton and Stedman households on several occasions. So they knew each other's strengths, interests, and weaknesses—a knowledge that would be invaluable upon the field of battle. In the regiments of the North, man had to acquire this knowledge, and under conditions that were less than felicitous. Furthermore, the northern regiments were filled with descendants of Englishmen, Welshmen, Scots, Germans, Dutch, Irish (though much less willingly in this case). They had no shared knowledge; no shared culture; no shared expectations. Thus they were a collection of weak atoms, not molded into a single molecule. This would come—indeed it would, as Mr. Stepton had seen—but the South started with a great advantage, which at least one of their leaders knew how to exploit.

"I'll be damn glad when we get to those Yankees," said Roscoe. "I ain't got any flesh left on my rump. Just you wait till you start cavalry training, Gervase. Up, down, on the left, on the right. Trot, canter, gallop. And all without saddles. And God help you if you fall off with Jones looking on."

Gervase was a better horseman than Roscoe, and Roscoe knew it, and Gervase knew that Roscoe knew it, so he suspected that his friend was deliberately instilling apprehension, or, at least, trying to do so. He had rarely used a saddle since he was a boy. But he had not yet realized that the essence of cavalry training, any military training, is repetition: Do that again and again and again, until you don't think about it, until, even when the salt sweat is in your eyes and your head is reeling, you do what you are told, and your men do what they are told, without thought, without any form of conscious decision, so that thought and decision can be left for more important matters.

"I got a gun just like the Colonel's," said Roscoe, and plunged into the tent. He came out with what seemed to be a miniature cannon, but that was, in fact, a Le Mat pistol. It fired nine bullets, and had a special barrel underneath the ball barrel that fired a charge of buckshot. "One of the boys fired this yesterday, and it dislocated his arm. It ain't dislocated mine yet. And it won't. Here, look!" Gervase realized that the weapon was loaded, and he was to be given a demonstration. A fat bird, black, a crow, obscene, was preening itself on the top of a tent pole. Roscoe took careful aim, holding the weapon with both hands, and pulled the trigger. There was an enormous bang. The bird, unharmed, flapped off in leisurely contempt. Roscoe, meanwhile, was picking himself out of the dirt and holding his left wrist with his right hand. Gervase laughed. "Have you dislocated your arm, soldier?" he asked. Roscoe, angry and bellicose but unable to do anything about it, looked at his friend. The anger rapidly turned to apprehension as a voice echoed down the line: "Mr. Stedman, have you been firing that damned gun again? Come here, sir. Run, sir, run." Major Jones stood upright, hitting his thigh with a riding crop. He was a figure to cause apprehension. "When I say run, I mean *move*. And you too, Mr. Stepton. I'll wager that you are not guiltless." They reached him and stood before him. "At attention, attention. You were both at Lexington, so you know what I mean by attention. You think this is a picnic. Doubtless you would like ladies to witness your gallantry. You . . . soldiers! You are two boys. Yes, gentlemen, mere *boys*." He seemed to spit out the word. "You put the camp into alarm. You waste ammunition. Is this the action of soldiers? The colonel shall know of this. Stand there until I fetch him, and, gentlemen, pray do not move a muscle—not a muscle." He strode off, turning his thin back on them, not another word.

"Old bastard," said Roscoe.

"Christ, it was a stupid thing to do."

"I just wanted to show you my gun."

"Well, now you've shown me." The sun was hot, and Gervase

felt the sweat rising at the roots of his hair. When he was hot he went very red in the face; he could feel the redness spreading over his cheeks. The sun continued to shine; they continued to stand; neither Major Jones nor Colonel Stuart put in an appearance. They stood for one hour, without hats, without protection. Both of them were swaying on their feet. Gervase felt his vision blurring. The tents were beginning to wheel around him in great arcs and shifting circles. The sweat had disappeared by this time and had left a smelly dryness. His eyes seemed to be filled with sand, his mouth with soil. His knees started to buckle. He felt a hand beneath his shoulder, and a calm voice, calm yet cold, said:

"Hold up, Lieutenant. You've got to learn in the Army." There was no great sympathy in the voice; there was a recognition of the justice of the punishment, but some touch of human compassion, perhaps a small feeling that Jones was being excessive in his retribution. "And since I know your father, I wouldn't want to see his son collapse on the dirt like a schoolboy."

By now Major Jones had returned. He cried out in frustrated anger.

"You there, damn you, get away from those two young officers. Leave them to stand. Who is it? I might have known. Indeed, I might have known. You'll be before the colonel, Mosby, within the hour." Gervase croaked a reply.

"He was only helping us because he knows my pa."

"I don't care a damn whether he knows every member of your family. And you keep your mouth shut, you young cub. Stand up. Get your shoulders back. Back, back, back. As for you, Stedman, get your knees straight. Mosby, report yourself at the guard tent under arrest."

"No," came the reply, soft, utterly determined, brooking no response. It appeared that Jones was about to have an apoplectic fit.

"No? No!" There was a pause while the major gained control of himself. "That's mutiny. You could be shot. And, by God, I'll have you shot, Mosby, I'll have you shot."

"I see no need for you to repeat yourself. And, Major, we draw no pay in this regiment. We are not in the presence of the enemy. So you try to shoot me, and I'll leave. But I don't think you will." By now, a number of men were gathering around. The small crowd gave way as Stuart thrust himself through their ranks. Roscoe chose that moment to faint. Stuart looked at the prone body with a slight smile. "Mr. Stedman needs more discipline, Major Jones?" He did not wait for a reply. "I think he's had enough. And I shouldn't shoot Mosby. He has some skill in getting the bullet home first." He walked up to Gervase, who was swaying on his feet. "Yes, sir, I know it's hard. But Major Jones was right. Don't forget that. He was right. Now go and put your head in water. And, John, take Mr. Stedman and do the same for him." Gervase noted with some surprise that Mosby took the use of his Christian name with a casual acceptance strange in a mere private. He turned and saw that Mosby had a pistol thrust in his belt, and another down his boot. The face was long, unbearded, and stern. It was a cross between Stuart's own and Jackson's. And his respect for Jones increased, for Jones had not hesitated to berate a most formidable and heavily armed man, a man moreover who was known to shoot those who took too many liberties with him. Gervase realized that Jones, too, lived for an ideal: the perfection of the military life. But his conception of a perfect army was a collection of automata, who responded like machines to a word of command. He was hard, but his hardness was superficial. He was a fine trainer of cavalry, but he was not likely to make a great captain in war. He was too inflexible. He saw why men loved the colonel. But he also felt that the colonel was exploiting his own position: He allowed Jones to draw the hatred upon himself, and then Stuart could intervene with some act of compassion or mitigation. Gervase could see the sense of this, but he felt that it showed that Stuart lacked some touch of moral courage. It takes bravery to be hated. He saluted and walked as steadily as he could over to the water butt and plunged his head into the cool depths, shaking his blond hair when he came up for air. Mosby plunged Stedman into the same water, and he came up spluttering and beginning to swear with his usual mildness of outrage. Mosby held him by the collar.

"Don't shoot that pistol again, Lieutenant, until you've made your right arm a little stronger." Those words probably had more effect than Jones' punishment—but then, without Jones' punishment as their prelude, they would have had no effect at all. Gervase was starting to understand something of the nature of preparation for war. Meanwhile, in Washington, General McClellan was being very merciful to all his men.

2

To Imitate the Action of the Tiger

On Sunday (the brigadier won't like *that*, thought Gervase) the 1st Virginia Cavalry was drawn up along the Warrenton Turnpike. Gervase stood by the head of Avenger, and saw that his troops were lined behind him, attending to their horses, laughing or smoking. They trusted him. At least they had elected him to the command when the colonel had proposed his name. He was no less sure of himself. The training that Jones had given them had increased their confidence in themselves as cavalrymen: They could perform all the required maneuvers, they could hold their heavy sabers at arm's length for ten minutes or more. And they had not yet seen a battle. They were sure of the skills of a peacetime army, and they believed in their cause. Surely that was enough. They believed in Jeb, too, for the command was now wholly his; Jones had been left behind at Richmond with the recruits and the remounts.

The sound of gunfire thundered to the north. Strange rumors had filtered back with the wounded. On the high hills over the Bull Run were crowds of Yankee reporters, politicians, dames, and virgins. They had spread fair white cloths on the grass and produced hampers packed with good food—chickens, corn, butter, and bottles of wine. Then, with hastily converted opera glasses, they had turned their attention to the battlefield, awaiting the entertainment of the destruction of the rebels—for, after all, there were far more Yankees than rebels on the field. America had not seen a battle since 1812—only heard of some skirmishes in Mexico. There could be little doubt of the result. Overwhelming numbers, a righteous cause. What more was needed, by God? Mindful of the Sabbath, some preachers were holding forth to the civilians, who were too full and too replete and too confident to give much attention to the words of the divines. Horses were grazing by carriages decorated for the day—the day of reckoning for the rebel armies. And, indeed, the events had so far justified them. The further confused noises suggested that the Yankees were drawing nearer.

Gervase had never seen artillery firing before. He was puzzled, even though he knew something of the theory of gunnery, by the fact that the gunners did not seem to see their targets. Nor did they often hit them, either, but the waiting troops were not to know that. The great bangs, and the hard smell of cordite and gunpowder, were comforting. Gervase mildly wondered whether he might be killed, and dismissed the thought. He did not know death other than as a word.

The wounded were something of a shock. Some conformed to his idea of what wounded soldiers should be: They lay on stretchers, or on the ground, silent, white, with the occasional prayer or moan. But some had little idea of how to comport themselves. They screamed and blasphemed. Gervase had thought that wounds were usually decent. He shuddered a little at smashed heads; at men holding in their intestines with their hands, and the blue-red guts spilling through the fingers. They saw a battery that had been hit by several balls. There were hands, heads, and legs lying on the ground. Gervase could not think of them as the remains of living persons like himself. They seemed to be wax models, cast aside by some wearied clown. The eyes in the heads were blank, without feeling or quickness just like the statues of which he had seen illustrations in books his mother had shown him. But his troops were bearing up well; there had been no cases of cowardice—not, indeed, in the whole regiment. Roscoe galloped up to him, laughing. He was accompanied by Josiah Tate, who had not been to Lexington. Josiah was a religious boy, like the brigadier, he was troubled by fighting on the Sabbath. It was less virtuous to send a soul to heaven on Sunday, Gervase supposed. Was God too busy to receive them?

"How are you, Gervase?" asked Roscoe. "Josiah here wants to pray, so I said we've come along to see you." Roscoe infected the world around him with a sense of happiness, but a happiness touched by irresponsibility. He was incapable of being anything other than a joker. This had its uses, as the colonel knew. Except for the artillery, the battle seemed very far away. Gallopers thundered by, raising the dust, which smarted the eyes. Wounded men limped back, or were carried. But Gervase hardly felt involved yet. Like the Yankee picnickers, he was a spectator. It was the last hour of his youth, the last hour when he could avoid the questions to which each man is subject merely because he is a man—questions about the world, and questions about himself. The cannon to their left discharged in unison, and Roscoe's horse reared.

"I should dismount," remarked Gervase affectionately. "You don't want to be thrown before the battle begins, do you?" Roscoe jumped down. He looked up the road. He sneered—as far as Roscoe could sneer.

"Here's our ally," he said. He pointed to the figure of Major Buxton of the Grenadier Guards, who was picking his way mincingly along the road. He paused by them, and spoke in his English drawl. He had a small, stubby mustache, and he was smoking a cigar.

"Plenty of fun up front," he said. "*Not* like the Crimea. But then I never understood much about war. Big armies; plenty of chaps to shoot and be shot at—that's soldiering as I know it." He smiled appealingly. "Your colonel says I may ride with you. Not my thing really, cavalry action. Just a Guardsman, you know. Still, my heart's on the right side, I think. Good dust up." Roscoe grinned.

"Yes, very good dust up." Gervase was no diplomatist, but he knew that the English were important to the Confederacy. He spoke more acceptingly. "I'd be pleased to have you with us, sir." Gervase naturally deferred to age, and he could not recognize a fool when he saw one, albeit it a gallant fool. They were near to some trees, tall elms. There was a crash and a splintering noise. Gervase watched a cannon ball bounce down the road, on the hard mud of the turnpike, and smack into a horse, which collapsed in bloody jelly. The trooper had swayed aside in time.

"Things jollying up," said Major Buxton. Gervase raised his voice and called to the trooper to fetch a remount from the center at Manassas Junction Station. Major Buxton drew on his cigar. "Your chaps are bearing up damn well," he said. "Even though your discipline is pretty poor, they seem to know the score." Gervase turned toward him with a rebuke on his lips, but recoiled slightly before the unspeakable calm of the English eyes. "Nervy? Best to do something during this wait. A game of cards?" "No," said Gervase. He found himself trembling. The Englishman laid his hand on his arm, soft yet insistent. "No need for any worry. It's the waiting that wears upon one." A stilted address, but the involuntary trembling in Gervase's muscles stopped. His heart, which had been beating very rapidly, calmed down. Then Stuart's galloper (who was, as might be expected, John Singleton Mosby) came down the road and pulled up in a flurry of froth and dust.

"Mount up," he called out. "All officers to the front to the colonel." Gervase swung himself into the saddle. Together with Roscoe and Josiah and the egregious Major Buxton, they galloped up the turnpike toward Mathew's Stone. The major fell behind a little. He called after them. "I say, no need to gallop. A canter will do at this stage. Save your horses." Good sense indeed, but the boys in the last half hour of their adolescence were not likely to listen to mere good sense. War had nothing to do with good sense, but with the utmost, with chivalry in its naked majesty.

At that moment, another cannon ball came over the trees. It was rather less considerate this time, but took off Major Buxton's left arm. He fell off his horse with a most undignified squeal and lay writhing on the road. Gervase reined in and ran over to him. The blood was pulsing from his stump, and Gervase knelt beside him. The blood covered his face as it fled from the arteries. Gervase wiped it from his eyes with his gray sleeve and bent down to hear the last words.

"Through the Crimea to die in a damned American battle," the man whispered. "What a waste! What a bloody waste."

"Mount up, sir," shouted Mosby. "You can leave him until later." Gervase pulled Avenger to him. The horse was nervous at the noise and shied. Viciously, Gervase pulled his head down and clambered into the saddle. The Englishman lay on the hard

ground and died. He was surrounded with blood. His cigar still
smoldered. It was an end as gallant and pointless as his life.

They reached the clapboard whiteness, now stained, of
Mathew's Station. There Jeb waited for them, plumed hat, Le
Mat, seated firmly on Virginia, whom he had on a tight bit. He
smiled at his young officers. "You be pleased to hear, gentlemen,
that we have been placed under the command of your old lecturer, now Brigadier Jackson. The Yankees have broken through,
and Jackson's brigade stands between them and victory. When
he holds them—not *if*, but *when*—we'll get about their asses.
And remember, gentlemen, this is a battle. You are here not to
wound, not to capture, but to *kill* Yanks." His smile became almost grotesque in its fierceness. "Now go and *kill them*. Move
your troops up to the crossroads north of Dogan's. Quickly."

It is a commonplace of description of battles that the individual knows nothing of the general engagement; he is caught up in
the fury of individual combat and, at the most, company
skirmishes, while the pattern of the battle is lost to him. This was
less true than usual of the first charge of Gervase's regiment.
Stuart had them drawn up at the edge of the oak woods south of
the Sudley Pike on the Bull Run River. They were at the extreme
west of the line, and could see something of the shape the battle
was taking. With absurd bravery the Union forces charged. But
the raw infantry were not able to sustain themselves under fire.
On the other hand, the Confederate infantry were no more cool
under cannon fire. They fell back; sometimes the retreat turned
to rout. However, in the center stood Jackson's brigade, and
Jackson was not accustomed to panic. Confederate leaders kept
pointing to his men: There the name "Stonewall" was born. And
the Union troops, meeting a resolute resistance, lost heart and
fell back. Again, some turned the withdrawal into a rout. They
began to run, flinging their weapons and equipment to the
ground. Some men climbed trees; some hid behind fences, vomiting their fear onto the ground. But some responded to their commanders, and made a fighting retreat, taking up defensive positions, and turning their weapons (which they had retained)
upon their pursuers. To the northeast of the 1st Virginia Cavalry,
an extraordinary body of men were behaving with intrepid bravery, almost as if they were seasoned troops. It was necessary to

break them, and Stuart was chosen for the task. Cautious as ever, Jackson detailed an infantry regiment to support him—which was just as well. Stuart rode up the gray-black ranks and shouted to his men.

"Boys! Listen to me! We've got to bust up some firemen. They call themselves *Zouaves*. I ask you, Zouaves! But they're nothing but the New York City fire fighters. There they are in front of you, dressed in red, so you can see them plain and easy. Their commander is Colonel Ellsworth. Now let's see their asses, boys." At which he turned, his plumed hat rakish, his saber in his right hand hung down by the flank of Virginia, and began to canter toward the red mass a few hundred yards in front.

His regiment followed him. Gervase found that his troop was in the front of the leading company. He drew his saber, and relished the feel of the rough handle resting in his hand. Avenger strode out, snorting at the nostrils, the finest black horse among fine black horses. They seemed to cover the ground at extraordinary speed. He expected to see the red Zouaves increase their pace, fling their weapons aside, and run. But he could see officers, little dolls, waving their arms, brandishing pistols, and many of the red dolls turned. They took up a position behind a hedge that ran along the line of the west flank of the Confederate line. There was a shattering crash, and Gervase heard a strange whistling fill the air around him. After a second or two he realized that it was the noise of bullets. The trooper next to him screamed and slumped over the saddle. His horse careened onward. Gervase heard the noise subside behind him. He was filled with nothing but exhilaration; this was glory. He felt a tugging at his right shoulder and, glancing to the side, saw that he had a hole in his tunic, jagged, rough, torn by a bullet. They were fifty yards away from the firemen. He expected that the civic officials would turn and run. They did not. They stood at the hedge, and once again the whistling filled the air. This time it was louder, insistent, violent, threatening. His sense of glory began to be qualified by some other feeling, less definite but no less real. Not fear, not apprehension, but an awareness that he might be killed, that *he* might scream and flop forward on his saddle, and that the choice did not lie with him but with that Chance that directs bullets in their course and that is no respecter of persons. He yelled. They all yelled—that tremulous, vicious, violent outburst of air that turned many a Yankee stomach in fear and loathing.

Suddenly Gervase felt as if he had been struck hard on the left hand with a stick. He glanced down and saw that the hand was covered with blood. He did not hesitate, he did not retard the momentum of his charge. He looked down and saw a face, a mere blur, gazing up at him, waving a rifle with a bayonet affixed to the barrel, which looked dangerous. He swung with his saber and saw the eyes disappear in a smudge of red. The air was filled with whistling, screams, and the roar of cannon. He swung his saber again. It struck nothing but air. He was moving through the Zouaves at an enormous pace. He checked Avenger at the very moment a bullet struck the horse and he sank beneath him. He rolled aside with a skill half intuitive and half the result of training. He found himself in the midst of the Union infantry, who were engaged in hand-to-hand struggles.

He was not afraid. He could not, at this time, understand what it was to be afraid. But he needed time to think, and he had no time to think. He dragged at his pistol, a solid Griswold and Gunnison revolver, sound in its brass frame (No. 103), and without aiming, fired the weapon. The recoil bashed against his palm and the shock went up to his elbow. This was no good. He had to think. It was at that moment that a Zouave, a veteran of many a fierce fire in New York City, smashed his rifle into the back of Gervase's knees, and he sank to the ground, involuntarily letting out a cry. He turned and saw the young fire fighter, and fired his pistol into his head at two feet distance. His gray tunic was covered with the grayer mess of brains. The man, in his dying gesture, clasped Gervase around the knees, a clutch that was difficult to remove. As he leaned down to pull the hands away from his knees, he looked up to find a young Zouave coming at him with a bayonet leveled at his breast. He flung himself sideways and the red figure ran by him, checked himself, and turned, swinging his rifle high into the air in order to face the bayonet once more at Gervase. The dying man's hands were tight bands around his knees, the fingers intertwined and locked in blue determination, an intention once formed and now executed when the vital source of motive had disappeared the corpse. Gervase flung himself forward, and the bayonet passed over his head. He struck upward with his hands, taking the Zouave in the groin. He gave a stifled groan and toppled over on the ground beside Gervase, who seized his rifle, despite the now acute pain in his left hand, and swung it like a club. It struck the Zouave on the side of his head, but his kepi acted as a softener to the blow. His eyes were glazed; he blinked; but he began to pull himself to his feet. Gervase knew that he would not have time to reverse the rifle and fire it. He struggled to find the catch to release the bayonet so that he might use it as a sword, but he was unused to the type of weapon. His hands, covered with slimy blood, slid around the steel helplessly.

The Zouave, still half conscious, looked around for a new weapon himself, and saw Gervase's saber lying on the ground. In the few seconds while he staggered over to pluck up the saber, Gervase became conscious of the appalling noise around him. Men were screaming—some in pain, some in fear, and some with the intention of unnerving their foes. The most intense noises came from the horses. He became conscious of thrashing and pounding hooves all around him; conscious of horses rolling on the ground and beating their limbs against the earth to relieve the intolerable pain. To his left a horse lay mute, its eyes like great glass bulbs, its stomach ripped open by a long bayonet and the intestines spreading in a mess of tubes and pipes and yellow oats partially digested. A hitherto silent self within Gervase began to scream, although he checked the emergence of the sounds. These vignettes flashed across his consciousness in the suspension of time while his conscious mind watched the Zouave pick up the saber.

While Gervase had been unfamiliar with the infantry weapon, the Zouave was equally unfamiliar with the cavalry piece. He stood irresolute, wondering whether to stab or swing with it. He made the usual mistake. Perhaps he had seen pictures of dashing cavalrymen slashing with their sabers from the saddle. He did not stop to consider that he was not in the saddle, but on foot. He swung; Gervase ducked again, and the blade whistled over his head. The weight of the saber swung the Zouave around, and he lost his balance. Gervase at last kicked himself free from the clinging embrace of death and, as the infantryman presented his back, he drove the bayonet into his kidney. He was used to the momentum that a horse gave to the weight of his blow, and was surprised by the effort he needed to give to his push. He felt the resistance of the red cloth, then the lesser resistance of the outer layer of skin, and finally the easy slide as the blade sunk into the left kidney itself. The Zouave went suddenly still, as if he had been struck by Zeus' lightning; the body went rigid, a stuck pig (but no pig; indeed, once a gallant though inexperienced fighter). He let out a high-pitched shriek, lost in the dissonances of the whole field, remained static for a moment, which appeared an hour to Gervase, and then toppled forward, the weight of his body drawing the rifle with him so that it sprung up and struck Gervase a glancing blow on the cheek and bruised him.

Would this never end? Another Zouave came at him the moment he had dispatched his first opponent. The man was running with his rifle and bayonet poised. He had lost his kepi, and Gervase could see his frizzled ginger hair, his green eyes wide and bereft of feeling or reason, lost in berserk fury of the battle. He had ten feet to cover, and at five feet his head disappeared in a bloody mess. Gervase, on his knees, was covered with the bloody matter. He looked up and saw Roscoe grinning down at him, his face powder-stained, holding the Le Mat smoking in his right hand, a saber in his left.

"Didn't knock me over that time, Gervase," he shouted. Then he careered off on his horse, after the running red figures, and plunging toward the gap in the lines that the charge of the 1st Virginia Cavalry had made; for the Prince Rupert of the South had made the same error as his Cavalier predecessor: He had allowed his regiment to charge headlong, and they had not known when to stop. They had torn a hole in the Union line, and poured through it. Now they were in open country and without order. But now the merit of Jackson's prudence became clear. The 33rd Virginia Infantry, strangely dressed in blue uniforms (a source of ready confusion to the Federals), began to advance and take over the ground itself. The western flank was safe.

Gervase rose to his feet. He staggered forward, and then recovered himself; he was drained of physical power. He looked around the field, which might have been a beautiful sight if one was only concerned with colors. There were black horses, gray men with yellow-and-black facings, men in red and blue, men in dark blue uniforms—all painted with red—all lying in patterns that stayed motionless or twitched and writhed. Men were pulling themselves to their feet, or to their knees; remaining there or falling forward onto the green grass. Men were wandering over the field without direction, meaning, or purpose, intent only on escape from the place of turmoil. Gervase vomited.

A battlefield is a fearfully *haphazard* place. Smoke drifts, bullets fly, men die, without any sense of order. The will of the commander is something impalpable, far away, which imposes itself through the minute links of order and counterorder, away from the mess and panic and suffering, though always conscious of their reality. Later in the war, Gervase was to see the control exercised by the greatest of captains, and to see the intellectual passion of war in action. But at this stage of the conflict neither of the commanders could exercise such control: Their troops did not respond other than sluggishly to their wishes, and they themselves were inexperienced in the complexities of command. They unleashed their forces, and then waited, helplessly, for a result. The South had won the fire battle of tactics, but their command, the glamorously named Beauregard, had no ability to initiate a strategic victory. And so this field was more than usually haphazard. Cavalry were learning to charge; infantry to maneuver, resisting and advancing; the staffs were learning how to sort the chaff from the wheat. It was the testing time of men and armies and, although both failed the test, it was inevitable that this should be so. The profession of arms does not yield its inner secrets on the parade ground. Not only were armies finding themselves, but men were as well. The illusion of glory had evaporated with the coming of its reality. Nothing is so different from the image of war than its true being. First Manassas was a battle of discovery.

Gervase felt himself being raised, firmly but gently, and saw a stretcher bearer from the 33rd Virginia at his side. The man led him over the field toward Mathew's Stone, where the field hospital had been set up. Gervase glanced down at his left hand. The

middle finger had been cut in half. From the bloody mush, blood
pumped with an automatic remorselessness, apart from his will.
The hand throbbed in great waves of pain, which surged from
his heart and down the intricate and numerous nerves of his left
arm. He knew, as he looked around him, that his was not a serious wound; he could see plenty of serious wounds around him.
Most piteous were the calls for water, for the day was hot and
the sun was fierce in the blue immensity of the sky, a nature pitiless to fragmented and yearning men. They came toward the
stone house where the hospital tents were established. But before they came there they met a mounted staff, which was picking its way over the battlefield. The general in their midst,
unadorned, saw Gervase and rode over to him. Gervase saluted,
a compliment gravely returned. Gervase looked up at his old lecturer in mathematics and artillery at Lexington.

"Wounded, Mr. Stepton?" asked Jackson.

"A mere wound in the hand, General," replied Gervase. The
words were difficult to force from his mouth, but he kept his
voice steady. This was not easy; he wanted to lie down on the
ground and weep. The energy of battle had seeped from him; he
was in the grip of shock and exhaustion. And yet it was less than
an hour since he had gone into action. And he suddenly thought,
Where is Roscoe? Where is Josiah? Roscoe had saved him, and
treated the salvation like a game. But without that play he
would not be talking to Jackson. The sudden horror of what
might have been swept over him like a sea of nausea.

"Give thanks to the Lord," said Jackson. "Give him thanks, too,
for giving us this glorious victory. Let us not speak praise to ourselves, but rather to the Lord for delivering them into our hands.
And see, Gervase," he said softly, "I have not escaped scatheless
myself. We are of a kind, though I fear you are in a worse state
than I." And he held up his own left hand. The knuckle of his
long middle finger was breaking through the surrounding blue
flesh. Gervase was fascinated by the sight of this wound, so
much so that he hardly noticed that the general had called him
by his Christian name. That Gervase was to remember later. A
wounded soldier broke in upon them; he was lying broken upon
the ground, a bullet in his spine. He was not calling upon the
Lord, but voicing a stream of obscenities and blasphemy. Jack-

son rode his horse over to him and looked down at the face twisted with the jagged thrusts of the unbearable. Jackson's voice was stern as he spoke.

"Pray, man," he said. "Do not disgrace your regiment. Pray to the Lord of mercies that he will cure or release you." And, perhaps strangely, the man fell silent. In the murder of a battle, the calmness and confidence of a great captain radiates like a ripple in a quiet pool; it creates a center of peace in the flatness of despair.

"Get to the surgeons, Mr. Stepton," Jackson called back, as he urged his horse into motion, and his staff bunched once more behind him, and his hungry eyes ranged over the field, down to Bull Run and over to the high hills beyond. These hills were now empty of picnickers, empty of carriages, empty of celebration; only a few dots, which were the tiny figures of fleeing men, punctuated the green slopes almost lost in the blue haze of late afternoon.

The stretcher bearer took Gervase up to the hospital tents, and a deeper dread seized him. Here he was in no danger—at least, not danger such as he had faced half an hour before. He did not know of gangrene, so he did not fear it. But he feared the prospect of a clinical pain, a pain that he had to watch being inflicted and that was for his good. When the body and mind are alive with passion, danger passes by like an unseen ghost; in a hospital it looms like a great statue of marble, omnipresent. As a boy he had known pain when he had fallen off his horse, when he had been bitten by a dog (thankfully not rabid), when he had fought with his friends and their sense of competition had overcome them and they had hit too hard. But in the hospital tent it was different. He had gone into the hot belly of the tent. Here the screams were more daunting than on the field. They were confined, not lost in the air, not mingled with the hiss of bullets and the whinnying of the horses. Here the noise was wholly human; here Gervase, who knew his Bible, began to learn the penalty of Adam. A doctor came over to him. The man was wearing a leather apron. He was covered with blood; his face was bloody, his apron was scarlet punctuated by gouts of purple, and his hands literally dripped blood. He was wiping them with a red cloth as Gervase came to him. The doctor spoke brusquely.

He had to be brusque, for this was his battle; this was the time when he could not think except with the passion of his profession.

"Let me see, sir. Left hand, second finger. Serious laceration as far as the knuckle. I can't save that, sir. It would turn gangrenous. The hand will recover. Be thankful its the left and not the right! You are not left-handed, sir? Good. Drink this." He handed Gervase a bottle of whiskey. Gervase, his stomach a whirling ball of emptiness, drank the burning fluid. He felt it course down his throat, scalding as it went. "More, sir, more. That's it." Gervase felt the whiskey acting on his empty stomach. He tasted bitterness and vomit on his tongue, wet with whiskey yet dry with fear. He did not see two members of the Medical Corps approaching him. They moved silently, delicately, ambassadors of pain. "Warmed you up, eh, sir? Hold him!" The last order was snapped out, and the Medical Corps men grasped Gervase around the arms, while one grasped his left arm and pulled him forward to a deal table, soaked in blood, over which an attendant had halfheartedly thrown a bucket of water. His hand was placed on the wood, and the doctor brought forward a small saw. He separated Gervase's fingers and brought the blade to bear. He began to saw with great pressure and at great speed.

"Mother!" cried Gervase, losing control of himself before he knew it. He recalled his mother's hand on his head when he had measles as a child, the cool lemon water she brought him. It was as if hot irons were being driven into his arm. The sawing ceased and the doctor flicked a wand of flesh onto the sawdust under the table. He took a needle and thread from the lapel of the coat under his apron and brought the two flaps of skin together, and began to sew them up, neatly, expertly, like a woman with her linen.

"There, sir, a neat job, although I venture to say so myself. You comported yourself well, sir. And now, if you will excuse me, I have other patients." Gervase did not appreciate the studied civility of the doctor's address, but he would have missed it had it not been there. Indeed, this decorum, this illusion that one gentleman was doing another a service, made the operation bearable. It brought civilization into a place that was the negation of all values. This was present to Gervase as he slumped forward in a faint, and was carried by the medical men to a corner of the tent where they laid him upon the ground to sleep himself back to contentment and reconciliation with his disturbed being. He had acquitted himself well, but he had learned that there were limits to his capacity, limits to every man's capacity, which is the essential feature of the human condition. The greatness of war lies in the humbling of the imagination; it teaches us that we are but finite in our bodies whatever may be the vaunting of our souls. So ended the Battle of Manassas Junction, for which, as Jackson wrote to his wife, "all the glory is due to *God alone*."

3

A Sylvan Scene

Gervase chose to ride South from Richmond to Sweetwater. "Get home for a week, boy," Stuart had said to him, and then switched easily to the formal mode of address. "And present my affection to your father and my respects to your mother." Gervase had bought a new horse in Richmond, a tractable mare with great haunches, and called her Lenore. He was a reader of Edgar Allan Poe, although his father smiled at this curious taste for the Gothic. And certainly, Gervase thought, as he trotted down the Newmarket Road, it does not look as if the Red Death has come to us yet. The farm workers were laboring in the fields; some black, but more white—farmers on their own patch. The only difference from the previous year was that there were more women assisting, and the men were older; gray hairs did not preclude strength, however, and skill was substituted for mere brawn. Their sons were away at the war, but they did not think they would be away long. As he turned off down the River Road at Bailey's Creek, Gervase began to recognize many of the faces, and shouted greetings, which were joyfully returned. Old man Mouton came across to him.

"You were at Manassas, Gervase?" he asked.

"Yes, sir," said Gervase.

"You sure whipped those Yankees," said Mouton with a grin. "Down here we heard that they couldn't stop running until they reached Washington." He spat. "Yellow, I say."

"No, Mr. Mouton," replied Gervase, "they're not yellow. They may have run, but they're not cowards."

"That's as may be," said Mouton skeptically. "If a man runs in a battle, then he's yellow." He looked down at the ground, playing in the earth with his hoe. "I'm sorry about your hand, Gervase." Gervase smiled his thanks. It was impossible to communicate the complex truth of a battle to a patriot such as Mouton; to him, all Yankees were yellow. No, more: Anyone who ran was yellow, and he would have been even more ready to condemn those Confederate brigades that had poured back over Bull Run in the opening stages of the engagement. He would have condemned them himself three weeks ago, before he realized that a battle exerts sudden and arbitrary pressures upon certain units, which the individual will cannot resist. To run is not always cowardly; only to the listener to rumor, or the reader of newspapers. He saw Mouton's daughter walking across the baked field toward them. She, too, was clearly helping her father in the fields, even though she was of Gervase's circle, and therefore a "lady." The first and most important quality of being a lady is not to care about its exterior manifestations. Deborah Mouton had the soul and spirit of a lady, but she didn't care about washing for herself and her father, or riding about in trousers. He found that the "idea" of southern womanhood was too often confused with the absurd trappings of excessive gentility. The simpering belles might dance away the night in Richmond or Charleston, but they would not be of much use, nor much respected in the farmlands between the James and the Chickahominy. Mouton, however, after waving to his daughter, was not disposed to give up his strategical speculations. "No, we won't have the Yanks down here yet a while," he said with satisfaction. "Not after the whipping General Beauregard gave them. A fine man, General Beauregard." Gervase saluted Deborah, and she grinned at him. Her face was even in feature; her hair red; her face was freckled, but the tan of the summer sun had given her a light brown hue. She had, as have most redheads, a delicate complexion, and the skin was peeling; it must have hurt, but she did not seem to care. Gervase had known her since boyhood; he was rather afraid of her vitality which bubbled over like a clear-

water spring. He admired her energy, for, since her mother's
death she had sustained her father and forced him to apply himself to the running of the farm when all he wanted to do was sit
down in front of his white house from ten o'clock in the morning
and drink whiskey, leaving all to Charles, his loyal but somewhat
feckless Negro overseer (though, of course, Charles was free, as
were all Mouton's black workers—as were the workers of Gervase's father; they had freed their slaves way back in the early
forties; Virginia was not fighting for the perpetuation of slavery,
but for the perpetuation of freedom of decision). Deborah drove
her father with affectionate but forceful words; she had not let
him slide into *accidie*. After a year or two he no longer wished
to, and since he was an intelligent and responsive man, he gave
his daughter the credit for his moral salvation. He looked at her
gently, as if she were a friend as well as his blood. The James
River curved around his farm, and the ground needed constant
draining; the woods were thick, but gave place to maintained,
clean fields, and the ground sloped gently up to Malvern Hill, on
which sat the whiteness of Binford's house.

"You might yet see the Yankees here, sir," said Gervase. "There
are plenty of them. And Mr. Lincoln's not the man to give up.
But we'll send them back home again. Now good day to you, sir.
Deborah." He touched his wide hat again with his right hand. "I
must be off to my parents." "Come over to see me this evening if
you have the time," Deborah shouted toward his retreating back.
"Tell us about the battle. Daddy wishes he'd been there." Gervase did not know; Mouton did not know; Deborah did not
know: They'd all be "there" soon enough. Gervase urged Lenore
into a canter. He did not wait for the turn off Quaker Road up to
Willis Church, but went over his own fields. The fields of his father, true, but in this county there was no great distinction between the generations except those that were required by civility: The fields were those of the Stepton family, not his or his
father's. The same was true of the fields alongside, which were
those of the Stedman family. They were all bound to the soil—
just as much as the slaves had been in the old days of bondage.
There was a community between the land and those who worked
upon it: Each owned the other, and this intercourse established
a slow-moving, patterned way of life—the times of the plow and

harrow, the times of the ax and halter, the times of the barn and the scythe. These were their fundamental realities; their "style" something above and beyond that to affirm their "humanity," that there was a difference between them and the animals Gervase could now see lowing and lazing under the trees in the tranquil heat, seeking shadow and fulfillment. He suspected that the Yankees did not realize why the South was fighting: The Yankees saw everything in blacks and whites, in terms of great moral dilemmas. There was nothing of moral dilemma in himself; there was a mere recognition that this land was in his blood and was in his father's blood and would be in his children's. Which made him think of Deborah, and he kicked Lenore in the sides and leaped over a tangle of boughs that covered a twisting stream, affirming his manhood. The sexual had barely entered their relationship in the last years. It had not been wholly absent, however; as she grew up, her breasts ripened, her gaze became more charged with meaning. But they knew how to take their time in Virginia—suspension of action in the interests of a greater intensity of prepared, nutured and educated feeling; to be direct would be so crude.

His father was standing outside the house talking to his stable boy, Henry. His father saw Gervase come from some distance, it was plain, for he raised his right arm in a wave and came striding forward into the meadow that ran down to the Sweetwater. As he saw his father coming into the grass with the house behind him, Gervase felt his eyes blur with tears. It was not held shameful to weep; now he had a greater intensity of thankfulness at the contemplation of the ordinary, for he might so easily not have contemplated it ever again. He pricked the horse into a gallop, splashed through the warm water of the Sweetwater, clambered up the bank and over the field, and jumped off his horse. His father embraced him, gripping him hard; after a moment they parted. His father looked into his eyes.

"Welcome home, son."

"It's good to be back, sir."

"Let's look at your hand," said his father. His skin was harder than Gervase's, but he took the left hand tenderly into the cradle of his own. The skin was still red, with white ridges down the cuts.

"The surgeon has done a good job, Gervase. Real neat. Thank God you didn't meet some butcher." Gervase laughed.

"You know, sir, I think all surgeons are butchers. Even the good ones. You have to be a butcher to carve up flesh." His voice became more somber. "And they had plenty of flesh to carve." His father looked at him sharply.

"How was the battle?" he asked. They all asked this—ladies in Richmond; the horse dealer in Richmond; even beggars in Richmond. But they thought they knew, like Mouton. His father was less easy to deceive.

"The Yanks ran," replied Gervase. It was the easy answer. His father had never been satisfied with easy answers.

"So did some of our boys, if I've heard it told right." His father was in some ways unwilling to probe like this. But he was a skeptical man, eager for the truth even when it hurt, because the hurt of truth is ultimately finer than the spiritual lassitude of comforting lies or half truths.

"Yes, they did," replied Gervase. "If it hadn't been for General Jackson's brigade, then we might have broken."

"And why didn't you push them back to Washington? You're cavalry. You should have done it. I wouldn't have thought Jeb would have let them rest until he saw back home." Gervase felt a weariness of spirit. How could he tell his father of the weariness that follows a battle; of the confusion; of the lost purposes? He evaded the question.

"You can't blame me, sir. I was having my finger hacked off in a tent." His father bridled.

"I'm not *blaming* anyone, least of all you. You weren't the general. But it seems to me that Peter Beauregard isn't the new Napoleon that everyone says he is." His father refused to give the Louisiana general his French name; he always anglicized it. This was not arrogance, but a casual assumption that his own way, his own language, was the right one to pin down the truth. If he had been required to write to Beauregard he would, of course, have written out "Pierre Gustave Toutant" in full—but not in talking with his son. "I didn't see General Beauregard during the action," said Gervase, "only General Jackson; and he pursued with his brigade."

"A brigade commander can't win a battle," replied his father with a wry and rather bitter smile. "Thomas Jackson couldn't gain the field for us at Manassas." This stung Gervase.

"No, but he stopped the Yanks getting it."

"You're right there." His father was a fair man, always.

Gervase looked his father in the eye, embarrassed. Yet it must be said: "Roscoe Stedman saved my life. I'd have been spitted on a Yank bayonet but for him." His father looked at the ground and, as was his habit, drew a pattern with his toe in the dust.

"You'd do the same for him, I don't doubt. That sort of obligation is not without precedent between soldiers."

"But Father," said Gervase urgently, "Roscoe *likes* battles. He was laughing all the time through Manassas. He laughed as he killed the Yankee who was coming for me. I can't laugh during a battle."

"I'm glad you can't," replied his father. "You can't laugh because you see the pain as well as the glory. Roscoe is a very brave young man, and no one has more reason to feel gratitude to him than I. But he's limited. Should a general laugh during a battle? William Pendleton prays before he shoots his pieces, or so I've heard tell. He says, 'The Lord have mercy on their souls. Fire.'"

"But he's a minister. I'm no minister."

"Everyone is near to God in a battle. So to laugh is only a way of concealing that fact—or, perhaps, of learning to reconcile one-self with it. Don't feel that Roscoe is a better soldier than you are—nor that he is worse. I've never been in a battle, but I try to imagine it. Every father must try to do that, son." Gervase was white, not with anger or effort but with a sense that he had never had before of a barrier that it might be impossible to sur-mount.

"No one can imagine a battle who hasn't been in one."

"Perhaps you're right," his father replied. "But soon we may all be in a battle. When the Federals come again. And come again they will. You can be sure of that. I told you before you left that Lincoln wouldn't leave off. He'll *never* leave off until we're finished. And when they come again, where will it be? Answer me that."

"Ask the generals," said Gervase.

"I don't need to. It'll be here. Just here. The Army may have come to us, but the Navy didn't. Go down to Harrison's Landing and look to the sea. You can see the white sails. Next time they'll use the water. And then who'll be in the battle? You needn't reply." There was a pause. "I'm thinking of sending your mother to Richmond. She won't go. I advised Mouton to send Deborah with her. She won't go either. So I don't get very far." Once again that wry grin. His father looked so young when he grinned, so old when he did not. "So we're stuck with the ladies." He paused, this time without a grin. The cry of the workers in the fields came in the faint warm breeze—a cry of seasonal delight, utterly unrelated to the war. "I'd be grateful if you'd do your best to persuade them. Both of them." "Try persuading Deborah," replied Gervase. "Or mother, for that matter." "These women let us run the details of their lives," snapped his father. "But when we wish to advise them wisely over something important, truly important, then they refuse even to listen to us."

"That's women," said Gervase. His father replied with unwonted violence.

"What in the hell do you know of women, Gervase?" His son was long in replying.

"Nothing." Pride required a qualification. "Or next to nothing."

"Not next to nothing," rapped out his father with authority. "What you said first. Nothing. Oh Gervase, Gervase, you're the southern soldier to the core; you are truly chivalrous. But war ain't chivalrous. You read the history books. You know that armies destroy homes, burn farms, kill citizens whether they mean to or not. Most soldiers don't laugh during a campaign. They kill. And they like killing those who can't shoot back because there is less danger that way. I don't say the Yanks will be worse than us. We'll throw up some brutal trash, believe me. Probably from the cotton plantations down South." His father's face took on the look of contempt habitual to the Virginia aristocrat when he spoke of the Deep South. "But so will the Yanks. And they have this capacity for turning murder into a crusade. And, I tell you, they'll be here before the year's out. You may whip them back, but they'll be here. And I want your mother out of it. Mouton wants Deborah out of it. And they won't go." Suddenly his father seemed to become aware of a fact to which the urgency of his own thought had blinded him. "How's your hand?" It was throbbing; the pain still lanced up the arm. "I am a damn fool. Come inside. And you'll want to see your mother." Together they passed between the small, delicate white pillars into the cool of the house. There were the french chairs, the great polished desk, the white curtains hanging to the carpeted floor, the books. The house was civilization; it was very like a European house, and yet there was a subtle difference, an informality of arrangement, and a lack of false precision. Gervase flung himself onto a deep chair. He found that he was trembling. It was a continual wonder to him that there were times when he could not control his body. He had thought it was always subject to his will. He felt sure that Brigadier Jackson never let his body take over from his mind; that schooling and drill book and Bible were a constant and infallible discipline. Gervase was still inclined to hero-worship men whom he could not comprehend. His father could have told him the truth, which was different, and he could have told him that this weakness of the body did not affect the fundamental heroism of men, but rather increased it. But his father did not know all his thoughts. His father poured out a whiskey into a finely cut glass and added a dash of spring water. "Here, son," he said gently, "drink this." Gervase put out his left hand to take the glass, and then lowered it, and accepted the drink with his right hand. He knew that he must not become self-conscious about his left hand. Deformity was horrifying to him; he was lucky that it was only a finger. But, as he quested for perfection in other spheres, he found it difficult to realize that his perfect body grotesquely lacked a finger. He seemed to be departing from that ideal self that he had always imagined for himself. His father had poured a whiskey for himself and sipped it, looking down at his son. Gervase could see that his father was undergoing some tension, and that he hesitated before speaking. At last he managed to do so: It was another problem for Gervase to see his father at a loss.

"You're twenty, son, just twenty, but twenty nonetheless. I want you to marry Deborah Mouton."

Before Gervase could reply to this somewhat startling request, his mother came into the room. He was glad: He did not know how he could have replied. He did not reject the idea; it appealed to him profoundly; but the manner of its proposal daunted him—and the scurry into his deepest emotional hiding places frightened him. He had never discussed the sexual with his father, no, not the thought of marriage. And *why* should his father suggest this somewhat extraordinary course? For the normal reasons? And what might the "normal" reasons be? But now he was caught up in his mother's waves of feeling. It was only five weeks since he had last seen her, on a brief furlough, when he had escaped from Grumble's clutches for a few days, but he was surprised at the change in her. She was his mother. She had always been withdrawn, a somewhat remote figure of perfection. He lived on a farm; he knew the processes of parturition. He had seen the bull serve the cows; he had seen calves born in a bellow of pain and rope around the hooves and straining blacks at the end and his father giving careful directions in the lamplight and the sweat and broken waters. He knew, or he supposed that he knew, that human birth was the same as this. His mother had borne him in the same sweat and blood and strain, though without the rope, and with Dr. Foote officiating instead of his father, with gentle words, as befitted this exile from New Orleans who had learned his medicine in Paris and then, for God knows what reason, chosen to practice it in Virginia. "Fuite" changed to "Foote." But his association of his mother with all this—with begetting, conception, and birth—was purely conceptual. And since he was virgin himself, he could not make the mental leap in reality. His mother had always been, to him, the image of a remote, cold, yet tender perfection. She was there when he had wept as a little boy, when he had cut himself or fallen from his horse. She was much less of a guide and an authority than his father, who had set the disasters of childhood into a context of moral and emotional reality. His mother had somehow been above reality. Of course, he was an Episcopalian Christian. Yet if he had been asked to describe his idea of the supernatural, it would have been in terms of his mother. And now she showed the scars of a great humanity. Her hair, which he remembered as pure black, was tinged with gray; he could see lines in her face, on her forehead. Her eyes were puffed out, as if she had been continually weeping. She advanced toward him with hesitation, and, with a side glance, he saw his father's look of anxiety, as if he too were witnessing a diminution of his mother, a transmogrification from perfection into personality. His father did not look as if he was shocked as Gervase himself was, but as if he was frightened, as if the expected order was falling down like a great building, a temple, which suddenly, for little reason, collapsed on itself, architrave mingling obscenely with lintel and hammer beam. His mother came over to him and took his left hand. She leaned forward and kissed it.

"My poor Gervase," she said. "My poor, poor Gervase."

"It could have been much worse, Mother," he said. A demon, a cold, hard demon took hold of him. "It could have been my head, it could have been my stomach, it could have been . . ."

"Don't!" said his father sharply. He touched his wife on her bare shoulder.

"We must be thankful that it was merely the finger."

"Thankful!" she returned with something like hatred. "I didn't bear Gervase to give his body to surgeons."

"He gave his finger for Virginia," his father said coldly. Then Gervase was profoundly shocked. His mental universe suffered a jarring and painful extension.

"To hell with Virginia," said his mother. "My son is more important to me than Virginia." His father took refuge in sarcasm.

"So with many other mothers. If they all showed your weakness, then the Confederacy would be lost in a few weeks." His mother bathed his left hand in her tears. Gervase put out his hand and touched her cheek. She looked up at him, and he saw the pain of love. He had always associated love with happiness, and, suddenly, realized that love must draw upon pain as well as happiness if it is to be worth the name.

"Mother," he said, "why not go to Richmond and stay with Aunt Maria?" Aunt Maria had married a Richmond corn merchant and lived in a fine town house. She had, in his father's opinion (she was his sister) coarsened the stock by marrying out of the land. He was wont to refer to her husband as "Maria's tradesman," but he had made no attempt to cut himself off from his sister and, when they visited the estate of Sweetwater, he was scrupulously polite to both of them in his high, ironic way. He came of a generation that saw irony as the only civilized way of expressing moral discontent.

"And leave your father?" she cried. "Leave this house?" The

two seemed to be without difference in her mind. But to her
what mattered more than her husband or the house or the fields
was her son. She had lived a privileged life. She was the daughter of Pounce of Fairfax County; she had lacked nothing. Indeed,
all she lacked was a moral sense, which was not to say that she
was amoral. She was an incarnation of that style that is Virginia.
Her morality was propriety, an insistence on what was proper
down to the last, precise, infinitesimal detail. She had never
known what she valued to be threatened—and, for most of her
life, what she valued most highly was herself. But the war, and
the Battle of Manassas Junction, had made her realize that she
valued her son more highly than herself. She had only known
pain once in her life, when Gervase was born. And the pain
anointed him with value. She had worried herself into illness all
the time he had been away from them. She thought she heard
him coming in the door, she thought she heard his voice, his
horse's hooves thundering, his body splashing in the Sweetwater.
All these were illusions. And she did not possess the ability to
find a community in anxiety and sorrow. When Mrs. Stedman
came over, she refused to see her; she feigned illness. Her neigh-
bors (and her husband to begin with) thought that there was an
element of vanity in her sorrow. But there was not, as her husband soon realized. She was quite selfless. If her reasoning
powers were scant, her imagination was active. When she heard
of the battle, she rehearsed each shot to herself, she saw in her
keen eye every saber stroke. And on a visit to Lexington she had
taken an instant dislike to Professor Jackson. She thought—rightly
—that he was cold; she thought that on the field of battle he
would not hesitate to sacrifice his men to his tactical conception,
though she put it much more personally: "He'll kill Gervase."
Not even the homely domesticity of Mrs. Jackson could eradicate
this impression. She saw her son's corpse in a thousand dreams:
Each time it was bloodier and more defaced with wounds.

And since she had never before met pain, she had no mental
apparatus to conceal it. She lacked Stoicism: She did not want
her son to return on his shield. So she remained in her room with
her black servant Maria, weeping, burying her head in the fine
feather pillows, biting the sheets, screwing her body into strange
shapes, constantly imagining the worst. When she heard that he

was wounded, she flew at her husband and beat her delicate fists against his broad chest and scratched fiercely—and with futility—at his golden beard. War was made by men to satisfy the passions of men. She saw no reason to succumb to the masculine idealism, despite her husband's long and reasoned arguments. Like her husband, she could not see war as glorious; unlike her husband, she could not see war as necessary.

Gervase felt oppressed by the atmosphere. It almost approached his beloved Edgar Poe. Indeed, he had hoped to lie on his bed as he had done a year ago and read his books. There were rows of books both in his father's study and in his own room. But he could not bear this intensity, this Gothic furor, this new fall of the House of Stepton. He looked up at his father with meaning in his gaze.

"Deborah Mouton asked me to come over to see them," he said, almost with sullenness.

"Then you must go," his father said urbanely. "No member of the 1st Virginia Cavalry disappoints a lady." The urbanity was fatuous but useful.

"And what about this lady?" his mother cried out. She burst into tears and clutched Gervase close to her. He felt the wetness of her tears on his shoulder. She was breathing hard and began to scream softly and clutch at him as if she were choking for air.

"Asthma," said his father briefly.

"Gervase, Gervase," called out his mother, lonely as the dog howling in the blankness of night. He embraced her, and then put her arms from him.

"Mother," he whispered, "do not distress yourself." He had not imagined this turmoil on his homecoming. He had thought that he was returning to tranquillity. Most soldiers do, because they forget the stress that absence creates in the hearts of those who love them. He held her almost at arm's length.

"Mother," he whispered, "I love you. Do not cause me to lose faith in myself." His father moved forward and took the heavy, dead weight of the despairing woman in his arms. "Go to Deborah," he said, "and don't forget what I said. There are other places to grow up besides the fields around Manassas Junction." His father's voice was fierce, not with indignation or anger but with urgency—an urgency directed at the need to preserve his

fields, his home, and, ultimately, his son. His mother appeared to
have fainted. She was slumped down in his father's strong arms.

Gervase ran out of the window doors. There was a group of
black workers gathered outside. He greeted as many of them as
he could by name. "Hello, Henry. Hello, William. Hello, Tertius.
Hello, Jim." They waved to him. He laughed to himself: The
Yankees are fighting to "free" them, he thought. Free them from
what? They all grew up with me. If Father whipped them, he
whipped me too when we did wrong. And he whipped me just as
hard, and just as soft too. And Henry couldn't take a whipping,
so Father didn't really whip him but pretended to, and everyone
was satisfied. And if they worked hard, then Father worked just
as hard. And when Ezekiel (which name had *not* been given to
him by Father) showed that he was intelligent, then Father sent
him off to Aunt Maria's tradesman in Richmond and he was ap-
prenticed in the corn merchant's and now had married with
three children and a house of his own and no shanty either. And
when the Yankee armies came to the Bull Run there was no rising of the blacks. They didn't see General Scott as savior and
redeemer any more than they had seen John Brown as Jesus
Christ—John Brown, who loved his mother and slobbered over
her much more than he slobbered over any Negro. To prove
himself to himself, Gervase took a flying leap at Lenore and
landed on her back, though he nearly didn't, because the mare
was not used to his ways yet and shied away from him. Henry
called out.

"You nearly took a fall there, Mr. Gervase."

"Damn nearly," shouted Gervase. He had read *Uncle Tom's
Cabin* and it had made him very angry indeed: He had never hit
a negro in his life. That, of course, was not true. He had hit Tertius very hard when they had fought in the barn one moonlit
night over the carcass of a young deer that they had hunted together. Both boys had shot together, and both claimed the victim. Both believed that they had succeeded, so the only way to
decide the matter was to fight. They were both twelve. He had
hit Tertius very hard indeed, but Tertius had hit him even
harder, and he had lost consciousness. Toward the end of the
fight his father had come into the barn, which smelled of new-
cut corn, and watched. The blacks had wished to scatter, but his

father had motioned them to stay where they were. When he
woke up he saw his father looking down at him. Even then there
was the wry grin. His father drew a circle in the dust with his
toe. "You lost a fair fight, son," he had said. Gervase had felt hurt.
He wanted to assert his white supremacy. He told his father so.
"Don't be a damn fool," his father had said. "Where do you think
this is? Alabama?" And that had, with circumspection, taught
him a lesson. He did not believe in white supremacy any longer.
And now they stood and shouted and cheered while he rode off
down the sloping meadow to the Sweetwater and once again
splashed through the water, which was rather chillier now since
the dusk was coming on and drawing long pen-oil black lines
across the cool sky. He galloped off toward the Mouton farm, and
felt strangely excited.

The dusk light of Virginia made every tree and bush and fence
and building seem cool and permanent. He wanted it to stay that
way; he wanted to live under the softness of Malvern Hill forever. He did not want the Yankee armies to come here with their
cannon and their hard twanging voices and shatter that peace
because he realized that when it had gone it could not come back.
He did not even want his own armies to march by Willis Church
and down Quaker Road, because any army would spoil this
landscape and he loved the fields and the determinate sky and
every fallow and rise was sanctified with the angel light of his
childhood. The birds and the small woodchucks called to each
other in the coming night, and the world lived in the aura of its
own gentleness.

The Mouton farmhouse was not as grand as his own family's.
It was a farmhouse, and not the American approximation to a
Cotswold manor house with a working home farm. But it was
large: The stables meandered away from the dwelling building,
and the solid huts for the black workers ran along that edge
where house became field and living ceased and fertility began.
As was usual at this hour, Mr. Mouton sat on his rocking chair
drinking his third whiskey—his daughter allowed him four except on festivities, when he took six, and rather larger ones. He
had a hard head. Opposite to him was another rocking chair,
which was empty, but Gervase knew better than to take it, because that was Mr. Mouton's living memorial to his dead wife;

occasionally he pushed the chair into gentle motion with his foot and glanced surreptitiously at it with eyes under his lowered lids as if he thought that he might be laughed at, although he knew he would not be. He sat with Gervase in silence for some minutes. Neither man experienced any sense of wasted time; chatter is left to the uncivilized.

"Not long at home, Gervase," said the man mildly. "Your mother troubled?"

"Yes, sir," replied Gervase.

"There's few of us that ain't. Except Deborah. Nothing worries her. And that troubles me, just as your father is troubled. We want the women out. Your father say anything about Deborah?"

"Yes, sir," repeated Gervase. The man ruminated a moment or two. "You're both plenty young to think of marriage in the normal way of things. But nothing is normal anymore. And if the Yankees come here and anything should happen to me . . . well, it would be a comfort to me if there was some kin to whom Deborah could turn. There would be no need for . . . well, you take my meaning, son?" Gervase thought that he might do. "Not that I think the Yankees will come. But they'll try; and boy, you heard the news? We've formed a new Army of Northern Virginia just to protect our own country. And Peter Beauregard" (Mouton shared his father's habit) "ain't going to command it. They've given the command to Joseph Johnston." Gervase had often heard the name of this eminent general when he was younger, but it evoked little for him. "He's a cautious man," went on Mr. Mouton, "too cautious by half. But he'll have Jeb and the boys to give him a little dash. And your professor from Lexington." Gervase was tired of discussing the war. He wanted to talk of Deborah; more, he wanted to talk *to* Deborah. He felt as if their fathers were using them—wholly altruistically, of course—as pawns in the game of dynastic safety. They had discounted both their feelings. He knew, or thought he knew, what he felt himself, but he knew little of what she felt. He had played with her as a sister, and three quarters of him still felt of her as a sister. But the other quarter was beginning to clamor. She came out into the soft and palpable darkness and stood behind her father with her hand on his shoulder, caressing his neck with her slight but hard hand.

"We aren't tyrants," said Mouton resolutely. "Work it out between yourselves." And he heaved himself from his rocking chair and walked fairly steadily into the house. Gervase was suddenly struck by this solidity of shelter: Here they all spent so much time walking into shelter. For weeks he had been used to a tent. Deborah remained standing and looked him in the eyes. It was now so dark that he could only see her face as a blur. The night insects had started their thick, buzzing cacophony. He knew that the rituals required him to take the initiative, although he felt strangely averse to doing so, for he knew that she, in some indefinable fashion, was stronger than he. And in the last weeks he had acquired so many new experiences that like a remount under cannon fire he shied away from something more. He was like the flinching Lenore.

"Shall we walk down to the river?" he asked. Here the "river" meant the James. Funny, only a few miles north the same word meant the Sweetwater. But the habits of his whole life had habituated him to this peculiarity, and that a different image flashed before his mental eye did not make him start. What *did* was that he caught a glance of the Sweetwater too; that the perfect separation had collapsed to some degree. With an effort of will he saw only the James once again, but it disturbed him; it showed the earthquake tremors in his sensibility. As they moved out into the darkness, she took his hand. Her grip was not soft: She did not let her fingers lie flaccid in his, but rather took his fingers in hers and squeezed them, communicating something of the urgency of her feeling through the gesture. He had never kissed a white girl yet. He had kissed a black, when he and Roscoe and Josiah had determined to explore the secret regions they had talked of until they were sick of it. Each boy had kissed her. She was perfectly willing, because boys from Virginia did not indulge in mass rape in the fields, whatever their great-grandfathers might once have done and whatever their dissolute cousins might be doing now in the cotton fields of Alabama. Gervase found the experience physically exciting but spiritually debasing. He could only put his body where his affections lay. And he felt something for the quiescence of black Miranda lying back on the dry, sweet-smelling straw in the barn but certainly not love, not even when she reached for him and caressed him in a manner calculated to make him forget his romanticism. But nothing then could make him put aside this romanticism; his idea of love and sex was from literature—he needed an element of strength and mystery. So he had drawn aside and let Roscoe take over, who inherited more of the eighteenth-century traditions of Virginia, even to a certain coarseness of speech that Gervase wholly eschewed. Once Roscoe had said to him when they came after a hard ride with the hunt on a spring day, "My, Gervase, you smell like a nigger in church," and Gervase had turned aside as if struck, although Roscoe had meant no harm. He was too fastidious.

Now the darkness enclosed him with Deborah. She turned toward him, and they stood close together. She leaned forward and their shoulders touched and her loins brushed against his, her knees, too, as if she were sagging. He put out his arms, only to steady her, and found that she responded by moving close to him and he could smell the freshness of her hair, but smell too a deeper, female smell. She wanted to melt into his strength, but he stood aloof, full of desire and fear. He took refuge in a matter-of-fact coldness.

"They want us to marry." It contained no invitation, only a verbal response. She sensed his resistance and moved away from the closeness of the embrace, and yet not losing contact with his body entirely, perhaps knowing that this tantalization provoked Gervase to more lust than direct invitation.

"And don't you want it?" she asked. He assumed that by "it" she meant marriage. And once again he tried to sustain the mastery of his will. "Yes." He paused, and heard some animals plunging about in the long grass nearby, and the very distant slap of the waters of the James against the mudbanks. "If you will take Mother to Richmond." Even for Deborah this was too much. She flared up and moved away from him.

"Is that *all* you want?" He could not reply, and she was affronted. She determined to wound him. "Roscoe wanted much more than that." She could not know what he owed to Roscoe.

"Then marry Roscoe."

"Roscoe won't marry anyone yet, or I would." But he felt no jealousy. "If Roscoe won't marry, then why should I?" She mimicked him in her reply; the hurt came through.

"Because your father wants us to marry."

"And what about your father?"

"He could ask until doomsday and I wouldn't do it for him unless I wanted a man. But that ain't you, even though you are dressed in your pretty gray uniform with its black ribbons . . ."

"Facings."

"How in the hell should I know what you call them!" He had humiliated her. And he could not see why. Only the war took up his thoughts. If he edged toward tenderness, his ears became full of the cries in the hospital tent at Manassas and the cruel civility of the doctor as he took up the little saw and brought it down on the bright bone. Gervase was committed to the bright bone, not the bright hair. He would not marry her to a possible corpse. And he could not think of her as a wife. He could think of no one as a wife in these months. After the war, maybe. Once again, she moved closer to him.

"Don't you want what I have?"

"What do you have?"

"Oh, love and obedience and comfort and all the things the parson talks of. But you know, Gervase, you must know. Don't say you've passed all your twenty years without knowing what a man and a woman do together? What Roscoe wanted to do with me. What all men want. Even the blacks when I walk past them, though I know I shouldn't say that, though no one can stop them looking, poor creatures that they are. I want to give myself to you, Gervase. I want to bear your children. I can feel your looking shocked. But why, for God's sake? Don't you want me even a little bit?" He could hear her weeping, and he moved forward and took her in his arms. Her breasts swelled beneath him, and he could feel the outlines of her loins sharp and moving against him. But it was useless. He could feel that bayonet sliding into the kidney of the Zouave. He could see the man in the silhouette of torment.

"I'll marry you to protect you, Deborah," he said. "And don't take that for nothing, because after my own kin, you mean more to me than any other person alive or dead. And I promise you that I'll love and cherish you. But in these days I can't offer you any more. After the war . . . maybe. But we shouldn't talk of after the war, because I don't know when this war will end or whether it ever will end. And I don't know what we will be when the shooting stops. But as for other . . . well, that I can't offer you because that's not choice but passion, and I have passion in me." Her reply was as bitter as she could make it.

"Did the battle scare you so much, Gervase?" He tried to be honest, and yet no honesty could reach out between them.

"I suppose it did." But it hadn't, not in the way she would take it.

"Most soldiers, most . . . men want nothing else when they come home after fighting. God, Gervase, if the South has to rely on *men* like you, then we might as well surrender to Abe Lincoln tomorrow." His voice was very weary.

"As I said, you'd better marry Roscoe." For the first time she raised her voice.

"I don't *want* Roscoe. Do you think he hasn't asked for it? A hundred times! I've had to fight his hands away from the place I was *giving* you. I'm *not* your sister, whatever you may think or want, and I've never thought of you as my brother. I was keeping myself for you, Gervase. Pure and chaste, as the ladies say. I don't want to be pure and chaste with you, Gervase. I want . . ." and she leaned forward and whispered in his ear, while he could feel the hot salt of tears on her face and the heat entered the words she whispered and that made him flinch because he did not know that girls could use such words and he would never have used them himself, and in his mind all confused were his father's words and her father's and a part of him that responded with unholy zest and all the other parts that drew back, a snail's antennae horns creeping back into the shell that he called his duty and that was nothing but an evasion of that maturity he dare not face because he had had to learn a new maturity on the battlefield already and that was enough for him, and he realized that he was losing something precious that would never be offered again and that however much his sword might protect Deborah what she wanted was more than protection and that *more* he could not give her because the blood of her maidenhead was something that he could not and would not shed until there was tranquillity once again when he could relish himself as a man of peace among the fertile fields unravaged by hooves and bullets and cannon balls.

"I'll marry you to protect you," he repeated.

"Go to hell," she spat out at him. "Go back to your daddy from Lexington and your perfect Colonel Stuart. There's something *wrong* with you."

"Good God Almighty," he cried out, "I'm giving you myself. But I have my duty too, and if I give myself without my duty as well then you only have half of me or less in these days."

Her voice was hard. "That's not enough, Gervase. Nothing like enough. And don't worry about your *mother*. I'll take her to Richmond if the Yanks come. But with soldiers like you, full of duty and honor and without the guts to love, there won't be any Yanks about here." He did not even notice her lapses in logic, nor, for that matter, his own. He turned and walked away into the anonymity of the night, which caught him up in its immensity. The throbbing in his left arm reminded him that, after all, he did have a body. But, apparently, all it could do was hurt him. He did not think that he had done wrong.

She ran back to the house; she ignored her father, who had surreptitiously taken an extra glass of whiskey, but still had wits enough to look at her in surprise and frustration and curiosity; she ran to her bedroom and flung herself onto the bed and let the tears soak the pillow with its fine embroidery her mother had stitched and gave a muffled "Get out" to the black maid who came in tenderly but left in a huff of understandable rejection. Deborah wanted Roscoe to come home. She pressed herself against the bed and wished with all the intensity of her tenderly hot being that Roscoe would come again and let his hands explore the places she had forbidden him. She did not think she had done wrong, either.

Enveloped by the climate of his father and mother, Gervase did not have long to enjoy this renewal of his childhood. On the third day of his furlough there came a weary trooper from Stuart telling him to return to duty. But not with the regiment. Stuart had responded to the request of the new commander of the Army of Northern Virginia and assigned him as a galloper to General Lee, political adviser to President Davis. Like Hector, Gervase buckled on his greaves afresh.

4

The Science of War

In some ways the next ten months were most frustrating for Gervase. He was at the heart of the Confederacy, but he did very little. His chief was called upon to advise President Davis on military matters, but it was clear that the President, who was not modest as to his own military abilities, having graduated (and with no small success) from West Point, did not take the advice very seriously. Indeed, he was wont to refer to "Granny" Lee in disparaging tones, and preferred to associate with Joseph Johnston and Jeb and Thomas Jackson and Peter Beauregard. Richmond was a hotbed of intrigue, who's in and who's out and his chief's resolute refusal to take part in such intrigues generated both respect and impatience from his staff of young officers. They did their best to intrigue upon his behalf, but Lee did not relish such support. So it seemed as if they might spend the war among the streets of Richmond, aimlessly bickering and scheming in the lower levels of government for a man who showed a curious sense of paralysis when it came to grasping real power. The small campaign that Lee fought was not particularly successful, but Gervase was not present. He was laid up with a fever, nursed by the devoted matrons of Richmond, who would have preferred him to be wounded *properly* so that their sense of tending the gallant might have been fully requited. But the days in Richmond were not without some significance, both professional and personal, for Gervase, as we shall see.

But the initiative lay with the Illinois lawyer in Washington.

In response to his appeals, men flocked to the colors, starry-eyed, dreaming dreams of romantic glory. They wished to free the slaves if they came from Massachusetts; they wished to preserve the Union if they came from halfhearted Maryland. But they wanted something; often foul-mouthed (like all soldiers), they were inspired by a genuine ideal, a vision of what they thought America should be, and, with all their human weaknesses (and they were many) they were prepared to lay their lives on the line for that vision, which is why even the humblest pioneer among them merits a footnote in the history of America. And Lincoln had found his Napoleon, albeit a young one, in the president of the Illinois Central Railway. Fortuitously, the President himself had acted as lawyer to the Illinois Central in the days of peace, and was acquainted with the administrative abilities of George Brinton McClellan. These administrative abilities were very real. He showed more insight into the needs of a citizen Army than others, such as Kitchener, were to show later. McClellan realized that his Army had to be trained and supplied and molded into a cohesive unit. This he proceeded to do. He put off the importunities of his civil chief as long as he could. Mr. Lincoln still nurtured a suspicion that all his troops had to do was cross the Potomac and march South to Richmond and the war would be over. Did he not have factories? Did he not have men? Did he not have a Navy that could prevent all matériel from reaching the South? What more could his generals want? He was bid to pause, it is true, by the failure of his arms in the smaller engagements, but this did not diminish, in his heart of hearts, his faith in sheer size as the instrument of victory. He held a sledgehammer in his hands. The South was a nut that he had to crack. George McClellan only had to swing the hammer and the South would fly into fragments. Patiently the railway chieftain explained that war was somewhat more complicated; that raw troops ran away when they were fired upon; that men must be molded into tight formations before they could be exposed to battle; the staffs had to be trained to administer them, and that it took a skill that lawyers and bankers did not possess innately to maneuver masses of men in action. The President was skeptical, but he listened, withholding final judgment. But George McClellan knew that his gaunt and bearded chief yearned for

the day when his blue-coated boys would surround Richmond
and bring Jeff Davis begging for mercy to the peace table. And
the mob of politicians behind the presidential back were even
less patient. Being a politician too, Lincoln could not afford to
ignore them. What, after all, was the real cause for delay? Patiently, George McClellan went on training his men until the day
was at hand when he could take his soldiers down to Richmond,
as the President desired so ardently, for he knew that all the
President respected was success; he knew that the President,
with rather less reason, thought himself as good a soldier as his
generals and as good a judge of military skill as Jefferson Davis.
After all, if a man can learn law he can learn strategy too. Lesser
men who failed Lincoln were removed from their commands and
sent to fight redskins in the West.

At last George McClellan was prevailed upon to move his
Army of the Potomac. In April 1862, under the enormous
firepower of federal gunboats, he disembarked his troops at Fort
Monroe and worked his way up the Yorktown peninsula. His
skill at training troops now paid dividends—a metaphor of
which both he and his chief approved. The Confederate Army
was forced back toward Richmond. Joseph Johnston was flabby
in its defense. And *he* was not going to take any advice from
Granny Lee, who had lost West Virginia in the opening months
of the war. Gaily he went his own way. But the gods saw fit to
take part. On May 30, jaunty as usual, Joseph Johnston rode up
to the line to inspect his dilatory and confused battle; well did
he need to see what was going on. But a federal sharpshooter
saw him before Johnston saw the battle. He was seriously
wounded and was unable to exercise command. After a night of
troubled self-examination, Jeff Davis saw that he had no choices
open to him. He gave the command of the Army of Northern
Virginia to Granny Lee. Richmond was under the guns of the
enemy; the inhabitants scurried around the streets to the sound
of cannon fire; the less courageous were making preparations for
a withdrawal to the West or the deeper South (but such were
few). It seemed that Richmond was about to fall, whatever ges-
tures Thomas Jackson might be making in the Valley of the
Shenandoah. Mr. Lincoln sat down to write a magnanimous
speech of victory, and George Brinton McClellan was preparing

to enter Richmond on his horse Daniel Webster. He was not prepared to let his favorite mount, Burns, have this honor, since the brute bolted after his oats whatever the occasion.

Meanwhile, Granny sat down with his staff to consider the situation.

In the previous winter, Robert Lee had assembled his staff in the evenings, and they had discussed topics of war. This might have been boring to the younger men, but it was not so. Lee would sit at the table, after he had eaten a simple meal, and, holding a glass of water in his delicate hands, would put problems to them. He did not defer to their answers, but he respected their solutions, often pointing out in his quiet voice where they had fallen into error. He *never* raised his voice; he was never irritable. Gervase sometimes found this degree of self-control quite terrifying. It was not that Lee was detached; he clearly cared deeply about his men, although as yet they were not *his* men. At times Gervase found that the man's faith in his own destiny drove him to fury. He had no command. When he had commanded in the field he had hardly been crowned with the laurel of complete success. And everyone knew that Scott had asked Lincoln to offer him command of the federal Army, too. Granted that he never referred to this himself, but he knew that others were aware of this, and Gervase suspected a deep vanity in his character. His very quietness bespoke a sense of his own infallibility. But one night Gervase was compelled to modify his opinion. They sat at the table, and Lee threw a question to him.

"Gervase, you were at Manassas. How would you deal with a defensive line that was firmly established and entrenched? How would you compel them to retire and leave the field to you?" Gervase had not wasted the months of comparative idleness. He had read some Clausewitz. He answered briskly. "Intensive artillery preparation, sir. Then a firm attack of infantry. Once the infantry has weakened the line, loose the cavalry upon them." They called Lee "sir" at all times; he referred to them by their Christian names when they talked informally. To Lee, they were gentlemen together. The reply was gentle but uncompromising:

"But the enemy possess more cannon than we. What if their counter battery fire can silence our pieces? And what if the infantry sustain unwarrantable casualties when they make their attack? Then there is no way for the cavalry to move. What would you do then?"

"Give firm orders for the infantry *not* to fail, sir."

"Gervase, Gervase, you trust too much to the power of the will. Yes, yes, I know that Napoleon talked of the overwhelming power of *morale*. But however brave a man may be, he cannot charge an unbroken line supported by artillery. So you would lose your men—gallantly, it is true, but you would lose them nonetheless. A dead soldier will not thank you if he has died to no purpose—and make no mistake, you will kill him to no purpose. A pile of corpses is the result of improper thinking. Reflect, gentlemen, ours is the only branch of philosophy where men *die* if we think foolishly, if we are misled by idle theory. And think too of the nature of our thought. Other branches of speculation require that the opposition should be brought to agree. We must never agree with our opponents; we must constantly surprise them. We must always employ the *ruse of reason,* because we play with men's lives, gentlemen. Our passion is their life. So think again, Gervase, and think more carefully."

"You evidently set a premium by surprise, sir."

"Surprise above everything, Gervase. We are not butchers. It is very easy for a general officer to be a butcher in modern warfare. The power of the defensive weapon is much greater than that of the offensive arm. The cavalryman is helpless against entrenched infantry. The enemy must not know where the blow will fall. And it must not fall on the front best defended. It must fall on a flank. Let the enemy know that in theory. But never let him know *which* flank. And when the blow falls, his line will reel. Then and only then may we attack him from the front. Then we may release our cavalry to pursue him."

"It is academic, sir."

"Indeed, Gervase, very academic. But as we sit here in Richmond and think about these matters, let us not forget that the intensity of our thought may not only mean survival for our country, but also life for many brave men. I think we owe that to God." The general did not often refer to God, unlike Thomas Jackson, which made the general's infrequent references all the more telling. But then, said Gervase with scorn to himself, you

didn't do too well when you were in contact with the blue bellies, did you? He had lowered his eyes, and raised them to see
Lee looking at him with affection and question in his eyes. But
what did he care for General Lee in January of 1862?

5

Winter of Discontent

During this winter Gervase surrendered himself to lust. The brothels of Richmond knew him well, impelled by a desperate intensity that sprang from his desire to forget what he had done to Deborah. He never referred to her in his letters to his father, nor did his father refer to her in his replies; his father's letters were filled with news of his mother's decline into a depression that brooked no alleviation or respite. Gervase had *respected* Deborah too much to touch her, yet in his imagination he yearned for her. He yearned especially for her *cleanness*. But what he could not take from her he could take from others. He wished to debase himself whatever the cost. So varied were his activities that it was a miracle that the surgeons were not required to cure him of the incurable. And he was compelled to exercise prudence, for General Lee was notoriously prudish in this respect, and he would not have been kept on Lee's staff had it been known that he had had commerce with women of the kept houses—let alone if he had acquired syphilis! Deborah tormented him: She had offered herself, and he had refused. He could not now imagine the scruples that had led him to abstain. Her red hair, her brown, tanned skin hovered before his eyes in sleep, and he walked the streets of Richmond to exorcise it. He lost sympathy with the brothels hosted by white women, and went to the Negro brothels. One especially was his favorite. It was a somber yet solid house. The reception room was furnished in French style, and the coverings were in red velvet. He had an especial whore whose name was Estella. She was very kind to him.

One night he lay naked on her bed. They had made love twice. She spoke to him softly. "You know, Captain Stepton, sir" (for Gervase had obtained a promotion), "you don't like having me one bit. I can tell that, boy." He relished her mixture of admiration, by the use of his rank, and her cunning reversal of the roles by calling him "boy." She gave him a glass of warm champagne, bitter to his taste. "You should be with some fine, clean white woman."

"Why, for Christ's sake?" Gervase hated to blaspheme, but he did it to plume up his will, to prove to himself that there was nothing sacred left.

"Because it's all over so quick. You get into me and you spend yourself before I can count up to ten. Real men can take much longer." Gervase rolled over on the bed and looked down at his manhood, detumescent, resting from its imposed duty of horror, its sacrifice to the imposed purity of the woman he truly adored.

"You're such a fine woman," he said.

"Oh sure," she replied, without believing him. She was very experienced in the ways of white men who needed to work out their guilt. At least Gervase was conventional. Some were not, as the weals on her backside bespoke clearly enough. He leaned over and touched her breasts with a sudden gesture of tenderness. He repented at the purity of this feeling of tenderness and pulled himself off the bed and hauled on his trousers. He felt for some money and gave it to her.

"You don't feel like paying me in Yankee dollars, sir?"

"Why?" asked Gervase.

"Because they'll be here soon enough." He hit her as hard as he could, and she cracked her head on the headboard of the bed. She recovered herself and smiled at him.

"Now, was that what a *gentlemen* would do?"

"I'm no gentleman," he replied shortly, and pulled another two dollars from his pocket and threw it at her in sudden fury. She smiled again.

"Is a punch in the teeth only worth two dollars?"

"Yes, to you," he said. He put on his coat and made for the door. He had drunk very heavily of poor wine. He paused at the

basin and vomited brown muck into the broad bowl. The smell
rose and hit him. He vomited again. Estella cried out in vexation.

"Now, who'll clear that mess up?"

"You can, for all I care." He saw Deborah by the door and
pushed his hand out toward it. The image vanished. Black sex in
a dark house: the fall of the House of Stepton, creaking and
groaning in muck and sweat and sperm and cries and groan
and saliva and brownness. At least there was nothing *wrong* with
him, not in the way Deborah implied on that night in the Geth-
semane of offering and renunciation. And what did he care for
Estella, lying back on the bed with a smirk and a bruise? Those
who live by the penis shall die by the penis, to borrow a phrase
he had heard Roscoe use. Roscoe had a turn of phrase. He had
only seen Roscoe once since Manassas, and Roscoe was withdrawn from him. Christ, who wasn't?

He descended the broad staircase into the reception room,
which had leaded glass windows like a church. There were three
men lounging on the sofas, who clearly made up a party. Quickly
scrutinizing them to see that he didn't know them, Gervase went
over to them. One had a whore on his knees, her legs spread. He
was touching her. An older man was exercising the show of
authority.

"Well, well," said the man, "an officer of the 1st Virginia Cavalry. Boys, we've clearly come to the finest cathouse Richmond
has to offer us." He staggered to his feet. "I'm honored to meet
you, sir." Gervase looked at him with distaste, although he realized that few men had less right than he to show, or feel,
distaste.

"I don't have the honor of your acquaintance, sir," he said.

"Nor I you, soldier boy," the man replied. "But call me Billy.
I'm but a mere captain, like yourself—at present, sir, at present.
I have hopes, however; high hopes, indeed, that I shall do great
things by our glorious cause. Jesse, I wish you'd leave that black
bitch to herself and emulate the example of our friend Cole
here."

"What in the hell does *emulate* mean?" asked the very young
man who was at work on the young black whore.

"You're asking the right man," said the older figure. "I shall tell
you. Once more I shall become a schoolmaster, though then I

was called Charles, and I hope you won't forget it, Jesse. Emulate means copy. Try to do the same as our dear boy, Cole."

"Fuck Cole," said the youth.

"Forgive me, sir," said the incongruous Billy. "My men lack the graces of you Virginia boys. They walk in beauty like the night. But they fight well enough, well enough, sir. They strike terror into Yankee hearts, especially the hearts of their women-folk." Gervase felt an instinctive disgust rise within him. He assumed his most aristocratic air.

"Do you hold a commission in our Army, sir?" The man called Cole let out a guffaw.

"Sure he does," he says. "Don't you know Captain Quantrill, boy?" The word "boy" is heavily charged in the South. Gervase might tolerate it from Jeb or Grumble but not from this unwashed lout, who spoke with a heavy western accent. He moved forward in anger and found himself staring down the barrel of a Colt revolver. The elder man tutted deprecatingly. "It don't do to annoy my men, sir. They take offense right easily. But tolerate them, sir. They are good in the field."

"Don't apologize to that lump of crap, Billy," said Younger. Jesse was staring at Gervase with what he felt was envy; Jesse liked the uniform. "You must excuse Mr. Younger, sir," said Captain (shortly to be Colonel) Quantrill. "He comes from a rougher world than you and me. But he inspires real terror in Yankee breasts. You know the Yanks still try to colonize the West? They still send out their wagon trains? We see to it that they don't arrive on *schedule*." He laughed. Younger laughed, and Jesse grinned. Quantrill suddenly changed to a horrid mirth. "We kill the men and we rape the women, sir. Right good sport it is, too." Younger put away his Colt with rather less speed than he had produced it. Suddenly Gervase realized that this set of despera-does was not to be taken for the group of clowns that he had assumed. He felt the presence of danger, even though they were on "his side," which was some comfort. Quantrill noticed a change in his manner.

"Ah sir," he said with exaggerated politeness, "I see that you perceive the difficulties, not to say the embarrassment, of your dilemma. Now, we three are nothing but bandits, shootists, call us what you will. Even though I have high hopes of President

Davis who sees, shall I say, the difficulties and realities of the position of the Confederacy. My, I am speaking around about. But
we've nothing to lose by being seen in a Richmond cathouse.
You're a gentleman, sir, and you have a good deal to lose. What
would General Lee think? Or General Jackson? I tremble to
think, sir. So please don't look at my boys as if they were dirt, sir.
Because they ain't dirt, sir, even though they don't wear the
pretty uniform of the 1st Virginia Cavalry, deep as is my respect
for the gallant General Stuart. And I must say, sir," he added,
widening the scope of his rebuke, "that I'm surprised to see a
member of such a gallant and noble regiment in this here house,
having it with bits of nigger meat. I thought you gentlemen did
your loving with the fair damsels of Virginia, sir." Gervase
started forward. "I should strongly advise against such a course
of action, sir," said Quantrill with a smile. "You yourself, without
doubt, would never shoot a man in the back, nor would you kill
a man at odds of three to one. Cole here, and Jesse, and, to tell
you the plain truth, myself, have no such scruples. If you lift your
fucking hand to me I'll kill you and throw you in the street like a
piece of nigger shit. And now, sir, if you've had enough black
cunt, I'll bid you a fair good night, with wishes for the safety of
the Confederate cause." Gervase felt a wary hopelessness flood
over him. How could he connect this ruffian with the calm words
of the general? He remembered the solemn pause after Lee had
referred to God. What had that to do with this man, with the
gray-tinged man who sat fingering his Colt, and the youth with
barely a beard whose hand was up the black's skirt while she
squirmed on top of him and put her hand on his crotch? Where
was the connection? Perhaps in himself: the man who thrust
into Estella to drive away the image of Deborah. As if telepathic,
Captain Quantrill (Christ almighty, they held the same rank!)
put his face close to that of Gervase.

"Doubtless you are thinking, my pretty little horse soldier, that
you and I have little in common. And that you have even less in
common with men like Cole here, and young Jesse. Well, let me
tell you, *sir*, that war is a great leveler. You can shoot your
mouth off with General Lee or General Beauregard or General
Johnston all day. But where do you come by night? To a nigger
cathouse to sample nigger sex. And I spend my day sending Yan-

kee settlers to hell and cutting the throats of Yankee deserters and staking them out and cutting them a piece to make the others think that Indians have done the desolate deed, sir. And where do I come of a night when I journey to Richmond to seek the thanks of President Davis? I come to a nigger cathouse to get some niggers. Sir, we both copulate; that there is what we have in common; it hangs in the crotch. I don't know how long it hangs. How long does yours hang, Cole? *At present,* Cole, when you are, so to speak, not in the line of battle." He laughed. Cole sniggered. Jesse guffawed. Gervase looked at them with horror. A sense of his own debasement swept over him.

"If we share the same cause," he said, "then God forgive me."

"A commendable sentiment, sir," said Quantrill. "Very commendable indeed. History will tell which of us gave more to the Confederate cause. Pray present my respects to General Jackson when you see him. He also thinks that the Confederacy is endorsed by the will of God Almighty. Truly, sir, I do myself. Jesse," he added, "get into that whore if you want to: Do something, for Christ's sake, because I can't abide the smell, boy, I just can't abide the smell. No more can the captain here, I'll warrant. And pray, sir," he said with exaggerated respect, "please remember that you are one of the few men who've looked down Cole Younger's gun barrel and lived to tell of it after." He bowed, grotesque, supreme, creator of mythology, an eternal disgrace, as Gervase felt, to the cause he held sacred. And the communicator, to hell with it, of truth. He never saw Captain, later Colonel, Quantrill again. It was ironic that the history books should link their names together. But the sober historian of plain fact must record that melancholy truth. Perhaps Quantrill was right: What held them in common hung between their thighs.

On the night of May 30 came the news that Joseph Johnston was wounded beyond immediate repair and that General Lee should take over the Army of Northern Virginia. When the trooper who had carried the message had withdrawn, Lee sat silent. He looked up at them.

"Perhaps a few minutes in prayer, gentlemen?" They all bowed their heads. Then Lee rose. He walked over to the map that always hung on the wall of the room in which they dined.

He looked closely at the map and turned to Gervase, who stood at his right hand.

"What would you counsel, Gervase?" Gervase looked at the blue flags that denoted federal troops, and his heart, almost literally, sank within him. "I cannot tell, sir." Lee smiled and brought his hands together, kneading them.

"The situation, gentlemen, is by no means hopeless. At best, I shall have destroyed George McClellan's armies within a month. At worst he will be on his way back to Washington with his tail between his legs."

A member of the staff snorted, and changed the snort to a cry of surprise. "But how, sir? How can any man achieve that?"

"I shall," said General Lee. And Gervase let his spirits rise with those of his chief, triumphant, free, like a bird, exultant, above the mire of the confusion in which he had struggled like a man in quicksand for months on end.

"Let us survey the situation in the widest terms, gentlemen," said Lee with the unnerving calmness. He placed his head on his hand and gazed at the map. Then he looked around them all, not forcing their eyes to drop, linking the eyebeams in a community of thought. "Reflect. We have everything to lose, and George McClellan thinks that he has nothing but victory in front of him. But George McClellan is afraid of me. I say it without vanity. And we must arrange for Jeb to make him even more afraid. But that's a detail. The essential point is, gentlemen, that we must annihilate this Army. If they lose this Army then whatever they do on the Mississippi will be of little use to them. Now, George thinks that invests Richmond. But he can't walk home easily. We can cut him off in the North between the rivers. He can't wade all his men through the Chickahominy and the Pamunkey. So if he retreats, he must retreat South, to his boats at Fort Monroe, or, if he is in *real* trouble, then he can bring his boats up to Harrison's Landing." Lee placed his finger on the map and lightly touched Oakland Station, where the Chickahominy rises. "Between *here* and Harrison's Landing we shall destroy them. We shall force them to retreat between the Chickahominy and the James and turn their flank each time they pause. If they have no Army left, then they are finished." There was a silence in the air; it hung, thick and heavy as the dust. A fly buzzed as many men

began to die in their thoughts. Lee smiled at them, that lazy and
reserved smile that he used when he was contented, but the
smile took on a twist of bitterness. "There's a long drop between
the thought and the execution, gentlemen," he added quietly.
"And we can't fight him for a month or so. The earthworks must
stand in Richmond for some weeks longer, and Magruder must
hold him in the trenches. I shall confer with my divisional generals in about three weeks, if we can get them here by that
time. The most difficult to find will be Thomas. Gervase?" Lee
leaned forward and brought his heels together. "Go to find
Thomas Jackson. Bring him here with the Reverend Dr. Dabney,
too." He laughed, without malice. "Only Thomas could make
his chaplain his chief of staff!" They all laughed, not as syco-
phants. "You'll find him in the valley; where, I'm not sure. Don't
ask a Yankee general." They laughed, this time with full satisfaction. "And now . . ." They turned back to the map and
picked up rulers and tapes. Gervase saluted and walked from the
room.

Gervase determined to enter the Valley of the Shenandoah by
the Rockfish Gap. He had ridden hard until he reached Mechum's
River Station, and the wooded immensities of the Blue Ridge
Mountains stood above him, inviting, the trees dark and cool and
shady. Behind them: What? At Mechum's River there were supply trains, hospital tents, wounded men half on the way to recovery, and masses of prisoners waiting to be moved along the
railroad to Gordonsville and the junction with the Virginia Central Railway. Gervase went to speak to some of the prisoners.
They were loosely herded together and guarded by a few men
with fixed bayonets who sat playing cards much of the time, yet
did not relax their vigilance. Gervase found that Jackson's men
were not accustomed to relax their vigilance: his hand lay heavy
upon them, and he did not rescind the sentences of his courts-
martial. The men seemed to relish the fierceness of their chief,
now firmly fixed with the name of Stonewall.

The prisoners were dazed. In some ways they were relieved to
be freed from the turmoil of battle. And Gervase noted that they
had suffered the worst of reverses. They had lost faith in their
commanders and in themselves. A grizzled Yankee sergeant from

Maine whose hand was wrapped in filthy red bandages (or, more accurately, rags) spat in the air and said: "Oh yes, sir, we was coming down the turnpike from Smithfield and marching in close order and General Frémont he comes galloping by and he waves at us and shouts out, 'We've got old Stonewall on the run and just step out and you'll see those gray backs' and we are cheered—*cheered*, by Christ—and think that we can have something to drink and even a woman maybe and we stepped out even faster and then, by Christ, there was Jackson's cavalry at our backs—our *backs*, man—as we came into Kernstown. And we thought the old bastard was legging it down the turnpike in front of us. I didn't get no drink and no woman and no victory either and now I'll rot in some prison camp and I bet you two bits, sir, if I had it, that General Frémont galloped back quickly enough up that fucking valley." Gervase noted the grudging admiration: The Yankees seemed to think that Jackson was some sort of magician. Gervase went out and bought a bottle of whiskey and came back to the sergeant and gave it to him and said: "For as many of you as can find a use for it." They crowded together and the sergeant took a long pull before handing it to the nearest prisoner. He grinned. "It ain't going to be as easy as we thought, sir. No it ain't. But we *will* do it, you know."

Gervase rode out of Mechum's Station in the evening, and the clouds hung with curious delicacy over Rockfish Gap. All was still and silent. Lenore loped along in a gentle canter, her shoes sparking fire from the occasional flint in the road. The natural beauty was unspoiled except for the occasional shoulder strap, or pack, or shirt that had been discarded by the prisoners in their exhaustion. The country had only been gently touched by the war, not raped. He penetrated deeper into the forests, and the great trees, now filled with solid shadow, began to hem in on the sides. He felt that he was being watched, though by whom he knew not. The valley campaign was so fluid that he might be riding into Frémont's Army, or into Jackson's. He had no way of telling: He would not know until he struck some troops.

Once a shot rang out, and he heard the bullet whistle by him. He stuck his spurs into Lenore and rattled along the trail, which was now descending. There was no pursuit, no challenge. He could tell that it was a rifled weapon, which made it more likely to be a federal. But even that supposition was now faulty, since Jackson had captured enough stores from the enemy to equip his Army for the whole campaign. Mr. Lincoln's factories in Pennsylvania were working very hard to equip the Confederate armies. In the noisy fury of the insect night he settled down to sleep, Lenore tethered to a branch, his revolver near his hand, fully loaded, his gray cloak wrapped around him, though leaving his right hand free for immediate action. He laid his saber on the ground before him. He fell into a sleep packed with dreams of Deborah. But the pure white air of glory in which she walked was pockmarked by the crawling paws of Quantrill. He found himself dreaming too much of Quantrill. And he heard his father's voice echoing with a booming loss of meaning among the great trees. He was a light sleeper, but the hand suddenly touching him on the shoulder woke him entirely and he jerked into an instinctive leap, but the hand was very firm. So was the other hand, which held a revolver pointed at his eyes.

"Who are you?" a voice whispered in a Texan accent. "Name and regiment."

"Gervase Stepton, to see General Jackson from General Lee." The hand relaxed its steel grip. Gervase had a bruise on his shoulder for several days.

"Well, Captain"—for his rank had been seen—"we happen to be in Yankee country, and we'd better get out of here." Gervase saw that he was in the company of a small, almost dwarfish man who wore no uniform and hence no badges of rank or identification. The man looked up, sharp and foxy. "Don't you worry who I may be, Captain. I'll tell you that General Jackson don't get his information by listening to the fucking wind."

There were traces of dawn in the sky—lines of oyster pink fragmented by the level branches of the trees. The man whispered again. He always whispered, as if he had an impediment in the throat and could not speak up.

"General Jackson's in Luray. We'll ride just below the tree line. From General Lee, you say. Then I'd better get you there in one piece." Gervase reflected. Luray? That was on the east of the Massanuttons. If Jackson had changed his line of march so radically he must have some complex maneuver in mind. Rather too complex. The two men saddled up—or rather, Gervase put his saddle on Lenore, and the dwarfish man swung up and looked down on the taller Gervase drawing the girths tight. The man was almost completely bald, which added to his grotesqueness. Gervase calculated that he must be about forty-five. Gervase also noticed that he had stuck his gun into his boot. The boots were wide at the top and came up to the thighs—though they were probably designed as knee boots.

"I thought the Texans were with General Lee," Gervase remarked.

"Sure they are, Captain. I'm on irregular duty, you might say. I watch the Yanks for General Tom and report to him. *Personally*." A shade too much emphasis, perhaps. And Gervase had never heard Jackson referred to by the sobriquet of "General Tom"; Thomas, yes; Jackson, yes; Stonewall, yes; but "General Tom," never. Yet this name might have sprung up among the valley soldiers. And was this man a soldier at all? Jackson was, he knew, a literalist. If he used spies and why shouldn't he?—then they would hardly report to him but to the Reverend Dr. Dabney, major and minister. Gervase spoke with deliberate mildness.

"I expect you see more of James Dabney than the general." The man nodded with eager jerks of his little head. He stuck out his white-coated tongue as he spoke. "Sure thing, Captain. The major and I have some fine old talk, and he tells me where to wander when the general wants news. Yes, sir, James Dabney and I have spent many a night by the campfire and planned my little walks in the forest." The Texas accent accorded ill with this pompous and false choice of diction. It was as if the man wanted to be taken for a *genuine* southern gentleman—noble in speech, articulate, and civilized. And he had not corrected Gervase when he called Dr. Dabney "James"; indeed, he had repeated the error, as if a man who had come anywhere near Jackson would have known Robert Dabney's Christian name.

Gervase realized suddenly what a catch he would be for the Federals. He had not seen himself as an important figure in the war, merely an appendage of his chief. But the Yankees would think that he was much more than that. He knew Lee's mind.

And the gleam in the eyes of the bald, filthy-mouthed dwarf suggested more than a patriotic zeal to perform his military duty expeditiously. It suggested that love of gain that was not unknown to the Yankee mind.

But could he kill a man for mere suspicion? Coming from the chivalry of the 1st Virginia Cavalry, he took men at their word; moving in the rarefied air of the staff, he saw men as pieces in the great game between Robert Lee and George McClellan. Then Gervase remembered Billy Quantrill. This was a side of the war he had shut out into brothels, dark imaginings, and uncontrollable dreams. But it was there nonetheless. It was there on the Confederate side. He had met Billy Quantrill—oh yes he had—and it was foolishness to suppose that such dirt could not touch him. The man swung his horse into the track before Gervase, who drew his revolver and leveled it at the man's back. "Turn around, Yank," he said. He shot him immaculately in the center of his shoulder blades. The Griswold and Gunnison was not as powerful a revolver as a Le Mat, but the impetus of the shot pushed the balding dwarf askew onto his horse's neck. He let out a whistling screech which was checked by the upward rush of blood in the throat. Slowly he reeled off the horse and collapsed on the track, striking his cheek on a piece of flint, which drew the last fleck of living blood from his expiring body. As Gervase pulled him up by the collar, his weary eyes began to haze over, and he framed his jaw and pursued his lips in a last question. "How did you know, Captain? How in the fucking hell did you know?" Gervase replied coldly, with no trace of sympathy for this ludicrous half man who had deceived him for about a minute and a half. He couched his reply in moral terms.

"General Jackson's men don't say 'fucking' to their superior officers," he said. "And they clean their mouths, too." The man became dead weight. Gervase released his grip, and the falling head struck a larger rock with an ominous "clug." Not that it mattered if his skull was crushed now. From the white sky, which was full of the rich rays of the sun, Gervase felt Billy Quantrill smiling upon his pupil. Gervase was *learning*.

If the man had said that Jackson was in Luray, then it must be that Shields or Frémont was in Luray. So Jackson must be on the other side of the Massanuttons. Gervase would have a long ride.

He swung up into the saddle and took off without a backward glance at the doll spread over the dust and rock. Surreptitiously, the first fly landed and began to crawl up his nose. A second, bolder, landed on the eyeball and began to lick away the moisture.

6

The Plume of Will

As he entered Jackson's camp at Harrisonburg, Gervase witnessed a sight that was new to him: a man was being executed. He had slept on sentry duty and had been condemned by a field court-martial. He had carried his coffin to a bare wall against the church and, as Gervase came up the turnpike from Mount Crawford, he was standing waiting to receive the fusillade of bullets from a platoon of his comrades drawn up in front of him. The Reverend Dr. Dabney was exhorting him to repentance and promising him salvation. The boy—for he was no more—was ashen gray and trembling at the knees. A dark patch on his uniform around the loins showed that he had urinated in fear. He was nodding vigorously at Dabney's admonitions. The boy was convulsed with animal terror; he did not care that he was a man and had an immortal soul (perhaps? maybe?), but he knew what extinction would be. Thus was the end of his life—for a trivial slip. But are any slips trivial in war? Gervase thought. Oh no, that is the fineness of war: It makes every action significant. In peace, there is a graduation of actions. A man may sleep and be blameless. In war, even the most trivial of acts becomes charged with a significance far beyond its intrinsic importance. War is life at its most extreme and at its most intense, which is why it is the most important of all experiences, and why a man who has not been tested by war is but half a man. There was a sharp command; a ragged volley rang out; the body lay twitching on the brown grass covered by the shadow of the church. The officer in command of the firing party walked slowly forward and placed his revolver at the back of the boy's head and pulled the trigger and scattered the gray brains on the hot earth. The other men looked on impassively.

Gervase found himself comparing the scene with that at the hanging of John Brown. The world declared that to die by the bullet holds more dignity than death by the rope. Gervase doubted this. Death is death—the limit of all experiences. Both the scaffold and the firing party bring a certainty of time to the man who is about to die. He is not afflicted by that uncertainty that hovers over the generality of mankind, who do not and cannot know when or how they will die. So the man destined for execution can prepare himself, steady his will, and harmonize his nerves; the manner of his death is no longer chance but choice. Even in battle soldiers can hope. But when the judge says "Tomorrow at dawn," then hope evaporates; the condemned man is left in the clarity of his own will. Gervase did not know whether he should envy this sunlit clarity or fear it. But, at all events, the firing party were not stung by these metaphysical wasps. Gervase galloped down the gentle hill into Harrisonburg. The firing party shouldered their arms and marched off toward the tiny tents laid in rows of bivouac.

Gervase saw the general's standard and made toward it. He dismounted about fifty yards away and walked his horse toward the table, which was set up with its map in the town square, and he prepared to greet the officers he knew. He felt a presence at his side and turned to face Dr. Dabney, who was holding his prayer book in his hand.

"A sad business, sir," said Dabney, with real regret. "But discipline must and shall be preserved. The lad came from this very valley—from Staunton, in fact—and his mother was here last night, interceding with the general. But he will not relent in such matters. Hard as it may seem, he is right. Our God is a just God, as well as a merciful God. War makes us see *only* his justice." Gervase nodded. It seemed fair enough to him. He was not coarsening in moral fiber: He was accustoming himself to reality. The officers stood by the table. Gervase saluted them. "I've come from General Lee," he remarked casually. "I have a message for General Jackson." Captain Tate jerked his head toward the tent, where Gervase saw Jackson's feet sticking out parallel to the earth. He was kneeling.

"The execution?"

"Yep," said Tate. "If he executes a man he prays for a while to send him off to heaven." There was no cynicism in his reply. Gervase, despite his idealism, was less easily convinced. It is easy to be stern, he thought, and then appeal to God because in that way you are absolved from all guilt and you can keep your Army afraid and disciplined and reconcile your conscience with that Christian God, which is only a fancy name for Necessity and which employs Billy Quantrill and which makes me shoot little men in the back because the cause is what matters I suppose and keeping the cause above everything else requires that we should find a way of making it all bearable to ourselves and religion is Jackson's way and perfection is Lee's way and I haven't found my way yet though I'm looking hard enough and I'd better not choose Billy Quantrill's way.

The officers stood shuffling their feet and twiddling their hands. They found it difficult to endue discipline with metaphysical implications. If a man slept on duty he died: fair. If he was shot he was shot. But did the general need to pray about him? But their faith in Jackson transcended their moral and religious scruples. Perhaps the men would accept discipline the more easily if they knew that the general prayed for their immortal souls, even though his God had already decided for all eternity whether or not they should be shot or rewarded with a medal. Jackson's heels moved forward, and he came from the tent. He looked at Gervase. Gervase had never doubted that he would be recognized and be addressed by his new rank.

"Captain Stepton, welcome to the Army of the Valley." He turned to his staff. "Captain Stepton was my pupil at Lexington." Several men grinned. Jackson did not. He was displeased.

"Since a man has just died, I see no reason for thoughtless levity, gentlemen. We were compelled to shoot him. That is no reason why we should not mourn his death." Like schoolboys they dropped their eyes and looked ashamed. They *were* ashamed; they were smoldering wood in the presence of a brightly burning moral flame. It was difficult to meet his expectations—too difficult.

"Your news, Captain Stepton?" Gervase gathered himself together. "General Johnston has been shot, sir," he said. "General Lee has been appointed to the command in Northern Virginia. He requires the presence of Major Dabney and yourself in Richmond as quickly as you can manage it." "Robert Lee?" said Jackson, with a note of incredulity in his voice. "*Robert Lee?*"

"Yes, sir." Without a word, Jackson turned his back on his staff and walked back into his tent. His shoulders were hunched in what might be fury.

"The general don't like to be subordinate," said Tate, "except to God."

"That's easy enough," replied Gervase. "We're all subordinate to God."

"Just so," said Captain Tate, shrugging his shoulders. "But, after all, the general has won his laurels here in the valley. General Lee ain't won a thing as yet."

"He will," said Gervase.

The group of officers was disturbed by a cloud of dust that approached them, concealing within its particles a thunder of hooves and a raucous rebel yell. Troops looked up from their bivouacs expectantly, although there were some groans, since they had had little sleep in the past weeks.

"That noise betokens Captain Stedman," smiled Tate rather grimly. "Even on night patrol he is incapable of approaching without this touch of the clown."

"You have Roscoe, then?" asked Gervase eagerly. He had not seen his friend for months. He also disturbed his dreams. Had he had Deborah yet? Roscoe would not waste time. He pushed these thoughts down into the deeper pits of his mind. Roscoe himself emerged from the swirling dust as he pulled his horse to a stop with a pressure that pulled the animal back on its haunches and almost caused it to fall; this coincided with the re-emergence of Jackson, his beard pointing like that of a sniffing bear.

"Treat your animals better," said Captain Tate. Jackson looked at Roscoe.

"Yes?" he asked baldly, without expression, yet quivering in his hands.

"General Shields is on his way, sir," said Roscoe. "Cavalry detachment ten miles down the turnpike. Keeping between the road and Dry River Gap with his infantry." Roscoe laughed in his high clear voice. "They all look very happy. They're coming to get us!"

"Trumpeter!" shouted Jackson. The trumpeter, a boy in a worn gray uniform, came running. You ran when Jackson shouted. "Arouse the men." The clear calls of the bugle (for the title was something of a misnomer, and conferred dignity) rang sharply and briskly through the morning air. "Major Dabney." The chief of staff brought his prayer book from behind his back, where he had been holding it, and following the example of their commander, the officers of the staff sank to their knees. Gervase caught Roscoe's eye, and the flicker of a wink passed over it. Such levity displeased Gervase, who still preserved a belief in decorum. But, after all, he had shot a man in the back only a few hours before. He sank his head forward, until his neck ached with effort, and pressed his hands together until they were white with the effort. The pain eased some of his guilt. Major Dabney was not forgetful of his military function, and so prayed briefly. When they arose, the camp was one of scurrying order. Horses were being assembled in lines; the infantry were running to their platoons, the platoons forming into companies, the companies stretching in the long, gray battalion lines. It was quite clear that everyone knew what to do. And then did it quickly. Roscoe ran over to Gervase and embraced him. Roscoe's body smelled of sweat, horse, and cordite. The stench of man was very powerful, and Gervase's nostrils crinkled. Roscoe guffawed: His voice was deeper. "I ain't been out of this uniform for a couple of weeks, Gervase," he said good-humoredly, the fighter to the staff officer. "We don't get baths in the valley like you do in Richmond."

"They don't get many in Richmond now," replied Gervase, thinking of the great earthworks, the little children, young girls, crones, and aged patriarchs carrying barrows and spadeloads to make General Magruder's lines safe and solid and that the staff knew that these lines were, in a military sense, quite useless against determined attack, and that all that preserved Richmond was George McClellan's failure to grasp the same point. Gervase

thought of a city shimmering in fear with the single resolution
that they would not acknowledge that fear to themselves or to
the enemy.

"And why are you here, Gervase boy?" said Roscoe, breaking
the short reverie. Gervase was beginning, a little, to resent this
assumption of military superiority, as if he had done nothing. He
did not pause to wonder why Roscoe might be trying to rile him,
as he surely was.

"I've come to fetch General Jackson to a conference with General Lee," Gervase said somewhat abstractedly.

"Lee? Why Lee?"

"Because he commands the Army of Northern Virginia."

"Lee? Granny Lee? You must be joking me!"

"No."

"But why in the hell should Lee command? The general here
has won about ten battles in the past month. He has President
Lincoln shitting himself every afternoon about his precious capital."

"I think General Lee will surprise you, Roscoe." Be mild, calm.

"Christ, he'd better. Some blasted engineer. I suppose he can
build good bridges."

"Come on, Roscoe," said Gervase placatingly. "You've met
Robert Lee. You know that he'll make a fine commander."

Roscoe hit one glove hand against another. "We've *got* a fine
commander. He says it's all from God, and it may be, though I
couldn't care a damn so long as he wins battles. But to put this
engineer over Stonewall! Jeff must be insane."

"I think you'll say different in a month." But Roscoe was not to
be convinced. Both men walked over to their horses and swung
up to the saddle. Roscoe loosened his saber and checked his revolver loading.

"You'll stay, Gervase. See a real battle with me once again?"

"Sure," said Gervase. "I'd be honored."

"There's not much honor in battles," replied Roscoe, and urged
his horse forward. "But at least you'll see what the general can
do, and you can tell Robert Lee that he'd better resign and hand
over to Stonewall."

Roscoe was quite right. By the end of the day General Shields
was legging it back up the turnpike, leaving the detritus of de-

feat behind him: rifles, ammunition, horses, food, cannon, groaning wounded, and the ragged dead. Thanks were, as usual, given to the Lord. That night, however, Jackson did not mingle with his staff but stayed in his softly lit tent with Major the Reverend Dr. Dabney. Whether Dr. Dabney was repenting his arrogance or subduing his will Gervase did not know.

They sat in a cool, tall room in Richmond. In the distance rumbled what in peace would have been taken to be thunder and was now to their changed sensibilities known to be gunfire. It was June 23: Monday. There was Lee, with his divisional commanders: Jackson, dour and uncommunicative; Magruder, his eyes twitching with pain at his stomach complaint; A. P. Hill, eager to speak and offer ceaseless and useless opinions, yet inhibited; Longstreet, calm, supported by an inner moral strength that was not accompanied by strategical vision; Huger, stolid and seemingly dependable. They were accompanied by members of their staff, but the room was large enough for them all. The atmosphere was not friendly. Magruder spoke up, belching a little between sentences:

"It won't work, General. Oh I can do my part well enough, since I have to hold a few trenches. But no troops can maneuver as you are asking them to. And General Jackson has to move his Army from the valley to Richmond in less than a week."

"He moved himself in just over a day," replied Lee. "So he can move his Army in seven times that space of time." He looked over at Jackson, who said nothing and merely nodded. He was not going to help Lee out of his difficulties. Why should he? A. P. Hill put in a quick word.

"Robert, you can rely on the troops' courage. But are they experienced enough for this type of battle?"

"The troops don't trouble me," replied Lee. "You do. All of you." The silence flattened the room. They were hostile; he had attacked their professional confidence and competence. Jackson kneaded his hands together. There were oily beads of sweat on his forehead. Lee went on, giving his beatific smile (or so Gervase thought; the judgment did not become universal until sometime later). "Pray do not misunderstand me, gentlemen. If I were facing Wellington, Caesar, Hannibal, and Scipio, I should say the same. It is a very difficult operation of war, and, so far, out staffs, and we ourselves, have not performed very difficult operations of war." Lee then made a mistake. Gervase recognized it immediately; perhaps Lee did himself, but he had to press on. "General Jackson here has won some magnificent victories. But they are victories of tactics. Their only strategical effect has been to keep Lincoln worried about his fair capital city. We must now combine our efforts to destroy the whole Union Army of the Potomac, as they call themselves. And that will require co-ordination such as has not been seen since Waterloo. Therefore you must accept my plan—as it stands, with no modification, because it is the best plan that I can give you. And I can promise you that it will give George McClellan some moments of thought."

The commander of cavalry spoke up, flushed, eager, impetuous, as Jeb always was. "To hell with George McClellan *thinking*. John Mosby led me around the whole blasted Union Army, and I hardly lost a man. I suppose that's just a *tactical* victory, sir! All we need to do is hit McClellan and go on hitting him." Jackson winced at "to hell." Lee looked at Stuart.

"Yes, Jeb," he said, "it was just a tactical victory with a strategic purpose. The purpose was mine; the tactical execution, yours. Unless you can see that division of responsibility, you cannot hold command in a great army. You are only fit to be a bandit raider." Stuart's red face went pale. Then, slowly, the blue flooded back into the veins and he grinned.

"I reckon you're right, General," he said. Jeb was a fair man, and realistic.

Magruder was neither fair nor realistic. He peppered up like an angry cockerel cheated of his tread.

"You have insulted us, sir! Many of us have faced the enemy longer than you have. Many of us held commissions before the war. Damn it; you doubt our professional competence."

Jackson spoke, his voice somber with anger; the veins were rising in his neck, melting into the flecked black beard.

"Do not be illogical, General," he said slowly. "You cannot object to the plan on the grounds of its complexity and then claim that you are competent enough to execute any plan of war."

"Thank you, Thomas," put in Lee.

"I was merely keeping the discussion within the bounds of sound reasoning, General," replied Jackson. Lee could not help his flush. Gervase was consumed with anger at the viciousness of his old professor—for, curiously, he saw Jackson as old, though he was not.

"Let us accept General Jackson's point, then," Lee said. "This is a complicated plan. I know it. You know it. The troops will not know it, but they will do as you order. It is complicated because it requires all of you to be at the right place at the right time. But if it succeeds, then we can annihilate the Army of the Potomac, and the war will, at bottom, be over. Gentlemen," he raised his voice in appeal, "we *must* attempt a battle of annihilation. George McClellan can afford to wait. We cannot. Our people are frightened and near to panic. We must drive the federal forces away from Richmond. If this battle goes as I wish it, then they will never return, because there will no longer be a federal army. If—and pray do not feel affronted by my stress upon that if—if, I say, you give me of your best, then we can succeed. It is surely worth the trial?"

Loyal to his simple nature, Jeb rushed in where Magruder feared to tread. "Of course we'll give you our best, Robert," he said. He looked sideways at Magruder. "At least the cavalry will do so." The other generals, skeptical, sour, deflated, yet lacking the ability or the will to confront their commander, clanked to their feet. Jackson looked at Lee with his lids lowered, almost dreamily, visionary. "You were always a perfectionist, Robert. You build perfect bridges in Mexico. Now you give us a perfect plan. But you do not take into account the weakness of men. They do not relish perfection."

"You do, Thomas."

"Perhaps I doubt myself a little more. And perhaps I trust in the Lord more than my own skill." Lee bit back a reply that Gervase saw springing to his lips.

"You will give me your best, Thomas?" There was almost a note of pleading there, a supplication to the one proven commander. Jackson merely nodded in reply. Clearly, the Lord had not made His will clear. The generals saluted and, as their staffs fixed times for further conference, left the room. Lee sat down at the table when only Gervase and two other officers remained.

Lee hit the table with his clenched fist. His face was white and his nostrils spread white; his breath came quickly. Clearly, his left arm was in pain, because he raised his right hand and rubbed the upper arm.

"Will they help? Will they give of their best?" he asked. Asked no one, asked everyone.

"I don't know, General," Gervase said. "The soldiers will. And I think the generals will. Only the battle will show."

"Only the battle," Lee murmured. "There won't be only one, you know." He looked up at Gervase, and his voice took on that metal quality of cool impersonality that he always used when he had bad news to impart.

"You know that the Federals have occupied Sweetwater and all the farms around Malvern, Gervase?" he said. "I had inquiries made. Neither your family nor that of the Moutons was able to reach Richmond. I would grant you leave to try to penetrate their lines if I were able to do so. But I cannot. You are one of the few who know my mind for the coming struggle." Lee chose his words with a slightly pompous care. "But more than that: You are the only officer who is closely acquainted with both General Jackson and myself. You must convey my will to Thomas Jackson, and no one can do that better than you. So I cannot release you. But," and he became more lively, "if we have luck, or God, or whatever you wish to call it, on our side, there will be no Federals in Malvern within a few weeks. And George McClellan is no savage."

"Unlike John Pope," put in Rooney Lee.

"Not even Lincoln would entrust an army to that scoundrel," replied his father. "He couldn't fight a battle either." Gervase nodded; if there was a time for patriotism to destroy all tender feelings, this was it. If anything (which he dreaded in his heart) had happened to his family, then there would be a proper time for anger later. But he had to ask Lee a question; he was still enough of a respecter of Jackson for that.

"Is your plan too perfect, General?"

"Of course it is," replied Lee. "But in our condition, will anything less than perfection serve our turn?" And he smiled without humor. His eyes were very cold.

7

Conceptions All Awry and Lost

Despite Lee's careful arrangements, it was, of all men, George McClellan, hesitater extraordinary, who began the engagement. Perhaps he had heard that Jackson's Army was moving from the Valley toward Richmond? Perhaps he was tired of waiting. At all events, McClellan decided to put an end to what he thought the futile resistance of Richmond. He had heard, from refugees, of the parlous state of the town; he exaggerated the apprehension, and the ceaseless goading of Lincoln from Washington began to affect his *amour-propre*. McClellan ordered General Hooker to step out with his division down the Williamsburg Turnpike and enter Richmond from the south, by way of Rocketts. Perhaps McClellan expected little resistance. Then he was disappointed. Hooker's division ran into heavy fire, and the Federals crouched along the ground, seeking cover under trees, where they were wounded by splinters, or lay in the open, where they were wounded by bullets. At midday along came General Marcy, George's chief of staff, who was so horrified by the sight of dead bodies that he ordered Hooker to step back equally briskly toward Fair Oaks Station again. But by this time George himself was stirred and, arriving on the scene, ordered Hooker to turn around once more and renew his attack. The raw federal troops had dust in the nose, dust in the eyes, sweat in the crotch, and sores on the feet. But they turned around and marched back again. George (who was no fool) gave them some cannon in support, and the Federals ran into battle with balls whistling

over their heads. General Huger's troops withdrew before the
determination of the troops and the scythe of canister fire. But
by now the sun was going down behind the little white spires of
Richmond, and General McClellan thought that his soldiers
should rest. He was always very considerate and very prudent.
Gervase had been with Lee during the day, and the general had
shown no signs of apprehension.

"Only a twitch," Lee said. "Nothing but George twitching."
When night fell he called for Gervase, who was eating beans in a
small restaurant.

"Tomorrow," he said, "we'll give George a surprise. Gervase,
get out to General Jackson, and above all, above all I say, make
sure he arrives on time. If he is late, it will cost us the engagement."

Gervase set out to the North. He rode through the streets of
Richmond. Women clutched at his horse; men shouted at him;
children were huddled against houses in corners, crying. Someone called:

"When's the General going to attack?" Gervase ignored the
cry. They would know soon enough. Once a deserter came at
him out of the shadows, drunk and staggering. He pawed at Gervase's horse in the deep darkness of the outskirts of the town. He
put up his face in cowardly supplication, and Gervase kicked
him with a boot he freed from his right stirrup. There was a
crunch of bone, and the man fell backward, putting his fingers to
a mouth that spouted red, so colorful it shone even in the darkness. Gervase touched Lenore on the neck, and the horse sprang
forward, leaving the man writhing on the street, calling out to
God and the devil and shouting obscenities. Gradually the town
fell behind him, giving way to fields lit silver by the moonlight,
ghostly, still, without a flicker of war. Gervase cantered north
along the Deep Run Turnpike, south of the railway line that led
up to Hungary.

In his tent the general was on his knees and clenching his
hands together in what he wanted to make a prayer but could
not and he thought of sending for Dabney but Dabney would be
no use because no man could come between him and his God
and his God was silent in the empty skies and only his heart

spoke to him of glory, the glory he had won and should win more, but Robert Lee had the command and all he could do was to obey, he, who had become a legend in a year of war, and who relished being a legend and who wanted no other legend to set against his own, and who hated his pride but at the same time could not control it, and whose hands clawed out to his Bible and opened it at random, or as the Lord directed in the Spartan tent lit by a single lamp, and he read, "Awake, awake, put on thy strength, O Zion; put on thy beautiful garments, O Jerusalem, the holy city! For henceforth there shall no more come into thee the uncircumcised and the unclean. Shake thyself from the dust. . . ." This was plain enough, as the Federals in the valley had learned, crowing into a town one day and belting back North the next, and surely he had not ignored the Lord, at least in his words and actions, and the Lord had rewarded him with luck and with victory after victory and he had never claimed them for himself but always given to the Lord, though he chastised himself in his own heart because he knew that *there* he praised himself and his soldiers not God, because he wondered truly whether he believed in God, at least now success had gleamed upon his helmet and he was not an obscure professor in Lexington but the stone wall of the Confederacy, and he told himself truly that he did not envy Robert Lee who was a fine gentle man, but did they need gentle men now the days of battle had come and the unclean and the uncircumcised had to be cast from the land and he suddenly thought that he was not circumcised himself and he pushed his nails into his palm until the blood showed through the blue flesh because such a thought was foul and unworthy of him and he had to be worthy of himself because he was the commander of the valley who had to subordinate himself to Robert Lee, to *Robert Lee*, and what would the Lord say to that, not that the Lord was despised by Robert Lee, but he was not loved too much either, or at least it seemed so, because Robert was no Presbyterian and creed *did* matter, and the belief inspired the sword, so an officer who blasphemed should lose his sword and march in the dust and shame at the head of the column, yes, for discipline was the mark of a stern and just God, and his knees ached but he held himself in the posture of prayer and cursed Gervase Stepton who had brought

to him the message of his subordination, and he had to think of
detail, of how he would move his Army from the scene of his triumph into Richmond where Robert Lee would command him,
not God, and he felt his beard rough against his hands as he
buried his face in chagrin and fury and prayed for humility,
which no general should yearn for, because humility is weakness
and he knew no weakness, he was brusque, he was hard, he was
unflinching, he was cold and savage, though compassionate toward his stricken foe and he had not seen his foe other than
stricken, nor would he, and now the damned lamp was flickering
and like to go out, just as his own fame, and the cause too if it
were left to Robert Lee, and the bile rose in his throat. What is a
man? flesh, fur, and feces. Did European generals think in these
terms? Never, they were worldly men; he knew, for he had an
observer from the Prussian Army with him, and that man had no
love for the Lord; for himself the elect Thomas Jackson, he
wanted nothing but to be back in the white-walled church with
his wife and sing hymns and pray and love his wife with all the
permitted ardor of his loins, but the Lord God of battles had indeed sent him to battle like Gideon and he could not turn from
his destiny and he would see to it that no other man turned either; human kind could not bear the reality of war: They wilted
in weakness, and needed to be forced to bravery by discipline
and example. His officers would beg him, "Don't expose yourself,
General, don't, we need you," and the wind of the bullets whistled by him finding as often as not a red home in a nearby body,
and the pleas were sweet in his ears, because if God wanted him
to die then die he would and one sin from which he had never
suffered was fear; he despised any man who was afraid; if they
showed it in battle he shot them; their mothers might weep and
wail and write him letters and sob in his presence and he showed
them the face of General Thomas Jackson and they acquiesced
in the justice of the Lord, and he gripped his hands together
even harder together until the bones showed because he knew,
without introspection, the final truth about himself: that he did
not see any difference between himself and God; that was why
he could be so humble before the Lord and tolerate the mouth-
ings of Dabney, because Dabney was really praying to him,
not God, because in those black skies there was no God but the

will of General Jackson, whose arms had triumphed over the unclean, even that man in Washington in whose home state he had himself been born; he could not humble himself before another *man*, even Robert Lee; he had no need to humble himself before Stuart or Magruder or Huger or Hill because they were very unlike God and did not threaten his self-esteem; yet a general must value himself; he was no strategist like Robert; but he had won; many a field had been left to him, broken, deserted, scattered with debris; his young officers worshiped him; yes, he did not flinch from that word. Why should he? Because he was worthy of worship, and if Robert won his battle it would be *his* Army that did it for him. Yet could he exert himself for Robert as he exerted himself for his own colors? Could he demand that his men should die for Robert? For Virginia, oh yes, but what was Virginia compared with God? He felt the need to urinate and rose from his knees. That, at least, he could not overcome. But Christ was *incarnate*.

The general walked through the streets of Richmond, unaccompanied by his staff, unmounted, anonymous as he could never be two years later, hearing the chatter and watching the soldiers lounging about who saluted his rank but not yet his spirit, seeing Negro servants scurrying upon errands that would save their owners and frustrate the liberators and he scrutinized the faces of the old patriarchs sitting on the steps sipping Bourbon and cogitating upon success or failure and he leaned over the balustrade by the river and watched its oiliness crawl toward the Atlantic and his thoughts became abstract and he wondered upon his destiny and the will of God or chance that had placed this city and this country in his hands and he smiled as he saw the phantasm of glory hover about him and glamor in the air and then melt because that ghost was not wanted and he thought too about science and war and the nights he had spent with Clausewitz and how little they counted when compared with his resolution, which he did not doubt, really, although flickers trembled through his stomach and he felt his temples throbbing and became conscious, as he did at moments of high tension, of the thump of his heart against the wide bones of his ribs, which were stout enough to withstand the terror of failure, but he hesitated most of all for his subordinates for he did not doubt their resolution and bravery and patriotism but he did doubt their science and he remembered the words of his English visitor who assured him that one army corps from England or France would decide the war in a month and he wondered whether this might be true although neither the English nor the French had excelled themselves in the Crimea but at least he could maneuver a trained army with confidence and these lean men who would spill their blood for him could not be maneuvered with such ease and they hated digging and left it to the slaves because that was after all what slaves were for, and they did not realize that slaves would not dig with determination because they were not to fight in the trenches they scraped from the soggy earth, and slaves could not realize, as soldiers should, that this was a war of the defensive rather than the offensive, and that the rebel yell that scored the air could not win battles even when followed by the resolute bayonet, and he tried to put the smell of animals and streets away from him because he dedicated himself only to victory, nothing mattered but victory, and history showed him that victory depended upon the leader and he was the leader, not Thomas, however much Thomas might resent it, which was a puzzle because before the war Thomas was the most self-effacing of men but victory might turn anyone's head and he hoped Thomas would not try to frustrate a rival hero, not that he thought himself a hero, because he did not believe in heroes, only men who did their duty, and duty was hard enough and did not consist merely in charging into rifle or canister fire or even dying for the cause, but it also consisted of thinking, and arranging food and bullets and cannon balls and medical supplies and arranging for the possibility of defeat for no general could be a great general until he had commanded an army demoralized by disaster and he wanted to be a great general, not for himself, nor his wife, nor his children, nor even Virginia, but for some ideal he was gradually forming, a cold ideal of truth to the self, for he could appraise his own abilities and he knew that he could and should beat George McClellan and anyone else Lincoln sent against him and that truly Lincoln was his enemy because Lincoln stood for a democracy without style, homespun, wisecracking, and homely while he, respecting the ordinary man, held that

style and order was in the essence of man's dignity, and he did
not see these terms as empty but rather real though not visible,
and he made his thought cut deep into this mysterious area of
dead bodies and blood and commitment where a general must
walk open-eyed and without fear but always with compassion,
seeing gray bodies lying twisting on the earth, without arms,
heads, legs, torn, gouged, tormented, for war is terrible, which he
knew to be a cliché but not therefore less true as he had pointed
out often enough to those solemn-faced boys at West Point ten
years ago who wanted warfare to be reduced to a set of geomet-
rical rules that couldn't be done because the great general has
flair and luck, as Napoleon had always asked of a general, "Is he
lucky?" and that was the question the next few days would
answer for him—whether or not he was lucky, for upon his luck,
as well as his skill and his sleepless nights with *Von der Kriege*
when his eyes ached and his wife yearned for him in the empty
bed he had made strategy second nature to himself at the cost of
migraine, and he saw the great gap between his own human reality and the coldness of conception, for he too sniveled in a cold
and evacuated smelly feces and urinated and coughed phlegm
and scratched himself when he itched and saw women in his
dreams but all that had to be expunged and cut from the image
of himself that he would present in the world, especially during a
battle, when the wilting soldiers wanted to see a man like God at
their head, and he had to make himself like God though he knew
he wasn't, just as Wellington and Hannibal and Napoleon hadn't
been, but he knew that Wellington and Napoleon could allow
themselves a leeway of humanity, which he couldn't, because he
depended on dignity, an aloofness that could counteract Mr.
Lincoln's intimacy and directness, and Lincoln could go on
failing and failing while he couldn't lose, lose men or guns or
supplies, and couldn't allow himself a richness of life and imagination but only a purity and coldness, and the life of the river
and the fields and Arlington and the complexities of peace had to
give way to the only service of his life, which was the service of
war.

He saw a soldier in his cups kick a Negro who was carrying a
keg of gunpowder.

"Stop that," Lee said. The soldier wheeled around with a

curse, but then came up into a salute, which the general returned slowly. The Negro looked up at the general with gratitude. Or was it only relief? Slaves? He had none, unlike some of Mr. Lincoln's generals. Lee spoke gently:

"Get about your business, boy." The soldier grinned at him.

"They need a kick up the ass, General."

"So do we all," he replied, "but before I give it I'll be damned sure I'm worthy to do so." The soldier was clearly puzzled, and the general regretted that he had ventured upon morality.

"Save your kicks for General McClellan." The soldier spat in the mud of the cobbled road.

"Just wait for *General* McClellan to come to us," he said. "There'll be plenty of kicks for him."

"I hope so," said Lee, "I hope so." He walked on.

General McClellan slept soundly and dreamed of politics.

Generals Magruder and Hill and Huger all had a drink, the first two together and the last alone, and tumbled into their beds with some dignity but little introspection.

General Stuart inspected his horse lines and then talked with John Mosby, who was no officer but whom he had determined to commission in the field in the coming battle.

The soldiers slept their several sleeps, caught in the cage of radiance that was each man's dream. Tomorrow General Lee would take the initiative at Mechanicsville and endeavor to decide the fate of the Confederacy by a decisive battle. The various gods played dice in the heavens. In Richmond, babies wept.

Gervase expected to meet Jackson's patrols after an hour or so. He did not. Occasionally he saw some cavalry, in small bands, in the distance, galloping along, hooves deadened by the grass, splashing in the small streams, cracking the branches of dead and fallen trees. The moonlight made all uniforms silver, so he could not tell which side they were. Their actions seemed aimless, so he sought neither direction nor information. It was better to be safe than sorry, he thought, comforting himself with a truism. He felt calm about both his mission and the coming engagement. What was another battle? The South needed a battle, and he felt that they would win. He, at least, believed in his commander. And he believed in Jackson. His fears for his mother, for his father, for Deborah were all suppressed. In a sense, he had no time for them. He rationalized the callousness by thinking that only by fighting could he free Sweetwater and Virginia from the hordes of Federals swarming over his own fields. But he knew that this was only a fraction of the truth. He did not really care. Like his commander, he had set out on a quest for the perfection of battle. This took up the full strain of his emotions. He was becoming intoxicated by warfare. The sight that would sweeten his eyes was a row of dead Yankees, not the brown cows of Sweetwater; his nostrils would relish the putrefaction of McClellan's soldiers, not the smell of hay in the meadows of his boyhood. And he knew that an aide-de-camp had the authority of a general behind him. He intended to make Jackson *move*, for his emotions about his old instructor were mixed: He feared the man's vanity. He knew that truly vain men were only impressed by their own impulses which Jackson called the will of God. And Gervase had grown skeptical of that childhood God.

By four in the morning, when the rising sun heralded the day of Lee's first great engagement, Gervase was thirty miles north of Richmond. His bones ached as if he had influenza or the clap; at least, he assumed this was what the clap felt like, for a pure southern boy like himself (as he told himself wryly) couldn't know. The skin on his inner thighs had rubbed away, and each step taken by Lenore was scathingly painful to him. He could see no dust but, about a mile away, he could see smoke rising from numerous fires, dirty gray against the faint blueness of the sky. He put his spurs into Lenore, and that took some willpower, I can truthfully say. After a writhing gallop of three hundred yards he came upon a picket, a leveled rifle, and a voice saying:

"Who's there?"

Gervase replied briskly: "Captain Stepton, 1st Virginia Cavalry. I have messages for General Jackson." The voice replied, quavering, young, the voice of a boy.

"What's the password?" Gervase did not know. How could he? (Lee had no radio, like Eisenhower or Bradley or Patton.)

"I don't know," Gervase snapped. "But I tell you General Jackson will be damned mad if you don't let me through."

"I only know that General Jackson will have me shot if I *do* let you through," replied the voice. Carolina, was it? Gervase slumped wearily on his horse.

"Fetch Captain Stedman," he said. "Or Major Dabney. Or get the general himself."

"I ought to shoot you." Gervase lost his temper.

"Go ahead. Shoot me. Lose the war for the Confederacy." There was hesitation in the reply.

"Wait there, Captain," the appeal sang up with the birds in the morning air.

Gervase waited, Lenore pawing the soft ground. After a minute or two he was greeted by a boyish cry.

"Gervase!"

"Roscoe." It was strange how they seemed to meet at every significant moment before a battle, and, luckily, during some battles. Gervase shook Roscoe by the hand.

"Come to the general. He's having breakfast." Gervase walked his horse along by that of Roscoe.

"God knows what the Feds are doing down by Malvern Hill," said Roscoe.

"George is no barbarian."

"But his men can be. Your mother didn't go with Deborah to Richmond?"

"Did you think they would?"

"No." They rode on and came upon a pleasant scene. Thomas Jackson was sitting with his staff at a fair white table, the sun shining through the trees, the coldness of dawn giving way to the heat of the new day's sun. Gervase was horrified. He turned to Roscoe.

"Why aren't you moving?"

"Moving, hell. We've done some fighting, Gervase, and not been on our asses in Richmond." There was a strange calm about the staff as they picked up bread and broke it, chattering about the past, what they had just achieved in the valley, how many Yankee generals had fled from them, how many weapons they had captured. Thomas Jackson looked up at him fiercely. His eyes gleamed. Gervase tried to clear away his old memories— fear and apprehension and respect. He spoke quietly.

"General Lee assumed that you would be on the march now,

General," Jackson merely smiled at him. Gervase heard his voice rising.

"There is some urgency, General." Jackson lowered his heavy eyebrows. "Don't give me a lesson in the science of warfare, Captain Stepton. I know that there is a need for speed. But I can find few guides. And you must remember that *my* men have been fighting."

"But a general engagement is on the point of opening!"

"Don't try to teach me, sir!" The voice was angry, now, sharp, unlike the calm he had always found in Jackson. "Have some food."

"I don't require victuals, sir." Dabney turned to his chief.

"Captain Stepton has been in Richmond, sir." They all laughed. The echo of the laughter swept around the table. Gervase felt his hand clenching.

"Sir, I am instructed to pass to you General Lee's order that you must be ready to attack General Porter at your earliest convenience. General Hill's division is already in position." Dabney began to knot his forehead in some anxiety.

"Perhaps we should be on the move, General."

"When we're ready," said Jackson. Gervase strained his voice.

"But General Hill and General Longstreet are both waiting for you, sir." He threw caution to the winds of the past. "The orders carried by an aide-de-camp have the force of those of the commanding general himself, sir. *You* taught me that!"

"So I did, you impertinent young man," smiled Jackson. With no great haste, he rose to his feet and told Dabney to see about the move. It was growing hot. The scent of flowers lay on the air. It was humid, and the lungs began to feel heavy and clogged. Dabney scurried away, and soon a bugle began to pierce the air with its urgent frenzy. Jackson looked at Gervase.

"Does that satisfy you, sir?"

"It will when we hit General Porter, sir."

"Don't push your good fortune too far, Captain," replied Jackson. "And since you've come all the way from Richmond to Ashland to tell me to get a move on, perhaps you would be so good as to ride with Captain Stedman's company at point and tell him the way to go."

Gervase saluted. "Willingly, sir," he replied. Jackson nodded, his absent expression coming and going like a moral headache. He sat down again, and picked a piece of bread from the table, toying with it, breaking pieces off and rolling them into tiny balls, which he then brushed to the ground.

"Tell me, Captain Stepton, do *you* think General Lee's plan will defeat the Army of the Potomac?" It was a most improper question.

"Yes, sir. I do."

"Maybe, maybe," said Jackson, brushing off another ball of bread. "We shall see." There was a silence. "You had better join Captain Stedman." Gervase saluted and left the hero of the valley meditating.

Roscoe had his company mounted and ready to go. Behind them on the road other companies were forming, some cavalry, some infantry. Gunners were limbering up their pieces and pushing the horses by their great rumps to get them between shafts or at the end of chain leads. Yet over all there was an air of lethargy, no sense of urgency, no real determination or will. It had been different with Hill's division when Gervase had been there two days ago, with a message for the commander, and Hill was no Jackson—merely stolid and brave and obedient.

"Get going, Roscoe," said Gervase.

"Don't give me orders," snapped his friend in reply. "Because you're General Lee's messenger boy doesn't give you any right to tell me what to do." And Roscoe turned his horse away to speak to a sergeant. Gervase waited for him to return. It took five minutes. Roscoe was his friend; he could be blunt with Roscoe.

"What in the hell's wrong with you all?" Gervase asked with sibilant anger. "Why can't you get moving? It's as if you wanted to lose this battle. And don't tell me that you've been fighting in the valley. We all know that. Everything depends on this division, and you're wandering around like niggers who are drunk." It was a sign of Gervase's fury that he used that word.

"Oh what the hell," said Roscoe. "Stonewall should be in command. We don't know what we're doing, where we're going, or what Granny Lee hopes to gain by this engagement."

"That's because Jackson hasn't told you. He knows well enough."

"He don't believe in the engagement."

"Why?" said Gervase. "For Christ's sake, tell me why!" Roscoe's anger had left him. His smile came back and he grinned at Gervase, showing his teeth like a healthy horse.

"Search me," he said. "I'm only a captain of horse, not a confidant of the great ones like you."

Gervase looked at him intensely. "Robert Lee is a genius," he said. "A military genius like Hannibal, like Wellington. You've got to believe in him. You must."

"Perhaps I will," said Roscoe. "But he ain't done much yet." He turned toward his company and stood up in the stirrups. He called out in his strong voice. "For . . . ward!" They moved forward at a walk. They stayed at a walk.

"Aren't you going to trot?" asked Grevase with some irony. "Trot at least. I don't expect you to gallop yet."

"Where's the enemy?" replied Roscoe. "But just to please you, friend." He motioned to his company sergeant, who gave the order. Roscoe glanced across at him as they trotted abreast. "I hope you know this Hanover County. I'm damned if I do."

"Haven't you a guide?"

"I had," said Roscoe, "but you were so eager to be off that we seem to have lost the bastard." To the southeast there was, suddenly, the sound of cannon—not a full bombardment, but the intermittent crash of single guns. "Well, there's your direction," said Gervase. "Ride to the guns, as they say."

But, as Roscoe had keenly noted, this was easier to say than to do. The tracks ran across each other in crazy patterns; some petered out after a few hundred yards; some led straight up to the Chickahominy River, and then abruptly stopped; occasionally there was a ferry, but Gervase knew that they were at this point needed on the south bank, not the north. Once they came upon a farmer, calmly working his fields with his daughters about him in orange dresses. Gervase called to him.

"Where's Mechanicsville?" The man paused with his scythe.

"Well, there you have me, Major . . ."

"Captain."

"I'm right sorry. Mechanicsville, you say, north of the river. Well, take that there road you're on now and then ask someone else when you get toward Richmond. I'm no hand at directions."

"No, you're not," said Gervase. One of the girls called out.

"Keep on, Captain. About four miles and then cross the river.
God go with you." Gervase sighed in relief. They moved on. The
dust rose from the hooves of their horses. Gervase glanced back
and saw the company stretched out over about a mile.

"Close them up, Roscoe," he pleaded. "I'm not ordering you.
Please. Please. Christ Almighty," he cried out, "this was to be a
battle of annihilation, and it all depended on your precious
Stonewall. He's failing us, can't you see? He's failing us."

"Don't quarrel, Gervase," said Roscoe. "Stonewall won't fail
you." He turned back. "Close up, damn you. Close up. Keep
them in order, Sergeant Ambrose." The cannon fire was now
more dense, and columns of smoke could be seen to their front.
They could hear the bursting of the new Yankee shells.

It was eleven o'clock and they began to run into the supply
lines of Hill's division, men toiling with ammunition and food
and water. The heat slammed down onto the dry foreheads, and
the sweat broke out all over them. They crossed the Chickahominy just east of the Virginia Central Railroad bridge and came
upon line upon line of Hill's men, drawn up in fours, leaning on
their weapons by the roadside. There were jeers.

"Where's fucking Stonewall?"

"Why are we waiting?"

"Here come the valley boys. Only three hours late!" Gervase
turned to Roscoe. "Stay here," he said. "Keep them formed up. I
only hope the general bothers to turn up."

"He will, damn you," said Roscoe. "It was the first time he had
spoken to his friend with bitter anger. Gervase ignored him and
galloped forward past line upon line of dust-brushed men, some
silent, some singing, some leaning on their guns. Only the artillery had work to do, slinging shells back at Porter's artillery
behind Beaver Dam Creek. They were stripped to the waist, carrying the balls up to the cannon, the officers giving the command
to fire with a swift downward movement of the sword, followed
by the great crash. Occasionally a ball came hurtling their way.
Gervase pulled Lenore around a great gap in a waiting infantry
company, where the surgeons were at work patching up the men
before they were moved back. Gervase noted with a scientific curiosity that wounds from the guns were different from the slices

of swords, or the small smash of the musket. The guns crushed men to pieces with the weight of metal; they pounded flesh until it was, quite literally, jelly.

This was no skirmish; this was no amateur affair, like First Manassas. This was real war. He saw Hill's standard in the middle of an infantry brigade and he galloped toward it, forcing his horse through the packed ranks of waiting men when they got in his way. Hill was by the standard, rubbing his gauntlets together and slapping them against his wrist, touching his saber, letting his eyes roam over the Yankee position. When he saw Gervase he let out a cry.

"Give him passage, give him passage!" Gervase rode up at speed and pulled Lenore to a savage halt. He saluted. Hill flicked his hand in reply, but did not stand upon ceremony. His staff crowded forward, a bevy of horses foaming where the cruel bits held them still.

"Is he here?" said Hill. "Is he ready for action? I can't keep my men under this artillery fire for much longer. Why didn't he come with you himself? Speak out, man!" Gervase hardly knew what question to take first.

"No, sir," he replied, "General Jackson is not here. Only one company of his cavalry. His division was on the move when I left him. But they fell behind me very rapidly."

"Good Christ Almighty," shouted Hill, his face flushed and furious, "didn't General Jackson understand that this maneuver is the essential part of General Lee's plan? If I don't attack soon, I'll never force Porter from the flank position at Beaver Dam. Any first-year student at the Point could grasp that. It does not take either a hero or a military genius. Doesn't General Jackson realize what he must do?"

"He does realize," said Gervase. "I told him."

"Thomas is no coward," said Hill more softly. "He will march toward the guns. Did he have guides?" he shot out.

"Yes, sir." Hill was silent. He looked at his staff, but they did not speak. He turned back to Gervase. "You must ride back to General Jackson. You must"—he spoke very slowly—"insist upon speed, the utmost speed, on his part. I can rely upon you, Captain Stepton. Look!" He pointed to the east. "I cannot take that position with my own division alone. It cannot be done, sir. Yet it must be taken. If General Jackson does not arrive by midday I shall attack by myself, and my division will be destroyed. Tell that to the hero of the valley. Be off, sir. And with best speed, sir, best speed."

Gervase pulled Lenore around and galloped off. He passed Roscoe's company at full speed and raised his hand. Roscoe waved back. Gervase made off up the same road, but there was no sign of Jackson's division. The dust had settled again, and so dense were the trees that he could not see the cloud of dust that meant that the men were on the march. He had expected to find Jackson within a mile or two, but the country was deserted. He passed the field where the farmer had been at work with his daughters, but they had gone away—to eat their dinner, he surmised, and laughed. But the day was not giving much place to gaiety and laughter. He pulled to a halt and meditated. He could strike yet farther west, but he had to assume that Jackson had at least started his march. He would turn north. There was another of the multitude of tracks heading north (Gervase calculated the direction by the sun). He cantered along the track for a mile or so, sniffing the dust, which made him cough and irritated his eyes. The air was even more humid now, and his eyes watered. At least he was not being shelled. He must be near to the Chickahominy. He thought he could see the gleam of water through the trees. Suddenly he heard a voice:

"Hey, look there!" He peered through the dust, thinking it must be Jackson's advance guard. As the dust began to settle he was disabused of this notion. The soldiers were mounted, and they wore blue. Soldier blue, now here I come. He drew his saber and pulled Lenore around. Behind him were four Yankee soldiers. They all had carbines, and they looked as if they had been trained sufficiently to know how to use the damned things. He would be ripped open in a second. He laid down the point of his saber. So be it. This was the chance of war. His general would lose, and that was that. He clamped his teeth together and rode up to the soldiers. One was a captain, like himself. Gervase handed over his sword, and the man took it. He spoke to Gervase in his harsh Connecticut twang.

"You put me in something of a dilemma, sir. I cannot spare men to guard you, since I am on patrol work, although returning at this time to General Porter. I am not willing to kill you here and now, but I shall be compelled to do so unless I receive your parole." Better live to fight another day, thought Gervase.

"You have my word of honor, sir." He lowered his eyes. The captain gave him back his sword.

"Here, Captain, you ain't going to take the word of this Reb sod, are you?" A sergeant was speaking.

"Of course I am. Don't you know that the word of a southern gentleman is legendary, Sergeant Holstein? My name is David Kinser, sir." He even held out his hand. Gervase took it.

"Gervase Stepton," he replied. The other looked at his uniform. "First Virginia Cavalry, I see. Are you with Stuart still?" Gervase bridled a little.

"I don't have to give you information, sir," he replied.

"Let me work him over, Captain," said the sergeant.

"Don't be absurd," said Kinser. "And no, Captain, you don't have to give me any information. And now I think we'll return to the more welcome side of this river with the Indian name." He rode forward, and Gervase followed. Together they plunged into the river, which was deep here and refreshing. David Kinser chatted away happily to Gervase. He clearly found his sergeant somewhat tedious, and was glad to have another gentleman with him. He would, however, not have relished that term, for he was most democratic and full of ideals—the other ideals, of which Gervase's father had spoken. "It was a fruitless patrol, Captain," said Kinser, "quite fruitless. General Porter was somewhat apprehensive that General Jackson might be hovering on the flank. But he's nowhere to be seen. At least," he said with a smile to which Gervase could not resist a reply, "*I* can't find him. Perhaps you would have better luck in your own country."

"I can't find him either," said Gervase. They clambered up the bank of the Chickahominy. Now they skirted north. The Yankee was a good officer. He drove his men hard. The sound of cannon had become continuous, and they found it difficult to speak. Now they were, after a ride of an hour or so, at General Porter's. It was almost two o'clock. Cannon, cannon, but no infantry fire. No yell.

Somehow Gervase could not believe in his captivity. At this stage of the war the reality of exchange was always present. He

knew that Lee would capture a Yankee to hand over in his place.
It might take a day or two, even a week. At all costs, he must not
give them the knowledge of his position, for that would provide
invaluable information, first to Porter and then to McClellan. He
must pretend to be an ordinary cavalry officer, a mere Roscoe
(he remembered that phrase of his thoughts later) until the battle was concluded.

"I must report to the general," said Kinser. "Will you accom-
pany me, Captain Stepton?"

"Willingly," said Gervase. At that moment a shell burst above
them, and fragments of metal pattered about them. A piece cut
Gervase on the cheek, and he wiped away the red with his
gauntlet. Sergeant Holstein had been struck more seriously; a
fragment had pierced his groin and broken the back of his horse.
Kinser dismounted and helped the writhing man to the ground.
His cry for stretcher bearers was answered quickly—more
quickly, Gervase realized, than would be the case in the Confederate Army. All seemed confusion. He could easily have turned
and galloped away. But was not the word of a southern gentleman legendary? Holstein was borne away to God knew what
ghastly fate. Kinser looked at him quietly.

"Thank you," he said. "You could have got away then."

"You said it yourself," replied Gervase. "Our word is legendary." Kinser laughed affectionately. They trotted through the artillery lines, their ears ringing and painful, to the small hillock
upon which General Porter had his headquarters. Everything
was well ordered. There was a tent, and a small desk before it at
which the general sat, smoking a cigar. He was a big man, even
in his chair, abrupt and laconic of speech.

"Did you find Jackson?" he asked Kinser. "Come on, man, be
quick. I've plenty to think about." I'll bet you have, thought Gervase, perched on this floating flank.

"No, sir," said Kinser. "I couldn't find a sign of General Jackson." "He's around somewhere," said Porter. Then Gervase realized how much fear the great Stonewall caused them. They saw
his ghost—no, his reality—in every corner. "Damned if I know
where he'll appear." It was almost three o'clock, and the sun had
turned in the sky.

Captain Kinser gestured toward Gervase. "I captured a Confederate officer, sir. A Captain Stepton. He gave me his parole, and observed it when he could have made his escape."

"More fool you," said Porter. But he meant this as a jest. "You can take him down to General McClellan's headquarters down by Harrison's Landing. You've done well, Kinser, and you can enjoy the ride." It was almost twenty miles, and Kinser was clearly pleased. Suddenly Porter stopped speaking. He rose from his chair at the desk, which had been placed so that he could see the battlefield in front of him. "Christ Almighty," said General Porter. "Jesus Christ Almighty."

The Yankee position was along Beaver Dam Creek, around Ellerson's Mill. They had done their best to make their position impregnable. Geography had aided their endeavors. In front of the creek, on the Confederate side, there was a swamp of several hundred yards. Then there was the creek itself, then a rise in the ground up to the Yankee positions. The rise had been piled with logs and dirt. Companies had been stationed so as to obtain both frontal fire and enfilade fire. Artillery were dug into pits so that they could shoot chain shot and canister into any infantry entering the swamp. The Confederate artillery had hardly dented the fortifications. General Porter was no amateur at warfare.

His ejaculation had been prompted by the sight of General Hill's division rising from a frontal position and plunging forward into the swamp toward the Yankee lines. They let out the rebel yell, better co-ordinated than it had been at First Manassas. They spilled forward in a gray mass, dots for faces, little sticks for rifles. They sank in the swamp as they came forward, and men climbed on the shoulders of their comrades as they sank, always going forward, dispirited by neither death nor wounds. "Give me a glass," shouted Gervase. He pulled a telescope from an astonished staff officer and scanned the Confederate ranks. Not one of Jackson's regiments was there. All Hill's. Gallant, impetuous, loyal Hill. "Give that back," snapped the outraged colonel. Porter rushed out orders. "Give it to them," he said, "give them all we've got. They're not touching our flank, the fools. They're committing suicide." And indeed they were. Heroic, glamorous, and futile, Hill was fulfilling Lee's command that Porter must be attacked in the first engagement and driven out of Beaver Dam Creek. Hill had waited for Jackson, but Jackson had not come. So Hill would do the job himself. Or die. His men were now doing the dying. The swamp was covered with gray bodies. Gervase could not see the wounds, he could not see the stigmata of death, the bullets flying, the canister shot like a scythe in the ranks. He just saw the doll figures toppling over, toppling, one by one in droves, like hunted beasts, like rabbits, oh all comparisons fled his mind in the torrent of steel that flew from the Yankee positions. Still they came on. Utterly futile.

"Well, that's a good beating," said Porter with satisfaction. Gervase turned away. He felt a hand on his shoulder, and Kinser was with him.

"Your soldiers are very brave, Captain Stepton," he said.

"Damn fools, too," said Porter.

"General . . ." pleaded Kinser. The general fell silent. And he looked down at the thousands he had killed. The day was most certainly his. Another patrol leader rode up in the roar of fire that continued, when would it stop, oh God let it stop pleaded Gervase with his silent God.

"General Jackson's at Hundley's Corner, sir," said the leader of the patrol. "But he ain't moving." Porter visibly blanched. "He may not move today, but he will tomorrow. We'll get out of here tonight. See to it," he said to his staff. And then he turned to Kinser. "And get that Reb to General McClellan." Gervase thought, with great bitterness, that the great Stonewall's mere name had achieved what Lee wanted. He had done nothing at all; he had let Hill's soldiers die by the thousand, but he had forced Porter to retreat because the bayonet of his reputation lunged at the federal throat. But what a way to win! The gray masses twitched and turned and groaned and cried and died in silence on the muddy expanses of the swamp before Beaver Dam Creek. It was a strange victory.

"David," asked Gervase, for they were now on terms of friendship, "would you object if we turned down to my parents' farm at Sweetwater? I have felt no little anxiety about them since the beginning of this campaign." Kinser somehow expected Gervase to talk like Dr. Johnson, and he acceded to the request. Kinser answered quickly.

"Of course I don't object. Why should I? You have my sympathies in that your family is mixed up in the messy business of war. I am thankful that we are spared that in Connecticut."

"General Lee may get that far," said Gervase. For a moment David took him seriously, but then he grinned.

"Lee won't want to get up North. He wants to keep us out of the South, that's all." They had ridden through Glendale and turned to the south among the familiar fields. It hardly deflected them from their journey to Harrison's Landing. They had heard the sound of cannon to the north for the past three days, for they had ridden slowly. But they had only had the garbled reports of the wounded and staff officers riding back to General McClellan. At all events, the cannon was moving closer, so Gervase surmised that the disaster at Ellerson's Mill had been recouped. How, he could not imagine. Perhaps the troops were learning that General Lee was not a mere theorizer. Perhaps even Thomas Jackson was learning that lesson. Gallant and heroic and famous subordinate commanders needed to learn their place.

Here was the field where he had won the pony race in 1856, with his mother clapping and Deborah shouting and waving her arms and his father trying to hide his pride and not clapping at all despite his mother's digs in the ribs and even verbal expostulations. The white church steeple shone in the sun, a point of direction in more senses than the geographic, a needle to pull the heart. The place was swarming with Yankee soldiers, Gervase noted. They had thousands of men about. He said so to David.

"You have more men to feed you than to fight."

"Not quite," Kinser replied. "But General McClellan likes good organization."

He certainly did. The streams that cut this area of the country were muddy, their sweetness gone. The Yankees had erected countless bridges. Everywhere were dumps of ammunition and food. The fields were deserted, sometimes stripped of grain, and barns were often burned.

"Regrettable, indeed," said Kinser. He couldn't find the right words, thought Gervase. Some houses were burned too, and his anxiety began to rise in his throat. He voiced it.

"Oh no," said Kinser, "our men would not touch women and children. Nor old men."

"Not if there were officers like you about," replied Gervase. He smartened the pace, and Kinser, understanding his apprehension, cantered with him. They went down the remembered roads, with the remembered shadows and known sunlight upon them. The house should be in sight soon. The tips of the roof, then the sheds and stables and cottages for the servants, all painted in fresh white, every year his father insisted. The trees would cast their welcoming shadows around about. The little field with the cattle would slope down to the Sweetwater River. The Yankees would have taken the cattle, he knew that, because any army was entitled to live off the land to a certain degree, even if they had ships calling every hour with supplies. He strained his eyes for the tips of the roof. He kicked Lenore into a gallop.

"Not so fast," panted Kinser. "All will be well, I can assure you. General McClellan gave the strictest orders about looting."

"What do I care if some looters hang?" cried Gervase. "If they've done the looting already!" Still he looked for the tips of the house, but could see nothing. He rode as fast as he could, risking a bad fall, and Kinser fell behind. So Gervase came upon the sight alone.

The house had been burned down, and the cottages. The cattle had disappeared. The meadow had been used as the camping ground for some regiment that had now moved up to the front line. A latrine had been dug along the bank of the Sweetwater. He took all this in with a single glance. He did not slow up his pace and was at the house fully three hundred yards before Kinser could catch up with him. He found plenty of Yankee soldiers about, one, an officer, wearing the badge of a provost marshal. Gervase jumped from his horse and looked at the charred ruin, the paradise lost forever. Then he saw four graves at the edge of the field, marked by crudely carved crosses. He walked into the house, the timber peeling in black charred fragments, the furniture hurt by fire lying at absurd and foolish angles. By this time Kinser had reached him. David spent no time with him but walked across to the provost marshal. They whispered together for a minute. Then Kinser came over to Gervase and took him by the arm and led him from the house. He was wholly considerate. Gervase felt utterly numb. "What happened?" he said. "What in the hell happened?" Kinser looked at the ground, scoured by horses and men's hooves, defaced a few yards ahead by dung.

"It's a complex business, Gervase," he said. "It's damnable, utterly damnable. Some men from a New York regiment got hold of some liquor. They got drunk. Then they came up to the house. There was an elderly man here and his wife. They had another old man, too, with his young daughter. They were taken with the liquor, Gervase, they weren't proper soldiers any more, you know. Well, they got into a brawl. They killed the elderly men. And then they . . . well . . . they took liberties with the two women. Both of them are dead too."

"They raped them?" asked Gervase.

"Yes," said Kinser bluntly. "But rest assured, justice was done the next day. They were tried by court-martial, and General McClellan confirmed the sentences the same day. The men who did this are buried at the back. They were hanged immediately."

"Hanged?" asked Gervase dully.

"Yes, yes," said Kinser. All Gervase's childhood and youth came into one image and smashed into his brain. Deborah had known nothing but the panting lust of Yankee soldiers, his mother had fallen beneath their fumbling bodies, his father had died at their hand, and old Mouton, poor drunken fool. All he had valued was already responding to the tiny teeth of the worms under those crosses out front. The grass had gone, the cattle had gone, the water was fouled, nothing could ever be the same again, he could never be the same. Memories swarmed about him, but he did not know which to choose. He left them, let them flow into the air and mingle with the thud of cannon.

"Gervase, please accept my apologies, regrets. Oh, what can I say?" Kinser was clearly deeply distressed. As he ought to be, thought Gervase.

"You can say nothing, David," he said, "nothing at all. I know you would not have done this, and I know that you would never have permitted this. He was my father; she was my mother; I was to marry Deborah. Perhaps."

A new voice cut in, strong Ohio tones. "We hanged them well and good, Captain. You can see the graves out back. They died bad, like most rapists and killers." It was the provost marshal.

"Oh, what do I care how they died?" said Gervase. The tears were hot in his eyes. The provost marshal turned aside with embarrassment. Dead, they were all dead. What did he have left now? Nothing. He had not even loved Deborah. She had known no love but the hot thrust of Yankee drunkards. They had held her and pulled her legs apart in pain and filth, panting whiskey and lust over her sweet face. Could his men have done this ever? Yes, oh yes, because war is war and fury and foulness.

There was a commotion in the grounds outside. Horsemen were moving about. Gervase, like a ghost, turned to pass into the meadow, newly foul and lit by the old sun, wondrous form of a nature polluted. It was a general and his staff. The general was quite young and looked down at him from a brown horse. The general called over to another officer.

"Are those ships here yet, Brampton? I'll know the reason why if they are not! It's that man in Washington, I tell you. He'll leave us all to die under Lee's cannon. Well, at least we shall defend Malvern Hill to the end." He turned his face to Gervase and focused on him. "You are Captain Stepton. I cannot too deeply regret what occurred here. You know the malefactors have been punished? So they shall always be under my command. My sympathies, sir, my deepest sympathies." And he swept his horse away and cantered over the meadow with his staff. One officer remained behind.

"We have arranged an exchange for you, Captain Stepton." He scribbled on a piece of paper. "If you take this to General Porter at the front he will allow you passage under a white flag. My sympathies, sir." He saluted and handed the paper to Gervase. Gervase sank to his knees and felt the arm of Kinser about his shoulder. He did not know for whom he should weep. At least they were now all in the past, where his memory could hold them in perfection and no one could touch them.

Captain Stepton was exchanged on the day after the battle of Malvern Hill, and, at his own request, he returned to the 1st Virginia Cavalry. He was tired of staff work, and Lee was somewhat embarrassed by his presence: He was a reminder of Jackson's failure at the battles during the seven days that had saved the South. Gervase served with distinction in the Second Battle of

Manassas. He was promoted to major. His heart did not leap up when Lee invaded the North. It was as if he had a foreboding of what was to come. At Antietam he was by Roscoe when his friend received a rifle bullet in the throat. Shortly afterward they were captured by Yankee infantry, for both had had their horses shot from under them. It was with something like relief that Gervase marched toward the rear. There was none of the civilized grace of exchange this time.

8

Stone Walls Do Not a Prison Make

They drew up into the sidings by Fort Delaware in a long train consisting of cattle trucks; the sun shone merrily.

The journey from the front had been one of discomfort increasing into horror. When they had been pushed and poked by the bayonet along dirt tracks until they were out of the dull sound of the cannon, a medical officer with squinting eyes had made a desultory attempt to separate the seriously wounded from the unscathed. It was very desultory indeed. He was a harassed man. He walked down the line and pointed with his short stick at anyone who could not stand and had an obvious wound—a missing limb, some disfigurement of the face, the appearance of interior organs through the uniform. These men were taken by stretcher bearers and put in a long line by the side of a ditch. Gervase never heard of them again. He was not afraid; capture seemed to have numbed his capacity for fear; here was a sense of finality, of completion in his mind. Naturally, it wore off soon enough.

Then they marched. They marched about twenty miles, continually being urged to greater speed. Men stumbled and fell to their knees, at which they were struck by rifle butts and either rose to their feet or were slung to the side of the road. If they were pitched out of the line of march then they were hit on the head by one of the provost staff so that they could not make off. This discouraged dissimulation. The provost staff hit prisoners on the head very hard indeed.

The landscape, nondescript, made no impression upon Gervase. It was like the landscape behind any battle front, littered with ammunition, piles of stores, stacks of rifles, dirty tents, the occasional body covered with canvas. Gervase was more concerned with Roscoe. Roscoe could not speak. The fragment had pierced his throat, not to produce gouts and gushing of blood, but doing its work invisibly, slicing the vocal cords. Roscoe gurgled. He gurgled at the medical officer, but that official had been left unmoved. His bodily strength did not seem to be diminished to any marked degree; he was not exhausted; he marched with Gervase step by step, right foot after left, looking up with puzzled and unfocused eyes as the provost staff exhorted them forward.

"Get a fucking move on, you scum!" Some were of German extraction but had acquired the most striking adjective in their new tongue.

Once a general and his staff galloped past them. Gervase recognized General Hooker. General Hooker did not recognize him. He did not spare a glance for the prisoners, who were bundled off the road to make way for the entourage speeding to control the action. When General Hooker had disappeared in a cloud of dust, which he left lingering in the air to clog their nostrils and parch their throats, they started to march again, putting the left foot in front of the right again and again until the action took on the wearisome monotony of a metronome.

They reached a railroad siding. There were many other prisoners already assembled there, and a train was backing a long row of cattle trucks along the solitary line. Federal troops stood behind them in their sober blue, but to Gervase's weary eyes they were black dots against the turmoil of activity among the civilian railway staff. One prisoner, driven wild by thirst and weariness, swung a blow at one of the provost staff. Without much ado he was propped against a wall and shot. He slumped down like a silly doll. At a shouted order all the prisoners squatted on the dirt, a mess of gray on the sandy ground. The sun did not relax his attentions, but Gervase sweated no more, for the moisture had oozed from every pore in his body. Roscoe did not understand the order, but Gervase pulled him down by his side.

Roscoe stared at the ground. He gurgled again, whistling too, through his throat.

There was no attempt to separate the officers from the men. Gervase felt that this was right and proper, it fitted the decorum of things. There is no rank among the defeated; all that matters is the fact of defeat and the capacity to endure. A boy from Texas who is captured in his first engagement can do as much in defeat as a general officer. Gervase felt like tearing off his badges of rank, but the effort would cost him too much. How tawdry appeared the brave insignia of the 1st Virginia Cavalry, that fine black against the weathered gray. The train clanked to a halt, and the provost staff moved forward, waving their clubs. The men were urged into the cattle trucks. The doors had been slid back, but there was a gap of about five feet between the ground and the vehicles. The men had to push and pull each other up into the trucks. Gervase took Roscoe by his knees and pulled him up and pushed him forward. A burly sergeant from Alabama took Gervase by the right wrist and hauled him after; he stumbled forward into the hot darkness of the still air, which smelled of cattle, but which was giving way to the smell of men. The prisoners were, largely, silent, although one man was weeping and laughing with alternating hysteria, and another was vomiting in the corner. The acrid smell drifted slowly through the unmoving air. Gervase propped Roscoe against the tough wooden wall as near to the sliding door as he could get. Many others had the same idea, and Gervase had to kick and push to retain his position. He did not try to use his rank. If the Yankees did not recognize it, it would be fruitless; in any case, he did not wish to claim some superiority based on a skill in the field they had left behind them. He tried to think of Deborah, who was dead, and his father, who was dead, and his mother, who was dead, and Sweetwater, whose buildings were shattered by cannon and consumed in fire. It was as if the whole texture of his being had been consumed on that day in Malvern Hill. During the battles he had lived upon the spiritual capital of the images his memory offered; in defeat, even memory and imagination failed him. The provost staff slid the doors tight, and Gervase heard the wooden bolts slide home with a thud. The closing of the doors did not, however, signify the movement of the train.

They were encapsulated. They were pushed together so that they could barely move, about fifty men in gray uniforms stained with powder and sweat and in many cases blood. Many men now felt natural needs, and they had to give way to these needs; they were, in some cases, men of delicacy, but the demands of the body were imperative. Gervase saw that Roscoe's pants were stained around the crotch with urine. Roscoe had pulled his knees up to his chin and held his arms around them, hugging himself into a ball. Gervase dominated his body until his bladder was too much for him. But he felt no disgust with himself; only a wet discomfort. It was as if he had fallen into the Sweetwater up to his waist. He seized that image and held onto it! Soon it fled among the twittering groans of the other men.

Nobody was prepared to exercise any command. What commands could be given that might have any meaning? Gervase nudged the man next to him, who had been standing against the wall. He keeled over, and Gervase saw that he had died, silently, without fuss, without protest, with only a silent endurance as his companion. The truck shuddered as the engine eased forward. Then it stopped again. There was the sound of hooves outside as a troop of cavalry rode past. It was in another world. Cramp was setting in, and with these sharper pains, despair, a despair that became vocal. Why can't they move us? was the question implicit in all the obscenities and blasphemies. But the noise was not like that of the battlefield, where one could ignore pain in the vigor of energy. It was a cry that rose from the paralyzed will. They had become animals.

Like his companions, Gervase was thirsty. He wanted no more than a cup of water, a dirty Army canteen filled with green standing water from a pool, but he wanted that very badly. He tried to generate saliva in his mouth and on his cracked lips, but he could not; his dry tongue tasted salt as it caressed the salty lips. Roscoe could not have drunk in any case. Gervase glanced at him and saw that he was asleep or unconscious, it was hard to decide. Even though the mind was consciously blank, the gurgling went on. Gervase was surprised to find that he did not care. Here was his closest friend, suffering, maybe dying, yet he did not care. He marveled at his own selfishness and condemned it with quiet anger, yet this did nothing to change his feelings.

He did not want his companions dead; he did not want them to
be happy; he did not care, for he was sunk in *accidie*. The air became hotter in the railway truck.

It did not grow cooler when they began to roll along, clanking
over the rail joints. They moved very slowly. The rhythm became hypnotic, and Gervase found himself losing awareness of
himself in those iron poundings as the wheels clacked and hammered on the iron. It was as if his very being had ceased to be
anything but an identification with sound; he had become
decarnalized. Occasionally there was a thumping on the roof of
the truck, and Gervase knew that federal soldiers were guarding
them from the top of the train. The thumps of the feet were a
distraction from the reality into which he had sunk himself. The
dead Georgian (for so his facing declared) lay beside Gervase,
his jaw dropped, all surprise and wonder and quickness gone
from his eyes. Gervase shifted him with his heel. His feet hurt.

It was peculiar how these little rushes of pain recalled him to
the complexities of his real situation. Sometimes for a minute or
so he would think: Where am I? What am I doing on this railroad? For Gervase had not grown up with machines, but with
animals; he was adjusting the fibers of his nerves to the new
modes of existence that hitherto the war had not presented to
him. Sabers and cannon and rifles were machines too, weren't
they? But hallowed machines. They were sometimes blood-
stained, but not acrid. Their car was near the engine, and the cut
of the smoke began to seep through the ill-fitting boards. There
was something immemorial about the smell of dung; this was the
perfume of the new Yankee world.

He would have liked to take off his boots and get the air to the
sharp blisters. There was no room. He was hemmed in by the
crouching Roscoe and the corpse. He shifted his buttocks,
scratched at his legs and armpits, which were infested with
creeping insects; he breathed in wood smoke and vomit smell,
the bouquet of excrement, as the train crept North. The journey
took twenty-seven hours, and six men died. After a while they
organized themselves to the degree that they handed the corpses
over the heads of the living and piled them one on top of another at the end of the truck. This did not give them much room,
but it gave some. Gervase could flex his knees at the least.

In the last hours of the journey before they reached Fort Delaware, he thought Roscoe was dying. He had gone not white but gray, and his eyes lost all focus. Gervase gave him his hand, and he clutched it with surprising strength, digging his black nails into Gervase's palm. Roscoe tried to speak, but only that gurgling came out. There was, undoubtedly, a mute appeal for sympathy, and Roscoe had saved Gervase at Manassas, but what could he do for his friend in this oven of degradation? Nothing. Roscoe, once the southern cavalier graceful with uncontrolled energy, had become a baby with a baby's demands, selfish, coded, intrusive. Gervase had no time for anyone but himself. Brotherhood was a tedious distraction in this wasteland of muck.

Shifting and shuffling, the train clanked to a halt. There was shouting outside and the sound of running feet. They waited an hour. Then the bolts were opened and the doors slid back. The sun shone merrily, and its rays pierced the soft balls of the prisoners' eyes like heated needles.

The journey in the train had been a suspension in time, hung poised between the flurries of action, where the body had been, as it were, hung up in chains and the mind left with its own despair to reflect upon impossibilities. The very noise of the engine and the wheels on the track had conspired to form an auditory image of a regularity stretching into eternity, free of the changeableness that constitutes the hazard of life. Now the noise became utterly irregular. Screams and orders broke out, barely distinguishable from each other in wording but clear in import. Out. Out. Quick. Out. Move. Get on. Move. Damn you, move. Quick. Out. Fuck you, out. Leave them corpses alone. Leave the carrion. Don't worry about them dead trash. Out, move. Move, out. The sun speckled the dirt. They tumbled down from the truck, many falling on their faces, feeling the earth in their mouths. Gervase fell to his knees and cracked his left kneecap against a stone.

"Get up on your feet, Reb!" He felt a rifle butt strike his ribs, and he hauled his body to its feet. He swayed. Pins and needles —of a more severe kind than he had ever known before—were shooting through his calves. He groaned, but the groan was cut short by further orders.

"Line up, line up, line up." Around them stood federal sol-

diers. (Were they the same as those who had put them on the
train? Once again that sober blue dotting the field of vision.)
The soldiers handled their rifles with rather less familiarity, because they were not line-of-battle troops. Stumbling, crawling,
staggering, the prisoners formed some sort of line in front of
long, deep-brown sheds. Gervase pulled Roscoe with him. Roscoe kept falling to the ground, and Gervase had to pull him to
his feet. Finally, he slid his right arm around Roscoe's shoulders,
gripping his torn tunic under the right armpit, and dragged him
along toward the line. Roscoe surrendered any attempt at effort,
and his toes drew crazy patterns in the dust, scrawling like a
giant insect. He tried to speak. Some noise came from his lips,
grotesque, ludicrous, courageous. Gervase could hear him saying
again and again: "God, God, God, God, God." Gervase reflected
that God had been noticeably absent from the scene since their
capture. Perhaps He preferred to be with General Jackson.

They formed a line, remnants of proud regiments, ragged, no
dressing, wavery, men smashed in the face and battered in the
mind, puzzled, resentful, hangdog, fit to be whipped, starving,
twisted by thirst, with shit in their pants and piss on their bellies,
without food, without sleep, flogged by time like wild dogs panting and rabid, the vomit caked on their gray chests, bending forward because their lungs were choked and their stomachs empty
and howling for food, their muscles trembling. The line was
straightened by the rifle butts of the guards, older men, men
without concern, with faces anonymous, men used to dealing
with cattle. A sergeant major bellowed at them.

"Listen here, you men. Listen good." A dapper figure advanced and stood in front of them at twenty yards' distance; his
uniform was clean, his golden badges of rank (he was a major)
shining in bravado to the sun. He held a cane in both his hands
at the level of his loins. His fingers clutched the wood with
venom and determination. He spoke, caressingly yet with a voice
of no pity; he faced a mass without identity.

"You men are now at Fort Delaware." His voice had a trace of
Germany, forests of Silesia, in its harshness. He smiled, but with
no welcome. "The rebellion is over for you." His face twitched
again—in disgust, as if the smell was too much for his delicate
nostrils in his pudgy nose. Even at that distance Gervase could

see the hairs starting from the base of his nostrils, like a pig. "Not that you could do much for General Lee and his Army in your state." A wave, involuntary, shuddered through the line of a hundred men. "You'll hear the rules soon enough. All I tell you is this: Obey them." A man slumped down in the middle of the line. One of the soldiers walked over to him and brought his rifle butt down on his outstretched fingers as hard as he could. The noise was both a thud and a crack. The man did not stir. The soldier kicked him, viciously, on the head—with such force, indeed, that the body turned over and the eyes stared up at the cold blueness of the sky. The major laughed. "I'll tell you this, men: You have to be tough to last out in Fort Delaware. That one wasn't tough enough, so you can bury him when you get into the camp. He'll have plenty of company." He reached into his pocket and took out a length of cord, about a yard. "Now look hard at this, Rebs. If you try to escape, or if you sass the guards, you'll get to know this cord. Yes you will, I can tell you that for sure." He looked around them, letting his eyes linger on certain figures in the line. "I see that there are officers among you. Well, there ain't no officers in my camp. Of course, being officers and gentlemen, you may be exchanged. The generals might fix up a deal among themselves. But until that day comes you are just prisoners to me. Scum, Rebs, shit, muck. Call yourselves what you want. I don't care how many slaves you owned in the fine fields of Virginia." He shook a little, and his face, brown as it was from the sun, went pale. "And get this: My name is Major Hass, and every one of you, whether private or colonel, will call me 'sir,' and if you don't, I'll have you whipped. Or give you the cord." One of the federal soldiers laughed. "You see, my men like the cord. They like to watch. And get this, too: If you're sick, you die or you get well. I've no medicines to spare for you. So keep yourselves fine and healthy, boys." His voice had become jocular again. "There ain't no camp hospital. Just work and the graveyard, see? Take them in." The sergeant major waddled forward. So grotesque, Gervase thought. We came into this war for glory? Christ alive. He shouted.

"Right form!" They shuffled around, some supported, as Roscoe was, by their fellows. "March!" They began to move; it seemed an amble, a country walk, but every step was pain. They walked away from the sheds and the railroad track, hearing the hooting and the clanking grow fainter behind them. The country was again nondescript. Does a landscape only seem significant if you look at it with a full heart? thought Gervase. My mind is empty, and so is the land. Or is all the North like this, a great camp to suppress us and beat us to our knees? The weight of Roscoe became intolerable, and he slipped. They both fell. A guard was on them in no time. "Up, up, up!" he yelled, waving his bayonet near them. Gervase became conscious of the Alabama sergeant near him. "I'll take the captain, Major," he said, and lifted Roscoe. Together they pulled him onward, and once more the feet scrawled their craziness in the dirt. Everything seemed to be repetition now. "Sergeant Lyon, Major." Gervase could not speak from his cracked mouth, but he pulled his lips into a grin. With a similar gothic effect, the sergeant smiled back. His teeth were very yellow. Clearly, he chewed tobacco, thought Gervase. He'll have no tobacco now, and Gervase laughed aloud, with a croak. "That's better," said the sergeant, all unknowing.

They approached a great gate, an entrance to an enormous compound surrounded by the new sort of wire the Yankees used, with spikes sticking out at every inch and in all directions, spikes an inch long with a vicious point, against which the horses of Jeb's cavalry (How long ago? How long?) had torn their flesh with whinnies of brute pain and reared and plunged and flung their riders down to the bayonet or the bullet or the gouging point. The compound had ten rows of this wire erected continuously on great wooden poles, nailed neatly in rows eighteen inches apart. Against the wire appeared blotches of faces, the prisoners he supposed, gazing at them silently as they approached. At about every hundred yards, there was a high wooden tower with federal soldiers in it, shaded from the sun by a quaint thatch, looking down at the prisoners along the sights of their rifles.

They filed through the gates. The prisoners became clearer, worn, ragged, listless, their boots often coming out at the toes. In the center of the great compound was a neat military house, surrounded by yet more wire, with the flag of the United States, bright and clean, flying stiff and proud at the top of a flagpost.

This house was the only decent sight. Tents, hovels of crazily leaning planks, holes in the ground covered by cloth, even great-coats, afforded the prisoners the only shelter they would find at Fort Delaware.

"Halt," yelled the sergeant major. The line, having achieved its own momentum, began to slow. "Stop, stop, stop, fuck you all. Stop, you bastards!" The front rank was brought to a halt by the easy expedient of having its members knocked to the ground, so that the following rank stumbled over them, and motionlessness, like a wave, surged back over the line. The sergeant major bellowed. "This is Fort Delaware. Find yourselves a place to live. Your fellow Rebs will tell you when you can eat. Dismissed." They dismissed, the line, which had achieved some life of its own, disintegrating into tiny units, which drifted toward the impassive groups who watched them. Gervase and Roscoe and Lyon and another Alabaman called Connor walked together. They meandered between the holes and the huts until they found a patch of ground that was unoccupied. A group of prisoners watched them. None offered information; none offered assistance.

"What do we do?" asked Lyon.

"You dig," replied a Carolina voice. "You rest, and then you dig."

"With what?" said Lyon.

"If you can find a spade, then use a spade," came the reply. "If you can't, you've got hands, ain't you?" Gervase sank to his knees with exhaustion. He envied Lyon the initiative he did not have himself. Lyon walked away from them. Was he deserting them for more active companions? Gervase could hardly blame him if he did, but in no time Lyon was back, holding a plank, some remnant of a demolished house perhaps, a library or a door. Did it matter? He began to dig in the sterile earth.

"I'll take an hour," he said dryly. "You take the next, Connor. And the major can take the third. The captain's in no state to dig." And so they dug. When his turn came, Gervase laid Roscoe on the ground in the most comfortable position he could find. It was so hot that he took off his tunic and made it into a pillow, which he placed beneath Roscoe's head. There was some blood on his neck.

There was blood on Gervase's hands when he had finished his hour. After a few minutes his muscles cried out and flames consumed his fingers. His nails cracked, one after another, and a long spear of wood drove itself into the tender flesh beneath the nail of his little finger on the left hand. The ends of his fingers were too tender to touch even velvet, if he had allowed himself to think of that. But he could not.

"Why don't they help us?" he asked Lyon. The sergeant had found enough saliva to spit.

"I reckon they want to see if we'll last out," he said. "Then they'll help us. But we'll have to last the night. And I doubt the captain will." The darkness was falling and the air growing colder. Not too cold to a normal body, but to exhausted flesh it was icy. Gervase held Roscoe close to him so that they could communicate the warmth of their bodies. They had tumbled into their pit, which was about five feet wide and three feet deep. At least it protected them from the wind, which freshened at nightfall. And, at dusk, the Carolina man brought them some soup: thin, weak, a few lumps of corn and other indistinguishable vegetables floating in the fluid, but at least lukewarm and digestible to their weak stomachs. They drank it greedily, but Gervase made sure that Lyon had the first drink. He, after all, had shown his strength when they needed it. Lyon looked at him, but did not refuse the eminence thus proffered. The Carolina man had looked at their refuge.

"It ain't bad," he said. "You'll live your first night. And don't think that there's food for breakfast, because there ain't. One meal a day here. But they parade you at dawn. And watch out for the Welsh sergeant. His name is Sebbs. But you'll learn that soon enough." He squatted near them and brought his face close to Gervase. His breath smelled, but then, thought Gervase, so must mine. "This Sebbs likes to kill a Reb a week. How's the war?"

"It goes on," said an anonymous voice.

"It'll go on forever," said the Carolina man. "And my name's Ogden." Gervase wondered whether the name was supposed to confer infallibility upon the opinion. Perhaps it did. Any thought seemed possible in Fort Delaware. The war was no longer a thought that could inspire him. For the first time in months his hand hurt him. He looked at the white wound. How long ago was Manassas.

At dawn they were woken by bugles. Or rather, before dawn, when the sun was merely peeping up in the eastern sky and sound folks were abed and the new day of suffering had not begun, and not by one bugle only but by a counterpoint of bugles, one calling to another and forming a set of discords like the battle call of a horde of barbarians. The prisoners, like foxes or rabid dogs or earwigs under stones, crawled blinking from their lairs and drifted toward the smart house at the center of the fort. No one walked with purpose here; all drifted, without motive or intention or purpose or determination, the men with broken boots dragging their feet, those with greatcoats lucky enough to protect themselves from the wind. The civilians were the luckiest of all, for they had had leisure to collect clothes before the provost men came to arrest them; Mr. Lincoln did not relish northern Democrats who expressed sympathy for the southern cause, and so he gave them the opportunity to meet their southern friends in Fort Delaware and share the style of life that they claimed to admire. If they lived, and if they expressed lively repentance for their mistaken ways, then they might return to their homes in Connecticut or Rhode Island. The trouble for them was that once they were in Fort Delaware it was difficult to let Mr. Lincoln know that now their minds were right and that they saw matters as he wished them to be seen. In Fort Delaware they tended to disappear, to be swallowed in the gut of the federal military machine and ground to offal by the powerful walls of the military stomach. It was unfortunate indeed, but they were soon forgotten, and when the vineyards had to be trampled, then the grapes had to be crushed. In wartime, a touch of ruthlessness does not come amiss, as John Brown had known quite well when he rode screaming into the devilish slavers on the banks of the Pottawattamie. Yet the civilians were accorded certain privileges. They stood apart at muster, in groups, not lines. After all, they had not borne arms against Mr. Lincoln and Mr. Stanton, and so their penance might be mitigated. Gervase stood at his first muster next to Lyon and Connor and adjoining the Carolina detachment, who looked to Ogden as their leader. Ogden was a little man, with darting eyes and a cynical and rough tongue, but he

did not give way to the Yanks. They stood for thirty minutes in
the cold dawn, with federal soldiers in front of them and behind
them. Major Hass did not arise for muster, but the sergeant
major did, and the lesser sergeants who controlled each division
of prisoners. Sergeant Sebbs walked along the ranks. He paused
by Gervase. His voice was rather lilting, and Gervase felt that
suddenly he might break out into song. His eyes belied the impression of his lyrical voice.

"Why you holding that man, soldier?" It was the first time
Gervase had been called "soldier." He did not relish the experience. He did not know what to reply, since, if he did not hold
Roscoe, he would fall to the ground. So he made no reply. He
was rewarded with a stinging kick on the shins.

"I asked you a question, soldier."

"I'm holding up my friend." Sergeant Sebbs was a connoisseur
of voices.

"Oh my, a Virginia gentleman," he said. "A major." He peered
forward, as if his eyes were weak. "And the 1st Virginia Cavalry.
The regiment of General Stuart and the raider Mosby. Well, I do
declare." He kicked Gervase again and, as he doubled up,
brought his gauntleted fist into Gervase's face. "There aren't any
officers and gentlemen in this camp, Major, sir." Roscoe had
fallen to his knees. Sebbs turned toward him.

"Get up, you." Roscoe looked up, mute and suffering.

"Reply when I speak to you, Reb," he said. Gervase swallowed
the bile that made his mouth bitter.

"He has a throat wound, Sergeant," he said. Sebbs turned his
cold eyes on Gervase.

"I wasn't aware that I spoke to you," he said. He raised his left
hand, and two federal soldiers came running forward. Sebbs
smiled.

"The major don't know our ways yet," he said. "Show him the
cord." Gervase could feel the men around him rise as if to resist,
and then subside. What could they do? And, in any case, what
was the cord? As he was pulled forward, he saw Lyon lean over
and jerk Roscoe to his feet. Roscoe swayed, but he remained upright. Then a voice rang out, pompous, well-modulated even in
its anger, accustomed to the hustings.

"Sergeant Sebbs, I must protest against your submitting this man to punishment merely for assisting his friend."

"Protest away, Mr. Howe," shouted Sebbs in a high-pitched reply, "you ain't in Congress now."

"If I were in Congress," came the angry reply, then I can assure you that you would not be here. You would be in prison yourself."

"I *am* in prison, Mr. Democratic Congressman Howe. And so, by Jesus, are you.

"Now shut your mouth or I'll report you to the commandant." Howe's voice rang out confidently to Gervase.

"Endure, sir, endure. Your action does not go unnoticed, neither shall it be unrecorded."

The soldiers placed Gervase under what appeared to be a gallows. God, they're not going to hang me, thought Gervase. But the crossbeam hung over no trap. The soldiers held his arms out in front of him, and Sebbs approached drawing two lengths of cord from his pockets. He took Gervase's left hand and tied the cord around his thumb, jerking the knot tight. He did the same with the right thumb. Then the cord was flung over the crossbeam and Gervase was pulled up until he was standing on tiptoe. The weight of his body was supported by his thumbs. If he removed the tips of his toes from the ground he would break the bones in each thumb. In spite of himself, he groaned.

A mangy little dog trotted out of the main compound and came and snuffled affectionately about Gervase's foot. Then, insouciant, he lifted his back leg and urinated over Gervase's feet. Sebbs guffawed. The soldiers smiled. The prisoners remained silent, except for a faint noise, like wind in reeds on a dark day, which sidled among them. The civilian prisoners, from whose ranks the unknown Mr. Howe had spoken, looked somber.

"You'll stay there an hour, Major, sir," said Sebbs. "Then you'll learn our proper ways. You fine Virginia gentleman, only fit for a dog to piss on." He turned back to the prisoners. Only his division remained, for the sergeant major had dismissed the rest. He shouted at them, his voice infused by an anger that cut through the diminishing darkness. "Look at him. Jest look at him and learn your lesson. You can all stand here until I cut him down.

And if any man falls over I'll have his thumbs too." Lyon kept
Roscoe standing for almost an hour, though Gervase never knew
how.

What a small vocabulary for pain he possessed! Soon his lungs
began to strain for breath and his heart pounded against his
meager ribs. The thin blood raced around his veins and he could
feel insensibility flooding his head with massive steamclouds of
obliteration, yet never losing the burning in his thumbs, the aching in his wrists, the twisted grating of his shoulders in their
sockets, the foolish effort that he had to make successful to keep
his toes, peeping through the ripped leather of his boots, on the
ground. He lost awareness of time, judging it only by the thud of
his heart and the rasping indrawing of breath. Pain established
its own clock. After a few minutes he ceased to anticipate; he no
longer said, "I must endure until it is over." He said, "I must endure." For the first time in his life, he lost all hope. He entered
the black cavern of despair and called for a death that would not
come. The men watched gravely. After Malvern Hill, he knew
that he could never love again; now he knew that he could not
hope. All the great words by which he had lived—honor, glory,
belief, loyalty, devotion—exploded like a shell, annihilating
themselves, becoming a bloody thought in a red shade.

Sebbs had a sense of wry humor. He leaned against one of the
uprights and had his breakfast brought out to him. By the standards of the elegant meals at Sweetwater it was nothing, fit for the
pigs. But standards had changed since those days, and Gervase,
even beneath his pain, stirred for this mess of eggs and beans.
Sebbs shoveled the food into his mouth with a dirty fork and
kept up a chatter. There seemed, at least to him, a bond between
himself and Gervase, their two spirits glued together by pain.
"Hurts now, does it, Major? You should have answered me right
off. That's the trouble with you officers, you think a sergeant's
below you, inferior, it may be. But it ain't like that here. That's
why my father left Wales. He didn't like kneeling down to the
English. And that's why all these Irish come over the great
ocean, tossing in boats packed like sprats. They don't like the
English. I'll wager that you come from good pure English stock.
All you Virginia gentlemen do." He chewed vigorously for a minute or so, and then wiped the fork against his trousers. He was

less fastidious than Major Hass. Perhaps the latter's German stock had something to do with it? No time for speculation. Up on the tiptoe, and the big toe almost buckled but not quite. Sebbs grinned. He had a very engaging grin beneath his Celtic hair, although his teeth were twisted and the upper incisors rotten. What details to notice! "I'll wager too that you'd like to kill me. Or hang me up on that there beam. Sebbs the Death. What a name! But you won't, because you'll rot in here while your General Lee loses his armies. You should jest see the factories we have up here in the North. All them cannon jest waiting to blow you gray boys to pieces. And all the *men* we have too. You look surprised, Major, sir." Gervase had no time for surprise, no inclination either. "Oh yes, you'd like to string me up there too. And you're wondering, I'll bet, that I can talk so good. You Virginia gentlemen, yes, from the 1st Virginia Cavalry, all your black horses too, you always think it's a marvel that a northern sergeant can even *speak*. You think we're jest like your own niggers. Well, I ain't no nigger. Not that I care about niggers. That's for President Lincoln to worry about, see? You have them and whip them, he'll free them. What does that matter to me? But it matters to me, Major, sir, that you should reply when I speak to you. See?" He came up to Gervase and made as if to kick away his feet from under him. Gervase braced himself. Sebbs drew back. "Had you worried then, Major? Praying a little to God up in the skies? You believe in God? Sure you do. All gentlemen do. God belongs to Stonewall, doesn't He? I don't hold with God, cause I heard too much about him in chapel when I was a kid. My father, he believed in God. But he didn't live in no war, Major. He lived in the fine old days of peace and blessed the good God who'd brought him to America away from the wicked English who wouldn't listen to him when he spoke in Welsh. Poems in Welsh, would you believe it? Oh Major, you make me sick. Look at this here Fort Delaware. Is God about here?" Sebbs grinned again and came near to Gervase so that their eyes were about six inches apart. Then he spat in Gervase's face. The fluid hardly made any impression. Gervase did not even feel humiliation. Once again Sebbs made as if to kick his feet away. This time he did so. He yelled to the division of prisoners.

"You can cut him down! Run!" Gervase felt the thumbs gradu-

ally pulling themselves from their sockets. Red-hot sabers sliced
down his arms; he desperately struggled to regain a foothold,
and had, indeed, given up even the desire to save his hands
when he felt Lyon's arms around his waist and the weight came
from his thumbs and that caused for a moment even more pain
and he was left with a dull throbbing. Lyon held him while the
hands of the Carolina boys scrabbled at the knots that supported
the cord.

Gervase wept. He buried his face on Lyon's shoulder and
wept. The men turned away from the sight, embarrassed yet
tactful, compassionate even in their anger. Mr. Howe stood some
twenty yards away and muttered to himself. He was an impres-
sive man, rendered ludicrous by his inability to realize that he
was now not what he once had been. Lyon carried Gervase back
to the pit, where he lay beside Roscoe until the sun reached its
zenith.

"Mr. Stepton, sir, you are but half a man," said Jeremiah Howe
sententiously. "Courage indeed you have, and honor, and taste.
But you have no ties, sir, nothing upon which we may build a
permanent commonwealth. You are a monk, sir, a monk of war.
Even your General Lee has children. He does not see military
devotion as an end in itself, as you do."

They had been in Fort Delaware for two months. Fall had
come, and it was growing colder. Cold in the heart, too, since
Lee had retreated back toward Richmond, and victory had
receded like a wave on a shingle beach, dragging the pebbles
with it. Roscoe had recovered some of his strength, but not his
voice. Gervase, Lyon, Connor, and Ogden's Carolina boys had
worked out a sign language that enabled him to communicate
most of his wants. On most days he sat, haggard, lethargic, listless, his legs swinging on the edge of the pit, which they had
covered with planks and scraps of canvas filched from odd areas
of the camp. Gervase had recovered himself, at least outwardly.
Inwardly, his eyes saw nothing but the dust of an immense
desert—or rather what he imagined to be an immense desert,
since he had never seen one, an image of desolation culled from
his nursery books and tales of grizzled explorers whom his father
had entertained at Sweetwater in the dead days.

"I am no monk, sir," he replied. "I have known love." Mr.
Howe dropped his magisterial tone and patted Gervase on the
knee.

"I'm glad to hear it, boy, I'm very glad. And will you enter the
nuptial state when you leave this dump?" Gervase smiled at the
abrupt switch from the verbose to the colloquial.

"She is dead, sir."

"Tragic, tragic," muttered Mr. Howe. Gervase, primed by his
father to precision, could not forbear reply.

"No, sir, not tragic. Meaningless. Absurd. She died at the
hands of General McClellan's troops, although they had no wish
to kill her."

"What evokes pity, my boy, is tragic."

"I must disagree, sir. The tragic has an air of nobility about it.
Deborah's death was not noble."

They used this stilted form of discourse because it gave them
both reassurance. By day they were compelled to listen to the
commands and abuse of Sebbs, and the guttural observations of
Major Hass who, though he might have left his homeland, had
not abandoned its military traditions, even though he did not
display them on the field of battle and showed scant desire to do
so. Both Howe and Gervase found a solace in using a language
that predated Mr. Lincoln's America—that had dignity, even if it
had magniloquence, and grace, even though it might possess an
intrinsic falsity. Language is the last refuge of the defeated, as
Gervase had observed to Howe when Howe had expressed his
contempt for Poland—a country that only lived in its language.

"Ah, but you do not know the Poles, sir. Only a trickle—so
far."

"Perhaps the future of this country lies with them, sir. And the
Irish, the Germans, and the Welsh."

"No, not the Welsh. *That* I cannot accept." Gervase laughed.
But when once he had laughed with his father, Gervase's eyes
had laughed with his face, but now they remained cold. But
Howe waxed voluble.

"I wish you could come to Massachusetts, sir. To my own
hometown of North Adams, deep in the hills and woods. Ah, for
the smell of those woods in the fall, the glory of the leaves. I can
hardly forgive Mr. Lincoln, our revered President, for depriving

me of that sight. Gold, red, brown: a magnificent orchestra of colors. Naturally enough, they have despoiled North Adams now. It manufactures weapons and acts as a holding place for the bullion of our unworthy cause. I knew the manager of our bank when he was a small boy. And now he sits on Mr. Lincoln's gold. A waste, sir, a waste." Gervase noted the fact. Although he might no longer believe in glory, he believed in victory, a victory achieved by death. He addressed Mr. Howe.

"Pray forgive me, sir, but may I ask a question of you?" The man nodded, confident of his ability to answer anything. "How is it that you, a man of Massachusetts, could feel sympathy for our cause? The men of Massachusetts are our most bitter enemies. Thoreau, Emerson, the female author of *Uncle Tom's Cabin*. I treat her as a man, of course."

"There, sir, you strike me to the quick. I believe, sir, in property. And slaves are property. I would not see you deprived; I would not see myself surprised by the soldiers of Mr. Lincoln seizing my goods. No, sir, we must stand together for the sacred rights of property. As our Constitution declared before your Jefferson altered it. And I despise idealists," he added with fervor. "They are not gentlemen. Just as those who opposed my Tory ancestors were not gentlemen. Merely frontiersmen." Gervase could not resist his reply.

"I own no slaves, sir. My father freed them all."

"A mistake, sir, if I may make so bold. The black man is born to servitude. The measurements of his cranium show a distinct inferiority to the white races. Phrenology, sir, is a decisive science."

"I didn't see any difference in their heads," said Gervase mildly.

"Niggers is niggers," said Lyon, who had remained silent. "There ain't no white woman safe from them. Any white woman who has a nigger ain't satisfied with a white man anymore. I should know. Christ, I should," with vehemence.

"While deploring your language, Mr. Lyon" (for they eschewed ranks), "I must, perforce, agree with your sentiments." Gervase stayed silent. Such rubbish was not for him, but without Lyon he could never escape from Fort Delaware. And that he had determined. Not for glory. Not because he wished to support the Confederacy again. Not for General Jackson. Not, God save him, for General Lee. But because he wanted to kill Yankees. All with the face of Sebbs. He wanted to drive his saber into them, he wanted to slice off their heads, their arms, their legs, he wanted to make them stand on tiptoe with cords around their thumbs, he wanted to burn their houses, kill their children, rape their wives. No, he could not do that. His organ of masculinity (he could not put it to himself more crudely) would never stir again. He would not know woman, as Adam had, and as Roscoe had. Gervase's lust lingered on the delights he had been offered and had spurned. He despised himself for that, since Sebbs, with his uncanny insight, had seen this weakness. One morning at muster.

"You dipped your wick, Major, sir? I'll wager not. No southern belle opened her legs to you, Major? I suppose you spend your time with niggers. Now, that I wouldn't do. Would you, Sergeant Lyon?" Before he had the answer he knew he would receive he cut in (because, yes, he was afraid of Lyon), "I'll bet you wouldn't. You're no *gentleman* like the major here." And then Sebbs walked away, because he did not wish to hear Lyon reply, since he knew that Lyon would not defer to him, and then he would have to punish Lyon, and, somehow, he was afraid of Lyon too much to punish him, and then he would lose face with his own soldiers, and Sebbs was a prudent man but a vainglorious leader who did not wish to lose face. He preferred to taunt Gervase, because he knew that Gervase had too much innate delicacy to reply to him in his own coin. Yes, and too much sensitivity to let the lash of words slide away from his nerves. Lyon would hit back, but Lyon would not really care. And Sebbs was wary of Connor, too, because the canny wit of Connor somehow left Sebbs baffled. And, perhaps because of some leftover scruple from those Celtic delicacies left in the mountains of Wales, he left Roscoe alone too. Certainly it wasn't his wound. But perhaps it was Roscoe's dumbness. Sebbs loved to draw close to a man he was tormenting and look into his eyes. He could read eyes like a book. So he could have seen Roscoe's pain if he had wanted to, but it would have been only his pleasure. Sebbs was an actor; he

liked a wide audience, and so Gervase, who flinched and responded and played an involuntary farce for the gallery, was his
favorite target, butt, clown. His mind churned with insults.

"Was your Daddy one for the niggers, Major Stepton, sir? Perhaps you have some nigger blood in your veins yourself? Touch
of the tarbrush, as they used to say back in the old country. Heh,
heh? Answer me, damn you." Or "How many little nigger Step-
tons are there running about them there hills in Virginia, Major
Stepton, sir? Look at him, boys, he's clenching his hands. He'd
like to hit me. Hit me, Major, sir, and I'll have you shot." Then
he looked meditative. "No, I'll not have you shot. I'll give you
the cord again and pull your thumbs from their sockets." Or:
"The major won't tell us about his nigger sidekicks. The major
don't like women now, the major likes men. Do you feel safe,
boys? I wouldn't feel safe with Major Stepton around my
ring. But perhaps you southern gentlemen"—he spat—"don't
care about that there form of activity, as you might put it." Gervase was continually astonished by the real rotundity of Sebbs'
rhetoric. The man was no illiterate. Indeed, in order to make
himself more democratically acceptable he endeavored to make
his voice more coarse and his vocabulary more thin than it actually was. He seemed drawn to Gervase with an unnatural intensity. "Yes, boys, the major ain't natural, I'm thinking." And then
he would put out his hand and touch Gervase on the face. Once
he removed the glove and ran his finger nail down the stubble on
the face and chin. His eyes glowed. He spoke softly. "The major
and I understand each other, don't we, Major?" He moved close
and Gervase smelled his breath, suggestive of rank potatoes; the
lips came much closer. "Oh yes, the major and I understand each
other very well indeed." And the other men would look at the
ground, and scuff their feet into the dirt, and cock their ears to
hear the cold wind yelling through the wires or the rain water
seeping down the wooden walls of the half-derelict huts. They
never mentioned Sebbs' insinuations—none, that is, save Mr.
Howe.

"The fellow is a scoundrel, sir," the congressman expostulated.
"A veritable scoundrel. He impugns your moral character, sir. He
impugns your manhood."

"Yes," replied Gervase. Curiously, these sexual innuendoes did not affect him so much as the jibes about his courage, his origins, his class. He knew that the men would pay little attention to them; he knew that they did not even pick up Sebbs' dirtier handfuls of muck. Then came the day, the day when they could no longer doubt.

It was late October. The sleet seemed to have that day a peculiar venom, cutting into their faces, slicing across their eyes. The men, numbed, wandered around the camp area, beating their arms about their bodies. Gervase wandered toward the wire, accompanied by Roscoe. Roscoe rarely left him now. And although Roscoe could perform the more simple tasks of humanity—he could lie down and sleep, he could urinate and defecate —he could do little else. Gervase had to dress him; to give him his soup with a crude wooden spoon, which he had carved with the edge of a billy can; Gervase had to escort him to the roll call and hold him when he looked as if he might fall, for Major Hass had none of the scruples Sebbs felt about the dumb. Major Hass did not care about an audience; Major Hass cared about his duty, interpreted with a cold Silesian precision. If a man fell once, he was whipped; if he fell twice, he got the cord; if he fell thrice, he was put in the solitary box. And, after September, men moved straight from the solitary box to the graveyard, which bade fair to become the largest area in the camp. Occasionally, Major Hass felt some need to justify his actions. He would put on an unctuous expression at roll call, and, after recounting the latest northern victories, would add, "you men may think you are being badly treated in this camp. I tell you that it may be so." Usually they were too tired even to smile at this little joke. "But our own soldiers are receiving even worse treatment at the hands of your fellow Rebels. In your prison named Andersonville our brave soldiers die like the flies. Yes," he repeated with anger as he saw their indifference, "like the flies. And so," he boomed in what seemed genuine fury, "it is my duty to pay you back in your own coin. Our soldiers are fighting for their country. You are Rebels. Rebels can either suffer or die." He seemed to relish his fine periods, but this won no approbations from Mr. Howe.

"That German is no orator, sir," he said to Gervase. "No orator at all. I'll wager he has never read a word of Tully." Gervase remembered that his father called Cicero "Tully" and he turned

his eyes, misty with the image of memory, toward the gray sky.
Howe, as always, saw the point. "But I see that I have distressed
you, sir. Pray forgive me. Some memory of your early years,
doubtless. Pray forgive me, I ask it of you."

"Don't worry, sir," muttered Gervase. He found that he was
losing all his own grace of speech. He could not even match
Major Hass now.

The day. He stood with Roscoe near the wire, and he was
taken with the enormous sadness of things. Roscoe gurgled in
sympathy. Gervase became impatient with the sound; he wanted
to quiet Roscoe, to shut him up, comfort him maybe, but just
keep him quiet. He wanted to retire into the depths of his own
consciousness where he was no longer aware of the cold, of
Sebbs, of his throbbing hand, of the effects of dysentery, of his
own smell, of the animals that crawled in his crotch, under his
arms, in his hair; he wanted to reach that oasis of aloneness
within himself that he could still attain with great mental effort.
He touched Roscoe's hand, gently, persuasively. Roscoe fell silent, but, at the same time, there came a laugh from behind
them. "Well, ain't that a lovely sight. Do your know your Bible,
Major Stepton, sir? Of course you do, for I'll bet that you was
brought up on the Scriptures like every good Virginia boy.
Learned them at your mother's knee. When she wasn't looking
around for some buck nigger. I learned them real good in Sunday school. Christ, they gave you a beating if you didn't. Some
bearded Welsh bastard beating love into a rabble of kids with a
cane. And David mourned for Jonathan. Yes, he sure did, because they had a love passing the love of women. Ain't that so,
Major Stepton?"

"Yes," said Gervase in a low voice. He was so accustomed to
saying "yes" that he never gave a thought to any alternative. He
merely agreed with Sebbs and hoped that the man would move
off to the other duties he assumed that he had to perform at
some time or other. "Yes," he repeated. "I've noticed that you
seem to have a very special relationship with Captain Stedman
here. Perhaps it's your natural pity for the wounded. That I
doubt," Sebbs snapped derisively. Gervase raised his blue eyes
and looked around. Suddenly he realized that Sebbs had made a
tactical mistake. He was wont to torment Gervase *in coram*

publico, as Mr. Howe put it, in full view of others—in the middle of the walking area, in the pits, at roll call. But seizing the
sight of Roscoe and Gervase together, he had not been able to
resist a little game with just the three of them, at the back of a
derelict hut, by the boundary wire, but in a position where the
crazy leaning walls of the old hut shut them from the view of
soldiers on the high towers. Gervase knew the penalty for hitting
a guard, for attacking the sacred blue of the federal uniform. He
knew, but he no longer cared. He no longer cared about anything. Certainly not himself. His body had endured too much
physical and spiritual damage for him to feel any scruple toward
himself, his fellows, or God. They were all apart from him, his
own self most of all. He looked up at Sebbs, his eyes clouded
with cunning. "And what relationship do you have with me, Sergeant?" he asked softly. Sebbs looked surprised, as well he
might. He thought that he had broken Gervase. He had broken
many men before, but he had taken particular pleasure in breaking this one. He was not a man given to introspection, or to scrutiny of his own motives. Why did he like to destroy men, particularly those whom he knew to be his superiors? It was, he told
himself, just the proper task of warfare. Some fought at the
front; he fought for equality in Fort Delaware prison camp. For
Sebbs had a profoundly democratic soul. He hated superiority.
He hated those thousand natural decencies that some men possessed and that made them better than he. So he set out to destroy such men and reduce them to his own level. He was an
anarchist of the moral cosmos. Such terms were foreign to his
brain; he was good with his lips but not with his mind. And
there was a deeper reason, which he relished with his hand
under the blankets in the warmth of the night. He enjoyed
breaking men. He enjoyed seeing them whimper, lower their
eyes, draw back from his hand and his tongue. Sebbs, strange to
say, was a virgin; he obtained all the satisfactions he needed
from his work. He was lucky to have been born at the right time.
But that Gervase should turn on him like this! He had to show
how cool he was. He took an apple out of his pocket. "Well,
Major Stepton, I don't rightly know that I have any relationship,
if you want to use such a shitty word, with you. You're just a
prisoner, just scum, that's all, scum. Dung. Muck. Fucked out

from old Virginia, you might say. Sow's piss mixed with bull's
cock. That's your mother and father, Major. All from them fair
fields of Virginia. I like to see your back. Show you that you're a
coward, just like General Maude did to Lee. I like to show you
what you really are, soldier boy."

Gervase began to lower his head in the despair that had become habitual, the sickness unto death he now knew so well.
Then something went in his head. It was not a snapping or an
explosion or a conscious suspension of prudence; just the disap-
pearance of all conscious thought. Perhaps he had taken in the
fact that they could not be seen; afterward he tried to remember,
but he could not. While Sebbs was watching the effect of his
speech with his rat's eyes, Gervase hurled himself upon the
Welshman. The move was so unexpected that Sebbs was taken
aback—in more senses than one. He had not expected a physical
response; he had expected submission. He stepped backward
and reached down to his revolver. But his heel slipped and his
head struck the wall of the old hut. He could not retreat the necessary distance to avoid Gervase. And, by some mischance, his
revolver stuck in the holster, even though he had opened the flap
(which he never kept buckled). He had seen Gervase's eyes as
he came at him, seen them for a split second of terror, and realized that no appeal to prudence or pity or fear could possibly
work. He would have to fight. And he had little doubt that he
could smash an undernourished southern gentleman. As Gervase
flew toward his face he was aware of Roscoe's gurgling, and the
sight of Roscoe running away flashed from left to right of his vision.

Gervase's teeth caught his hand on the revolver and they
buried themselves into the flesh, a rabid dog hungry to break the
skin and inject its poison. Sebbs tried to shout, but Gervase had
pulled him down onto the muddy ground and they shuddered
together in silence, a silence broken only by the animal pants
and yelps. Sebbs was wearing strong boots and he managed to
kick Gervase hard on the shins. Sebbs felt the skin slide off under
the steel-tipped leather. Gervase let out no sound. Sebbs felt the
blood flowing from his hand, and he took a quick glance downward. He hand was covered with blood. That was strange, for he

felt little pain. But when he tried to move the fingers, to clench the fist, he realized that his muscles would not respond to the impulses of his brain. He brought his left arm around and punched Gervase in the kidneys: once, twice, three times. But he felt Gervase's hot breath near his face. Sebbs was lying on his back, and he knew that this was a disadvantage; he felt Gervase smash his fists on his nose, and the blood began to stream out of his nostrils. It also flowed backward, into his throat. He began to choke, and the fluid of panic flowed over him like waves of scalding water.

Gervase brought his knee up into Sebbs' groin, and the sergeant screamed but he could not be heard, for Gervase covered his face with his coat and the high-pitched screech was lost in musty cloth. He began to kick upward, but struck only the empty air. Gervase was sitting on his torso now, and he had one hand over Sebbs' face and the other around his throat. Sebbs realized with astonishment that he could feel the stump of Gervase's amputated finger on the left hand. The blood began to sing no happy song around his brain. He began to hear the pounding of his heart. He felt a strange inertia flooding his muscles. He began to dream back to the Welsh hills, to the boat tossing like a toy on the Atlantic swell, to the tall tenements of New York, to the words of Scripture that hammered in the voice of a Wesleyan minister into his inner ear, and all the clouds of uncertainty and fear of extinction and bitterness that he had made his mark on nothing, before he plunged into a rubber foam of blue density that wrapped him closer and something lighter and airy tugged away from the constrictions of his body. Gervase, realizing he was dead, strangled, inert, harmless, a doll, and began to gouge out his eyes with his thumbs. The splodgy lumps proved recalcitrant in their clinging sockets.

Consciousness came running back into his mind. This man killed his father, this man killed his mother, this man killed Deborah, burned Sweetwater; this was the Yankee soul, and he would deface it until all men could see the obscene parody of humanity that it was. He dug in his thumbs. Suddenly he felt a large hand at his collar and he was hauled away from the body. He knelt on the wet ground and wept; not a gentle weeping, but a mixture of panting and groaning with the heat of his tears warming his rough cheeks. He looked up, and saw, through a blur, the craggy features of Lyon looking down at him.

"Well, Major," said Lyon, "now you *have* done it." And awareness, the ability to calculate and make decisions, returned to Gervase. He glanced down indifferently at the body of Sebbs, which was all incongruous. How could he have been afraid of this thing?

"He had it coming," he replied to Lyon. Lyon grinned, slowly and with restraint.

"He sure did. But what's to be done now?" Gervase realized that Roscoe had brought Lyon. And, not content with Lyon, he had brought Connor, some of the Carolina boys, and Mr. Howe. They all stared at the scene in silence, a menacing tableau. Gervase began to feel impatient with them all, an impatience bred of the realization that he was dead unless something could be fudged up. And suddenly he did not wish to die. He wanted to live, to have a purpose again, now that this ludicrous old man of the sea had been pitched off his back into the inhospitable waves. "What's to be done?" He laughed. "We have to get out. Unless you want to see me at the end of a rope. And you don't, do you?" They made no sound, nor did they make a motion of their heads. Old Howe (was he so old? Just older than I am, thought Gervase. Can anyone be older than I am?) stuttered a reply.

"Nobody can get out of here, Major Stepton."

"Nobody has yet, Congressman," said Gervase.

The federal soldier came upon them so suddenly they all were taken off their guard, except Lyon. He was carrying a carbine, but the sight of a sergeant lying dead momentarily disconcerted him. He began to raise his weapon, but by then it was too late. Lyon had broken his neck with a single blow, and they dragged his body to lie by Sebbs'. A pretty pair. Even Howe could smile now.

"We seem to be assembling a trophy of the slaughtered, Major Stepton. I suppose," he added, "that this makes us all accomplices. If you hang, we all hang."

"That's it," said Gervase, with the lighthearted note of hysteria in his voice. "If I hang, you all hang. So we must get out." The second incident had taken place so quickly that they were all somewhat stunned by it. It lacked the high drama of the fight with Sebbs. It seemed a mere triviality, although, in effect, it was more serious, since it involved them all. Howe fondled his large jowls and shot his shrewd eyes from one to another of his unwonted southern comrades in arms. (Yes, for now Howe has seen battle, thought Gervase; at last he's been in the firing line, and his words can have some bite—if he ever utters any more except at his trial, he added as an afterthought.) There was silence, save for the wind and their deep breathing. Gervase suddenly realized that it hurt to breathe. He staggered over to the edge of the hut and pulled open his trousers. He urinated blood. Though he had not noticed it, Sebbs had hit his kidneys very hard indeed. But then, did it matter? If he was to hang, then broken kidneys weren't of any consequence.

"Listen to me, boys," said Howe, with forced avuncularity. "I think we can get out. But it won't be easy, it won't be easy, I tell you. But nothing venture, nothing win, as they say. Gather around me . . ." And gather around him they did. The sleet had stopped, and the sun, weak and yellow, peeped around the clouds, though it hardly shone merrily, as it had done in high summer, when they had arrived at Fort Delaware. Mr. Howe outlined his plan to them. There was a chorus of disagreement.

"We'll never fool the guards!"

"You need a written pass!"

"We have the wrong voices!"

"What about him? They'd never let him out!" pointing to Roscoe.

"Your points, gentlemen, are all valid," remarked Howe mildly. "But I would merely point out to you that this plan has a chance of success—if we move immediately. If we stay here, we face inevitable death. It's a chance against a certainty, and that's a bet I'm prepared to take. And I may add," he remarked with a deeper and gloomier resonance to his voice, "that if you don't try this, I'll go for the wall myself. I'd rather be shot by one of Mr. Lincoln's soldiers than hang on a rope for the staring crowds to gape at. Wouldn't you?"

"Yes," said Connor in his light Carolina voice, "I guess I would."

"As for voices," added Howe, "I suggest that Major Stepton, if he has recovered himself, should be in command of our little party, for he is an educated man, a man of quick wits, who can simulate enough to trick a Yankee guard or two. And I would further suggest that Connor takes the other uniform. He, too, is not without a subtle ability to think faster than our friends who wear Mr. Lincoln's uniform."

"I'll take your word for it, Congressman," grinned Connor.

"But it will need speed," said Howe rapidly, "speed, I say. We must be out of here before they find these bodies."

Like toys wound up and released from the restraining hand, they sprang to work. Sebbs and his fellow guard were stripped, and Gervase put on Sebbs' uniform. Connor put on the other's. In normal times both would have found the clothes a tight fit, but not now, with their bodies emaciated, thin, cold, shrinking, undernourished. Gervase felt, for the first time in many months, a rising of the spleen, a gaiety, a zest for life. He pulled the Yankee belt tight and adjusted the revolver over his left thigh. Once more they gathered as a group, looking at each other with a certain degree of wonder and suspicion. Sebbs was naked (they had all agreed on that!), and the other soldier was dressed, albeit somewhat haphazardly, in the clothes Mr. Howe, who was now himself wearing a motley of borrowed gear. "We had better leave the bodies in the hut," said Howe. "That may delay discovery for an hour or so."

"Oh yes," said Gervase. He noticed that the soldier who had so suddenly and so fatally come upon them was wearing a bayonet. He smiled at his companions. "Lyon, put that Yankee in the hut. I'll take Sebbs." Lyon dragged in the young boy whose eyes pleaded foolishly with the empty heaven, surprised at the nothingness he had met in the final moment. Gervase pulled in Sebbs' body. In the dark of the hut they were together. Not all the warmth had seeped from Sebbs yet. It was almost as if there were some life in the man yet. As Lyon turned to leave his burden, Gervase said: "Send in Connor." Lyon looked surprised, but nodded. Connor came into the dark. It was darkness visible. Gervase had remembered that the young soldier had carried a bayonet in a long scabbard. As Connor came in, Gervase leaned forward and pulled the bayonet from its sheath. It emerged with an oily slick. A little flicking sound, ha, ha! Gervase took it in his right hand and grasped Sebbs by the hair, pulling his head upright. He leaned forward and whispered in the cold Welsh ear. "For everything, bastard." Then, with a single blow, which took some strength, he cut off Sebbs' head and placed it on the naked chest, plumb between the nipples. From the severed veins and arteries the blood oozed very slowly, purple in the gloaming. Gervase laughed and laughed and laughed. Lyon came into the hut and shook him. "Get hold of yourself, Major," he said. "Get hold of yourself." He looked down at the severed trunk with distaste. This was not how the South made war. But then, Gervase was not himself. Lyon had sympathy, even if he did not have complete understanding. He put his hand on Gervase's shoulder and led him into the brighter light. Gervase looked at his motley squad. He entered into his role with a joyous accuracy. "Connor, take hold of that rifle properly! No, like the Yankees, man. You've seen them hold the bloody thing. You're in a Yankee regiment, not in a Carolina group now. They care about drill, not about how you use it." He assembled them with care. "Connor, take station at the side. Mr. Howe, take the front, please. Then you, Roscoe. And then Lyon. I'll cover the rear." He drew the revolver—some unknown make—from its holster. "Now move forward toward the gate." They tramped forward, out of that little hidden arena where destiny had decreed that their lives should change: whether for better or worse, who could tell? They covered the long area of exercise, passing the pits scraped in the ground, going by the ramshackle hospital shed, marching with straight back by the central administrative center, all the time moving toward the gates where ten Yankee soldiers lounged on their weapons with the ease of security. As they approached, a sergeant major moved ponderously forward. He stood directly in their path.

"And where in the hell do you think you're going?" he asked.

Gervase knew that Yankee sergeant majors liked to be called by their ranks. He put a snap into his voice.

"Working party, Sergeant Major. Down to the docks." The sergeant major walked around them, his face skeptical. He stopped by Howe.

"This man's a civilian, ain't he? They don't go on working parties. And where's your written authority from the major?" Gervase thought quickly.

"This ain't no civilian, Sergeant Major. It's a soldier. A traitor soldier, what's more. A civilian died and they gave him the bastard's clothes. The major said you'd know about us. Loading a frigate with medical supplies for General"—he paused briefly—"Sheridan. There's a ship at the docks. Must get away by nightfall."

"Your voice ain't right," said the sergeant major. "It sounds like a Reb." "Oh, don't come that," said Gervase. "Please, please, Sergeant Major. I'm from Maryland, and everyone thinks I'm a Reb. It's enough to make me join General Lee, the way you all mistake me." The sergeant major was clearly unsatisfied. He walked around the group several times. Luckily, however, he had not summoned aid from his command. He looked at Connor. "Speak, you," he said. "Say something." Connor stood like a landed fish, his mouth open. Gervase put in quickly. "He ain't too clear in the head, sir. That's why he was put on the prison duty." Then he realized that this was hardly tactful. The sergeant major hardly spared him a glance. He kept his eyes on Connor. "Say something, soldier," he snapped.

Connor did his best. He tried to imitate a Connecticut accent, but it was hardly successful. "Yes, sir," he shouted, at least preserving a becoming brevity.

"Another Reb accent," said the guard commander. "This is too much for me." He was looking up to his soldiers, about to shout out a command. Gervase moved close to him.

"You a family man, Sergeant Major?" he asked softly. The noncommissioned officer appeared surprised. Involuntarily, he replied, "Why, yes." It was a fine Ohio accent. "You got kids?" "Three daughters." "You want a son?" "You bet." Gervase wondered whether the threat was necessary in the face of this amiable exchange. He decided to play safe. He put his hand down to his revolver and murmured words of comfort and good cheer to the gate commander.

"Unless you let us out, now, I'll shoot your crotch to ribbons."

"Understood." The sergeant major went pale. He was no hero. He was, in fact, a man with a weak heart, who had been detailed to these duties because he could not face the rigors of the front line. In fact, to tell the truth, he looked as if he were about to have a heart attack. He was certainly not a man to play the heroic role. His face went putty gray, yes, gray or almost white, thought Gervase. "Get them to open the gate. And when they do, you come with us. You have my word that you'll be returned safe." The sergeant major nodded. He turned and bellowed to his men. At least it was meant as a bellow, but it came out as a croak. The wind obscured this subtle tonal difference. "Get the gate open for this working party. And I'm seeing them to the docks." The Yankee soldier slouched over to the gate and pulled it open. They marched out, the sergeant major accompanying them. "Tell them to shut the gate," said Gervase. "Shut the gate, you idle bastards!" the sergeant major shouted. The gate shut.

And so they marched out of Fort Delaware. All of them restrained the desire to cheer. They marched toward the Delaware River, preserving the proper decorum of the military order. The sergeant major, an elderly man of about fifty, deflated now, marched by their side. The landscape was still littered with boxes, piles of ammunition, silent locomotives, moving locomotives, and, in the relative distance, the masts and funnels of ships. They passed into the dark shadow of a warehouse. Gervase turned to the sergeant major and looked at him with a smile.

"Why are you at Fort Delaware, friend?" he asked.

"I've got a weak heart, man," said the noncommissioned officer. "It's what they call a murmur. They wouldn't let me go to the front lines. I wanted to do so. Christ, I did. I didn't want to be in no prison." "Let me cure your heart for you," said Gervase who smelled burning cloth and flesh almost at the moment he heard the crash of the discharge. The sergeant major remained standing for a curiously long time. Then he toppled over into the mud, his hand twitching toward a railway sleeper that was lying, for no apparent reason, on the ground. Howe looked around at him.

"Again, Major, that wasn't *necessary*." Gervase felt the anger bubble within him like a solution in a chemical retort. His father had used retorts—"alembics," he had quaintly called them—when Gervase was a boy.

"Shut your mouth, you blasted Yankee," he said, softly, sibilantly. "I'm getting you out of here."

"But Mr. Howe gave us the plan, Major," said Lyon. "Don't forget that. It seems you're getting a little trigger-happy, sir."

"Perhaps I am," said Gervase, "perhaps I am, Lyon. So keep your mouth shut."

Lyon looked at him but said nothing. They abandoned formation, for the clouds had returned, and visibility was low, and they walked almost abreast, although Gervase kept his revolver in his hand lest they were accosted. The masts and funnels grew taller as they neared the estuary of the river.

"Well, Mr. Howe," asked Gervase gaily, "what ship?" Mr. Howe looked thoughtful.

"If we can find one," he replied, "a Canadian vessel. That will take us North. Into neutral territory. And the Canadians, like the British, have mixed sympathies. They're priggish Scots, but they don't relish Mr. Lincoln."

"Who does?" said Gervase.

"Far too many for our comfort," replied Howe grimly. "He has the gift of the tongues, sir. That's not a gift to be despised in these days. He'll bind these states together with his silver tongue. I'll wager there'll be statues to him all over these *United* states one day."

"That implies our defeat," cried Gervase. "Will we be defeated? Tell me that, sir."

"Wasn't it inevitable from the start, Major Stepton?" said Howe ironically. "Glamorous and futile. That's the South." At which they fell silent. The funnels and masts came nearer and nearer. They reached the docks and marched along them, taking up, once again, the military formation. They passed four ships. The fifth read *"Thor: Montreal"* on its stern.

"This will do," said Mr. Howe. "And now, Major Stepton, perhaps you'll leave the negotiations to me. And all of you—pray that the camp isn't roused before this vessel sails. Happily, it looks full enough. Packed to the brim, one might say." He smiled at his companions. "I don't think you'll be much taken with Canada, gentlemen." He turned to the gangplank.

The soldiers, simulated and genuine, set down on piles of timber, while the sun declined in the livid sky. After about half an hour Mr. Howe came down the gangplank and motioned them toward him. He smiled with that touch of the pompous they had learned both to respect and love. He was also satisfied with himself, a mark of the true politician.

"He'll take us," he said, his voice plummy with resonant pride. "Luckily, he's Scottish—and remember, Scottish, not Scotch. But he'll take us. And he sails within the hour."

"Should we pray, Major?" asked Lyon. He had no irony in his voice. None at all.

"You can—if you want to," said Gervase. And they all turned up the rickety gangplank, the camp behind them, freedom before Sebbs a decapitated corpse, two dead bodies added extraneously, Mr. Lincoln's prison camp behind them, the open sea ahead, abstention from the war if they wished it, only a nightmare left, which they might suppress if it lay within their power to do so, but it did not, for Fort Delaware would lie within them even in the coming days of peace, a horror not to be controlled, the nightmare that would ride them through eternity, a foretaste of hell. Gervase pushed his revolver into its holster with a sigh of what might perhaps be taken to be relief, but which was truly only a suspension of action. For what the Yankees had done required much payment, far more than they had given, far more than the dead Sebbs, far more than the dead sergeant major (with three daughters and a murmur in his heart) from Ohio, far more than all the blood he could drink and draw. For although Mr. Howe had forgotten about his hometown of North Adams, Gervase had not forgotten. He had nothing to live for anymore; he had everything to die for, so long as he took plenty of Yankees with him. He was now devoted unto death. The sea washed and whimpered under his broken boots.

9

In the Land of the Allies

The *Thor* had carried them safely to Montreal. Except for a few days when they had tied up in New York, they had been free of the decks, pushed aside by sailors, and the butts of the captain's jests. But Captain MacWhit was a jolly soul, and his jests had no malice; they were, at least, easier to take than those of the defunct Sebbs. Lyon and Connor enjoyed the sea, as did the three Carolina boys. Mr. Howe grumbled but was unaffected. Gervase was seasick most of the time. He leaned over the heaving side of the vessel and flung the pea soup from his mouth. If he was not sick, he felt worse. He would eat, and sense poison settling about his stomach. He would go up on deck and stick his right forefinger down his throat, until, with little spasms, the stomach began to contract, and the gouts of warm soup, mixed with bile, trickled and then hurtled into the salty air toward the mirrored sea. Gervase became a connoisseur of vomiting. It pleased the captain to lean against the rail and comment. "How you boys in gray won any battles beats me, if yer throwing up all the bloody time." Then his better nature overcame him. "You're sure yer not ill, Captain?"

"Major," gasped Gervase.

"Sorry, son," the captain grinned. "I can't get hold of these Army ranks. And it don't seem right that you should have a higher rank than me."

Once, when he was feeling less queasy than usual, Gervase asked the captain why he had taken them with him.

"I can't stand damned Yankees," was the reply. "And I don't like this here blockade. Why, four years ago I could take my ship to New Orleans and all over the bloody ocean, but now the blasted Yanks come and push their guns out at me if I show my bow anywhere near the Virginia shore. Why you can't settle the affair without a war beats me. We did."

"You're still British," smiled Gervase.

"Not us, son," said the captain. "Not us." But it was quite clear that the captain did not think of himself as "Canadian" either; he was pure-bred Scottish. Eager to seek kinsmen, he had questioned them all as to their ancestry. Luckily, one of the Carolina boys was of Scottish stock and had a Scottish Christian name, Angus. The captain rejoiced and chose him as his drinking companion. Angus made no objection, although he did not like scotch whiskey as much as his Carolina mash.

"What I cannot comprehend," said Mr. Howe, "is why this man took us without fare. This vessel is hardly designed for passengers." And indeed it was not; they bedded down near the galley, though not with the crew.

"Ask him," said Gervase.

"I hardly think one questions charity," replied Howe in his most pompous manner. Gervase had no such scruples.

"It ain't no charity," smiled MacWhit. "When we get to Montreal there'll be some Rebs there willing to pay me for what I done. At least, Reb sympathizers. Exiled Copperheads or whatnot. Don't think I took you for no charity, son. If there wasn't some money in it for me, the Feds could have had you back at Delaware. But it pleases me somewhat to take their money for the cargo, and then the Rebs' money for your carcasses."

"Captain MacWhit, you are not a gentleman."

"I'm not indeed. Don't really know the meaning of the word."

That, as Gervase was to learn, was an adequate comment upon the Dominion of Canada, misty lump of ice in Queen Victoria's crown.

They crept down the St. Lawrence River. The fog swirled about them, and members of the crew were stationed at the bow, and to port and starboard. Their task was to announce the coming and going of icebergs. These came and went frequently, silent and ghostly, sometimes old and cracking, at other times gleaming with a peculiar emerald sheen. The sea was no longer clear, but flecked with lumps of ice and broken by small, gray-white waves, which smashed against the solid little lumps of cold. Captain MacWhit stayed by the wheel, and he was not very talkative. Nor were the crew. Gervase saw that they were like men before a battle. Even when they had no specific task they fondled coils of rope and chattered softly among themselves. Birds flapped out of the mist but rarely settled on the rigging. Occasionally, vast black mountains loomed up to the sides of the river, dark, anonymous, transient. Gervase stood on the deck with Howe. They were silent and heard the water slapping against the sides, with the tiny crunch, crunch of bits of ice.

"What a godforsaken country."

"My dear boy, you would hardly credit the fact that some of our politicians—from the Republican Party, I may say—wish us to take arms and conquer the land. When we have finished with our present troubles, of course."

"They can keep it," said Gervase.

"That's how I feel myself. Exactly so, sir."

They did not pause at Quebec, but the American party stood gazing at the squalid little castle, and the rather unimpressive cliffs scaled by General Wolfe in his attempt—successful, as it turned out—to keep Canada British and not French. Gervase remarked to Mr. Howe how many men had been engaged. The elder man whistled.

"You don't say. Well, warfare has certainly advanced since those days."

Gervase thought of the shattered walls of Sweetwater and agreed.

Roscoe was sitting upon a coil of tarry rope, playing with his fingers. Nowadays he rarely gurgled; his eyes were fixed upon vacancy, perhaps upon some inward vision, certainly not upon the things of this world. Gervase went over to him and put his hand on the thin shoulder and pointed up the green hill—green at least through the patches of early snow. "Quebec," he said. Roscoe raised his eyes and gurgled. His fists clenched. God knows why, thought Roscoe. The Canadians ain't Yankees.

When the ship docked at Montreal, Captain MacWhit's expectations were fulfilled. There was a portly figure standing on the quay (another Mr. Howe, perhaps; certainly a comrade in words, for the two fell to discussion right away) who came on board and entered into a further conference, this time with the captain. Money changed hands. The captain smiled, and he came to see off his little party of human contraband. "Good luck, boys," he said, the Scots accent intensified. "You'll be getting back to the war, I expect. No more heaving the guts up over the side, Major? You weren't made to be a sailor. Well, good-bye to you." And, solemnly, as if in a religious ceremony, he shook each man by the hand. Roscoe stared past him. "It was a damned good job you fell in with me. There's many a captain that wouldn't have looked twice at a dirty bunch of escaping Rebs. Many a man would have turned you back to the Feds to swing at the end of a rope." Gervase cut him short with abrupt thanks. He found the mixture of self-congratulation, mercenary achievement, and mock-piety somewhat distasteful. The portly man ushered them down the rickety gangplank and they stood, self-conscious, on the scurrying dockyard. The portly man spoke briefly, laconically, with a pronounced Georgia accent.

"You'd best be on the move, boys. Yes, yes, I know you'd like a rest and some food. Yes, food you shall have; I know you have short commons aboard ship. But then you must move South. To Toronto. It means another journey by boat, but we must have you South before this lake freezes over. You'll be of little use to the cause in this city of discontented frogs. Unless any of you are Louisiana men? No? I thought not. South it is. I shall take you to the coaching station and you'll ride to the head of Lake Ontario. When you arrive in Toronto you must meet one Henry Harris, who will supply you with all that is needful and give you some instructions. I could do that myself, but, yes, it will come better from Henry Harris. Oh, by the by, any of you of Irish stock? Come on, out with it." He spoke with a curious peremptory tone. One of the Carolina boys grinned sheepishly.

"Name?"

"Carey."

"Then keep quiet about it. If you're asked, say you're from Ulster—or your parents were. From the great"—he drew out the epithet—"city of Belfast. They don't like the Irish here in Canada. They are mostly Scots themselves. Orange lodges every-

where." Gervase wondered what an Orange lodge was, and involuntarily looked around for some orange buildings. The portly
man caught him at it and snapped, "No, no, it's a society. Almost
secret, yes. Anti-Catholic. They don't like Catholics either, so
keep quiet about that too, if any of you owe your allegiance to
the Scarlet Woman." Clearly, the portly man had been chosen
with some care for the Canadian work. He worked to a perora-
tion. "When you reach Toronto, wait for Harris to find you.
Here's some money to keep you in victuals. No drinking, mind
you, no whoring about the town." He looked at Gervase.

"As senior officer, sir, I shall hold you responsible for your
men."

Gervase looked the portly man over, from his balding, sandy
head to his shabby shoes.

"Sir," he said, "we are deeply grateful to you. But pray do not
prescribe my duties to me." The portly man looked flustered.

"No, sir, why, of course not, sir, I should not think of doing so,
sir."

"You have done," returned Gervase.

And so began another tedious journey. Gervase wondered if
there had ever been a time when he had not been on the move.
Shuttled from ship to coach, stuffed in the sweaty darkness of
the musty interior, swaying from side to side, bumping over the
rocky roads between the interminable pine trees and the squalid
little log cabins like those the black servants used in Virginia,
with the sleet a constant and unwelcome companion, chilling,
crawling into the bones and the raw lungs, coughing, sneezing
with cold and dust, wiping away the mucus that they could not
control, and the coach pausing while they scrambled out through
thorn-filled thickets to urinate, and a dull, dour people who
stared at them with offensive lack of interest. Then on to a small
sloop, which looked elegant, but combined with its elegance intense discomfort, pushed into a minuscule cabin with Howe and
Roscoe, when one could lie down, and barely sit down, and
Howe had dysentery and farted and cursed the while, and
Roscoe played with his hands. Gervase had somehow thought
that a lake would be less rough than the sea, but he was wrong
in that, and he started to feel sick again and tried to get up on
the deck with the sloop pitching and feeling for the companion-

way in the total dark, and when he made the deck being pushed back by a sailor with a Scots voice saying, "Get back down, you bastard," and trying to be sick on the deck of the cabin but splattering Howe and Roscoe, the former cursing and the latter utterly indifferent. And so, at last, they came to Toronto—or, to judge from the cries shouted on the dock, which was much smaller than that at Montreal, "Tronner." The captain of the sloop, a nondescript man who smelled of fish and dung, came to say farewell.

"You can disembark now. And thank God for that. I don't like running Rebs. Thank Christ when this war is over."

"Thank you for your hospitality, sir," replied Gervase. The captain looked at him queerly and turned his back. Lyon laid a large hand on his shoulder. The captain squealed.

"The major spoke to you," said Lyon.

"Yep, I reckon he did," said the captain. "I got a crew, you know, Reb."

"Leave him, Lyon," said Gervase. "He ain't worth it." Lyon spat on the filthy deck.

It was nine in the morning. They stood on the dock, once again, oh yes once again, among the barrels and ropes and detritus. Hell must be a dock, thought Gervase. The Ancients had something in their notion of Charon. Howe had not yet recovered, was strangely silent, and had his hand on Gervase's shoulder. Connor was leading Roscoe, who looked more than usually puzzled.

"Welcome to Canada, gentlemen" came a voice, apparently from nowhere. Gervase glanced around and spotted its owner leaning against a pile of boxes marked TEA in large burned letters. He was a tall man, lean of face, beaky in the nose, with long, tapering fingers, which were splayed at his sides to support his lounging gait as his shoulders rested on the boxes. "Or rather, not Canada, but Toronto. Tronner to the natives." The voice was cool. It wasn't Canadian, or didn't seem to be. It certainly wasn't American. It was English. So was the gaze: amused indifference.

But despite the indifference, the man seemed to be enjoying their discomfiture: merely for the fun of it. In more normal times, Gervase would have gone forward to shake him by the hand, to introduce himself. But on the gray dock with the biting

wind he let the tall man make himself known. He noticed that
the man's eyes had curious yellow pupils. After a moment or two
the man pulled himself forward off the boxes.

"My name is Harris," he said casually. "Henry Harris. Don't
call me Henry. You, I take it," scanning the group and fixing on
Gervase, "are Major Stepton. And you," again the eyes roved,
avoiding contact, looking through the object upon which they
fixed, "are Howe. The politico." He laughed, and Mr. Howe
flushed. Harris smiled, and the corners of his mouth twisted
downward in the smile.

"I take it that you dislike docks as much as I? Good. Then let
me take you to your lodgings. Not very handsome, I'm afraid.
But better than that boat. They tell me I should call all vessels
'ships,' but that is indubitably a boat. Damned uncomfortable,
I'll wager. And Captain Müller is no courtly host." He turned
around and walked off toward the edge of the docks, where railroad lines crisscrossed and, even now, engines were moving
slowly along, shunting vans which, apparently on their own
power, drifted along and crashed into other vans, setting up long
lines of goods, freight trains for the interior, if there was one,
which was hard to imagine. Gervase thought that Canada must
be nothing but docks, a country perched on the edge of cold
water. Harris slowed his pace, for Mr. Howe was hobbling, and
gestured Gervase to move to his side. Howe tried to catch up
but, with nice timing, Harris calculated the pace so that he and
Gervase always remained ahead, and so out of earshot.

"A Virginia man, I believe? On Lee's staff?"

"A long time ago," said Gervase. "A very long time."

"Ah well, times change," said Harris. "Comforting cliché, don't
you think? I'm afraid I haven't found you anything very princely,
but then you won't be in the odious Tronner for long. Not unless
you wish to sink yourself in the great Canadian mass, that is.
And I can't imagine anyone wishing that. No, we'll get you
warmly bedded down, and then we'll have a little talk about the
future. I think I can offer you something *enticing*. If you wish to
carry on the sacred struggle, of course."

"I suppose so." Gervase found the man's continual irony de-
pressing rather than cultivated. They were now at the end of a
long, straight street, which looked like a building site. Houses,

shops, offices, all with rickety notices patched onto them, stretched as far as the eye could see.

"Yonge Street. It looks young, too, if you'll permit me the pun. Not very attractive to look at, is it? But then, you see, Major, unlike your country and mine, Canada is a burgeoning place." He paused. "By your country, of course, I mean Virginia." Gervase had not doubted this fact, but he welcomed the scruple. They paused by one of the more rickety houses, built of old wood, already dark although the building itself was new.

"If you'll go in you'll find you're expected." He paused more significantly. "I should give you a warning: Don't think that because you are in Canada you're safe. The Federals have as many agents here as we do. And they don't like prisoners who escape and decapitate their guards. So they'll be after you if they find out your place of residence, as we might put it. So keep in the house, at least until I've spoken at length to you. This house," he gestured theatrically with the words, "is a well-known hostel—I think that's the new word, ain't it?—for migrants, transients. It should offer you plenty of entertainment. For the time being, it should be safe." With which he strode off down Yonge Street, his long legs loping, the air blowing from his lips like smoke puffs from a train and yet, withal, preserving a curious elegance among those who strutted and crawled along the half-constructed sidewalk.

"He might have taken us inside," muttered Howe. They ascended some dangerously insecure steps and hammered at the door. There were sounds of movement from within. The door, however, did not open. Gervase hammered again. This time the door did open, and he found himself facing the barrels of a shotgun, held by a sturdy middle-aged woman. Gervase could not help himself; he laughed. A dig in the ribs from Howe helped to recollect him. Howe himself spoke from the side. "We come from Mr. Harris." The gaping metal holes lowered out of sight, and the woman beckoned them inside with an irritable motion. They trooped under the lintel, Lyon stooping low. Howe, Gervase, Roscoe, Connor, Angus, Carey, and the third Virginian, Lexy, all stood packed together in a smallish room while the woman peered at them suspiciously.

"How do I know you come from Mr. Harris?" she asked.

"He brought us to the door," expostulated Howe. She grimaced.

"He has yellow eyes, and he's English," remarked Gervase.

"That's my boy," said the woman. "Call me Piggy. Everyone does."

Gervase thought that nothing could surprise him anew in this strange colony. He could not bring himself to use the name, no, he could not. Lyon had no such qualms. He asked her for something to eat.

"Why, sure," said Piggy. "Girls, girls!" There was movement to the rear and two ill-favored young women peeped through a tatty curtain that divided the front from the back. "Get these boys some food! And mind you, make it good food." Gervase suspected that they had been landed in a house of ill fame.

Ill fame it might be, but not bad food. They ate as they had not eaten for months. Even Roscoe showed interest. At first he had played with the toast and eggs, but Gervase took up a spoonful and thrust it to Roscoe's mouth. A look of something like recognition came over Roscoe's face, and he grasped the spoon and fork with determination, shoveling the stuff between his lips. They ate in silence, for their need was so great. After they had finished, Mr. Howe said, with repletion, "That was most welcome. Most welcome indeed." Piggy had been bustling about while they were feeding. With familiarity her features became warmhearted rather than irritable. Harris clearly paid her well, because she was solicitous for their welfare. Or perhaps it was that she was naturally of a kindly disposition. Gervase thought he would suspend judgment.

"Major," whispered Connor with his catlike sibilance, "I think we're in a whorehouse." Piggy was sharp of hearing.

"Whorehouse indeed!" she cried. "I'll tell you that this is a respectable place. That's gratitude for you. But I'll tell you this: My girls won't be ungenerous if you's feeling the needs of manhood. Most of my lodgers have been deprived for a good long time when they come to my door." She leered at them. Lyon was not slow on the uptake. He had been least affected by their privations.

"That's right kind of you, ma'am," he said. "I reckon I'll take some rest now, and I'd not say no to a sweet companion."

"Piggy, not ma'am," she said. Lyon, despite his earlier readiness, felt qualms before Gervase's eye. Gervase encouraged him.

"Right then, Piggy," said Lyon.

"You go and lie down upstairs, big boy," said Piggy. She raised her voice in a screech. "Peggy Jane, you go and make up the bed of this big southern gentleman." One of the girls in the back—Gervase could not tell how many there were—moved. Looking at his men, Gervase could tell that now that Lyon had broken the ice—the metaphor occurred naturally to his mind—they all wished to emulate him. Except Roscoe. Even Howe showed the glint of lust, and was clearly pondering how to square lust with dignity. Gervase helped him.

"You go to rest, Mr. Howe," he said. "You had a more exhausting time than us. You're an older man. We'll all understand." Howe drew himself up and padded over to the door. Connor and the Carolina boys had already gone. There was more sound of movement. Then Gervase heard creaking about him; laughter and squeals. Roscoe had fallen asleep in his chair. When he was asleep the air whistled through the half-healed wound in his throat, giving a strange, eerie sound, as if he were no longer human. When Gervase recalled the laughing, gallant boy at First Manassas, he wondered whether he was. He wondered whether Roscoe knew objects as objects, feelings as feelings, knew cause and effect, love, hate, patriotism, or whether a deeper *accidie* than his own had fallen on the lad. Piggy pushed her way through the curtains. They jangled when her portly frame had moved through, and the uneven floorboards creaked. She pushed the plates to one end of the table, but made no effort to take them away. Bits of bread, the half-wiped yolks of egg, and spilled coffee all decorated the table. Piggy leered at him.

"Ain't you feeling like some rest, Major?" she asked, with provocative glances.

"Later, perhaps," said Gervase. "And how did you know I was a major?" She did appear discomposed. "Mr. Harris told me," she said. Then how was it you didn't greet us as Harris's guests? thought Gervase. "I'll take some sleep here," he added, for she was girding herself up for an act of seduction. There was even more noise from the upper floors, and this may have had an aphrodisiac effect upon her. Gervase leaned forward and put his head on the table, buried in his arms. Soon he began to breathe in measured intervals, the deep rhythm of sleep. He heard Piggy moving around. After a while she said "Major?" very softly. He made no reply. He was very tired. Piggy had moved over to the other side of the room by the window, crude glass, inexpertly tacked into an ungeometric shape. He heard the rustle of her clothes; she was waving, or something. Now she moved toward the door. She was making a deliberate effort to tread softly. A slumber did my spirit seal, thought Gervase. The door opened, and from the sound of the boots one man entered, and on tiptoe, for Gervase could only hear the creaking of leather. There was a murmur, then Piggy's voice came clearer, though very low. "Mind you, I'll have no gunplay. Get them and get out. The major's asleep at the table. You don't need to worry about the other one. He's an idiot. An he's dumb." There was guttural grunt in reply.

Gervase was an expert in judging distances. He had been doing it from his childhood. He waited until the boot leather was about three feet from him, and then pushed himself back from the table, standing up as he did so. He was faced by a small man, of what looked to be Italian extraction. The man was holding a knife in his left hand, and the weapon sat there with a look of familiarity. The black eyes opened wide with astonishment. Gervase's sudden metamorphosis from sleeping victim to dangerous opponent had been too sudden for the man to take in. Exploiting this advantage, Gervase seized the knife hand and crashed it against the table with all the force at his command. The man yelped but did not let go. Gervase lifted the hand and repeated the downward blow. The fingers opened, and the knife fell to the floor with a clattering din. There were sounds of confusion upstairs.

They had been eating with sturdy forks. Gervase leaned over the recumbent assassin and picked up a fork. The hand was still open, and Gervase skewered it to the table with a single blow. The prongs of the fork, he noted with satisfaction, had passed through the hand and had buried themselves at least half an inch in the wood. Roscoe had awakened, for the tenor of his breathing altered. But he made no effort to help. He sat and watched. The man was screaming out imprecations, or pleas, in some for-

eign tongue. Gervase kicked him—once, twice, three times—just
beneath the kneecap.

"Keep quiet," he said. There were footsteps descending the
stairs. Lyon came into the room at a run, his shirt stuffed into his
trousers, fumbling with his clothes as he moved.

"Get that Piggy," said Gervase. And he was only just in time,
for she was almost out of the door when Lyon caught hold of her
dress and hauled her back. There was the sound of ripping cloth;
expostulations; a blow; a whimper; silence. Upstairs there was silence, and, after a while, one by one the men crept down, some
sheepish, some defiant, Mr. Howe truly discomfited. No politician likes to be taken in to so great an extent. Roscoe sat playing
with his hands; Lyon had dumped Piggy by the window and
deputed Lexy to watch over her. The other girls, in petticoats or
less, were twittering in the back room. Gervase sent Angus to
shut them up, and his abrasive Scottish tones soon assured the
men that this was underway. Gervase turned his attention to the
prisoner, who appeared to have fainted. Gervase slapped his
face. The eyes winced in the lids, which indicated that he was
engaged in deception. So Gervase slapped him harder.

"Do you speak English?" he asked. He was greeted by another
outburst of the foreign tongue. It was quite possible that they
had hired an assassin who did not speak English and who thus
could not betray them—whoever "they" might be. The only
question that mattered was whether Harris was, or was not, one
of "them." It seemed unlikely; he would hardly go to the trouble
of getting them from Montreal to Toronto merely to have them
killed, when he could have arranged a gang of French cutthroats
to do the job on the docks of Montreal. The man might be a
sneak thief. But that was unlikely. Piggy had let him in; Piggy
was in league with him. But that might be for the loot, nothing
more. But then why did she direct him to "the major"? Because
he seemed to be the most formidable or because he *mattered*
much more. They had to find out whether he knew Harris. He
looked down at the man.

"Harris? Harris? Harris?" Gervase said. Once more the burst of
unintelligible babble. Clearly a plea now. "Lyon," said Gervase,
"we must know whether this man knows Harris. Come and help
me. Mr. Howe, would you be so good as to watch over that lady

by the window?" Mr. Howe, his face a rich crimson of fury, moved over to her. Age would not hinder him, nor custom stale his watchfulness. Gervase spoke clearly to the man. "I don't know whether you speak English or not. If you don't, it is really most unfortunate for you. But I must know whether you are acquainted with a man called Harris." Gervase paused and then spoke very distinctly. "Do you know Harris? *Connaissez-vous Harris?*" His Latin was rusty, but that might be the nearest to Italian. He tried. *"Homo nomine Harris scis?"*

The man's eyes were ranging wildly in the sockets. He babbled again, and Gervase thought he recognized the word "Harris," though pronounced in a curious way. But if the man did know something, then to feign ignorance of English was the best way to conceal his knowledge and to evade exposure of this intelligence. Gervase had to be sure. Once, perhaps, he might have abstained from the methods he wished to employ; after Fort Delaware he had given up playing the game of war by the rules. There were no rules; or rather, rules were the luxury that Lee could reserve for himself in the quiet of headquarters or the elevation of a command station.

"Break his right arm, Lyon," ordered Gervase. "But do it gently, because I don't want him fainting on me." Lyon, nothing loath, moved forward, and took the right arm in his two great hands. He had decided upon the break at the elbow and slowly began to bend the arm backward. The man no longer took refuge in language, but screamed. Gervase picked up a piece of filthy cloth and put it over the man's mouth. His eyes were quite cold and expressionless.

"Nod your head when you want to talk to me," he said. "Do you know a man called Harris?" Lyon bent the arm back and back. The thrashing of the limbs became greater and greater, and Gervase had to hold his body against that of the recumbent man to prevent him tearing his left hand out of the table by main force, maddened by the pain in his other limb. But he made no sign of linguistic recognition. Gervase was about to tell Lyon to stop his efforts when there was a crack, and the man went limp.

"I guess he's fainted, Major," said Lyon.

"So he has," said Gervase. And Roscoe smiled. It was a smile horrifying to look at, and Gervase quickly averted his eyes. The whistling gurgle was fast and satisfied. Roscoe was creating a language out of pure sound. He was happy. They could all tell it: It radiated around the room. Gervase shut his senses to purposeless delight in suffering. Lyon was full of suggestions.

"I can wake him up, Major," he said. "There's a fire in the back room." "No," replied Gervase. "It will do no good. If he wouldn't talk when you were breaking his arm, he won't talk when you shove a red-hot knife up his ass." Lyon accepted this judgment, for he respected Gervase's judgment.

"The point is, did he know Harris?" reiterated Gervase.

"Oh, I should think that most unlikely," came an English voice from the door, and there was Henry Harris leaning against the jamb, his ironical smile playing over his features, the usual downward turn of the mouth. That he had a gun in his pocket Gervase could tell from the preternatural bulge. Gervase did not have a gun, and though Harris had shown little inclination to reach for his coat pocket, Gervase had learned a good deal of prudence. Harris spoke once more.

"A sneak thief, wouldn't you think? A common sneak thief? But let's not give him to the police. They can be damned unhelpful in this country. All too inquiring, you know. You might let Piggy go, Mr. Howe, I'll speak to her later. And discipline her." His voice was hard, and Piggy scuttled to the back room. "And now, Major, if you don't mind, I think we'll have our little talk now. Would you mind asking your men to leave us alone in this room? And, I regret, you too, Mr. Howe." Harris walked over to the recumbent foreigner and pulled the fork out of his left hand. "You're very resourceful, Major Stepton," he smiled. The others shuffled away. Howe looked as if he was caught up in events he could not control. Bafflement mingled with anger. Roscoe sat where he was. Harris said something in the same foreign tongue to the man, who had recovered himself, and he scampered out of the house. Suddenly, without warning, Lyon clapped his hand over Harris's mouth and pinned him against the table. He put his free hand to the Englishman's pocket and pulled out a pistol. He stepped back and handed it to Gervase.

"You'd better have the piece, Major," he said, and walked out. They heard his feet tramping up the stairs.

"You might as well give it back to me," said Harris. "I won't use it on you. My, how brave and sudden you Rebels are. No wonder Grant is having all the trouble he is."

"I think I'll keep the weapon," replied Gervase, "at least until we have had our talk. Then you can—perhaps—have it back." Harris sighed, as if at the ingratitude and foolishness of the world.

"Very well then. If you must." He moved to sit on the rough-hewn bench. He gestured Gervase to be seated. He nodded his head to Roscoe. "Does he matter?"

"He matters," said Gervase, "but he can't reveal anything you say. And I trust you'll say plenty." Harris grinned: infectious, schoolboy, very English, frank, without guile, trusting.

"Oh yes, Major Stepton. I'll tell you plenty, as you put it so quaintly." "And cut out the jokes," said Gervase. He felt the presence of the Englishman as wholly alien, utterly foreign, as foreign as the little, pathetic assassin whom they had maimed and flung away as a dog will discard the shreds of a chewed bone. He felt an impersonal gratitude to the man, no more. No warmth, no comradeship. No wonder they had fought the English less than a hundred years ago. And, in the Confederacy, they had had high hopes of the English. Had not Gladstone said they had created a "nation"? And then desertion. Abandonment, except for childish and clandestine operations like this. Though he had reason enough to be grateful.

"Let's begin with the Italian, shall we?" said Harris. "You know, the trouble with employing dagoes is that they always misunderstand very precise instructions. My Italian is good, really good, and then the slippy little bastard comes in here and tries to murder you. That Piggy isn't much better. Though, after all, she didn't know what was on, so she can perhaps be excused. He didn't know my name, by the way—Giovanni, that is. I called myself something outlandish. It's better that they know as little as possible. I say, this is going to be rather a monologue. Tedious, as you might expect. Let's warm ourselves." And he produced a hip flask, with two caps that screwed the one upon the other. "Rather neat, don't you think?" He poured brandy into the two alfresco containers and toasted Gervase. "To the Confederacy." They drank. It was the first time Gervase had tasted liquor in many months, and the brandy burned the back of his throat. He coughed violently.

"Sorry," said Harris. "I should have remembered." He looked significantly at Roscoe. "What about him?"

"No," replied Gervase. God alone knew what effect brandy might have on Roscoe. And yet, curiously, hardly had Gervase said "No" when Roscoe leaned over the table, grabbed the brandy bottle, and put it to his lips, drinking deeply. Both Harris and Gervase stared at him in astonishment.

"Can't do any serious harm, it seems," smiled Harris. "Well now, to my tale. Giovanni wasn't sent here to kill you. He was sent here to kill Howe." Gervase grasped the butt of the pistol, but Harris raised a restraining hand, accompanied by that infuriating smile. "No, please don't shoot me, and hear me out. You can't think that I spend my time in this godforsaken country helping Confederate soldiers for fun, can you? If you think that, you must have a very queer idea of me. For my opinion, anyone who spends a day in Canada longer than he needs to must be quite mad. London will be the happiest sight to me when I return. My dream of heaven is whatever isn't Yonge Street. But my masters have sent me here, and here I must stay. For the duration of your little bother at least."

"And who are your masters?" asked Gervase.

"Well, that would be telling, as we said at school. Shall we say that I have habits above my means, and my masters are supplying those means, which I shall enjoy when I return to England. You won't have read the newspapers recently, will you? Of course not. Tactless of me. But you may perhaps know that most of the mills in Lancashire are standing idle because they can't get cotton from the southern states. The operatives are very happy about it, apparently. They starve so that the darkies can be free. All very complicated—Ruskin and Cobden and Bright, you know. The lower orders are deuced difficult to fathom. May God put off the day when they will run England. Because, my dear fellow, that day will come. However, to take up my tale, the chaps who own the mills aren't quite so altruistic. After all the *brass* they are losing, as one of them put it to me. Quaint expression, ain't it? They had fair hopes that England would intervene on the side of the Confederacy, but that damned foreign bastard who's married to the Queen put a stop to that before he popped off. Actually, he might easily *be* a bastard, did you know?"

"I didn't," said Gervase. His interest in Prince Albert's ancestry was limited.

"After hope of intervention ceased, my masters thought they might give a little unofficial help to the Confederacy. Because, believe me, we have friends working for us in England, and with the Frogs, too. Put some spokes in the wheel of Mr. Lincoln. That's what my masters think. Yet there's deuced little I can do. Only organize some raids into the northern states. Puts the wind up the Yankees, you might say. I was talking to a lieutenant Young the other day. But I have even higher hopes from you. Of course, I supply the equipment, weapons, horses, and whatnot."

"I see," said Gervase.

"I don't think you do," replied Harris, insouciant as ever. He had made no attempt to go for the gun, either directly or by subterfuge. "Did Mr. Howe tell you anything about his native town?"

"North Adams?"

"I see he did. Well, you're being very cagey, so I'll fill in the details. North Adams is a railroad center in the North. That's quite important. But much more important is the fact that the place is the main bullion holder for the federal states. Far away from Mosby's raiders, I suppose. I want you to go and get that bullion." There was silence. "Of course, *I* don't want the damned stuff. That is for General Lee and the Confederacy. Give them a shot in the arm. Enable them to buy medical supplies, or ammunition, or whatever you need. If you raid North Adams and capture the bullion, I'll have a ship standing by in Toronto and in Boston. Oh yes, I have my ways, even in the city of Emerson and Thoreau. But what I want from you is the capture of the bullion. I understand that you were in the 1st Virginia Cavalry. We understand these things in England. I'll buy you black horses, and the proper uniforms I'll have made up by Jew tailors, and I'll supply you with guns, sabers, and ammunition. All I ask is that you capture that bullion. Take it for Lee, for yourself, or for whoever God cares for—but take it away from the Yankees."

"And why did you want to kill Mr. Howe?"

"Be sensible, my dear fellow. Mr. Howe is a Democrat, true,

but he's a native of North Adams. He's quite willing to rant about private property and the right of individual decision—but he's not likely to support an attack on his own hometown. You might have to kill civilians. . . . Regrettable, of course, but the Yankees don't seem to worry about it too much. Heard of General Sherman?"

"I don't need to know about General Sherman."

"Had experience yourself? Well, you'll know, then. But Mr. Howe would have scruples. I know he would. And we can't afford scruples."

"No, we can't. That's quite true," said Gervase.

"So will you do it?"

"Let me be clear in my mind. You want me to track down from the North into this place, North Adams. Attack the bank. Steal the bullion. Blow up the railroad if I can. Then get out through Boston or through Canada."

"That's the score," smiled Harris. "In a nutshell."

"And you'll supply what I need?"

"Yes, indeed."

"What if I'm captured? The Yankees won't be too kindly disposed toward me after Fort Delaware."

"That's your problem," said Harris. "You're a man of spirit and spunk. Don't get caught. I thought all you Rebs had patriotism by the gallon."

"We do."

"And, after all, one of General Lee's personal staff."

"I'll do it," said Gervase. "But no killing of Howe. Just keep him safe in Toronto."

"There's the telegraph. Don't forget the wonders of modern science, Major."

"I said keep him *safe*."

"Your risk then. I'll do that. And may I have my gun back?" Gervase slid the weapon across the table to him. He smiled. "I want a special revolver myself. A Le Mat."

"Will do," said Harris smugly. "I rather like that gun myself."

And all went as Mr. Harris said. He had words with Piggy, and they were not troubled. The girls were made free of the men. A man with a skullcap came to measure them for gray uniforms with black frontings. Harris was proud of that. "Do you know," he said proudly, "I've even found some black ostrich feathers for you. Just like the early days." They were given rations in leather cases. They were given water bottles, and bottles that contained other spirits, which Gervase smashed on a brick lying on the sidewalk outside Piggy's house. Mr. Howe was approached by a distinguished Copperhead in Toronto and informed that his counsel would be invaluable in the sessions of the expatriate Democrats, devoted to overthrowing Mr. Lincoln and Mr. Stanton and General Grant by rhetoric. Gervase recruited Lyon and the Carolina boys into the 1st Virginia Cavalry, a regiment that he no longer knew existed or not. And finally they set out by train, and then wagon, to the border of Canada, so that they might move down from Vermont into northern Massachusetts. Mr. Harris, sallow but cherubic with excitement, accompanied them and the horses, which were tied in line behind the wagon. "I just wish you had more men," he said, "a few more men."

"These will be enough," Gervase assured him. "Quite enough to raid a civilian depot." Even Roscoe gurgled with greater verve than he was wont, until they stood finally by their horses in the dark tip of the Green Mountains. Mr. Harris crowed with delight. He constantly evoked his masters and their pleasure. Gervase wondered how much Mr. Harris was to be paid. Not that it mattered. The rain was dripping from the enormous trees when Harris met them for the last time to say his farewells. He assumed a serious air. Gervase, too, was serious, touching the Le Mat that hung from his belt as it had done in the old days before the death of Deborah, before the death of his father, before the death of his mother, before the burning of Sweetwater. There they stood, seven of them, below the great trees that marked the beginning of America.

"Mr. Harris," said Gervase, "we must be grateful to you for all you have done for us. General Lee himself would wish us to thank you. You have restored to me, and to Captain Stedman, the insignia of our regiment. You have enabled these men to join our great regiment. I am truly grateful. And yet I cannot but reflect that you sent an Italian murderer to kill Mr. Howe, a patriotic American who had endured the indignities and horrors of Fort Delaware. And I also reflect that all you have done is in the interests of some English millowners who are only concerned with money. All Americans, whether of the North or the South, have fought for an ideal. The ideal of the North is mistaken, but an ideal it is. You sneered at Emerson and Thoreau. I think they are wrong, but I do not sneer at them. You once lectured me upon the need for safety, for security, for secrecy about our mission. I am a ready learner, Mr. Harris. We are, as you realized from the start, cavalrymen." Gervase turned to his men. "Mount," he cried. They swung into the saddle. "And now, Mr. Harris, I am going to teach you the first lesson in cavalry tactics. And your first lesson in idealism. Lyon, take off his head." And Gervase pulled his horse toward the track in the woods, but before he had gone ten paces he had heard the swack, thump, whistle, and rustling fall of a man who had no honor. He looked to his side and saw Roscoe's eyes shine.

10

To Ruin the Great Work of Time

Gervase had his black horse, the third, named Darcy, a stallion, and much of his uniform. This was rare enough for an officer of the Confederacy in the fall of 1863. As he remembered, when he had joined the 1st Virginia Cavalry in those heady opening days of conflict, the whole regiment had been mounted on black horses. He remembered, too, Jeb carefully inspecting each animal, hoofs, flanks, and fetlocks. Anything less than pure black would not do then. The feathers on the cap were often dyed, but not even the lowest trooper might have a trace of gray showing. Jeb had said (ah! far-off resonance), "You are the black-horse regiment of Virginia, and, by God, you'll be black—black horses, black plumes, black boots." But all was faded now, despite the late Harris's munificence. His uniform was stitched in places; it was so threadbare that the cloth barely held together. The tailor of Toronto had been out to make the quick buck, or pound, or whatever they called it. Even the cavalry standard he had in his saddlebag was threadbare, though the tailor had made it up afresh. Yet it would fly well enough when the time came.

They had made their way down from Canada slowly, keeping to the tracks in the woods, living off the land. When they were still near to the border, he would send Lyon off into a village to buy supplies. Lyon was a capable mimic and could mute his Reb accent and take on the linguistic guise of a Yankee. And, after all, Lyon only had to say "I'm from Maryland" and nobody would doubt him. They might suspect him a little, feel a twinge, but they had no grounds for action, for Maryland was a neutral state. It might support the Confederacy with its heart, but the divisions of Yankee soldiers swarming over its every mile discouraged its declaring its allegiance openly.

It was mid-December now, and had been raining for several days. The wind was keen, although the trees sheltered his band of seven horsemen. But these great trees retained the water. The drops hung on the brown boughs and fell onto their thin clothes. They were always sodden, always cold, usually hungry. Harris's rations had given out sooner than they expected. Gervase made the men walk their horses for half the day. The horses were still exhausted, because fodder was more difficult to obtain than food. Harris had not thought of that. This damned iron-cold North. It was like the hearts of its people. Hard, inflexible—Sebbs incarnate in natural objects. He saw that Roscoe was staggering in his gait. The boy was young—so long from First Manassas, as he kept reminding himself. He should never have brought Roscoe on a mission such as this. Gervase called out some encouragement, and realized that his voice was nothing but a croak. He had had a cold for the last week. His limbs ached; his head throbbed; he felt as if acid were running in his veins. He continually wiped the mucus from the tip of his nose. His upper lip was raw and bled. The outer skin had quite disappeared. He did not dare to shave, and the men had followed his involuntary example. They looked like ragamuffins, just as the Yankee cartoons depicted the Confederacy and its soldiers, cartoons etched with that mixture of fear and contempt they had come to expect from Yankees. He remembered Sebbs. He also remembered that first battle where he had lost the finger, which still throbbed. Women dressed for a picnic flooding back to Washington from their confident seats on the hillside where they could watch the Rebels thrashed. They had run back to their houses quickly enough!

None of the men, not even Lyon, knew of their mission. If Gervase were to be killed on the journey, they had been instructed to make for Canada again, or to Boston, where Harris said there was a ship—and thence to the Confederacy if they could, for the sea offered no safe passage. Gervase remembered the sea and its discomforts. Whatever transpired, it was not to be the sea for him again. He had the only map. Only he knew where they were and what their purpose was far behind the Yankee lines. They were deep in the enemy's heartland. The enemy? Gervase distrusted such terms now. They spoke the same language as these Yankees—a language similar, as Harris's was not. Maybe it was a question of attitude, a way of looking at the world, call it "civilization" if you will. The Yankees would not give an inch (except on the battlefield, he thought; they'll run fast enough then; but that was in the early days of the war). All matters of principle, right and wrong, fixed before time began. And all the right on their side, of course, discovered by that lunatic who lived on beans by Walden Pond and saluted the dead spirit of John Brown, whom Gervase had seen swing on the end of a hempen rope, and women like the virago author of that sentimental tract, who, yes, Mr. Lincoln had told, had begun the big war. Old hypocrite. That demagogue from Illinois whose apparent humility covered a depth of pride at whose altar thousands had to die. The Yankees had no gaiety, none of that spirit that Jeb showed when he waved his plumed hat at McClellan's horsemen charging toward him on the banks of the Potomac. Jeb had waited until they were well within range before signaling his farewell and plunging his horse under the stream until he emerged above the surface and their erratic pistol bullets fell wide of him. Gervase's own horse shivered under him; he felt the quivering along the whole of the rough flank. He patted her gently on the neck. They were near enough to their destination now. Only one more day, a dash, and then, please God, a return to their own kind.

He could smell himself. He could smell sweat, feces, urine, and horseflesh. It was strange how the intimacy of his own odors did not offend him, and yet, when the other men approached him, he almost retched with disgust. He could see that they felt the same. Because they were indeed soldiers of the Confederacy they did their best to control their feelings—not because he was an officer, for Roscoe was an officer too, but because Gervase was their leader. Although they were reduced to the level of animals, their lower clothes smeared and soaked with excrement, they knew now that they were living a myth. They knew that their own mission, because of its hazardous nature, must be a significant part of that myth. His motley crowd of Virginians, and Carolinians turned Virginians, might eat their food raw, tearing at the bloody flesh with stained teeth, wiping their asses with leaves and handsful of grass, facing each day with a resolution tapped from God knew what reserves within themselves; but they were part of General Lee's Army. Most of them were, at bottom, religious men, who had crowded around the fires during that first winter while preachers harangued them under the dour yet approving gaze of old Thomas, now dead. Yet God was only an occasion. General Lee was there. General Lee was incarnate to them, although they would have flinched from admitting it, afraid of the blasphemy. General Lee was Christ incarnate. The living Logos. And since, by implication (of a damned Englishman!), he, Major Gervase Stepton, was appointed to command them, he shared in this sacred atmosphere. Jesus, who could think of those Yankee incompetents, particularly the foolish General Pope, the incompetent and defeated, as if he were God incarnate? This was part of the trouble with the Yankees. They saw God as expressing himself only in principles, not through men. They had not read St. John's Gospel. The only "things" they recognized to have value were machines and gold. Well! They would deprive them of some of them stock of gold, yellow dross, mandestroyer. Yet now the Confederacy needed money; to that degree they were already surrendering themselves to the new world of the Yankees. Otherwise he would not be leading his sad-faced men through the close trees down the red path of soft leaves. Once they had joked a good deal, laughing, whooping to be out of the unspeakable Canada (too loudly, until he rebuked them casually), giving with a new vigor that yell that made Yankee soldiers wilt with fear, although the trees were unmoved unless they sent back an echo as an ironic comment to men who attempted to disturb the solemnity of New England by anything so obscene as a burst of merely human sound unlimited by the metaphysical. The leaves deadened sound; there was a zero in the bone.

The old wound in his finger began to ache abominably. That wound from an early skirmish of the war, from toy soldiers dressed as French Zouaves! He remembered, too, the general seeing him before he went the lonely way to the surgeon's tent, and his screwed-up mouth as he said, in answer to the tender query, "Fine, General, fine." He had even felt religious and said a prayer or two, with the image of his family and Deborah floating in place of God. There had been plenty of praying in that winter, little blasphemy, though. And in those days they had some chloroform and ether for the seriously wounded, but now that sanctimonious bastard from Illinois who called himself the President of the United States of America would allow them no drugs and no medication through the blockade his dark ships maintained. It would end the war more quickly, he said, as his wife ranted on with the bottle at her side for liquor to squirt through her lips. Jeff Davis might be a fool at times—Gervase certainly knew that—but he was never a barbarian. In this way the grapes of wrath were sown, as the Yankee civilians liked to think; often they sang other songs. He saw that his men were drooping in their saddles; only Roscoe sat upright in the remembered posture.

"We should have a rest, Major," suggested Lyon.

"Sure," said Gervase. "Get a fire built and let's have something to eat, Lyon." Gervase realized that he never had found out whether "Lyon" was the man's Christian name or his last name. He always called him by it, and it had the affectionate ring of a Christian name by now. It had always been the practice in their Army. It did not harm discipline. The Yankees were very punctilious about rank. But then, they had little respect for each other as men, not when their generals were idiots or guzzlers of whiskey. Mind you, General Jackson did not call the men by their Christian names. It was an event to be pricked out in the memory to be so addressed by General Jackson.

They had difficulty with the fire. The wood was wet. The rain still dropped. But after a while there was a crackling, a new noise to add to the dropping and breaking and sighing in the great trees on the side of the mountain. They had withdrawn from the track into a clearing that had not seen human occupation since the days when the defeated Indians were trooping westward from the blankets infested with smallpox so generously given to them by Lord Jeffrey Amherst. Once the fire took hold the men crouched around it, holding out their hands to the meager warmth it offered, their dark faces stained by weather and suffering and endurance lit grotesquely by the weak yellow flames colored by an occasional spark, which sent an orange bead whirling to the sky. Mostly, however, the fire itself was hidden by the acrid smoke, which made Gervase's eyes water. He made a sign to Lyon, who handed around some pieces of bread. It was curious how they had fallen back into their military roles so easily. The men drank from their water cans, Gervase as usual guiding Roscoe's tin to his mouth and wiping away the dribble from his tunic. Angus had stolen a bottle of rye whiskey from a village three days before, and each took a sip. This time Gervase had to hold Roscoe's hand back. He could not be trusted with liquor. Perhaps it blotted away the pain, which must throb in his nerves? Of the others it was significant that no man took more than a sip. No man wanted to do so, for that would have deprived his companions of their share, and they were bound together now by so many memories of shared agony as well as by devotion to their cause, which they would not have put in these stirring words, except the old Gervase once upon a time, but which they all truly felt, even though they crouched like animals in the heart of a Yankee wood. Gervase sat among them and glanced from face to face. They looked back at him, expectant, hopeful in some cases—Lexy, for instance—that he might give them the news for which they all yearned, which was in fact the knowledge of what they had to do, for anything would be better than this endless tracking through the forests, purposeless to them though endowed, as they remotely surmised, with the word of their commander in chief. Was it, thought Gervase, or the mere prompting of English merchants giving some support to his own quest for renewed significance? He might as well tell them something now.

"We are three miles, more or less, from a town in Massachusetts called North Adams," he said. "The Yankees keep a store of bullion in the bank there. We are going to take some of it, and burn the bank about their ears." Lexy made a feeble attempt at a rebel yell. The others only smiled, except Lyon, whose face creased with prudent foresight.

"Bullion, Major?" he asked. "Won't that mean a regiment of Yankee soldiers?"

"Not that I've heard," replied Gervase. Lyon was no fool. "Nor
had our . . ." he pauses and minutely hesitated ". . . Intelligence. The Yankees think the gold's far enough away from us.
They didn't think we could ride this far." There was a low laugh,
satisfaction that the Yankees had been outsmarted. "They forgot
our Canadian friends. Friends, not allies. And our British
helper."

"Bastard," said Angus. They all laughed, both at his indignation and the memory of Harris lying munching the grass on the
Canadian border. But the men realized that the crisis was
approaching, the long delay of enduring and hoping and fearing
and wondering was soon to be over, and they would know exactly what they had to do, because instinct would take over from
calculation, and they would strike a blow and show their faces
and the standard and regain the dignity stripped from them at
Fort Delaware and no longer skulk within the shadow of the
great trees that grew on the dark mountain. Gervase had com-
pleted his penetrating scrutiny. They could be relied upon, weak
as they were, both to think and act. Except for Roscoe, and he
would keep Roscoe close to himself. They could be told.

"We ride into the town about the middle of the day," he said.
"Most of them will be eating then. We ride up to the bank, take
the money, and ride out. We ride east into these hills, but farther
south than this. We'll hole up for a day or two at a place called
Tannery Falls. Even the Yankees can't find us there. Then we'll
make our way, taking our time, along this road they call the
Mohawk Trail, and there's a ship waiting for us in Boston. If the
worst comes to the worst, we head back for Canada." He made it
sound so easy. Could he find Tannery Falls? Harris had made it
seem simple enough as they pored over a map north of the border, but these tracks and these woods seemed all alike. Then to
get to Boston! Through a countryside raised and inflamed,
doubtless, with righteous indignation. Just itching to hang a few
Rebel spies who were laden with golden coin. The Yankees
would run to recover that even more than to capture those who
had affronted the sacred dignity of their homeland. Gervase felt
in imagination the rough fibers of the rope gripping his neck as
he fell downward, and he shivered slightly. Better that than

Fort Delaware again, anyhow. But they were all shivering, for the fire was getting low. "Lexy," he ordered, "get some god-damned wood." There was a pause while Lexy, country boy as he was, scraped around to some purpose and came back to fling the branches on the smoldering heap. "When we leave the band we burn it," Gervase added. "There'll be a few Yankee soldiers around. Infantry. Old men and ruptured young ones, I guess." Perhaps. So he had been told by the untrustworthy Harris. Doubt seeped into him. But he would have surprise on his side. "And," he went on in a voice that he charged with solemnity, "don't shoot anyone who doesn't shoot at you. We don't fight women and kids, and we don't kill civilians."

"The Yankees don't care so much about that," snapped Connor, waspish, squat as he hunkered on the bracken.

"That's why we do," replied Gervase. "The Yanks fight anyone who gets in their way. We don't. Jesus, that's what the whole war is about." Was it? Once he had liked to think so.

"It's supposed to be about the niggers," said Lyon with a smile.

"So the Yankees tell the rest of the world, and all the bleeding hearts bleed a bit more with redder blood. But you know that the niggers have nothing to do with it." Did they? He had never discussed these wider issues before. And was he certain any longer, as they had all been certain in the intoxication of Manassas? "My father had no slaves at Sweetwater. He'd freed them all long ago. I lay you ten to one that none of you have slaves? I thought so. And what about our black workers? Fed, worked easily, given a good cottage. I've never lifted my hand to a nigger in my life. I'd as soon think of whipping a nigger as I would of whipping you." Quantrill's leer flashed before his eyes in the cathouse in Richmond. Didn't the very word "nigger" indicate something?

"You'd have a job, Major," grinned Connor.

"I'm too sensible to try. All this crap the Yankees talk about slaves. They force kids to work in their factories and they whip them when they're idle. I'll wager there are more children whipped in a day in this state, in the factories—sorry, in this *commonwealth*—than in all the parishes of Louisiana. But then

their professors put on their solemn face and talk about dignity
and freedom and liberty and the rights of man and the rest of
that crap." Was it? He wasn't sure any longer. His head buzzed
when he made moral statements. Once he would have had no
doubts. Thomas Jackson had no doubts and he was dead, shot by
an ironic bullet. "When men talk with big words you can tell
they are lying. Yankees always lie, even to themselves." Was he
honest now? He paused, ruminating. "If we succeed in this mission the Yankees will feel what war is like themselves. For a
change." His voice perked up. "They'll smell the smoke in their
own backyard. And now we'll get some sleep. First we'll pray."
Some of the men clasped their hands. Roscoe looked sightlessly
to the front. Perhaps he saw God already? All let their faces
relax, though not to a pitch on inattention, as if they were ab-
stracting themselves from their surroundings into a world which,
though impalpable, was real as this in which they sat as for-
eigners bringing fire and sword and destruction like Joshua to
the Cannanites. Gervase had learned much Scripture in his
childhood; at his mother's knee in Sweetwater in those days of
paradise past and never to return, before the Yankees forced the
war upon them (yes, that *was* certain!), and the resonant words
brought back to him the measured pace of the days of peace
when he was surrounded by love and security and was not always having to decide with such precision that lives, beating
hearts, and quick brains were dependent on his skill. The words
thrust the past into the heart of each man (even effaced the staring terror in the dead eyes of Deborah) and, in the frame of
memory, strengthened their resolution and convinced them of
the rightness of their cause by the very simplicity of its sustain-
ing structure:

The Lord is my light and salvation; whom shall I fear?
The Lord is the strength of my life; of whom shall I be
    afraid?
When the wicked, even mine enemies and my foes,
Came upon me to eat up my flesh, they stumbled and fell.
Though a host should encamp against me,
My heart shall not fear:
Though war should rise against me,
In this I will be confident.

One thing have I desired of the Lord, that will I seek after;
That I may dwell in the house of the Lord all the days of
my life.

"Lord, if it be thy will, grant us success in our work tomorrow.
Let the Lord God of Battles look with favor upon us. Amen."
They all echoed the final supplication, some tonelessly (which
did not betoken disbelief but rather an abnegation of the self)
and some with fervor (which did not betoken assertion of the
self but rather the losing of the world in the intensity of their
wish to unite their will with that of the Deity). "Now let's get
some sleep," said Gervase. "Try." The men lay down close together, with their feet to the fire, and Gervase laid his cloak over
Roscoe's shoulders. Lyon had detailed Angus and Lexy to act as
sentries for a start. The guard would change every two hours.
They all wrapped their gray greatcoats about them. Gradually
the leaves and bracken beneath them grew warmer with the
body heat, but they could not lose that dampness. Animals and
birds, though softer than they would have been in the forests of
the South, called out eerily. An owl was insistent. Squirrels scampered about in the dying light of the fire, foolishly thinking that
it was day, but, as the light disappeared with the glowing and
fading and turning to ash of the sticks, the creatures grew still
and retired to their own warmer nests, where they nuzzled with
close animal tenderness touching the flesh of their mates, unlike
the men below, to whom sexual renunciation was now a habit of
life and whose lonely beings were uncomforted by touch of hand
or lip or loins but who stirred uneasily in the hidden desires that
flicked their memories even in the bleak forgetfulness of sleep.
The horses were tethered, although they were now sufficiently
trained not to have scattered. Their breathing blew steam in the
tightening air, although this could barely be seen in the darkness. Some of the horses were wheezing. They might be called
upon to make an effort tomorrow that would be beyond them;
they would not only be forced to walk or trot or canter, but in a
fury of straining muscle they might also need to gallop. Gervase
thought of these matters, but kept an equal mind in times of
trouble. He had learned the words of Horace from his father as
they sat in the civilized study and constructed between them by
their words the great fabric of civilization that Gervase was now

fighting to preserve against the eel-like twisting of the categories
spawned by so-called thinkers such as Ralph Waldo Emerson.
Oh, Gervase read the words of the Yankee sage. He even had a
copy of "Nature" in the pocket of his greatcoat, picked up from a
stall in Toronto. He recalled his father, child of the Enlight-
enment of Jefferson, reading aloud some passages from this essay
and bursting into uncontrollable laughter. He called his son over
and read the words aloud. "And we are supposed to call this
'gentleman' a philosopher," his father had said. "Whatever sense
he talks he steals from Plato, and the rest is obfuscation and
cant. He was a Unitarian, I believe. No gentleman is a Unitarian
even though he may live on the banks of the Charles at Cambridge." But such common sense seemed remote in these great
woods and silent mountains where nature did seem the eidolon
of a God whose nature or personality was impossible to define.
Gervase grew nearer to the sensibility of Emerson. In the day-
light the somber beauty was mixed with a peculiar capacity for
destruction and hurt, and the loneliness shadowed the minute activity of the termites and the polecats. Perhaps the red slayer actually was wrong to think he was slain. Well, they would know
tomorrow. The men were stirring in their sleep. That Confederate soldiers were valorous in battle did not mean that they felt
no fear; they were merely schooled in a tradition that did not
allow them to show their fear. The Yankees were fresher, a raw
mixture. The battles they fought were on the surface, and their
emotions were the flags that were the supposed testimony of
their sincerity. They believed that their authenticity was
vouched for by the intensity of their expressions, whether by
word or action. Living on beans for a year! And by choice! Gervase fell into a partial sleep in which, as always, the balm of forgetfulness alternated with images of nostalgia and the pain of his
wound and the dribbling of his nose until the gray light began to
trickle with the water through the dead overhanging branches
and the day arrived creeping upon them stealthily so that they
could compose their features and their bodies into that image
they felt it proper to show to the world and to their comrades on
the single day of decision. Gervase pulled up his aching limbs
and walked over to his horse. He checked his Le Mat. Harris had

at least obtained him a good weapon, though not with one of the higher numbers. He opened his saddlebag and took out the standard of the 1st Virginia Cavalry that had been fudged up by the Toronto tailor (not a bad job, really) and walked over to Lexy. The boy was surprised.

"Take this, Lexy," said Gervase. "You ain't a Virginia man, but you've earned the right to carry this. They'll envy you in Carolina." He looked into Lexy's eyes. "Don't ever lose it. Not unless you're dead first."

"Not me, Major," replied Lexy, his face breaking into that country-boy smile that carried in it a drooping a fear of his own possible unworthiness for after all carrying the standard was a sign of trust since it incarnated the symbol of the greater whole, which transcended the mere individual being of even Gervase himself. Gervase looked at his troop and shook his head slightly. They all mounted at this agreed signal. Gervase walked along the rank of horsemen, formal now, as before the ritual of battle; he saw that they had all made efforts, pathetic yet worthy, to smarten themselves up, for after all they were about to ride into a Yankee town and show themselves to the enemy. Yesterday they had drooped in the saddle; today they sat upright. Gervase swung himself up and led the way along the track, Roscoe behind him. They sloped downhill steeply. The trees began to thin out until there were large clearings. At the edge of the last of these Gervase held up his gloved right hand. He looked down at the town of North Adams, which unfolded before them.

It seemed to spawn from the foot of a steep rocky precipice. There were the usual large Yankee factories, built of red-brick and blue-slate roofs, with tiny windows, barred. They looked like the prisons that they were. There was a canal filled with gray water that turned to a dirty froth of white as it poured through lock gates to supply the power that fed the voracious factories where children turned wheels and proffered material to the huge machines that satisfied the great proud purposes of President Lincoln. There were people moving down the streets, narrow and darkened by the high factories, except for the spacious Main Street, which was bedecked with shops and a restaurant and—large, ponderous, and powerful both in stone and influence—

the bank of North Adams. Two soldiers in blue with rifles
casually laid against the rough granite stone were lounging
about, minuscule when seen from such a distance.

There was a railway line, which skirted away toward Williams-
town. Even as they watched, a train, pouring out black and
sooty smoke in twisting of wheels and paroxysms of effort, began
to creep out toward the yellow-green plain, flecked with snow, in
the direction of the colonial seat of learning. The train was carrying freight—weapons of war and drab uniforms produced on the
forges and looms of the cavernous factories. In the freight yard
there were more soldiers in blue, although not too many, and
numerous workers, anonymous in their shirts and gray trousers,
who scurried about in tasks indecipherable to the untrained eye
but all fitting into the plan that industry carved on the brains of
its servitors. The town was like a great beehive without the gaiety of color. In the factories were the slaves. In the freight yard
too. The soldiers were drones, injured and weak and put aside
into this backwater, which was merely the bone marrow that
supplied the blood of the federal Army. Then there was the
great center of the town, with the solidity of achievement showing in stone and rotundity and monuments and cobblestones
scraped free of horseshit—clean and noble, like the cause so pit-
ifully served by the exploited. It was all so ordered, but it was
an order that chilled the bone. The figure of what is to come
when we lose this war, thought Gervase. For lose it we will.
What can gallantry do against this pattern and power? Here
were their principles reduced to stone and steel, directed to an
end very different from Ralph Waldo's principles of a universal
God of fertile, reflective Nature. Plato had certainly given place
to the practical Montaigne here! Jesus. The troopers sat silently
and stared down at the activity, fascinated, for it was so different
from the calm order of rural purpose that they had known at
Sweetwater, or on Malvern Hill, or on the farms of North Carolina. It was something utterly new; a massive energy; a machine
not used by men, but that consumed men, that reduced them to
nothing but parts of itself.

It was eleven-fifteen when Gervase began to pick his way
down the scaly rock path toward the town. He had pointed out
the position of the bank to his soldiers (as if they needed that!).

The town machine was not stopping, but it was losing momentum as groups of workers sat down to eat (not for long, of course, for thereby they would lose pay, and therefore money to put into the great stone bank, with its title incised pretentiously into a granite slab above the architrave of the massive doors). There was a light rain, which would make the cobbles slippery. But it was not heavy.

Women, with dark blue umbrellas, were still parading in small numbers. As the men crossed a little bridge over the canal they could see children playing, mostly in the dark side streets but some, more daring, venturing into the great thoroughfare itself. A few wagons were being hauled by dour horses. One or two more dashing conveyances, although hardly even primitive cabs, went bouncing along, as if eager to leave the cold and get warm within some womb of a building. Everyone wanted to get inside. The water of the canal swirled in sinister eddies beneath them as the horses picked their way delicately over the planks with a hollow sound. Gervase imagined his lifeless body caught in those twists of icy water and trembled. Lyon echoed his thoughts and murmured back to the men:

"Mind you don't get yourselves in that there river." Lyon did not recognize it as a canal. Why should he? He was new to the North.

They scrambled up the bank, slipping and floundering, but assisted by a road made out of rocks and cinders, cruel to the horses' hooves. Probably all the workers walked along the railway line, which went by the side of the canal until it stopped abruptly at two buffers set against the granite hillside. They walked their horses slowly along the side street until they were near the open vista of Main Street. Incredibly, they had not been seen, or, if they had, nothing untoward had been suspected.

"Lyon," said Gervase loudly, "when we get to the bank you stay outside with Lexy and Angus. Show the standard. The rest of you come in with me. Bring your carbines. Make sure they're at the ready, but don't shoot unless they loose off at you. Lyon, I'll leave the two Yankee oldsters outside to you. They're soldiers. If they resist, kill them. If they surrender, accept their word. But tie them up. The rest of you get to the vaults when we're inside. We'll take as much as we can. The rest we burn.

And remember: No civilians shot unless they draw on you. Even then, try to disarm them first." What absurd chivalry! This, after Sebbs and Hass! This was war.

But they must not, could not, would not ever fight this war like Yankees. He was not General Sheridan.

"Draw sabers, men," ordered Gervase. He looked aside at Roscoe, and found that, without assistance, he had drawn his saber too. Gervase felt the Le Mat in his holster, cold to the touch, comfortingly efficient, nine shells and a load of buckshot to take a man to pieces at ten feet. He felt as if he were back at First Manassas and the eye of Jeb was upon him. "Well, Jeb," he said to himself rather sadly, "we'll give this Yankee town a reminder of the name of Stuart and his black-horse regiment." He raised his voice. "Out into the street," he said. They filed out and took up line. He squeezed effort from his lungs, which had so easily cried out at Bull Run. "Charge!"

He urged his horse forward with his knees. The steed leaped between his thighs, and exultation took hold of him as he raised his saber to the regulation angle of ninety degrees. Connor gave out the rebel yell he had been saving up for weeks. Lexy held up the standard. Roscoe stared intently as his horse shied sideways and then righted itself. All of them let out cries and screams, a melody of savagery. Their speed whirlingly increased. Passion of violence took them; they seized the traditions of their culture. A frail old matron turned and saw them flying toward her. She turned to run and stumbled, struck by a god with thunder.

"Sweet Jesus," she shrieked, "Reb cavalry. Reb cavalry."

11

Steel My Soldiers' Hearts

Grote (once Gruit) Vansit (once Vanselt) was a deprived young man. He had traveled to the United States with his parents when he was a very young child; he could remember nothing of the flats, the windmills, the canals, and the tulips of Holland. He had grown up in New England, although his family had peregrinated, as was the custom, moving farther and farther west from Boston until they had taken up permanent residence in North Adams. His father, burly, and with an uncertain command of English, was a baker; his mother assisted at the ovens and kept a spotless home, showing by her actions, though not her words, that cleanliness was not next to godliness but, indeed, identical with it. He had been brought up as a regular churchgoer, his family having espoused the Presbyterian faith since it had a Calvinism almost as rigid as that of the Dutch Reformed Church. The parental discipline was administered with a kind but firm hand; he was surrounded with a real, yet undemonstrative, love. He cared very little for externals. He hardly ever looked up at the Vermont mountains or the northern Berkshires. His variety lay within. He desired to find moral certitude, and, when he had found it, to give this certitude expression in overt action. He craved martyrdom. He embraced the Abolitionist cause with great fervor in his late adolescence; he was inflamed by the heady rhetoric of Henry David Thoreau; he followed the subtle reasoning of Emerson with enthusiasm if not with understanding (a difficulty that he shared with many of the Sage's readers); he wept freely over *Uncle Tom's Cabin,* leaping in keen imagination from lump of ice to lump of ice with the fleeing slaves. He conceived a violent hatred for the South long before the war began. He was too young (by a few months) to vote for President Lincoln, but he was heart and soul, to the death, with the radical Republicans. He would force freedom for the slaves at the point of the bayonet, driving it home with the gusto of the saint convinced of unquenchable righteousness. He rejoiced at the coming of the war. He cared nothing for secession; let them go if they wished—but not until the slaves had been freed. It was a matter of deep disappointment to him that his parents would not open their house to runaways, but he compensated for the parental indifference (for they barely understood the points at issue—Dutch as they were) by sitting with the committees of the "Underground Railway," and sharing in the pontifical vaporizing that passed for realistic action among that body. Its rhetoric was spiced with frequent references to the Supreme Being, who, it was easily assumed, had a special concern for this little corner of Massachusetts. Before the war began, he had wept and raged and shouted when the hooligan Brown was hanged; he cursed the arresting officer, some Colonel Lee, with all the rich vituperation at his command. He had contributed three dollars to the fund that the murderer of Kansas farmers had collected in order to launch a bloody slave rebellion. Truly, in the souls of such young men as Grote Vansit, the spirit of the bearded lunatic had gone marching on.

Nothing could express his joy when the war finally came. His soul had yearned for a cause in which he might sacrifice himself (and, if possible, plenty of others) in blood and smoke, and in which he could bring death to Antichrist by bullet, saber, rifle, bayonet, or pistol. However, the Supreme Being had seen fit to order matters otherwise. Grote was very frail. He had often suffered from keen pains in his lower abdomen. His mother had declared that he was full of wind, or that he was constipated, and had prescribed, to scant effect, violent purges. To scant medical effect, it may be said, but the purges had an immediate effect, and many hours he sat upon the board, perched over the cesspool, crying out at the pain of his evacuations and declaring, between moans, his love of God, his desire to march with John

Brown, his desire to free the slaves, and his desire to die (the last wish had, it is unfortunate to relate, many causes). He was not flippant; he did not dance; his life was one of unremitting seriousness. He was ready for war. He was (if it were not a Roman concept, and therefore detestable) like a monk, ready to devote his total being to the struggle against the powers of darkness. His fury when the federal Army medical officer told him that he was too badly ruptured to serve with the colors knew no bounds; he protested, he wept, he protested again, more vehemently. The doctor was adamant. Grote would be more of an encumbrance than an assistance to the gallant Massachusetts infantry. Indeed, he might, by his sickness, halt the fine strategic plans of Generals McClellan and Pope and thereby give those Southerners an unfair advantage. He claimed that he would march until his guts dropped out onto the road, and fight until his stomach muscles burst—indeed, they had had good practice in the privy. But the medical officer remained adamant. Grote blushed when the women looked at him (he thought accusingly) in the street; he could not bear to watch the town's volunteers march away to join the infantry. When a regiment of New York State cavalry rode through the town he stood on the uneven sidewalk, clenching and unclenching his hands, red with embarrassment and hate and envy and staring at the regimental standard as if it were the cross of Christ himself. (That it truly proved to be when the New York cavalry charged Jackson's position at Fredericksburg. They lost all but a handful of men, and all but one officer.)

The older men in the town were sympathetic to his dilemma. He had disdained work in the bakery—his father did not need his assistance and was embarrassed by his son's enthusiasms. Grote had taken a position in the North Adams bank, for he was not without shrewdness and intelligence; he was merely without good sense. As further men had volunteered, with progressive diminution of enthusiasm, he had supported the cause by writing in the town newspaper. He had rejoiced in the death of Jackson; he had applauded the capture of Vicksburg; he had greeted the victory of Gettysburg with rhetoric more florid, if less memorable, than that of the leader of the federal armies. He was promoted in the bank, for elder men had gone off to fight. He was given the temporary position of chief teller in the bank. It was understood that he would relinquish this when the Rebels were defeated, but the understanding was loose, and, since many of his seniors lay under the earth near Antietam Creek, or at Chancellorsville, on that hill at Gettysburg, or along the Mississippi, it was unlikely that the war would bring him anything but good fortune in the material sense. Yet still he raged; at times he trembled and felt giddy with the intensity of his passion. As he saw the fatherless children he said to himself: I had nothing to lose, I could have died without loss to the world. In his words and his thoughts he was very gallant indeed. In his actions, too, for he kept a Colt by his side in the bank, and when some vagabond had attempted a theft, more foolish than dangerous, he had shot the man dead. He was commended by his superiors, and the town Fathers. In his dreams he saw the man crumble up; he liked to imagine that it was General Lee himself.

Grote was settling down to his meal on 11th November 1863, with some satisfaction. He had retired from the teller's desk in order to enjoy his repast, and was casually watching the few women and the single child who were doing business in the bank while he munched the fresh and salty bread from his father's oven. Curiously, as if by prescience, he did not feel his usual midday somnolence (he was acquiring the habits of middle age very rapidly, as well as the girth). He felt active, ready for anything, even if it was only another hobo who came up with a bearded and sordid face to demand a few dollars and won his death in such a foolish gamble. He heard the clatter of hooves in the street outside; he heard a single shot from a carbine; he heard a cry from a voice that he recognized as that of old Amos Howell, who was on guard outside, because he was fit for nothing else. He saw the doors burst open, and the teller (younger even than Grote) staring at some apparently unearthly apparition that had defeated his expectations and had reversed the possibilities of the universe. Hurriedly swallowing a large piece of bread, although he knew it would cause him much trouble on the privy plank later, he ran forward to the teller's desk and laid his hand on his Colt. He found himself face to face with Antichrist. Antichrist took the shape of a gaunt, fair-haired Confederate officer. Grote had studied the uniforms of the enemy, and he knew that the black plume and black frogging betokened the 1st Virginia Cavalry. Stuart's own regiment! He peered forward and squared his shoulders.

Gervase was glad that only one of the Yankee soldiers had offered any resistance. They were both old men, their hair liberally admixed with gray. But one of them had shown courage and fired at them. He hardly knew how to hold his gun, let alone aim it, and the bullet had flown away into the gray, cloudy sky without doing any harm. Lyon had jumped off his high horse and knocked the man over the head with the stock of his carbine. He collapsed with a moan, blood pouring from the light wound on his scalp, sprawling in an ungainly posture. The other man, uttering a cry that might charitably be interpreted as surprise and more harshly as terror, flung down his weapon and raised his hands as high above his head as the arthritic limbs would permit. Connor controlled the horse, which was jumping from side to side in excitement, with some difficulty, and grinned down at the terrified old man. "Don't worry, Pa," he said, "we won't kill you." The man looked even more terrified as Connor raised his carbine in a mock threatening gesture.

"Cut that out," snapped Gervase. "Tie him up." Connor, who was prepared for this, brought some cord from his saddlebag and expertly trussed the dodderer so that his arms were firmly pinioned behind him. Connor pulled hard at the knots as he fixed them. He had kinsfolk in Vicksburg. The soldiers entered the bank.

"Lyon," said Gervase, "get the president of this place and have him open the vaults." Lyon and Angus moved off; Roscoe stayed with him. Roscoe had his saber lowered. Soon Gervase saw a fat and vapid man moving to the rear of the building, waving his arms in protest—a protest that Lyon's carbine in his ribs adequately stifled. There were few people in the bank: three women, an octogenarian, and one six-year-old boy accompanying an attractive fair-haired woman who was obviously his mother. Gervase had drawn his Le Mat, but he held it down, pointing to the ground. He spoke in the best traditions of southern chivalry —oh yes, a code, but what, he thought, is civilization but a code respected by all? It was no role now, no act, but the reality.

"If you ladies would move over to the wall there, no harm will come to you. Truly. You have my word." The boy started to cry. Gervase looked at him and smiled. This might have been his child and Deborah's. He felt an onrush of tenderness that his duty should have forbidden. "Go on with your mother, son," he said. "I'll tell you what; when you're a man you'll be able to tell your own sons that you saw Jeb Stuart's black horsemen in North Adams. There won't be many that can match that." Curiously, or, in the widest human context, where man contacts man in the reality that words hide, not curiously, the little boy smiled at him. Gervase looked at the teller's desk and spoke more harshly.

"You keep quiet and nothing will happen to you," he said. "Make a move and I'll kill you." He looked at the tellers. One was a very young boy, who was clearly quiescent. The other was only slightly younger than himself. He stared at Gervase through crude spectacles, with a gaze of peculiar intensity, tinting his eyes with a color that might be called violent yellow, but was really nothing but the patina of fanaticism. This man is crazy, thought Gervase. He'll bear watching. He thought his warning worth repeating in personal terms.

"You especially," he said, "keep still." The fat president of the bank had by now opened the vaults, and Gervase could see that Lyon was supervising the loading of sacks with federal notes and gold coin. The myopic teller was still staring at him. "Peckerwood," the teller whispered. "Fucking peckerwood." Gervase was surprised by the language. (Did it indicate courage?) He was no Puritan, no prude, nothing so facile. But he was not used to hearing obscenity used to no purpose. Even when men were held down for the saw they did their best to control their tongues. And he did not understand the word itself. Then he remembered that it was a Yankee term of abuse of southern officers, particularly those southern officers who were supposed to own broad acres and many slaves.

"Keep your mouth clean, Yankee," said Gervase calmly. What had he to do with such as this? He learned very rapidly, when the strange creature produced a Colt automatic and coolly shot the small boy in the chest, and then turned the weapon on two of the women, who screamed at the impact of the heavy bullets and slumped down on the floor, clutching at their shattered lungs. There was only one woman left, and, equally calmly, he shot her. Before he could move from his trance of astonishment Gervase saw Roscoe's saber flash down on the man's gun hand. He saw the bright steel strike the flesh, and heard the crunch as it passed through the bone. The teller let out a piercing scream and watched, in fascination, as his hand left the rest of his body, still gripping the revolver, and fall to the floor as if it had a life of its own. It was grotesque.

"In God's name, why? Why?" cried Gervase, as he strode forward and took the almost fainting man by the scruff of his neck and hauled him up to his eye level. "They're your own people. Why shoot them and not me?" The teller looked at him through the glaze of known extinction and pain and suppressed joy at the achievement he had long yearned for and at last obtained.

"Because now they'll hang you, peckerwood," he whispered. "They'll know you for what you are, a killer of women and kids. A savage. How many slaves did you own, peckerwood?" A red rage grasped Gervase as it had taken Roscoe, and all thought left Gervase; he did not reason, he was merely seized by a passion at the injustice of it all. He raised his Le Mat, stepped back two paces, and pulled the trigger of the buckshot barrel. They spent a good deal of time later scraping Grote off the wall. But the boy and the women were dead. So finally and terribly and unnecessarily dead.

His mind still obscured by contrary passions, Gervase walked over to the bodies, already doll-like in the grotesquerie of death. The small boy had a red smear over his chest (the Colt is a powerful weapon), and the women were in ungainly postures, one leaning as if drunk against the white plaster wall. Gervase leaned down and arranged the corpses, still warm with the fled life, in more decorous position; he pulled the boy close to his mother. The whole incident had lasted only half a minute. Lyon came running from the vault, where he left the others loading the sacks. He paused at the scene before him.

"Jesus, Major, what happened?" Gervase looked up at him, desperately focusing his eyes on the remembered features, forcing himself to recognize that this was Lyon—yes, Lyon—in the hell that had suddenly engulfed him through no volition but that he had caused by his mere presence, allowing an occasion and a motive for irrational feelings to explode with some show of justification.

"That teller shot them," he said simply. Roscoe pointed at the defaced corpse with his saber. Then a snuffling noise came from his side. The old man was cowering away from him. He burst into frenzied pleas.

"Don't shoot me, sir. God, why in hell am I here? I'm only walking out, don't shoot me, let me live." The old man was gray with the fear of death; perhaps in the quietness of his bed he had prepared himself for his end, but he flinched from the reality painted in red about him and the vast and thundering cordite in justice of the world fixed in the symbolic corpse of a boy less than one twelfth his age lying with a trace of the answering smile he had given to Gervase still imprinted upon his lips and his facial muscles, although his eyes were now nothing but polished stones in a wilderness of oblivion.

"You old fool," shouted Gervase, his control loosening, "why should I kill you? You saw what happened. You can tell them. We didn't shoot anyone except the murderer. Your own kind did it."

"I won't tell anyone, sir," sniffed the old man, snuffling, with tears running down his face weatherbeaten and leatherlike through constant exposure to the harsh New England winds and snow and rain. "I swear before the living and the dead—yes, before God himself—I won't tell."

"But I want you to tell everyone," yelled Gervase, taking a step toward him.

"Everyone, everyone, everyone!" He felt a hand at his shoulder and turned to face the eyes of Roscoe filled with that purpose they had had at Manassas, restraining him, recalling him, pointing to the progress that is duty. The old man had backed away with a cry like that of a weasel in agony.

"I won't tell, sir. Believe me, oh believe me, sir." Clearly the old fool was too bemused to think clearly. His only image was of sudden death; he had no idea of responsibility; he would gladly tell the townsfolk whatever lies they wanted to hear, and Gervase knew well enough what that would be. The newspapers of the North would have a day of glory with this information of a brutal massacre. But it was fruitless to try to persuade the man.

He was sick with terror, weeping, and now about to fall at the feet of Roscoe, who kicked him away against the wall. This old man would be pliable to the creation of legend. Then a cry came from within the vault.

"Major, we've got all that we can carry." Lyon and the two others came out, dragging sacks. The sacks containing bullion moved slowly, and were only half full; the horses could not bear the weight of anything like a full sack. The fat president was pushed out at the point of Angus' saber. Gervase looked at him. Then he thought: How can I burn this place down with these bodies here? How can I deny this child burial? How can I char the fresh skin and consume his bones in the great ashpit of Jehoshaphat? I can't. And yet I must, because I am not here to carry southern chivalry into the North but to put their money to fire. Then he saw a solution. In this time, to think was to act.

"You smoke?" he said to the president. The man nodded, bereft of speech by terror. He took out some phosphorous matches. Gervase nodded to Lyon. They had agreed to this plan beforehand. The notes they could not take were scattered over the vault and Angus, helped, good God, by Roscoe, was engaged in tearing papers from the drawers of the large and pretentious desk in the president's sequestered office. The bank was snowed with paper, white and sterile. Gervase took the matches from the man's flabby, wet, and shaking hand and gave them to Lyon, who began to set flame to all the paper he could reach, beginning in the vault and moving backward into the main hall of the bank. Soon the flames were spinning around within the acrid, dense smoke that began to fill the room. The flames had got good hold, for, despite the rain, there was enough wind to fan them. Gervase turned to the president.

"We were going to knock you on the head," he whispered, barely allowing the official to hear in the increasing roar of fire. The fat and florid entrepreneur turned thinner and paler. "But we won't. There are three women and a boy." He pointed. "They were shot by your teller. God knows why. You may know, too. But you have my word that we did not shoot them. Not that you will believe me." Gervase's voice was plangent with bitterness, for who would have doubted his word in the Army of Northern Virginia? "Now, Yankee, you can make a choice. What is more

valuable to you: that this boy and his mother have decent burial,
or that you save your building? If you want to save your building, you'll run for help. If you want to save them, you'll drag
them into the street. You can choose." Gervase could not prevent
a note of compassion creeping into his voice; he did not intend
it, but humanity will out. "Believe me, I did not intend to force
such a choice upon you, sir." He turned to Lyon. "Let's go. Get
them moving." They all hauled sacks toward the door. They had
tied two together so that they might the more easily be thrown
over the horses' backs. The horses were fretting, pawing at the
cobbles as they emerged; the animals smelled fire. A crowd was
gathering—at a safe distance, Gervase observed. A figure in blue
with gold on his shoulders was gesticulating without much
effect. Clearly, his admonitions as to cowardice and exhortations
to heroism were falling on deaf ears. They mounted. Gervase
waved. "This way," he shouted. He pointed to a track that lay toward the mountains from which they had come, but farther to
the south, into the Berkshires rather than the Green Mountains
of Vermont. They clattered off over the slippery cobblestones.
The horses, bearing in some cases the weight of bullion, and in
all cases being tired by the day's activity, did not have that live-
liness they had shown in the morning. Gervase dug his spurs sav-
agely into his mare's flanks. They had already traveled about a
hundred yards and Gervase glanced back to see the fat president
run out of the bank wildly crying and waving his arms as if
pursued by all the demons of Stuart and Mosby and Lee painted
by the imagination of Harriet Beecher Stowe. The old man staggered after him, holding his hands to his mouth, until, overcome
by the effort of restraint, he leaned over on the cobbles and
vomited with feeble jerks. Then Gervase turned back to face his
front, when Roscoe's horse collapsed, its hooves shod badly, or
more likely worn through the long tracking, losing their purchase
on the slippery pavement.

"Take them on, Lyon," shouted Gervase. "Get them into the
hills. At least up to the tree line." Lyon was a good soldier and
he did not hesitate or pause or argue, as he might well have
done, but with a gesture and a shout drove the men onward. Lexy held the standard high. Meaning what, what, what?
The boy's body must be charred gray ash by now. Gervase

pulled up his horse and ran back the few feet to Roscoe, who was white as the chalk cliffs they had ridden past and the sweat stood out in drops from his forehead. The horse was bellowing, and urine and feces were pouring from it. Its leg was broken, and the gray-white bone protruded from the flesh and skin and jet-black hairs. Roscoe was trapped under the animal. Gervase pulled at the reins, but the horse resisted him with its head. It could not move its body. Roscoe could not speak, but he gestured to Gervase's Le Mat. He gestured with passion and urgency. Gervase ignored him and hauled at the dead weight of horseflesh. He could do nothing. Roscoe attempted to pull the Le Mat from the holster, and Gervase knew what he meant. Roscoe had always been kind to horses. He pulled out the gun, put it to the horse's head, and pulled the trigger. It was messy, and both men were spattered with blood and brains. The horse shuddered compulsively several times and then lay still with the occasional jerk of the leg, and so trapped Roscoe even more decisively under its weight. Gervase tried to lift the horse bodily. He could not. Roscoe was pushing him away, whistling, gurgling in his urgency. He waved to the hills, he punched Gervase. He even spat at him. Gervase felt the tears on his cheeks.

Gervase looked up and saw that the bluecoated officer had at last succeeded in moving a substantial body of men into Main Street. Cautiously, they were edging along the walls toward them. There was a report, and Gervase heard the bullet sing away far above him, but he knew that they would soon be within range, and however incompetent they might be as marksmen, they could hardly miss him eventually. Roscoe was going frantic in his efforts to get Gervase to leave him. Pain was crisscrossing Roscoe's face and bending his features.

"Listen, Roscoe, listen to me," said Gervase. "You are in uniform. There's a Yankee officer down there. Surrender to him. Raise your hands." He leaned down and took Roscoe's hand in his own. "God be with you, Roscoe. Nothing turned out as we expected, did it? But I don't think our kin need to be ashamed of us. Good-bye, good-bye." He pressed the fingers. Then he stood up, regardless of the futile bullets winging about, and saluted Roscoe. It was not an empty gesture. Into the movement of his arm went their youth and adolescence and tormented manhood.

Gervase kept his fingers at the brim of his gray hat and paused a
second in a respect that transcended pain and suffering and separation and the silence of the past weeks. Then reality hurtled
between them and he turned and ran for his horse and swung up
and drove the mare forward to the group that was disappearing
upward as the horses clambered up the slope in that ungainly
fashion horses have when they are faced with this difficult feat
and especially when the wet surface and clinging mud make
them slither backward recovering themselves and then try again
and yet again under the jabbing impetus of spurs pushed without compassion and without feeling for the horseflesh which
bleeds beneath the steel. Gervase got to the edge of the town,
where his men waited. They were above the houses and near the
tree line. They were safe from pursuit unless the Yankees had
cavalry, which clearly they did not. The large bank was burning
fiercely; the flames leaped with delight high into the gray air,
and the black smoke drifted over the town, darkening the whole
place. Various futile efforts were being made to organize fire-
fighting parties, and a curious engine had been trundled, by
hand, to the disintegrating building. But nothing could save this
bank.

Good, God-fearing, churchgoing, regular communicants came
up to Roscoe. They were led by an officer of the Army of the
United States of America. Roscoe threw away his saber (they
could see it clearly) and indicated by the language of gesture
(for he had no voice, no voice Roscoe) his surrender to this
officer and gentleman, who chose to turn idiot and deny understanding. The fat president, now florid again and newly valorous,
was shouting about money and murder, in that order. So his sensibility was arranged. A woman noted for her godliness leaned
down maternally and spat in Roscoe's face. Another, with quiet
deliberation, took off her hat. It seemed an absurd action. As
Roscoe lay under his horse, a boy from Virginia who had answered the trumpet what seemed centuries ago, she removed the
pin from her prim bonnet and stuck the pin in his face up to
about three inches' penetration. She had aimed for his left eye.
There were calls for a rope. Willing hands pulled the horse off
Roscoe, no burden now, and his crushed and torn ligaments were
exposed to sight. His spleen was ruptured; his left thigh was bro-

ken. A ginger-haired man emerged from a saddlery carrying a hempen rope. Ungentle hands picked up Roscoe and hauled him along the street, jolting his broken bones, which grated against each other, until they reached a warehouse, where there was a pulley for bringing up the sacks of wheat and corn. They threw up the rope to a grinning man, and he fixed it to the pulley. A noose was quickly tied and fixed around Roscoe's neck. They pulled him up and clutched at his feet. He was strangled. He turned blue. His tongue stuck out in the ugliness of death, dark purple with thick blood. The Presbyterian minister jerked at his legs, calling on the Lord.

Gervase pulled at his saber and turned his horse back down the hill. He felt Lyon's hand on the bridle. He hit at Lyon's gloved hand with his fist, beating at the massive limb. Lyon did not let go.

"Leave me, leave, Christ blast you," cried Gervase. "He saved my life at Manassas. He was brother to me. Let me die with him. Oh Christ, Lyon, let me die with him." Lyon hung on, and the others clustered around Gervase so that he could not return to North Adams and could not see the puppet on a rope, around which the assembled congregation were singing "The Battle Hymn of the Republic" with fervor. Lyon put his arm around Gervase's shoulder, and Gervase buried his face in the tunic of the big man. Gervase's sobs brought hot tears, and his shoulders shook.

"There weren't nothing you could do, Major," said Lyon. "Nothing at all." He stared down toward the town. "Fucking Yankee bastards," he said. Lexy lowered the standard. They stayed motionless for a moment, then turned toward the dark wood.

On that same day, November 11th, 1863, Union forces under the command of General Philip Sheridan, erstwhile merchant, pursuing the avowed policy of President Abraham Lincoln, devastated certain areas in the state of Mississippi. Many farms and houses were burned to the ground, and, as an accidental side result, ninety-three civilians were killed, among them twenty-seven children. Several soldiers of the federal forces were captured by the cavalry of the Confederacy; many more fell into the hands of groups of homeless civilians. None were harmed, and all were handed over to the regular forces of the Confederate States of America.

The farmers in Massachusetts had foretold that it would be a very hard winter. They were adept at reading the signs. They saw the amimals building their shelters earlier than usual; the birds who migrated South started almost three weeks before their accustomed time; flocks of them departed, wheeling in great clouds of black spots over the heads of the anxious peasants below. Prudent men searched the woods for extra stocks of timber. Weak places in the clapperboard houses were repaired; the windows in log cabins were covered carefully to keep out the prying winds and the clawing storms. Snow normally comes to Massachusetts toward the end of November. In 1863 it came early, melted, came again, left the ground flecked, and then returned with fury on December 15, in the evening hours. It began to snow lightly at about one o'clock. The light rain from the gray clouds gave way to swirling gusts of wet-blown snow, which fell from yellow-dirty clouds. Under this sudden natural onslaught the citizens of North Adams swiftly forgot the excitements of the day. They would, of course, be living with the effects for some time, since their bank had been burned to the ground. Nevertheless, they were (rightly) convinced that the federal government would recompense them in the light of their heroic actions —after all, unarmed townsfolk, merchants, ministers, schoolteachers, and the like had dispatched a fully armed Confederate cavalry officer (oh yes, they found out that he was Captain Stedman). The federal officer's report prudently abstained from mentioning the injuries Roscoe had incurred in falling from his horse. General Pope, in good odor again, had sent this report to the President himself, with the scrawled comment, "This is true bravery!" The President had agreed, and had said, with his gnarled solemnity, to the full Cabinet: "With the help of God himself, the people of this small town gathered, and, while showing great restraint, dealt out a righteous vengeance unto those who had brought murder and rapine to the place of their quiet and industrious labor." And, at the presidential request, the Cabinet remained in silent prayer for several minutes. Poor Roscoe did not merit the calculated rhetoric of Gettysburg.

These future events did not and obviously could not affect Gervase as he led his men upward and ever upward into the black density of the Berkshires, the men turning their faces aside from the whip of the jagged snowflakes. Gervase had memorized the map, but it was difficult to see even ten paces in front of him. And the snow obscured the tracks. They might be there, or there, or there. His eyes ached as he peered into the closely knit trees— far more closely bound together than the trees on the Green Mountains of Vermont, which they had known hitherto. The men made a sight that could not even attain the pathetic grandeur of a small patrol winding its way over the snow. They had disappeared from the sight of anyone except someone within ten paces of them. And even then it was possible to miss the way. Above the wind, Gervase called out:

"Lyon, where's Angus?" Lyon repeated the question to Connor, and he to Lexy. Angus had disappeared. His horse had padded away, silently, ghostlike, disappearing into the halls of white darkness. Real darkness visible.

"No," said Gervase, "we can't look for him. If we scatter we're all done for. Yes, Connor, I know he was your man. A Carolina man. If you want to go, I won't stop you. But you'd better not. He may meet us, join up again. Stragglers do."

"Angus ain't a straggler," shouted Connor. He needed to shout above the wind.

"I know he isn't," said Gervase, "but he's straggled, poor Angus." And that left the four of them. They padded on. To what? thought Gervase.

"Do you reckon we're on the right track, Major?" asked Lyon.

"I reckon so," replied Gervase. He could not justify himself now, even to Lyon. Gervase was so weary, with a deep wariness he saw reflected back at him from the eyes of Lyon. The cold was unnerving them. It had been cold in Delaware in the spring, but never this cold. The bitterness of a Virginia winter was nothing like this. It froze the blood and the bone marrow. But soon he should come upon a farmhouse—the last habitation before he turned South to Tannery Falls (so called, Harris had told him,

because, obviously enough, there had been a tannery there in the
old Colonial days). Two hours' riding in normal conditions, and
they had been riding four hours now. The trees enclosed them
claustrophobically. They yearned for a plateau, for some open
country. And suddenly the farmhouse was upon them. Dim
lights glimmered, and they could hear the lowing of cattle.

"We turn South here," said Gervase. And as they began their
wheel, a harsh New England voice rang out from the house,
muffled by the snow, but discernible in the harsh precision of its
twang.

"Who the hell's there? I got you covered with two barrels of
buckshot whoever you are, so you'd better not move." Gervase
turned warily toward the voice. It rang out again, the choked
threat covering fear.

"Don't you come no nearer."

"Listen, mister," replied Gervase, "I've twenty soldiers with me
here, and unless you tell me where I am, and shut your mouth,
I'll hang you from this tree here and burn your house." He
would, too, damn him. There was a silence. Then came a flash,
followed by a crack; then, incredibly, the fool fired the second
barrel.

Gervase saw Lyon look steadily to his front and put his hand
up to his chest and feel the red mush before he heeled over to the
side and hung from his horse by the right foot, twisted around.
The horse gave little nervous movements, and Lyon's great head
shuffled in the snow. Christ, would it never end? The second barrel had taken Connor, by the man's infernal luck straight in the
head, frontal. The skin was splayed out and the eyes were unsee-
ing and Connor screamed and screamed as he tore at the horse's
mane in his death agony. The horse, maddened, galloped off into
the darkness, and they heard it crashing through the trees, and
Connor's cries dying away into the night. Before he could do
anything, even draw his saber (which was his first thought and
would have been useless anyway) or his Le Mat, Gervase
saw Lexy fling himself off his horse and kick open the door of the
farmhouse and rush into the dimly lighted house. Gervase leaped
down and followed. As he framed himself in the door, the scene
was etched in a silence of terrifying stillness. A Yankee farmer,
about fifty, was lying on the wooden floor with blood on his

scalp. At the back of the single-roomed cabin crouched his wife, clutching two small girls to her, who were silent with an incredulous terror, for to them the greatest fear of their lives had been Dad when he said he'd give them a whipping with the birch twigs. Then movement began. Lexy was shivering uncontrollably. He put the barrel of his carbine against the forehead of the farmer, and his finger tightened on the trigger. *Oh let him, let him,* thought Gervase; *let him deny all we have fought for, and what Roscoe and thousands more died to prevent. No, I can't let him. I want to see this bastard dead, but I can't let him. Lexy had lost moral control.*

"Stop it, Lexy," said Gervase quietly.

"Keep out of this, Major," said Lexy. His features were delicate, like those of an aesthete created by Edgar Allan Poe. But there was resolution there, a resolution bred of his first real contact with the abattoir of uncontrolled battle. *And what would Robert Lee do with this situation, pray? Lexy had seen death, and he was going to deal it out. All can play at God.*

"Lexy. I said stop it. Stop it, or by God I'll shoot you myself. Did Lyon die for you to kill farmers?"

"Lyon *was* a farmer, Major," replied Lexy, turning agonized eyes on Gervase. "He didn't want no war. He wanted to be with his wife and his kids and his horses. Like this bastard here." He prodded the recumbent farmer with his carbine. One of the girls began to cry. She wailed in a high-pitched voice, wailed with hysterical terror. These were the devils in gray about which she had heard, and for whose defeat she prayed every night. And they had her daddy on the floor. "Listen to that, Lexy. Do you want that?" Lexy let his shoulders sag. He handed his carbine to Gervase.

"I guess I don't, Major. I guess I don't want anything anymore. I just want to sleep. Like I did when I was a kid." *Is all happiness in the past? Must it be there, where we cannot touch it, cannot grasp it ever again?* Without another word he went out. Gervase did not even hear his horse as it moved away. *Lexy would be white bones in the woods by the springtime. He wouldn't grow with the plants. Who would?* Gervase turned to the woman, who held her children like a frightened partridge.

"You will observe, ma'am," he said with great bitterness, "that

this brutal officer of the Confederate Army prevented one of his
soldiers from shooting your husband. You will further observe
that your husband had, without warning, and without provocation, shot two of my soldiers, who were my dear friends, and that
by the laws of warfare and by the civil law of decent nations,
your husband deserved to be hanged for murder." Gervase could
feel his voice trembling with indignation, fury, all the accumu-
lated terrors and anxieties of the day. That thin, godly face as it
concentrated its efforts on pulling Roscoe's legs. Oh Jesus. The
farmer was shaking his head to recover himself as he looked at
Gervase, not understanding, trying to grasp the inexplicable
chain of cause and effect that brought a soldier in gray to his
cabin on the first night of the great snow. His face was bemused,
silly in bemusement; it had that peculiar stupidity that mingled a
lack of intelligence with a disarrangement of whatever limited
faculties had been there originally. Yet he was the father of these
two girls. Lyon had been a father; Connor too. Lexy was too
young. Angus was close: He didn't know. Neither he nor Roscoe
had been permitted by the times to beget children. An excuse?
Oh, but much better that way. This Yankee fool probably
thought they were bandits, robbers, out to rape his wife and kill
his children. Gervase could feel the fear coming out of the man
like the smell of sweat. His own saliva was bitter within his
mouth. He could hear his own heart pounding with the effort of
self-control. Did they all think it was easy not to kill and maim?
The wound in his finger throbbed; he had been in the saddle for
so long, how long, God knew. His crotch ached. He walked over
to the man, picked him up, and steadied him against the wall.

"You have just killed a soldier of the Confederacy," he said.
"Two of them, to be exact. If this had been battle, you would
have been shot yourself by now. If this had been peace you
would have been hanged, for they did nothing to harm you. But
go down to North Adams and tell those godly citizens that General Lee's soldiers do not kill civilians, and never, never kill
women and children, whatever the provocation. And tell that
gang of murdering Yankees that we are only men. Whatever our
enemies make of us, we are only men, I tell you. Think of those
soldiers outside. They had families, had children. You give them
burial. Give me that in return for your life, which I am giving

you. Because, believe me, Yank, they didn't want to die any more
than you do." Gervase smashed his gauntleted fist twice into the
man's face; the gauntlet came away bright red with blood. The
man sank to the ground and the woman looked an appeal. "Oh
go to him," he said. She ran forward and began to wipe his face
with her blue calico dress. Gervase desperately wanted to be understood. It was a pain within him. He looked at the girls, who
cowered. He smiled. They cowered more. "When you grow up,
don't forget. Tell them all that Major Stepton didn't kill your
daddy. And, ma'am, tell them that he wanted to kill him. Very
badly." Gervase turned to the door and walked out into the
snow; he felt the hatred of the woman strike him in the back like
a bullet. She had understood nothing.

He called out the names of his men, but the wind flung back
the words, and the snow muffled his cries. In a primitive panic
he pushed his horse forward, digging his spurs into the tired
flanks. He moved only in tantalizing circles. The soldiers must be
lost in the woods, too; all of them racing around in futile circles,
crying like children for companionship, crying in vain. And he
had failed them; if he had kept better discipline, if he had kept
them bunched together, if he had not given way to anger, then
they might have held their ranks, supporting and comforting
each other as the Yankee winter hurled itself upon them. But
now they were destined to wander alone to a solitary death, to
topple from the saddle in hopeless weariness, and curl up in
some declivity like a woodchuck and wait for the paralysis and
the cold to numb them into death. After some time—What was
it? An hour? Two hours?—he gave up the search and let his
horse stumble onward, feeling his cold saber rest against his
thigh and the two books flap in his pocket.

In a futile gesture he reached up to his shoulders and ripped
away his badges of rank. He could no longer regard himself as
an officer of the Confederacy. Whether he had deserted his men,
or they him, no longer mattered. He returned to the great booming solitary world of his childhood.

12

One Impulse from a Winter Wood

Gervase found Tannery Falls the next day, when some sort of light came. He was leading his horse through the dense trees when the small stream he was following disappeared, very suddenly, from sight. It appeared to plunge downward to nowhere. But, having tethered his mare, neighing its protests, to a branch hanging low and weighted with snow, Gervase followed the stream himself. Frequently his boots slipped on the ice which covered the rocks like a patina of paint. Once he slipped twenty feet or more, vainly grabbing at tufts of vegetation, roots and thin branches from the bushes. He was struck sharply on the kneecap, and on the elbow, and he sat on a crude ledge—more of a pause in the precipitate descent—and nursed himself. He wanted to vomit, but he could not, since there was nothing in his stomach. He glanced upward and then, with sudden vertigo, downward. It would be easier to go down. He scrambled on, and reached a natural enclosure. Here two rivers, quite frozen, met. One came from above in the great fall, about two hundred feet of what would in warmer weather be cascading water but now held in a solid motion which suggested energy but did not move. Exploring to his right he found that the other little river led to another waterfall, smaller, indeed only about thirty feet, but sheer rock. This was not lighted at all; even in the summer it must be hidden from the sun, and the very ice was black and the snow shadowed dark.

He could not go on, so here he might as well stay. He would

be sheltered from the winds at least. There were trees enough to build himself a shelter. Life had once been a value to him, but he could see that it was to continue being an exercise. He could not explain to himself why he wanted to go on living. It would be so easy merely to lie down on the snow and surrender himself to sleep. In his exhaustion and emaciation it would come soon enough, and he knew that he would never wake up. He would drift off; it would be very cold for a time, but then his nerves would become numbed, and his feelings would sleep, too. No more images, no more guilt. At least, he had shed responsibility!

He heard a movement in the bracken, which was hard and brittle with frost. His fingers fell to his Le Mat and he drew the weapon. He held it very clumsily, because he found it difficult to bend his fingers. They were not yet frostbitten, but they were well on the way. A woodchuck came out of the bracken toward the water. He had thought somehow that they hibernated during the winter. Perhaps they did; perhaps he was mistaken. At all events he would not want for food, though fire would be a problem he would soon have to face. He put the barrel against his left arm, and took careful aim. The backsight came up into alignment with the foresight and the woodchuck flashed into focus at the proper distance. His finger began to tighten around the trigger. He waited for the crash himself. But then he realized that he could not kill the animal. It was not entirely physical, though his finger ached even from this tiny effort. It was moral. He would never kill again. And, after all, he was the intruder here. The woodchuck had rights of territory. Just as they had rights of territory when the Army of the Potomac came South. The woodchuck could not shoot him, but he wasn't going to employ Yankee methods.

He sat down on the snow and laughed, hysterically. Here he was in a northern wood, determined to live, and to live he needed food, and he refused the most obvious source of food because he thought it immoral to kill. He laughed again and the sound echoed in the frozen gulf. The echo was curious: it went up the great falls, and then darted round the corner to the sheer face. So there were three voices together in the rocky basin at the foot of the falls. This country must have some influence, Gervase thought. His mind moved slowly. He found it difficult to form his thoughts. Where had he read this stuff about not killing and not eating animals before? Of course, John Brown's friend, the bean-eater Thoreau. Well, that was a turnaround.

The woodchuck came up to a tiny hole in the ice and drank noisily. It kept shooting suspicious glances at Gervase from its hot little eyes. He beckoned to the beast, but it made no movement to him. Damn it, he thought, this isn't a dog at Sweetwater. It's a Yankee woodchuck. He rose, and the animal turned tail and rushed back into the wood, bashing aside the bracken and making a hell of a noise as it went back to its warm lair. He was alone again.

But he wasn't, as he soon realized. Though most of the animals might be hibernating, plenty were not. Trees were not exactly infested with birds, but the odd call echoed and replied. Gervase had been adept as a boy at imitating bird calls. He tried now. He couldn't quite catch the rise and fall, the exact pitch. He sat on a mound of snow, no, it was a softly rounded rock covered with snow, and continued to try. After about five minutes he was rewarded with a silence. Into the silence he threw his own call. There was a reply. He replied himself. Another reply came from behind him. It "meant" nothing, of course; he knew that. But it also "meant" something. It meant that he had established a community.

He looked up the falls. He could never get the mare down. She was half lame and tired. She could never get down; it would be condemning her to broken bones and screams and discordant lack of harmony. After a time, however, he wondered whether he would ever get up again himself. His boots kept slipping. He could not leave the course of the water entirely, for the undergrowth was so thick that it was like a stout fence to keep him out, to test him, to force him into the most difficult ways. But about halfway up he found some berries. They were of a sort that he had never seen in Virginia. He did not know whether they were poisonous or not, but he took the chance. They tasted delicious, something like an apple, more bitter, true, but with a subtle, haunting suspicion of some herb too. They gave him some strength—not physically, he supposed, but mentally; he imagined that he had been sustained. As he neared the top of the rocky face he determined to act with speed and without thought. He was being illogical, he knew, after his deliberations below. But he had no fodder. He could not turn the horse loose, for she would only wander to her death. He came over the top and saw the great bulb eyes of the mare staring at him in terror as if she had followed his thoughts all the way. He drew his Le Mat and shot her expeditiously. She collapsed with hardly a whimper, and the birds rose from the trees with a cackle. There was scampering in the undergrowth. Away from him. Could he not have lived upon berries? Yes, he could. But what could he have done with the horse? It was an act of mercy, he told himself. Only mercy.

He had a knife in his saddlebag, and he took it out to cut the flesh of the horse into manageable proportions so that he could take the pieces down the falls. The hot blood flowed red, and he drank it. The taste was salty, but otherwise quite neutral. He felt no revulsion; indeed, he seemed to be looking at himself from a distance, hovering above himself like his own ghost. And why should he not drink the blood? It was the last service the mare could do for him. And wasn't this what communion in that little white church in Malvern Hills was all about? Yet he could not imagine his mother seeing the transformation of the decorous priest carrying the wafers on sacrament Sunday transformed into this dark-stubbled creature in a wood of which she had never heard. He wiped the congealing fluid from his mouth with the back of his hand, and as he looked down at the gouts of red, his gorge began to rise. Yet it soon sank again. All he wanted now was calmness.

He left half of the meat at the top. If the animals took it, so much the worse. He calculated that, with berries and the flesh he could drag behind him, he could last the winter. He could not face going down and coming up again that day. If ever. When the spring came he would follow the river as it moved southeast. He strapped his carbine over his back and pushed his scabbarded saber down his trousers. That was going to be difficult, but he needed the weapon to cut wood for his shelter. He thrust his map beneath his greatcoat and filled all his pockets with ammunition. He filled a saddlebag too. Why? He had eschewed

killing, hadn't he? And then killed his horse. Well, that was the
sort of contradiction he might have to resolve in the coming
months.

The blood had given him strength, and though he still found
the descent difficult, it was not the exquisite torment it had been
the first time, weighted though he now was. He did not realize
how slowly all his limbs were moving, as if he were a very old
and very sick man. Indeed, he had grown so used to deprivation
that he found it difficult to describe symptoms of illness to himself, or even recognize them. He could hear the strokes of his
heart, and feel the blood as it flowed through his ankles; he
would feel sudden shooting pains in his head and think that he
was losing consciousness; he found it both painful and difficult to
breathe, and often he had a sharp, stabbing pain in his left side,
sometimes over the heart itself, and sometimes under it to the
left. For months he had concealed this from his men. They had
to think him in perfect health, or their very solicitude might destroy his determination. Now he had nobody to pretend to but
himself. And why should he pretend to himself? Because he had
been afraid of dying, and he found that he was no longer afraid
of dying. He had long ago concluded that men are not afraid of
death, but of dying. They are afraid of the saber blows, the bullets, the fragments of metal, the creeping diseases, the cancer,
the fever of childbed, the stroke in the head, the claws of angina.
They are afraid of disgracing themselves by fear in the face of
pain, by cowardice. Here he could not disgrace himself, for there
was no one to watch him, to give him that close scrutiny Thomas
Jackson flashed over an assembled company. Unless the ghosts of
Deborah and his father and his mother were flitting about this
little womb of rock in which he had taken up his watch? They
would not judge him harshly. And they weren't there. He had no
companions. That is why death itself is not fearful: It is oblivion.

He rested when he reached the bottom. Then he counted his
ammunition, gently turning over the little snub-nosed bullets
that could smash a man's flesh to pulp. He had twenty-three bullets for his Le Mat and ninety-seven shells for his carbine. He
would need them to make fire. When his limbs ached a little less
he picked up his saber. He walked over to a rock and hacked
away the ice with the pommel. Then he sharpened the blade. He

needed to repeat that many times before he had finished, for the blade was not designed to cut through wood but through clothes and flesh. He hacked at the branches, carefully selecting some thick supports, and then many thinner stems, so that he could weave them together into a close texture. He and Roscoe had made such houses in Virginia when they were boys. They had spent many a summer day doing so, while their two dogs had bounded about them. Gervase had a bitch; she was more obedient than Roscoe's male. What were their names? He screwed up his face in an effort to remember. But he could not. He could remember Roscoe, though. He could remember him as a ten-year-old boy better than at the moment of his death. When was that? Yesterday? The day before? Before that? He had not lost his sense of time, but it no longer came to him in linear sequence. Images from different years arranged themselves in a pattern, which was, he supposed, a pattern of significant feeling, not just this then that then that and then that. It hurt him to try to make the conventional order, so he gave up trying. He never tried again.

He needed fire. He sat in front of his shelter and tried to think of a way to make fire. He knew that the rubbing of sticks only works in the summer, when the wood is dry. He had to have a flame to start the fire off. He felt in his pocket and took out his two books. His small Bible, which his mother had given to him. He put that back in his pocket. And Emerson's "Nature." He looked around him at the trees and ice and snow and bracken and listened to the voices of the objects and the animals and the birds. Well, he didn't need any philosopher to tell him what it all meant. He would find that out for himself without help from Cambridge or Concord. He noticed that his hands were bleeding from his work with the branches and that he had lost the nail from the little finger of his right hand. Pinkie. Does the pinkie hurt? the nurse had said to him. Yes, Mammy Caller, yes, my pinkie hurts. At least he didn't have the second finger on his left hand to lose the nail. He looked at his disfigurement, and the deep shame he had felt about it for years melted away. As the snow did not melt. He began to tear up Ralph Waldo Emerson's "Nature" carefully, page by page.

He laid down a neat framework of branches, which he rubbed

as dry as possible. He then put twenty pages of Platonism on the
wood and picked up his carbine. He fired four shots as quickly
as he could into the pile. Much of the paper was blown away,
but a tiny flame from the heat caught at one sheet. He knelt
down and put others to the flames. Flame begot flame, and he
thought he might risk a piece of wood. For a moment he thought
it might have extinguished the fire, but it didn't, and, with some
hissing, it began to burn too, and then he put more paper on the
fire, and more wood, and after ten minutes or so he had a merry
blaze, which was as well, because night was beginning to fall.

The berries and blood and horseflesh had worked through him
and he felt the need to evacuate. He left the fire and walked to
the edge of the clearing. He was very fastidious. He had always
been fastidious, he thought, as he hitched up his greatcoat and
lowered his trousers. When he had been about fifteen some of
the boys in the county had fucked their way through every black
girl they could find, scattering mulattoes like corn broadcast.
Even Roscoe had not remained chaste. Gervase had; he had been
beguiled by the pure idea of southern womanhood, beguiled into
a self-denying chastity. Or was it beguilement? Perhaps he had
been right and they wrong; they certainly had talked of a sacred
affection with coarseness and brutality. But they had something
to look back on, and he had nothing. His sex at fifteen had been
furtive and private, and all his reward had come in the public
accolades he heard given to him for his propriety and virtue. His
rump was cold, and he could smell himself. Think: Those were
living berries and that was a living horse only eight hours ago.
To think so was to consider too curiously. Now, where had he
heard that?

He was in the utmost dark; the fire shed its glow about ten
yards away upstream. Suddenly he noticed two red eyes staring
at him out of the darkness, and, as he stilled his own breathing,
he heard little pants. He wondered what it was—a fox, he supposed, with a gray coat that they called white, because it was
winter. He pulled his clothing straight as gently as he could, and
then looked at the eyes. "Hey, hey!" he said. He needed the companionship, even of an animal, though he knew foxes were very
remote and timorous creatures. "Hey!" he said again, softly, trying to insinuate himself into the animal's confidence. He had

been good with the wild ones in his youth. The trick was not to move, not to raise the voice; to be infinitely patient. Well, perhaps not infinitely, but extremely so. The red eyes were still fixed on him, but moved a little nearer, not changing their angle. He heard the pad of paws and the tiny crack of a light stick. He kept on speaking, softly, meaningless words. He even sang some tuneless song in the lowest register he could manage. Finally, as his leg muscles were about to give way, the fox sidled into his sight. They gazed at each other. Slowly Gervase lowered his hand. No quick movements; nothing untoward; nothing to scare the creature. Suddenly the pale gray fox darted forward and sank its sharp teeth in Gervase's left hand. The hot breath covered his flesh. The teeth, like fresh nails, penetrated the skin and flesh, and the blood flowed. It hurt. The fox turned tail and with a flicker of the bush ran out of sight. Gervase heard it retreating for some time.

Gervase made his way back to the fire, and sat down. He tore off a part of his shirt at the bottom and wrapped the linen around his hand. It throbbed, but he was so used to throbbing in his left hand by now that he hardly noticed it. He was determined not to contemplate cause and effect. He knew well enough, but he forced it down. No. That was the sort of hypocrisy he was done with forever. He stared into the fire, the red ash lying at the center, the flames creeping along the wood that would soon itself be ash and go into the ground and make it fertile and help the bracken to grow and that would grow and then fall and rot and the cycle would go on and on. He did not blame the fox. Why should he? It was entranced by the unknown, and then frightened. It responded as it knew how. It was three to one that the beast was rabid. He lay down, his head resting on his saddlebag, and soon slept.

Gervase fixed a routine for himself. He learned, after a few mistakes, exactly how much wood to keep on the fire at night and how much he needed in the morning. He hacked a hole in the ice to draw up clear water to drink with his roasted horseflesh and red berries. He would sit for hours by the side of his fire with his greatcoat wrapped around him, and after a day or two the birds began to hop around to pick up scraps of his discarded food. Even the woodchuck came back once or twice. But mostly

Gervase liked to look at the birds, to trace their patterns in the snow, to talk to them. At first they flew away, shocked, frightened, but soon they saw that when he made noises he was not going to hurt them.

And this was a fine time to put his thoughts in order, to sit by the fire and meditate on the great matters that afflict humanity, to define duty and courage to himself, to understand love and hate, to contemplate what makes one man greater than another, what gives one man the power to endure where another will give way; to consider why men weep, and why they laugh; to scrutinize the difference between himself and the woodchuck and the birds; to search for God. He thought of discussing these topics with himself, but rejected the idea. He emptied himself of all thought. He sat by his fire and tried to think of nothing; or, if he did think, it was to summon an image and not to fuss about it and seek the whys and wherefores, just to live with the image itself. The issues of the war seemed futile, while his picture of Robert Lee did not. He allowed himself only one thought. He realized that during his life he had used, both in public and private language, the word "seemed" a great deal. It was as if he had been preparing himself for this moment. Everything that he had committed himself to was "seeming"; not merely a man like Harris. And Harris lived centuries ago.

It was New Year's Day 1864. Gervase woke up, feeling rather more cramped than usual. The frost had traced its delicate patterns in the trees, pieces of natural lace surpassing human ingenuity yet the result of nothing but chance. He threw some wood on the fire and walked over to his waterhole. He knelt down and lowered his hand into the water and brought it up to his lips. Involuntarily he spat it out. It was scalding; more, it was filled with writhing worms that had little faces and made as if to bite him. He thought that some of the worms were in his mouth, and he twisted his right forefinger about his teeth and tongue, scraping them off him. But he could not. They swam about his mouth and slid down his throat and whirled about in his stomach, biting at the walls. He fell to the ground and beat his fist against the snow. The worms multiplied within him. Already there must be thousands in his stomach. His stomach was bursting. They came out through his penis, hot and malevolent. They

were in his bowels. He pulled himself to his feet. He had to wash
them out with clean, cold water. But no water was clean and
cold. The worms swam in the stream, large and gleaming like sea
snakes.

Suddenly something hit him in the side of the head. He heeled
over. He got up again, and his legs buckled under him. He
crawled about by the stream. He had to have water. He would
die without water. His arms failed to support him and he lay on
the snow, moving in tiny little shoves from his boots. He began
to eat the snow, but that, too, was full of worms and had grown
hot too. He had never known hot snow before. He forced himself
to stand up. Now the strength came back to his legs. He ran
about in little circles. He ran up the dark creek and tried to
climb the sheer black face of the rock. He kept trying to get a
foothold and kept falling back and slipping down on the ice.
When he had failed for the seventh time he started to hit his
head against the black rock, and he cut his cheeks to ribbons. He
could hear the noises he was making, as if he were distant from
them. He flung himself into the trees and beat a way through the
undergrowth, his hands shredded. He was like an ape, curling up
and stretched out. He could feel his back arching. If only he
could have some water to cool him down. But no water came.
Instead, his flesh burst into flame as if it were hot coal in a steel
furnace. He tried to pat out the flames, but he could not; he tried
harder, punching his flesh with all his strength with clenched
fists. All his body bent to his blows, bruised, cut, agonized. If
only he could have water, he thought, as he heeled over in a
faint, his body exhausted, flaked out, done, smashed.

When he came out of the faint he felt like a baby, helpless. He
could hardly move a limb. The worms had gone; the coals were
extinguished, but he knew that they would soon come to life and
light again. He pulled himself up with the help of a smooth-
barked tree. He fixed his eyes on his fire and walked toward it. It
was as if he were drunk. He swayed, and his footsteps made an
irregular pattern in the snow. He kept falling to his knees and
trying to pick himself up. Finally he stopped trying and staggered on all fours toward his fire. He could feel the worms stirring again. His eyes no longer functioned, and the landscape
whirled around in cavorting circles. He vomited onto the white

snow, and the mess lay yellow and smoking. He crawled through it, smearing his gray greatcoat. Finally he reached the fire and flopped down, exhausted. He was not going to die of rabies. He had seen a black die of rabies. He was not going to let that happen to him. He fumbled at the holster in which he kept his Le Mat. He forced his eyes to concentrate as he checked that the chamber was full. He put the barrel into his mouth until he felt it touch the roof of the mouth itself. He licked the cold metal and pulled the trigger. He heard the hammer descending and the click of contact. Then there was a mere click.

The revolver had misfired, which was curious, since it was a most dependable weapon. Providence had taken a hand somewhere. Gervase was suspicious of Providence, but she, he, it clearly meant him to die of the wound rather than by his own hand. Perhaps, after all, he would not die of the wound. You can't recover from rabies, but, he told himself wryly, you can be mistaken in your diagnosis. He smiled, and slipped once more into a faint. This time he was vouchsafed no mystical vision, just a wet, cold emergence, and what seemed to be an old prophet, bearded, gaunt, sitting on a stump holding a gun that might easily be turned on him. Was this a vision? It spoke, which intimated an auditory reality.

"How long have you been here?" The vowels were long drawls. A Yankee clear enough. There was that clipped assurance to the voice as well; individuality and self-confidence, they called it. The man repeated his question.

"How long have you been here?" Gervase spoke very softly in reply because he had no strength to assert himself.

"Months." He might as well joke. "Years."

"Funny I ain't seen you before," the man said. "Seen some of your friends. Buried them decent." His eyes roved over the money and lingered on the gold. "Plenty of cash you have here. No place to spend it." He laughed, but the laugh was not malicious. "You the raider of the North Adams?" What was there to lose by silence?

"Yes," replied Gervase.

"You're a killer if the word's true," said the lean man. Killer of women and kids. Not that the word is usually true. You killed women and kids, Reb?"

"No," said Gervase. There was a silence, broken only by some snow sliding down Tannery Falls.

"It's droll," said the man, "but I have this feeling that I can know whether or not a man is telling me truth when he speaks. I ain't been wrong yet. And I reckon you are telling truth. I don't have much to do with them in North Adams. They'd be pleased to send me off to the war. And I don't care for either side. Not mine. And not yours. Burger's the name. John Burger." The sound trailed away as Gervase fainted again. What matter, he thought, I'm going to die. I've been bitten by a rabid fox. There is no cure for rabies. I shall die; not quick, but howling and screaming and flinging myself about like a demented clown. Let me die now. He emerged into the clarity of cold, the agony of bereavement.

"Kill me," he said to the man, who hadn't moved. "Kill me. I've been bitten by a fox."

"Well now," said Burger, "that might mean rabies. And then it might not. I've had a fox's hot teeth into my leg, and I'm still here. You needn't give up yet, Major, or Colonel, or Captain. A major, I should guess. And what's your name? These military titles don't fascinate me much. Tinsel. Silly bits of gold. They tried to have me in the Army. Said they'd send me to prison. But I don't want to kill. Told them so, but it didn't need my word to convince them I was a traitor and coward. So I took to the woods. Hard life, 'specially when you've lived in what they called the groves of academe. Yet I've managed. What's your name?"

"Stepton. Gervase Stepton."

"With that voice I reckon you're from Virginia. And I'm right? Fine state, Virginia. Damn me, I'm losing my accuracy. Commonwealth." His voice took on a rasping authority. "Come on, Stepton, wake up. Pull yourself together like the gentleman you must be. Don't sleep yourself to death like a child in the womb." Gervase put his head on his elbow and wept.

"Let me die."

"Stop that, soldier. Soldier gray, I must say, not that 'soldier blue' they sing about up here. You don't want to die. You needn't fear death. He's a sorry man who fears wood, stone, and, Zeus, death among mortal men. Recognize that?"

"No," said Gervase.

"Plotinus. It was one of Waldo's favorite aphorisms. St. Augustine died murmuring it. Not the Bible, mind, but a pagan sage. But if Virginia's far from you, then Cambridge is far from me. This war adjusts our style of living, Stepton. It sends us off into the wilds, wilds of consciousness as well as these trees. I like them no more than you like them. But we both have to live with them awhile. Not for long, if the news is right, which it ain't usually."

"What news?" Gervase muttered. Did he really care? A particle of his mind, just a particle, was left for others besides himself; the rest was consumed in the great sea of his own pain and deprivation. He wondered if he would ever know joy again. His capacity for endurance was at an end. His mind hammered against a blank wall of sorrow and meaninglessness; even the commonwealth, Deborah, his father, his mother were insubstantial spooks. Cold, wet, pain, and a mad academic formed his tiny world, and he raged against it with puny agony, which left nothing for anything outside the frail shell of his own consciousness.

"Get on your feet, Major," said Burger. "You need a bed. And some hot soup." Gervase pulled himself up and buckled at the knees. His hands clawed hard snow. Burger stood up, took him by the collar, and hauled him upright. Gervase vomited, smoking bile on the pure snow.

"That's messy, boy," said Burger. "Be sick without mess."

"I don't know how, Father," said Gervase in his solitary pain.

"Then you must learn."

Burger put Gervase's arm over his shoulder, and they staggered down the thin, frozen river, stumbling over skiddy rocks, letting the ice-bespangled trees slap into their faces, hearing the echoes of the feet on the hollow rocks.

"The money," said Gervase. "We can't leave the money."

"You'll have to do just that," said Burger. "And the way Grant's got Lee pinned down in the Petersburg lines, they won't be needing it in the South. They'll need it," he corrected himself with pedantic accuracy, "but there's no way, just no way, that you can get it to them. So forget it. I know men died for that bullion. Men died for those scraps of fancy paper. But they've died for less than that, so you can leave the money to disappear under the leaves and the bracken. That's a funny end. But not inappropriate, soldier." They staggered onward, Gervase hardly conscious as they came to a clearing where a hut was built of solid wood, skillfully hidden by trees and the edge of an overhanging rock. Burger had had time to prepare his retreat. He even had a truckle bed, and he dropped Gervase without ceremony onto the blankets.

"You'd better sleep—at least when I've seen to your bite." He gathered up some wood and kindled a fire. The smoke was acrid and filled the cabin with a blue annoyance. The fire glowed in its center like a cruel gem. Burger put his knife into the hottest part until it glowed too. He looked up at Gervase.

"Hold out your left hand," he said. Gervase flinched with every muscle. He could not bear any more pain. His heart pounded within him; he could hear his ears singing. His head was light, flying up to the clouds; the tremors of the flesh coiled about his body like snakes. He remembered the illnesses of his childhood, the shaded room, the jellies, the ice brought with great expense (plenty of that now). Oh, he had stood the knife at Manassas. But he was a little child again, not ready to enter the kingdom of heaven. He tried to cover himself with the coarse blanket. Burger looked at him without kindness.

"Hold out your left hand, you blasted coward," he said. "My, a southern gentleman can't take a little pain! Think of all those philosophers who talked of immortality on the rack. I had been told that General Lee's soldiers were wonders of courage. Clearly, I was told wrong. Perhaps you did kill those women and kids." He came toward Gervase, the red knife in his hand, a god of vengeance, but healing vengeance, some Harvard Asclepios in the dark woods where grew no golden bough. He shouted to Gervase.

"Hold out your damned hand. If you don't want to get well, then I can't help you. What's a little pain? Your mother went through more than this when she bore you. Get it out." In terror, Gervase stretched out his left hand, and the healing, cauterizing knife sent its message of pain to his overtaxed brain as he sank back in yet another faint. This time, as usual, God was absent.

When he came around he felt Burger's arms about his shoulders once again. He felt the taste of hot soup in his mouth and the impress of a wooden spoon on his lips.

"Drink it up," said Burger. "I won't tell you the ingredients." Thank God, thought Gervase. He drank a mouthful. He spat that out onto the gray blanket. "Sip it, boy," whispered Burger. "Sip, sip." Gervase obeyed, and the stuff stayed down. It tasted very salty. His dry mouth exalted in the warm liquid. It was a pleasing return to civilization. Cooked food. ·

"That's better," said Burger. "We'll have you well yet." Gervase glanced at his hand, which was black with burn—black, but not suppurating. Clean, though full of throbbing pain. He could compile a list of physical pains. And only he could know them, pains were private, pains were his alone, a treasure to be hoarded, unlike the bullion and cash he had lost. The hoard of private emotions grew into a great heap in his hot imagination. He lay down and returned to the bondage of sleep. Imprisoned, always imprisoned by duty or obligation or pain. Some were of less importance now. Yes, indeed.

His dreams were strange. Now that he had some degree of security, his mind ranged with self-indulgence. Deborah was alive; he had her in his sleep. Roscoe was alive; they rode through the plains of heaven. He tortured Sebbs in fine ways; he skewered him in the groin with a bayonet. He walked with elegance in the fine halls of Richmond. All the phantasms of the world of night swept over him; he was beaver and knight, Christ and Iscariot, Vergil and Aeneas. Occasionally he came back to the cabin and saw Burger looking at him quizzically, a probing gaze, a fine intuition of what went on in his toppling mind. He returned again and again to his childhood: This is *your* horse, Gervase; come home before the dusk, Gervase; sleep, Gervase; we love you, Gervase; tell me, Gervase, tell me everything; I love you, Gervase, will love you always, Gervase, you can have me, Gervase, why do you hesitate? Gervase, what is marriage? Gervase, words said in church, Gervase, touch me here, Gervase, undo these little knots, Gervase, there, Gervase, there; oh you damned romantic, Gervase; see how the niggers take each other, aren't they human; what does being a gentleman matter, Gervase; Roscoe will have me, Gervase; you are giving up so much,

Gervase; what are we fighting for? God and the Confederacy; be tender, Gervase. And Quantrill leering over the past, spitting on it, and smearing the spit with his index finger. "I train my boys good. They take what they want, Captain Stepton."

His periods of consciousness grew longer. Burger hunted and, since he appeared to be skillful, brought home game: little birds, chipmunks, and the odd fish. In the flickering darkness they talked. Or rather, Burger talked. He was a master of the voice. And months of solitude and academic deprivation forced him to talk endlessly to his captive audience. "As you'd expect," he said one evening, "since I was once paid to talk to students, to instruct them in right and wrong. All useless. I've learned more in the past year than I learned from my books. One impulse from a vernal wood . . . But I expect you know your Wordsworth. Oh yes, I could have bought my way out of the Army, but I chose to run from Mr. Lincoln's conscription, from Mr. Lincoln's war. And I wasn't going to fight for your side either, glamorous and absurd heroes fighting for a futile cruelty. Because, make no mistake, Major Stepton, that's what you are fighting for: black slavery. Disguise it as freedom and individualism if you will. Talk about your own moral purity if you will. But you are all fighting to keep our peculiar institution. The right to hang Nat Turner, and whip niggers if they answer you back. You may be a hero, but you no more think a black your equal than Achilles would have thought a Hittite slave was *his* equal. And *we* fight for our corporations, to make one great big country with bigger factories, bigger steel mills, bigger railroads. And no coven of planters is going to stand in the way of that dream. We'll have reduced even England to a satrapy in a hundred years. And neither of those ideals seems worthy to demand my life. So I fled. Simply fled, my boy, and took to the woods in earnest, like my friend Henry Thoreau." At which he laughed. He had a sardonic sense of humor, and when he laughed he twisted his hands together, cracking his knuckles until they seemed about to break. At night, before he went to sleep, Gervase heard him talking to the angels. "Just like Swedenborg," said Burger. "They have more to say than you, and it's a way of reaching heaven where the lion lies down with the lamb, and Grant kisses Lee."

Spring came to the Berkshires, and with the rain and filtering sunlight and rushing of the waters, Gervase felt a softening of his heart. He ceased to hate so much, and he ceased to fear. The geography of his feelings began to settle into firmer contours. He talked more with Burger. He watched the animals creep from their hibernation haunts. He let his eyes follow the energy of the birds, and he could hear their cries without screwing himself into a knot of bitter copperheads. Each year, he thought, the seasons return; I cannot never know a springtime in myself again, but that's no reason why I shouldn't enjoy the springtime of the world. But the Yankee spring was a slow process—slow, but inexorable, like all Yankee activities. Inexorable too was his physical recovery. He was still young and vigorous. Gervase felt that he had served a monastic penance of withdrawal. Burger had helped him; Burger was like one of his own mystic angels, without real substance. He ate Burger's food, laughed at Burger's jokes, shared Burger's reminiscences. But Burger never became real to him in the way that Roscoe, or even Sebbs and Hass, had been real. And yet Gervase recognized that by this very passivity Burger had served a spiritual office.

And his medical office had been no less effective; save for violent fits of trembling, Gervase had not been further troubled by the bite on his hand. The fox had been vicious but not rabid. When he trembled he would crouch on the damp moss and hold his arms around his knees until the paroxysm passed. He had warning of its coming: His head became light, and his balance began to waver. "It'll be with you for the rest of your days," said Burger in his comforting way. "You'll have to learn to endure it. There are worse states. Have you seen the inside of an insane asylum, boy?" Gervase had not. So he pulled his arms tight and thought how much luckier he was than a lunatic. For an optimist, Burger was very free with his counsels of endurance. Perhaps because he could endure himself, he was, in fact, an optimist. Gervase had to come to terms with his fragility.

"I know you've seen men cut to pieces in a battle," said Burger. "Seen them smashed by the cannon ball. You've seen the worst of man in that camp. But that's not the truly terrible aspect of man's condition. It's the unseen dread that creeps up on you, the pangs of childbed, the diseases that eat at your vitals when you are oblivious and then spurt pain all over you. When you expect nothing from your body, you will be able to control it. Treat pain as normal, boy. Hope for absolutely nothing, and then you might gain something you want. Your country's gone, your family, your so-called honor. That's just about the best state I can imagine a man to be in." General Jackson would hardly agree with that, thought Gervase. But he said nothing, for General Jackson was many years dead and gone. Perhaps he should have expected rather less, at least from his Carolina pickets.

It was in March that he felt sufficiently recovered to leave Burger. The man had so sunk himself into the life of the woods that he had become a part of nature. Gervase still craved for something of civilization. So when he was out hunting he borrowed some paper, which he tore from a volume of Coleridge, and wrote a letter:

"Dear Professor Burger [for Gervase felt the man set store by his academic title; most of them did]:

"Pray forgive me leaving you with such undue haste and for failing to observe the courtesies as I should. I must thank you for all that you have done on my behalf. Thank you for curing my wound, thank you for giving me the shelter of your home. You must have found me an almost intolerable burden. I lack your sense of humor. But I beg that you will remember that I have endured this war, while you have not, and that I have surrendered myself to my country, while you have only sought to keep your own integrity. Integrity is fine, but it is not, cannot be, enough. You talk to the angels. Let me talk also to the lowest of men. You talk very easily of pain, but I have yet to see you endure anything except its contemplation. I am now returning to the community this war has ravaged, and I will see what I can do to rebuild it. You have given me some hope, although I do not think that that was your intention. I am sorry to have defaced your volume Coleridge, particularly as I see him as a poet for the South rather than the North.

"I am, sir,
"Your most obedient servant,
Gervase Stepton"

Gervase picked up his Le Mat and stuck it in his belt. He would have to leave most of the money, but not all. The bullion he could not carry, but the Yankee dollars would be useful. He waded up the stream toward his old haunt at the foot of the falls. The bullion had sunk into the ground and disappeared. The sacks that had contained the notes were there. The sacks. Only the sacks. All the money had gone.

Wearily he tramped back down the stream. Animals flashed along the banks; rats and beavers; he trampled over the nascent dams. Birds called. Water flashed over clean little rocks. He checked his gun. The bullets were still in the chamber. He thought of risking a shot, but decided against it. When he came upon the secluded cabin, Burger stood abstractedly outside, hunkered before he rose. He had the letter in his hand.

"This book cost me three dollars," he said. "And I thought you'd be gone by now, boy."

"Don't call me boy," replied Gervase. "I'm not one of your Yankee students. Where's the money?" Burger smiled. An innocent, abstracted smile. "I wondered when our hero would get to that. I burned it. Buried the bullion and burned the notes. Money is evil. It rots the good sap of the soul. Fine phrase, ain't it? I thought the destruction of the God of Mammon might furnish my medical bill. Boy."

"You're lying," said Gervase.

"But you don't know that, do you? You haven't my uncanny skill at ferreting out the truth. I'm a piece of Nature, and I can recognize real Being. You can't, because you're still full of illusions. Boy. And why should I want money?"

"Every Yank wants money," said Gervase. "It's your substitute for honor."

"Now, that is a good aphorism," smiled Burger.

"You may not need the money on metaphysical grounds," said Gervase. "But I need it on practical ones. Where is it?"

"As I told you, I burned it. And I wouldn't let it corrupt your perfect soul. Truly, boy—don't you address your slaves thus?—I have only your heavenly good in my heart." Gervase's hand moved to the butt of his Le Mat. Burger, with detached irony, raised a bushy eyebrow.

"Where is it? Where is the money?"

"I burned it, Gervase. I burned it. Gervase drew the gun. A mixture of cupidity and apprehension briefly shadowed Burger's face, for, though a philosopher, he was no Stoic, and no martyr to be turned on the gridiron of terror. With a shrug of both resignation and contempt, whether for Gervase or himself perhaps neither man knew, he told Gervase of the hollow tree over the clearing where the notes were stacked and covered. Gervase took several thousand dollars and pushed them in a sack. He turned downstream.

"So," said Burger, with an edge to his voice, "even a Confederate 'gentleman' can't resist the lure of Yankee dollars. Stolen ones at that."

"But *you* stole them from me—or tried to, at least. Philosopher, or should I say casuist? How courageous are you, philosopher?" Burger's face remained impassive, though his eyes flickered a little. To conceal this, to keep some self-respect, he blinked rapidly.

"Good-bye, philosopher," said Gervase. "You should get back to Harvard. You can teach a course in 'courage.' You seem to be an expert now."

Before he left, Gervase recalled that here his men had died. Here, if Burger was to be believed, they lay buried, part of the New England soil, involved once more in the rhythms of inscrutable nature. He saluted, pausing before he lowered his hand. Though he was far from his regiment, he felt at one with them. The month of March had passed, and it was April 9, 1865. He turned his back upon New England, upon the Berkshires, upon the great trees, upon the little animals, upon the ambiguous philosopher who had not dared to face a battle, upon the cold and damp and pain and shivering fits and the desire to destroy his own identity. He looked forward and followed the stream, wherever it might lead him. Imaginary bugles soared in triumph among the branches.

13

In the Great Hand of God
He Stood

Gervase would have found it difficult to describe his journey back to the South. He lit upon a little New England town; he did not even bother to discover its name, and he bought a horse, a wary old horse that sufficed for his needs. He had learned to conceal his southern accent, which was never very pronounced, and nobody seemed to question his presence or make inquiries as to his destination. He learned that the telegraph had borne the news of the end of the war. Of course, some were fighting on, but Lee had surrendered. The townsfolk showed little triumph. They were learning to live with the memory of their dead. His horse ambled along the Mohawk Trail, among the big hills, still without living leaves, and he arrived at Greenfield. Here he sold his horse and took the Boston and Maine South. Burger had given him some civilian clothes in the early days of their acquaintance, but they stank, and he bought better garments. He sat in the corner of the saloon as the train crept south toward Springfield and Hartford. The train frequently stopped for, although the war was over, there were other trains carrying military equipment both North and South and, as if by habit, these had precedence. In the two towns he saw the great factories, indeed caught a glimpse of the arsenal at Springfield. Great piles of shells; rows of guns; heaps covered with tarpaulin; the enormous energy of a nation geared to war. "How could we beat this people?" he thought. "We never had a ghost's chance. All we had was our courage and determination." Every second man seemed to be wearing the blue uniform. They laughed and cursed as soldiers will; they talked of the battles that Gervase had never seen. One old sergeant—at least, he seemed old; so did Gervase, who was in fact twenty-three—included Gervase in the conversation.

"Christ, boy, I thought we'd never take those lines at Petersburg. I got two bullets in me: one in the ass, which hurt like hell, and one in the shoulder, which got me sent home. In one day we lost ten thousand. Ten thousand, I tell you. And those Reb soldiers had no shoes. They had no ammunition. They just stood by their trenches and fought like hell. We couldn't get near them. And old U.S. took Lee in the flank, or thought he did, and there the Rebs were. Lee outsmarted him. Rows of bayonets. Starving faces, but lines of bayonets. God, we had everything. Rows of cannon, rows and rows. We blasted their trenches to dirt. But they were still there. Old U.S. never gave up, though. He didn't care for our lives, but he never gave up. Ain't it dreadful?" Yes, thought Gervase, it is *dreadful*. I wonder when some Homer will come to make an epic of our sufferings, of their sufferings too. We are too close to the wounds and the bodies. We will have to wait half a century at least. For we *are* worth a Homer. We deserve never to be forgotten. Reputation, reputation, echoed from *Othello*. We don't need an impersonal Shakespeare: We need a Homer, a Vergil, a Milton. We need an epic poet, though I doubt whether we will find one. And not from our generation. We have been hurt too much.

New York was a mixture of smashed slum and burgeoning magnificence. There were signs of battle, and Gervase asked a passerby what had happened. "You weren't here, sir? The Irish, those damned potato eaters, refused the draft. They turned on the Negroes and hanged them from the lamppost. The President had to use cavalry and artillery—yes, sir, artillery—to disperse them. Damned cowards." So much for the great crusade, thought Gervase. Thin immigrants, pushed into a quarrel about which they understood nothing, and cared nothing, were to be pressed into Mr. Lincoln's armies. So they resisted, they fought, as they had fought the English over the water. And their new country had crushed them with even more expedition. All motives are mixed. He felt sure that Mr. Lincoln had felt great regret at so doing. Killing Americans: how very sad. He had killed enough for his lifetime. Yet New York was a revelation of what was to come. It sprawled, it meandered, it imposed its force and magnificence on the river and the land. It was not like Richmond (or his memory of Richmond). Richmond was a small town where everyone knew everyone else, or thought they did. In New York nobody knew anyone else. The city cultivated its own cold energy. But the energy was real enough. Gervase felt his own legs moving faster. He felt himself staring about furtively. He felt the need to mingle with the great crowd that surged about, down the straight streets and into the squares. Of course, they were islands of elegance, but Gervase felt that they would soon disappear. Once he had a shivering fit upon the sidewalk. The crowd parted to leave him some air. No one helped him; no one stretched out a hand. They left him to himself. Let him recover if he could. He did. If he had not, doubtless the city trash collectors would have come to collect him. And yet this energy was daunting; it inspired admiration even if it also inspired horror. Gervase could not have lived there, his father could not have done so, but he admired those who could.

To take a train South was not so easy. The military had the seats, and Gervase had to take a place in a converted cattle truck. He did not mind. He was surprised himself by how little he cared about his body now. He only shaved when the glances of the curious told him that he was passing the bounds of acceptable propriety. After all, their President looked scraggy enough. His indifference was genuine, not an attitude struck up, like Burger's. There were blacks on the train, but Gervase did not mind. He had never minded blacks. Why should he? They showed little exultation at the conclusion of the war for their freedom. Because, he thought, what could they do in the South but work the fields, and what could they do in the North but work the factories? They had gained very little by the war for their liberty. On the train he had another paroxysm of shivering. He almost lost consciousness. When he came back to the clarity of perception he found that his head was cradled in the lap of a black wearing the blue uniform. "Thank you, soldier," said Gervase.

"You from the South?"

"A long time ago."

"But you fought for us, man?"

"I don't know who I fought for," said Gervase. The black stared at him; the whites of his eyes glimmered in the half darkness as the train heaved and shuddered South. The truck stank of sweat.

"That ain't no answer."

"Isn't it the only answer?" It was the first time he had discussed philosophy with a black. The man stared at him while his great arms supported Gervase's head and shoulders.

"You fought for them." Gervase lost patience with deception. And he felt no apprehension because he felt no fear.

"Yes. I was an officer in Jeb Stuart's regiment." How strange. He called General Stuart "Jeb" to a nigger. But he would have done so five years ago, although five years ago no black would have held him in a dirty Yankee train.

"You're an honest man." And was it not strange that the black engaged in none of the gabbling talk of his race? (for Gervase still held to that absurdity). There was no "young masser" and other conventions of servility. They spoke as man to man, and Gervase again wondered that he felt no strangeness. "Honest, but it's all over now. General Stuart is dead. All your fine Army is gone."

"And what sort of freedom will you get?" asked Gervase.

"Me? Horatius Macgregor? Oh, I don't expect freedom for myself. But for my son. Or his son. You all owe us that."

"I didn't bring you from Africa," said Gervase. "I had no slaves. My father freed them all. I've never whipped a black in my life. Oh, I'm as pure as the lily in the field. But I'll take the blame. And I won't grudge you your freedom. I wasn't fighting to keep you enslaved. I was fighting for . . . well, what? . . . all that this *isn't*."

"This is America," said Horatius, incongruously named by some lover of Macaulay down South. "We'll make something of it. Together, man." "We'll try," said Gervase, and endeavored to sleep. They reached Washington, and Gervase found a pretty city of tin soldiers, scurrying about in their important business of administering a conquered country. He looked South. "We came

so near," he said. "So very near." And his hand throbbed with the
memory of that battle long ago. It was April 15, 1865. He had
made a good journey. But he had not paused.

There was a constraint in the air of the capital. Waves of emo-
tion surged over the crowds of soldiers and the few civilians.
Gervase noted, as he wandered from the station, that women
were weeping in the streets. He went up to one lacrimose matron
and asked the reason for her distress. In a high-pitched voice she
told him. "Those damned Rebs," she said. "Nothing can protect
them now!" Gervase leaned against a white-painted wall. In the
moment of his triumph Mr. Lincoln had been taken from them.
Gervase did not admire assassins. He felt nothing but an emptiness. Lincoln knew what he wanted. He made a profession of
caring. And Lee surrendered, and Lincoln was shot in the head.
And Gervase was headed home. He could not weep, but nor
could he cry out in triumph. Mr. Lincoln was only an idea to
him, an idea that embraced Hass and Sebbs and Burger and all
the toys soldiers in the cruel battles. At least Mr. Lincoln would
know what he had unleashed on his countrymen. His body was
smashed too. Gervase gave up the task of thought. He had
thought too much.

He had to ride to Richmond. All the trains carried soldiers. As
he approached *his* capital the ruins of war lay around him. Burial parties were still at work. Long rows of bodies, far, far longer
than he had seen in the early battles. Man had not suffered
alone; the trees were smashed, leaning like scarecrows against
the gray skies. The ground was pitted, and the holes filled with
greasy water. It was a landscape of death. There were cages of
prisoners. They were not the soldiers of 1861. They looked
starved. Their weapons were piled up outside the cages. Most
men were sitting hopelessly on the mud. Clouds of gray scudded
across the active sky. Nobody seemed very happy at Lincoln's
death. The federal troops were going through the motions of
sadness. Gervase heard the voices of colonels and generals and
chaplains wafting on the winds. He did not stay to listen. Often
he was stopped by pickets, but he gave them some story. "Yes, I
was up North and now I'm to go to Richmond. For General
Sheridan." They seemed to accept his word with a dumb
affability. The war, after all, was over. What was over? Nothing.

Pain hung like a miasma on the air. When he saw a hospital tent he rode a long way around to avoid it.

He came to the outskirts of Richmond. The city had been smashed to ruins. Thin women and girls roamed the streets, while columns of blue cavalry picked their delicate way over fallen masonry and splintered wood. All the landmarks of Gervase's youth had gone: the houses of his kin, the houses of his friends and fellow officers, the brothel were he had met Quantrill. Church spires leaned over at weird angles. Some buildings were still smoldering. Children played, content even in this squalor, played in little groups, asserting something about humanity, he supposed. Richmond had been an elegant town, and now, like the body of a fine and virtuous woman, she had been bayoneted to pieces. He looked around for a house in which he could sleep. He could not bear to return to Sweetwater. Not yet. After a time he would go back. He would farm. He would push the plow himself. He would take comfort in the seasons, however many were left to him. He would sink himself in the inanimate. Meanwhile, *sunt lacrimae rorum.* The rape of Richmond made his eyes itch as Mr. Lincoln's shattered brain had failed to do.

"Hey," came a call to him from a window. He looked up. There was a girl, dark-haired, emaciated yet beautiful.

"Yes?" he asked.

"Come in," she said. He wondered whether she was a whore of the conquered mistakenly calling for the protection of a conqueror. He gave her the benefit of the doubt. He swung down from his horse and tied it upon a crazily leaning post. It hardly mattered if the horse wandered away, though he would need a beast to haul the plow. The house was a mess. It had been both smashed by shells and looted by man. The girl, dressed in what had once been finery, descended the stairs to meet him. She extended her hand.

"Ophelia Robertson," she said.

"Gervase Stepton, ma'am," he replied, and took her hand. It was very cold.

"You are a Southerner, sir?"

"Yes, ma'am," replied Gervase. She was preserving the dead manners. She would have to learn.

"Will you honor me with your presence at dinner, sir?" she asked him. He nodded. Suddenly, without warning, she collapsed into what had once been a fine chair.

"They took everything," she said. She burst into a fit of weeping. "They took me."

"Soldiers in victory aren't very considerate." And his heart reached out to her. How old? Eighteen at the most. Younger, for war aged them all. He put his hand on her shoulder. She laid her hand on his; the flesh was cold.

"My mother and father died of typhus during the last months," she said. "We had no medicine. We had no food except the scraps I could gather. And we could not sleep."

"When did you last eat?" asked Gervase.

"A week ago. Perhaps it was a week . . ." Her voice trailed away. Gervase left her and wandered around the ruined house. In the kitchen there were pieces of bread. A bucket of water, which looked clean enough. He found a cup, china chipped at the rim, and filled it. There was a row of cupboards, one door leaning open in a crazy way. Inside were two bottles of whiskey. Miraculously moved or more likely just not found by the soldiers. He drank from the bottle himself and then poured a generous measure into the water in the cup. He took it back to Ophelia. He handed her the bread. She ate it. Then he gave her the cup.

"Drink this." She sipped.

"Liquor," she said, and screwed up her face. She looked as if she was about to spit the stuff out onto her blue silk dress.

"Don't do that," ordered Gervase. "Drink it." Her dark eyes became fiercely resolute, and she gulped down the fiery liquid—very fiery because it was very crude. Her shoes, which peeped under the dress, had been elegant, but were worn. Her body was young, and its contours should have pushed out the silk into sensual contours, but everything seemed to shrink away. She kept turning her eyes away from Gervase.

"Forget it all," he said.

"How can we ever forget?" she said with sibilant anger. "Ever. Ever. Ever."

"I've lost all I had as well," replied Gervase. "At least the war is over."

"The war will never be over. I owe *that* to my kin." She screwed up her face. "And if those niggers think that they . . ."

"Be quiet," said Gervase. "I understand. But be quiet." The drink was going to her head. She laughed.

"I thought you were one of us. And you're a nigger lover."

"I fought with General Stuart and with General Lee," said Gervase. "And I'm not a nigger lover. I'm not a nigger hater, either. We ought to try some more loving and not bother about the color of the skin. My soldiers didn't."

"I do," she cried out. And then wept more. "I'm all hurt," she said.

Gervase picked her up, wondering at her lightness. He felt her thighs under his hands, but marveled that no lust moved within him. He carried her up the stairs and wandered about the great landing, with torn carpets and smashed chairs, looking for a bedroom. He found one. The bed was disordered. He put her on the floor and straightened the sheets. He picked her up gently and put her down on the softness of the covered mattress. "Sleep," he said. But her eyes were already closed. He went into a nearby room and picked up a pillow and a blanket and returned to her room. He lay down and slept himself, oblivious of the continuous clattering outside as the cavalry moved in yet more men, and the tread of the infantry as they stepped out their triumph. The guns rattled over the stones, but they were not moving fast, for the last battle had been won. They slept for hours, and when Gervase awoke it was very early morning. Far away, bugles played tunes in military code, and, nearer, birds sang, oblivious in delicious innocence. She still slept, a girlish Deborah with her dark hair spread on the pillows and only a tightness of her mouth to suggest the pain and anger of her dreams. Would time smooth that away? Gervase wondered. Maybe. Time heals, though it cannot repair. He wandered down out of the house into the streets. Some soldiers tramped along, full of purpose. The few inhabitants wandered like frail ghosts. He sought a shop. He found one. Men were jostling at the rough counter. The shopowner was dealing out his wares with prudence.

"Only Yankee dollars," he was shouting again and again. "Just Yankee money."

"But these are good Confederate notes."

"No Confederate money is any good." And the crowd was so filled with despair that they took this judgment in silence, old women of twenty-five who needed bread for their children, emaciated men of thirty who had stood at the lines of Petersburg until their wounds forced them back to Richmond. Gervase walked up to the man.

"Bread," he said. "And meat if you have it." He laid ten dollars on the counter. The fat shopowner stared at them and licked his blubber lips.

"Where did you find those?" Gervase was too tired to explain.

"Bread and meat," he said. Someone in the crowd raised a shout.

"Traitor!" The muttering grew. He turned on them with a feigned fierceness.

"I rode with Stuart, damn you," he said. "I *stole* these greenbacks from the Yanks." The muttering died away. The man gave him a loaf and some repulsive red meat. Skinned rabbit, he assumed. He picked them up and walked out of the shop. He picked his way back to Ophelia's house over the stones and down the mangled street. She was awake and sitting in the chair where he had given her the whiskey. He handed her the rabbit.

"Cook this," he said. She opened her face in surprise.

"I can't," she said. "We had a darkie cook. I don't know how." Gervase turned on her in fury.

"Then learn," he shouted. "You won't have niggers for some while yet." He built her a fire in the untouched stove. There was plenty of wood about. They went about their domestic tasks. It was as if they were married. She did not cook the rabbit enough, and the meat, now pale, was very tough. But at least it was warm. She smiled at him.

"I told you I couldn't cook," she said.

"For a first effort I'd say you'll do well." He wiped his mouth with a fine linen napkin he had found neatly folded in a drawer.

During the next week they consolidated their oasis in the desert of conquered Richmond. They put from themselves the memory of things past and healed themselves with a routine that each adopted without any thought. Gervase bought food. He tidied the house, restoring the ruins to something worthy of habitation. Her cooking improved, and she began to take a delight in her work at the stove. She even washed their clothes. She stitched her father's garments so that they would fit Gervase's emaciated body. She did not speak of her father. From the scattered papers, Gervase gathered that he had been a lawyer. In the public world various decrees were posted, imposing curfews and giving directions about rations and the burial of the dead and the proper respect to be paid to officers of the Army of the United States. Occasionally Gervase saw a gaudy body of officers trot by, accompanying some general. Maybe the great General Grant. He gathered from gossip that a power struggle was taking place in Washington. It seemed so very far away.

Neither offered love to the other. It was as if the erotic had been drained from them. They touched each other. They kissed each other good night and embraced briefly in the morning, but there was nothing more to these embraces than friendship. They lived in complete intimacy of the body—complete save for the final molding. He knew when she relieved herself, and she knew when he did the same. She saw him wash, she saw him shave, he saw when her monthly period began and when it ended. But they lived suspended in an emotional vacuum. They had to enter the halls of affection before they could gasp in the dark corridors of love. As she washed her clothes she laughed.

"At least I won't be bearing a Yankee child." He did not pursue the matter.

It would have been indecent, would have broken the rules they had imposed upon themselves. They looked at each other's bodies, saw the hair, the flesh, the muscles, the worn skin. And they felt nothing.

"Good night, Gervase," she said each night.

"Good night, Ophelia," he replied.

After he had been in Richmond for ten days Gervase saw many copies of a new decree posted all over the town. At least he assumed it was all over the town from the number of copies between the house and the shop. It was signed by the hand of the general commanding and dealt with the requisition of houses for officers of the Army of Occupation. It might mean trouble. And, sure enough, it did mean trouble. Gervase had mended the front door to Ophelia's somewhat imposing house, but, on the sixteenth of May at about midday, there came a peremptory knock. It was swiftly repeated, and, without more ado, the door opened. A group of soldiers entered. A colonel, a sergeant, and an enlisted man. Ophelia moved toward them. The colonel spoke with some courtesy.

"My name is Hass, ma'am. I am afraid that I must impose myself, and two of my officers, upon your hospitality. I have recently been appointed to command the field police in this city, and I need a residence. You may be sure that I shall not trouble you, and shall inconvenience you as little as possible. Since I hold the command I mentioned you won't have any trouble from other soldiers, I can assure you." He gave his guttural laugh. The sergeant, like a good sergeant, laughed too. The enlisted man smiled deferentially. Ophelia bowed her head. None of them had noticed Gervase. "I can, of course, insist, ma'am," the colonel went on. "But I most sincerely trust that that will not be necessary. You will gain nothing but benefit from my presence." And he waited for her reply in quiet confidence. He turned and his eye flicked up and down Gervase, indifferently. "Your husband, I take it? He can stay, of course. Perhaps I should have addressed myself first to you, sir." The sergeant was slightly more prescient than his superior and pulled his carbine up a little, the more easily to deploy it.

Enter the torment of history once again. Oh, Roscoe, Roscoe. See the quiet cows of Sweetwater and the joyous face of Job as he moved to action. Sebbs. The quietness of the general as he planned the battle that could have saved us if Thomas Jackson had not betrayed him by dilatory marching and damned pride. There lay his mother and there lay his father and there lay his beloved Deborah and the Yankee soldiers hanged the rapists and they stood in the icy winds at Delaware and his thumbs ached in anguish. Oh my God, the God of my fathers and the God of battles, I shall avenge you all and take you into the peaceful plains of heaven. Blood, blood, there's blood on my hands. Roscoe, Roscoe, we grew up together: We climbed the same trees and jumped the same fences and endured the battles and you could not speak to me of your pain in the last days. And Deborah lay beneath the heaving Yankee bodies, what though they hanged for it, twitching their toes in their agony, as he hung up by his thumbs in the ice of Delaware, and Howe cried out vengeance that under the rule of Johnson and Stanton they would never find. Roscoe, Roscoe, here's the beaver dam; here's that nest we searched for—a hummingbird. You can't take that fence. I can, you know. They had both landed shaken and laughing. Let's go see Deborah. And the three of them had ridden back to Sweetwater in the soft sun of evening and his father had greeted them and the whole earth moved in a dance of elegance and gentleness and meaning and kindness. Oh Roscoe, Roscoe. "Oh no, Colonel," Gervase said softly, "you can take my wife's word as well as mine." The colonel was determined to make an impression of gentility. The sergeant was still suspicious. Gervase had to rub that away.

"Did you bear arms in the late struggle, sir?"

"Yes, Colonel, I bore arms in the 1st Virginia Cavalry." No quiver of recognition went over Hass's face. When you persecute thousands you do not remember a single victim. Unfortunately, however, the single victims remember only too well. "And you must have borne arms yourself."

"Alas, no, sir. I was . . ." a flicker of hesitation . . . "I was in charge of a camp for prisoners from your gallant Army. It was there that I learned to respect your Confederate spirit so deeply."

"I thank you, sir." The colonel was taken in by this fatuous charade. He probably thought that Southerners continually spoke in imitation of an eighteenth-century biography. The sergeant was clearly skeptical. "My house is at your disposal, sir." Of course, the conquered had no choice. No longer interested, the colonel turned aside and briefly ordered the sergeant to look the place over. For an instant the sergeant's eyes wandered up the stairs. Gervase picked up an old chair leg that he had overlooked in his cleaning operation and leaped toward the sergeant. The man almost got his carbine into the position to fire. Almost, but not quite. Gervase hit him across the face with the solid piece of wood. The man buckled forward and Gervase hit him again on the back of his head. He fell to the floor. The enlisted man, with the courage expected of a member of a regiment recently recruited from immigrants, made for the door. Gervase picked up the carbine and swung it like an ax at his head. The blow was badly aimed and took him on the shoulder.

It hurled the man on to the door itself. Gervase swung the weapon again as he rebounded and hit him on the back of his neck. He heard a crack and felt no pity. The man disintegrated into a blue heap. Gervase had heard noises behind him as he had dealt with those who were not officers and gentlemen. He turned, and saw Colonel Hass attempting to disentangle himself from a piece of cloth that Ophelia had thrown over his pistol hand. Gervase ran easily and lightly to the corner of the room where he had secreted his Le Mat. He took it from the drawer and pointed it steadily at Hass's chest.

"Stand still, Colonel," he said quietly. Ophelia's eyes gleamed with an unearthly light, the *gloria* of conflict.

"You'll hang for this," said Hass. "As certainly as there's a God in heaven, you'll hang. And, for Christ's sake, why? I wouldn't have troubled you. I wouldn't have raped your wife. I'm a policeman. I'm here to prevent that. What a foul waste." Gervase let the silence rest. The silence crawled about the room, and Hass's eyes began to flicker. Gervase felt his giddiness, but he controlled it. He forced the trembling out of his limbs.

"I was at Fort Delaware."

"Oh," said Hass. His eyes took on weary understanding. He made a mute appeal. Then he spoke. "I was only obeying my orders, you know. Whoever you are. And your own Andersonville was far, far worse, from what I've heard."

"But we aren't concerned with Andersonville, are we?" said Gervase.

"Christ, I know you," cried Hass. "And, by God, you're the killer of North Adams. You killed Sebbs."

"You have a good memory," said Gervase. "Now take out your gun and give it to my wife." Hass did as he was told. Ophelia held the gun as if she could use it. She probably could.

"This I have always found to be the case," said Hass didactically. "When it comes to it, the gallant southern gentleman is as ready as anyone else to shoot his enemy in cold blood. Custer hanged Mosby's men, and Mosby hanged even more of Custer's men. Gentlemen!" He spat.

"Colonel," said Gervase, "remember that you are in the presence of a lady."

"Not so," said Hass. "I'm in the presence of a Rebel *woman*."

"At Fort Delaware I was tortured," said Gervase. "That doesn't matter much. My friend was dumb. He suffered. We all suffered, and were treated like pigs without dignity. Sebbs died for his part. He died because I found him and he enjoyed what he did. You, maybe—maybe, I say—didn't enjoy it. But you allowed it. My dearest friend died because of you. And now, Colonel Hass of the army of conquerors, I'm going to kill you. But southern gentlemen don't shoot their enemies unarmed. I was brought up to a code of honor that you would think to be gibberish. You may be right. In the world you are making, you are certainly right. My honor has no place. I realize that. And this is my last act of honor and duty to my general and to my father and to my friend." He handed his Le Mat to Ophelia. "If he beats me, let him go."

"That'll be the day," said Ophelia.

"My dearest Ophelia," said Gervase with urgency, "you must promise me to let him go if he beats me. It must be honorable. It must. Otherwise all we fought for is quite meaningless."

"Very well," said Ophelia.

"She doesn't mean it," said Hass. "She'll shoot me the minute I knock you down."

"Clearly you don't know southern women," replied Gervase. "You are well fed, strong, a little older than I perhaps. But you have a good deal on your side. And you'd better try to kill me, because you can be sure I'll kill you if you don't." Hass grinned.

"I've wanted to fight throughout this blasted war," he said. "At last I'll have my chance." And he looked at Gervase thoughtfully. Then he ducked and ran full at Gervase, catching him about the knees. Gervase heeled over. Hass had the greater weight, and he was on top. He raised himself up and began to pummel Gervase in the face. Gervase fanned his hand and jabbed upward with rigid fingers. The forefinger caught Hass in the eye. He screamed and reeled backward. Gervase rolled to the side, as the chair that Hass had picked up in his fall landed just where Gervase had been lying. But Gervase was now at an angle to Hass. Gervase punched him in the stomach as hard as he could. The colonel doubled up and vomited a little. It's finished, Gervase thought, finished at last, at which moment Hass caught him an upward blow in the face with a swinging fist. The world went misty. At that moment, from a great distance, he heard the door open and there was a sharp crack, followed by a thump. Ophelia had clearly dealt with an intruder. Hass was breathing heavily and Gervase brought up his knee into the man's groin. Hass screamed in a preternaturally high-pitched tone. Hass fell onto his back, his knees pulled up to his stomach. Gervase hit him across the neck and he fell silent. He was conscious though, very conscious.

"You looked at Roscoe tortured by his wound," said Gervase. "You gave him no help, damn you. You *looked* at it all." The tears flowed hot and salty from Gervase's eyes. "You killed all the past I loved." Then, as the man lay moaning on the floor, he strangled him, penetrating through the folds of flesh on the neck and constricting the windpipe and the veins and arteries. The body ceased to twitch after a time. It looked like a puffed up clay figure. Gervase panted and fell breathless to the floor.

"The war's over, Ophelia," he said. She flung the weapons down and held him.

"You killed him," she whispered, "but you've also killed the men who raped me, and murdered your kin and your friend. I kept them out. Look." Gervase walked over to the door and hauled in a federal soldier who had been foolish enough to intervene, albeit without knowing what he was doing. He turned to Ophelia and kissed her, meeting her open mouth.

"They'll say we are too lucky," she cried.

"Who will?" he asked. "Men who sit in cabs and call to the horsedriver to turn back to their lodgings because they feel a passing lust. Men who are clever, oh so clever, but lack wisdom." For wisdom, he thought, is knowledge of the pattern of life; wisdom is metaphysics; wisdom is knowing that morality is eternal, and not the emotional whim of the moment; wisdom is seeing the One and making timeless assertions about God; wisdom is He who is.

"It isn't gratuitous, is it?" she asked.

"It is fulfillment," he said. And his manhood came to him, the manhood he could not find for Deborah, and he gently lifted her skirts and entered her, as she cried out a little as he touched the still tender bruises left by the federal cavalry, and put his seed into her forever, and she closed over his manhood, and they were healed and the joy of love engulfed them with its hot fluid and panting joys and they felt the limbs and flesh of each other's body and knew that God did not give man his flesh for nothing and realized in the panting and heaving that nothing is contemptible except cynical cleverness and held onto each limb, each stroke of flesh, each caress of tenderness, each penetration of joy, each adjustment of clothing, each bitter taste in the searching mouth, each contact of rough hair, each murmured endearment, each assertion of humanity, as the past fluttered away and the soft present fell in peace upon their clenched loins. They had incarnated the sacrament of a true and holy love, never to be alone again.

"The war's over, Ophelia, over and over. We'll go to farm." And that night they left the stricken city and made their way toward Sweetwater.